T. A. Hunter

The Master Code

The Master Code by T. A. Hunter
(Book 1.0 of The Code Masters™ series)
Copyright © 2022 T. A. Hunter
Cover fish Copyright © 2022 Son J. Nguyen

ISBN: 9798411080247

In the Near Future...

Exgenics is a privately held company founded several years ago by Dr. Ernesto Gerardo, a Nobel prize winning biochemist and genetic scientist who invented the Crickett gene synthesis system. This was one of those technologies that could change the world, and if harnessed carefully could prove a miracle breakthrough in cancer and other cellular genetic diseases. A company led by such an ambitious man would readily find investors and could easily capitalize his company to focus on both his immediate research needs and long-term goals.

Jason Dickson is a brilliant twenty-two-year-old engineering student with autism spectrum disorder who was convicted of malicious computer hacking in Federal Juvenile Court at the age of twelve. While a young boy, he suffered the loss of his parents in a tragic accident and was raised in the Tidewater region of Virginia by his grandfather, a widowed Baptist minister. Jason, his high school sweetheart Julie, and other local residents of rural Charles County are about to be faced with a set of coincidences and discoveries that force Jason to decide whether to break his court-ordered lifetime ban on computer hacking to uncover the mystery and crack The Master Code. If he's caught breaking the terms of his suspended sentence, he'll face a lifetime in Federal Ultramax Prison, but the mystery is dark, deep, and earth-shaking, so he must make his decision carefully and wisely...

"One Fish, Two Fish, Yellow Fish, Glow Fish!"
with apologies to Dr. Seuss

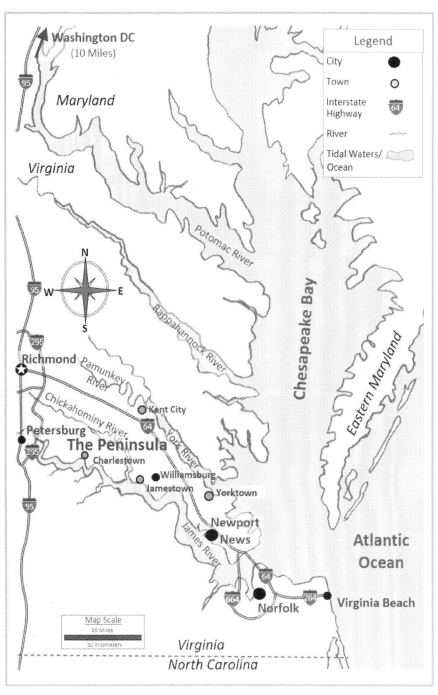

THE VIRGINIA PENINSULA AND TIDEWATER

DEDICATION

For Alex, Katie, and all my family and friends who thought I could do this.
Thank you for encouraging me to write my dream.

"Power makes truth, but sometimes the Truth is more powerful."
J. E. Dickson
55th President of the United States of America

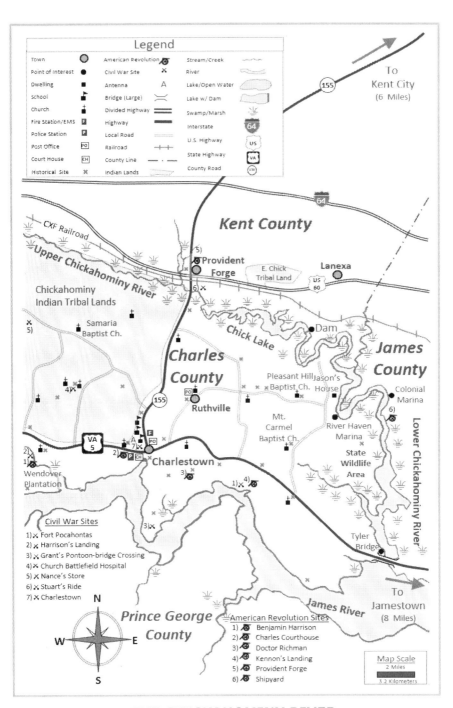

THE CHICKAHOMINY RIVER

Legend

Town	◎	American Revolution		Stream/Creek	
Point of Interest	●	Civil War Site	✕	River	
Dwelling	■	Antenna	A	Lake/Open Water	
School		Bridge (Large)		Lake w/ Dam	
Church	✝	Divided Highway		Swamp/Marsh	
Fire Station/EMS	F	Highway		Interstate	64
Police Station	P	Local Road		U.S. Highway	US
Post Office	PO	Railroad		State Highway	VA
Court House	CH	County Line		County Road	
Historical Site	✖	Indian Lands			

To Kent City (6 Miles)

155

Kent County

CXF Railroad

Upper Chickahominy River

Provident Forge
5)

E. Chick Tribal Land

Lanexa
US 60

Chickahominy Indian Tribal Lands

6) ✕

Samaria Baptist Ch.

✕ 5)

Chick Lake

Dam

Charles County

James County

Pleasant Hill Baptist Ch.

Jason's House

Colonial Marina

4) ✕

River Haven Marina

6)

PO
Ruthville
155

Mt. Carmel Baptist Ch.

State Wildlife Area

Lower Chickahominy River

VA 5

A
7) ✕
PO
F

2)
Charlestown

3) ✕

1) ✕ 4)

2) ✕
1) ✕
Wendover Plantation

3) ✕

Tyler Bridge

Civil War Sites
1) ✕ Fort Pocahontas
2) ✕ Harrison's Landing
3) ✕ Grant's Pontoon-bridge Crossing
4) ✕ Church Battlefield Hospital
5) ✕ Nance's Store
6) ✕ Stuart's Ride
7) ✕ Charlestown

N
W   E
S

Prince George County

James River

To Jamestown (8 Miles)

American Revolution Sites
1) Benjamin Harrison
2) Charles Courthouse
3) Doctor Richman
4) Kennon's Landing
5) Provident Forge
6) Shipyard

Map Scale
2 Miles
3.2 Kilometers

TABLE OF CONTENTS

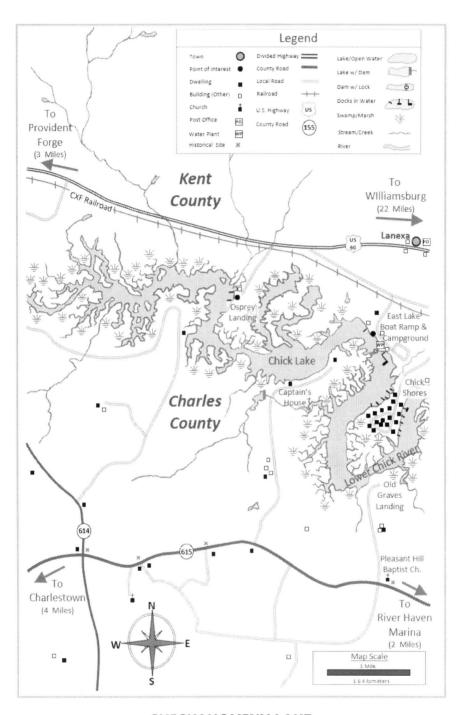

CHICKAHOMINY LAKE

Prologue

The Long Path Forward

Early morning, July 4, some year in the near future...

Jason gazed at the genetic letters and program words scroll in front of his eyes as he thought about the past week and how events had led him to this nexus of his life. Everything hinged on what he could tell Dr. Gerardo of what he learned about the Master Code. Grandpa's life was in his hands, and so was his beloved Julie, her parents, Doc, Nick, and even Rufus. What could he do? They'd been captured and at the point of Gerardo's gun, he had no other options. He stared further and soon his subconscious mind deciphered the enigma that had eluded Gerardo's brilliance. He now understood all. Grandpa was right. Sometimes the shortest moments of life are the most important. Death would come swiftly, but he might still save humanity from doom. He quickly made his decision with faith he'd made the right choice...

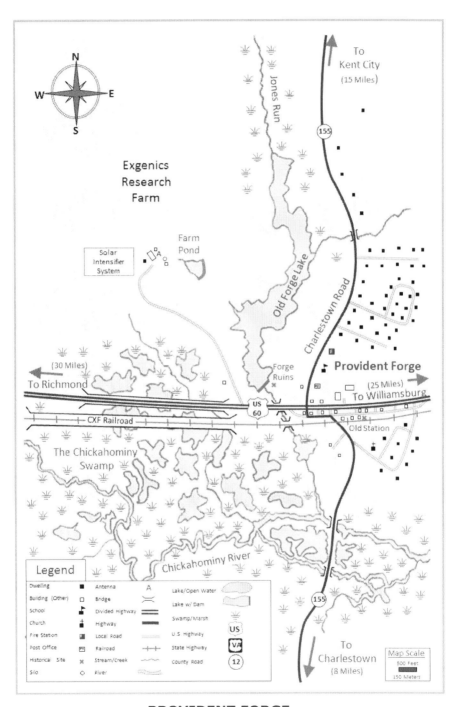

PROVIDENT FORGE

gcgaacgcgatggcgtaagcgatggcgaacgcgccgctggcgaacgcgtgcgcgaacgcgctgccggcgaacgcgatggcgtaagcgatggcgaacgcg

Chapter 1: The Research Farm

Exgenics Research Farm

Two years earlier in the near future…

Nikolai Abramovich was working the second shift in the Embryonics Lab of the large research building at the Exgenics Research Farm, a facility recently constructed by the lowest bidding contractor. The rain was pouring that spring evening and his wife, Elvira, was worried would be driving home a long way the dark, slick rural roads of Charles County.

As he went about his tedious lab work, he thought about how his life had led him to his present circumstances as an old man nearing retirement. He had come to America as a young Orthodox Jewish Russian émigré right after the breakup of the Soviet Union. Before that, he was a precocious, brilliant young man who'd passed the Russian university entrance exams at a premature age. He was only 15 years old when he entered university and was rewarded with an internship studying plant genetics at the Vavilov Research Plant Institute in the city of Leningrad.[1]

He remembered vividly the stories told to him by his babushka,[2] who survived the Siege of Leningrad during the Great Patriotic War against the Nazis.[3,4] She had worked at the Vavilov Institute with the other staff those

---

[1] Now the Russian city Saint Petersburg, often nicknamed the "Venice of the North."

[2] Transliterated Russian Language – бабушка: grandmother.

[3] Russian name for World War II; this was a patriotic war to the Russian people, who suffered immensely. It was a fight to the death for their nation to survive. It is estimated that 20 to 27 million Russians died of which only about 9 million were soldiers. (This equals about 14 to 18 percent of the total Russian population. In comparison, only 0.3 percent of the United States population died in World War I.)

[4] Two-million Russian civilians had not been evacuated before the city was cut off from almost all supplies for 900 days. The only meager rations for the besieged city were those surviving the Luftwaffe bombings of military supply truck convoys that sporadically came

endless, bleak days filled with hunger. As the siege began, the researchers met and agreed, swearing their lives at risk of certain starvation, to protect and guard their institute's valuable seed bank for future generations. Many did perish, as a slice of sawdust-filled bread was the only ration provided for those lucky and strong enough to survive.[5] Finally, salvation arrived as the Soviet Army liberators and heroes broke the blockade to begin their slow and grinding fight, marching westward to eventually defeat the Nazis with the help of their American and British allies. Babushka barely survived and inspired Nikolai, at an early age, to become a genetic scientist.

Even though Nick, as he now liked to be called, was a young scientist just out of university when he came to America, he didn't speak English at first and his Soviet education wasn't recognized by American academics. So, his background was underutilized in his new homeland. However, luckily, he found a lab technician job, but most of his career, he'd bounced from one company to another, since he wasn't satisfied working for others who didn't treat him as an intellectual equal or approve of his beliefs.

His life changed, however, when he started working with Dr. Gerardo, who at that time was just a college professor. Gerardo truly appreciated Nick's brilliance, so he'd worked for many years with Dr. Gerardo as a senior genetics technician while Gerardo grew to become a world-renowned genetics scientist.

Now, he was an old man and humble enough to accept that if he worked a few more years, he'd retire with his meager savings and a minimal subsidy from Social Security.[6] Fortunately, Nikolai and Elvira resided where the cost of living was low near Charlestown, a small town about a mile from the James River in Charles County, in what is known as the

---

over Lake Ladoga across an ice road during the long and dark Russian winters. This ice road was just a transitory lifeline, so the food supply situation was dire.

[5]At least 12 institute scientists were known to have died of starvation while guarding at least 5 tons of crop seeds and seed potatoes. A normal daily ration for most citizens was 125 grams of saw-dust-filled bread or about 300 calories per day, but soldiers and important laborers received double this amount. Exact numbers are not known, but more than a million citizens perished in the city, either from starvation, illness, or while fighting the Germans at the front. A dark truth was isolated incidents of cannibalism, but the Soviets usually handled offenders with an immediate death sentence.

[6] The minimum retirement age was raised to 80 by then to keep the Social Security system solvent. Although the Coronavirus Pandemic of the early 2020s and the vaccine deaths reduced the population, an economic depression followed that combined with demographics limited contributions to this continually financially troubled entitlement.

Peninsula of the Tidewater region of Virginia.[7] The Peninsula is located between the James and York Rivers and is partially bisected by the roughly 90-mile-long Chickahominy River, which the locals called the 'Chick', with Charles County on the south riverbank and Kent County on the north bank.[8]

Nick liked working with Dr. Gerardo and was always treated well. As a reward for faithful service, he was given a garden patch at the research farm just north of the old dairy barn. Nick already had a home garden, but during the summer would plant this 'bonus' garden at Exgenics before work. There, he planted beets and seed potatoes descended from those of Nikolai Vavilov, his namesake.

The modern history of the Peninsula started with Indian Chief Powhatan, Pocahontas, and the first English colony in Jamestown. The region became an economic powerhouse during the colonial period and was heavily involved in the Revolutionary War with the final Battle of Yorktown occurring nearby.[9,10] There were even multiple Civil War battles fought nearby in this area that had prospered from Southern plantations and the oppression of slavery.[11]

All that was long in the past and now Charles County was a rural, economically depressed region, bypassed by industry and much of modern

---

[7] Charles County is among the first colonial-era counties established. It has the third oldest county courthouse building in the United States and is the only county where three U.S. presidents were born. In the 2035 Emergency Census, Charles County still had about 3,000 residents. Large cities lost a greater percentage of citizens than rural areas.

[8] Kent County still had approximately 30,000 residents per the Emergency Census of 2035. Many residents commute by interstate highway to Richmond, the capitol of the Commonwealth of Virginia.

[9] The abundance of natural resources in Virginia and the New World flowed to the Old World and enabled the colonies to grow. The agricultural economy based on the plantation model using slave labor enabled wealth to flow to the area. Several signers of the Declaration of Independence had a connection nearby, including Benjamin Harrison, George Washington, and Thomas Jefferson. Benjamin Harrison owned Berkeley Plantation. George Washington married his wife Martha in Kent County. Thomas Jefferson, author of the Declaration of Independence, married his wife at her father's plantation named 'The Forest' in Charles County, but all that remains of that plantation now is an archaeological site.

[10] British General Cornwallis surrendered to General George Washington at Yorktown in 1781, ending the hostilities of the Revolutionary War. See Index of Revolutionary War Sites for more rediscovered historical details.

[11] See Index of Civil War Sites for more rediscovered historical details.

times.[12] The fisheries of the Chickahominy River once were a major industry, but the last fish cannery had closed many years ago as a result of declining fish populations caused by man. During the late-spring spawning season, great shad fish runs once fed the workers of the regional economic engine. However, a four feet high dam was hastily built during World War II to supply fresh water from a pumping station to the booming wartime Navy Shipyard at Newport News 40 miles away. The dam was a barrier between fresh water upstream and brackish, salty tidal waters that flowed downstream until the Chick joined with the James that emptied into Chesapeake Bay. This lower, widening tidal portion of the Chick meandered, forming a marshy estuary in many areas.

The dam, called Walker Dam, also had a lock for small boats to travel upstream during the low tides which occurred twice a day downstream. The engineers built a small fish ladder, as even during wartime, they knew the importance of the river fisheries to the war effort. However, the fish ladder was ineffective and the shad fish were decimated, so this was the area's sacrifice to defeat the Nazis. In the end, the dam was both Victor and Destroyer, the great shad fish runs were gone, and the river economy faded except for tourism, camping, and recreational boating.

Charles County's remaining economy was from agriculture and forestry of largely swampy and mixed pine-hardwoods. The lack of opportunities led to a sparse, declining population and many moved for better prospects to the nearby cities of Richmond or Norfolk. The remaining residents were descendants of the original farming settlers, the last rivermen, the local freedmen slaves from the Civil War era, and the Chickahominy[13] Indian tribe. However, this lack of opportunity was overwhelmed by the area's natural beauty, from the sunsets across the James to cypress trees near the riverbanks with nesting ospreys or eagles diving toward the deep waters and a tasty yellow perch.

⋈⟨⟨⊲⊳⟩⟩⋈⟨⊲⊳⟩⋈

Nick now maintained the robotic gene synthesizers at Exgenics Farm. The robots could rapidly synthesize DNA strands base by base and molecule by molecule creating new DNA sequences and genes with potential uses in curing diseases. This technology combined with computational chemistry, and artificial intelligence were the foundations

---

[12] The only industries there were a wooden pallet factory and gravel quarry. The pallet factory was supplied with local timber and the gravel quarry supplied crushed stone and gravel for road building in nearby counties, but both had become largely automated and so contributed little to local employment.

[13] Translation from native language: "People of the Coarse Ground Corn"

gcgaacgcgatggcgtaagcgatggcgaacgcgccgctggcgaacgcgtgcgcgaacgcgctgccggcgaacgcgatggcgtaagcgatggcgaacgcg

of Dr. Gerardo's Crickett technology. Nick also assisted Dr. Gerardo with genetic experiments, where synthetic genes were inserted into eggs. The robotic gene insertion procedure had been completed on a large batch of tetraodon fish eggs and Nick was decanting the eggs into an aeration flask, where they'd grow into full-sized embryos for further experimentation and analysis.[14, 15, 16, 17]

As Nick stood up from his lab bench carrying a flask of fresh embryos, he suddenly felt a brief weakness come over him. Perhaps he'd stood up too quickly or his blood pressure dropped, but his now old, wrinkled hand lost grip. The flask immediately shattered on the industrial tile floor and covered the tiles with the liquid contents, fish eggs, and broken glass.

"Cheort!"[18] he exclaimed and knew that Dr. Gerardo, who often had temper tantrums, would be really mad at Nick for screwing up the experiment. He began cleaning up the mess by hosing down the spill into the floor drain and carefully sweeping up the sharp glass shards. He thought for a moment, "Now what am I going to do? I can't afford to lose my job for such a big mistake." Then, he remembered his lunch to eat

---

[14] Tetraodon – Scientific Order that includes puffer fish and blowfish species (Tetraodon means 'four-toothed.' The two teeth on the upper jaw and the two on the lower jaw are slightly fused in the center forming a beak that works like a pair of pincers.)

[15] Bases are the individual nucleotide units of the DNA; A, C, G, T are the scientific abbreviations for the four nucleic acid molecules in the deoxyribonucleic acid (DNA) strands of every living cell. When these units are joined in a specific sequence, (three bases per codon) the DNA creates amino acids in specific sequences that carry chemical energy and regulate the synthesis of amino acids and proteins forming the structure of living cells. DNA sequences are like a program code and define the living cell, its functions, and, ultimately, the organization, chemical processes, and multicellular life.

[16] Crickett is the acronym for Concurrent recombinant integrated computed (DNA) kernel expression & transcription transfer

[17] Tetraodons are some of the simplest vertebrates with the smallest known vertebrate genome, were the perfect genetic model to study the effects on higher vertebrates of genetic variations and manipulations. Their eggs could be readily incubated in tanks and, due to their fast rate of growth, the fish larvae could be studied, if necessary, as juvenile or adult fish in short order. Tetraodons were among the first vertebrates to have their DNA genetic codes fully mapped for study. Tetraodons have 22 chromosome-pairs and about 25,000 active genes in their DNA code versus 23 chromosome-pairs and a similar number of genes in humans. Most of their genes are active and compact, without non-coding "junk data" DNA sequences, so their chromosomes are shorter than other more complex animals. Tetraodons have only 340 Mb of genetic information in their DNA while humans are nearly ten times more complex lifeforms since humans have more than 3.1 Gb of genetic code. Even after 400 million years of higher vertebrate evolution, about 75% of tetraodon genes are similar to human genes, so they still represent a good laboratory study model of the effects of genetic changes in humans.

[18] Transliterated Russian Language - Черт: Heck, Hell (mild swear word)

catgcgccgccgtattaaattcgcacccatgatgcgtatgcgatggaacgcatttgcgcgcatgcgccgccgtattaaattcgcacccatgatgcgtat

gcgaacgcgatggcgtaagcgatggcgaacgcgccgctggcgaacgcgtgcgcgaacgcgctgccggcgaacgcgatggcgtaagcgatggcgaacgcg

later at break. Luckily, his lunch box contained an unopened can of ikra,[19] also known as golden caviar. He thought the salmon eggs were similar to tetraodon eggs, so Dr. Gerardo would never know the difference if he switched them. So, Nick grabbed another incubation flask, labeled it "Lab Book 3, Experiment #247" with the correct date. He added the salmon eggs, some incubation solution, and placed the flask in the aerator/incubator for Dr. Gerardo to examine the next morning.

After his shift, he drove home that rainy night to his trailer home near the James and into the loving arms of Elvira for a late dinner of hot borscht[20] and cold fish salad. Little did Nick know that the shoddily plumbed floor drains connected to the building's storm drainage system.

Friday, June 25, two years later…

It was late in the afternoon, just before dusk, on what would become a dark and stormy summer evening. The purple-shadowed anvil of a distant thunderstorm was billowing in the southwest and slowly approached the Exgenics farm. Several years ago, Gerardo had needed a research facility and bought an unprofitable, abandoned dairy farm located on over 1,400 acres of fertile land on the north bank of the Chickahominy River.

Its barn, silo, and old farmhouse were in a state of disrepair, but with renovations suited his purposes. He converted the farm into a modern facility, constructed a large research building, replaced the decaying silo, and fully restored the old, faded, and tattered cliché of a red-painted dairy barn near the ridgetop. Dr. Gerardo also gutted and modernized the farmhouse so he could spend the night when working late, but it was also a relaxing weekend retreat from the city with his wife Marianna. A final new addition, near the barn, was a towering quantenna with a rectangular box at the top pointing north toward the horizon.[21] The quantenna

---

[19] Transliterated Russian Language - икра: fish egg caviar, usually salmon eggs

[20] Russian beet, carrot, and cabbage soup with sour cream (optional). Add stewed beef meat (optional). Salt and Pepper to taste. Garnish with fresh dill. Recipe varies.

[21] Quantennas offer the highest possible data transfer rate and fully secure communications between two fixed points. There is no known method to "tap" their quantum-coupled photon transmissions. A quantenna's transmitter and receiver operates using a beam of gamma-ray photons travelling at the speed of light. The photons are beamed from the quantenna to an identical quantenna located up to 150 miles away. The shape of the quantenna and the heavy element lead acts as a receiver to capture the gamma-beam while a supporting structural antenna tower that aims the heavy receiver and transmitter equipment toward the second quantum-coupled quantenna at the other end of the data connection.

catgcgccgccgtattaaattcgcacccatgatgcgtatgcgatggaacgcatttgcgcgcatgcgccgccgtattaaattcgcacccatgatgcgtat

ensured Gerardo the fastest possible, maximum bandwidth, and fully secure Grid link so his research proceeded rapidly in complete security.[22]

Just downhill from the buildings, he constructed a pond of several acres to contain farm runoff and for irrigation. A patchwork of fields surrounded the research complex and beyond were hardwood forests. To the south was Chick Swamp, a flood-prone open forest and to the east was Old Forge Lake and Provident Forge, a minor historical site.

Old Forge Lake, a long deep finger of water sticking northward onto the dairy farm's land, was built before the Revolutionary War by damming a creek, Jones Run, to form a 70-acre lake. At that time, the dam fed water via a spillway to a water-powered blacksmith's forge. The forge was constructed by a Presbyterian minister and his partner, a freedman blacksmith, Jacob Coleman.[23] Now, all that remained was the old earthen dam and spillway built from locally-quarried stone cemented with colonial 'tabby' mortar.[24]

Twilight was beginning to fade that stormy June night as the distant thunderstorm neared the Exgenics farm. The flashes grew brighter and the thunder claps louder in more immediate intervals as the first raindrops began spattering in ringlets across the calm surface of the pond and nearby lake. Soon, the crickets ceased chirping, and in the barn, a moo bellowed from a dairy cow fearing the approaching storm. Seconds later, another cow resounded with even greater alarm.

Suddenly, with a flash and clap, the quantenna blazed with a billion-volt arc and 10,000 amperes of fiery electrical plasma connected between the earth and the sky. The farm's pond immediately glowed with several hundred diffuse yellow spots. The afterglow soon faded just under the surface of the raindrop rippled water.

The rain fell in earnest that evening, turning into a non-stop torrent after the initial thunder diminished. Rain dropped in buckets and the farm pond, constructed by the same shoddy contractor as the rest of the new buildings, began overflowing, cutting first a small notch through the

---

[22] The Grid was still not as extensive in rural areas due to the poor economics of covering such large areas with Grid transmitters.

[23] During the Revolutionary War, the forge turned plowshares into swords (and rifled black powder muskets), but British Lt. Colonel Banister Tarleton and his horseback cavalry Tarleton's Raiders burned it to the ground in 1781 before surrendering with Cornwallis at nearby Yorktown just months later.

[24] 'Tabby' mortar, a mixture of powdered lime from burnt oyster shells, river sand, and crushed shells, was used in foundations of nearby colonial Williamsburg, Virginia. When mixed with ashes, this mortar is an excellent cement.

earthen dam which contained the rising waters. The notch quickly eroded into a gash that expanded into a wide gap. Soon, the dam's berm collapsed and a wall of water burst downhill toward Old Forge Lake.

Meanwhile, the flooding headwaters of Jones Run had poured into Old Forge Lake, but for some reason, this storm was different than the previous storms of at least 250 years. Maybe it was the rapid surge from the farm's pond and the floodwaters briskly rushing beyond the spillway's capacity. Maybe the old tabby cement failed. Whatever the reason, the lake's spillway and nearby dam suddenly burst with a low rumbling sound of crashing stones and a gushing flood of nearly 1,200 acre-feet of water ensued within seconds.

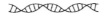

gcgaacgcgatggcgtaagcgatggcgaacgcgccgctggcgaacgcgtgcgcgaacgcgctgccggcgaacgcgatggcgtaagcgatggcgaacgcg

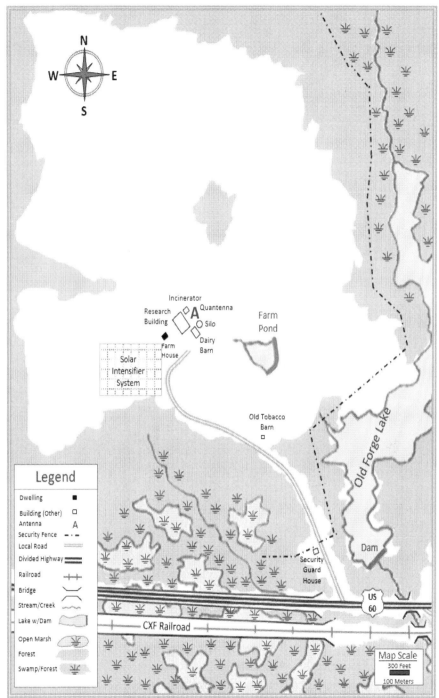

EXGENICS RESEARCH FARM

catgcgccgccgtattaaattcgcacccatgatgcgtatgcgatggaacgcatttgcgcgcatgcgccgccgtattaaattcgcacccatgatgcgtat

gcgaacgcgatggcgtaagcgatggcgaacgcgccgctggcgaacgcgtgcgcgaacgcgctgccggcgaacgcgatggcgtaagcgatggcgaacgcg

Chapter 2: Butterfly Effect

Old Forge Lake Spillway

5:00 a.m., Saturday, June 26, ...

At dawn's first light on this rainy, but soon to clear morning, Kent County Sheriff Albert Olsen used his e-screen to make a Grid-linked call to an old land-line telephone at the home of Charles County Sheriff George W. Coleman. Olsen, a descendent of Norwegian-Americans, spoke, "Morning George. Sorry to wake you."[25]

"What's up Al?" George replied to his friend after grabbing the handset of the princess phone on his bedside table.

"I just heard from Kent 911 Dispatch there's been a dam break at Old Forge Lake and a bridge washout. I'm going now to take a look, but it closed both the east and westbound lanes of U.S. Highway 60. A farmer said a flood swept away trees along the creek and tangled debris hit the bridges like a bowling ball knocking over anything in its path. Those old bridges just washed away."

"That sounds bad, Al. Is there any other damage?"

"I don't know George. I'm leaving now to look, but you check out your bank of the Chick just in case. Those highway bridges in Provident Forge caught the brunt of it. Luckily, downstream, there's just river meanders, swamp, and Chick Lake. So, you're likely okay."

"Thanks for letting me know to take a look, Al. I'll put my pants on, drive to Chick Bridge, then mosey over to give you a hand if you need it."

"That's a good idea. I still have to rouse more deputies and get them on their way to assist."

"See ya' in a few," Sheriff Coleman muttered as he hung up the telephone while slightly perturbed at waking up before sunrise. George

---

[25] The town of Norge in nearby James County was founded in 1904 by a "colony" of Norwegian-Americans who moved eastward from the Midwestern U.S. and consolidated with their families into the area which offered a better farming climate than the Midwest.

catgcgccgccgtattaaattcgcacccatgatgcgtatgcgatggaacgcatttgcgcgcatgcgccgccgtattaaattcgcacccatgatgcgtat

gcgaacgcgatggcgtaagcgatggcgaacgcgccgctggcgaacgcgtgcgcgaacgcgctgccggcgaacgcgatggcgtaagcgatggcgaacgcg

was a middle-aged local African-American who had joined the Army after high school. After two tours of duty and the war, he returned home with a distinguished service medal. Later, he was elected as Charles County Sheriff, served for many years, and was well respected by its citizens.

He still spoke the local Southern dialect, since some habits of a lifetime are hard to break. He enjoyed who he was and refused to change to fit in with others' lifestyle molds. He had an aversion to modern technology, which he avoided after seeing its vulnerability and unreliability in the Army. As a descendant of local freedmen, he thought modern technology was just a different form of slavery. In fact, he still didn't own an e-phone to remain free from the AI-technology he considered evil.[26]

His wife Olivia was lying on her side of their bed and softly asked, "What was that call, Honey?"

"It's work, Sweetheart."

"It's still early and it's your weekend off. It rained all night and today would've been a nice day to sleep in," Olivia replied as she put an arm over her husband's chest begging him to stay longer.

"I know, but it's my job and I gotta go to Provident Forge 'n check out the flood'n. There's been a bridge washout I hear." He clambered out of bed, put on his pants and rain gear, went to the kitchen, grabbed the wall-mounted telephone, and called his only full-time deputy, Jefferson James, to meet him at the Chick Bridge.

Olivia went to the kitchen and gave George a cup of instant coffee in a travel mug and a left-over country ham biscuit from the refrigerator for a cold breakfast on the road. She was used to this drill, one of the unfortunate side-effects of being married to a lawman.

George kissed Olivia goodbye, went outside into the rain, and climbed into his high mileage, antique 1979 Chevy Malibu patrol car with a sheriff's star, a county logo, and a rooftop rotating red dome-light. With a 350 cubic inch V8 engine and supercharged 4-barrel Quadrajet carburetor, it could nearly fly down rural roads. Similar engines had run a million miles, and George's car was nearly there. He liked the nostalgia and nicknamed it, "Ole Bessie" after his grandmother, keeping her waxed to a high gloss.

Luckily, George was a good mechanic, saving his impoverished county on vehicle maintenance. He loved such work, like it was in his blood, and upgraded the engine while largely keeping it in original condition. The only thing he couldn't repair was the police band radio, but Jason Dickson, a local young man and electronics wizard, made repairs to keep it working.

---

[26] AI is an abbreviation for Artificial Intelligence

catgcgccgccgtattaaattcgcacccatgatgcgtatgcgatggaacgcatttgcgcgcatgcgccgccgtattaaattcgcacccatgatgcgtat

11

Charles County could never afford the maintenance on newer police cars, especially those high-end electric-powered Supercruzer autoSUVs like Sheriff Olsen and his deputies drove.[27] George even maintained Deputy James' old, gas-powered 2030 Dodge Charger HP Police Turbo-Hemi-Special too, even though it was new compared to Ole Bessie.

Coleman drove toward Kent City along rain-soaked Charlestown Road, the only major road connecting the two counties. The road was fairly straight between swampy, flooded woods on either side. He soon rounded a bend and saw the smaller of two Chick bridges was intact. He drove another quarter-mile and stopped on the pavement, which was like an island surrounded by floodwaters. Yards away was remains of the second, longer steel truss bridge at the county line. The road ahead was washed out and the bridge collapsed into the muddy floodwaters. However, the northernmost pier was undamaged and the steel truss beams affixed to the north bank refused to release their grip, as a drowning man holds tight to stay above water.

Coleman radioed the usually lonely Charles County 911 dispatcher Mable Jones and she soon replied. He told her to tell Sheriff Olsen the Chick Bridge was out and send a deputy to the north bank. He sat quietly waiting and staring at the river while Ole Bessie's dome light rotated like a lighthouse beacon. Deputy James soon arrived and Coleman told Jeffrey, as he liked to be called, to install a barricade and contact Benson Thurmond, the county manager, to inform him of the emergency. George then climbed into Ole Bessie and drove a detour route toward Provident Forge. He backtracked on Lott Cary Road and turned north to cross upriver of the Chick Bridge by using the small Yadkin Road Bridge.[28]

Sheriff Olsen traveled in his nearly new Chiefmaster model Supercruzer with one of his deputies, James C. Jeffers, toward Provident Forge to survey the flood damage. As the Supercruzer drove itself south from Kent City, the rain was lightly falling when they saw the Old Forge dam breach and empty lake bed. The Supercruzer only drove a hundred yards further to the highway intersection when they saw more serious damage from the

---

[27] The proliferation of electric powered autocars, autoSUVs, autotrucks, and autodrones had been enabled by the advent of lightweight single-sheet lithium ion-doped graphene giga-capacitor technology which could store a large amount of electrical power and be recharged in a matter of minutes.

[28] Lott Cary was a famous freedman from Charles County who bought his own freedom, became a baptist minister, and was a missionary to Africa in 1821 where he established the first Baptist Church there, founded schools, and helped lead the new colony of Liberia for freed African-American slaves to resettle.

flooding. U.S. 60 highway to the right was destroyed, leaving a hundred-feet gap across Jones Run.

He verbally commanded the Supercruzer to park on the east side of the westbound bridge and the electric SUV carefully stopped with blue lights still flashing. Olsen soon received a dispatch from George that Chick Bridge also washed out, so he directed a second deputy, who was already en route, to install a roadblock there. He told Deputy Jeffers, "Luckily we have the I-64 interstate, so a detour won't be too bad while the Virginia Department of Transportation makes repairs, but it'll be inconvenient for the locals."

Deputy Jeffers nodded his head in agreement and added, "Yes, handling calls and patrols west of here will be difficult too."

Olsen next spoke, "E-screen. Real-time Sat-Map. Download and display image of current location."

The e-screen replied, "Local real-time Sat-Map image not available; next close-up satellite flyover imaging available at 4 p.m. Displaying present location 11 a.m. yesterday."

Sheriff Olsen frowned since he knew the Feds had access to 100% coverage, continuous satellite monitoring, but radar and thermal imaging were not readily available to local law enforcement without authorization and this morning was still cloudy. He briefly looked at yesterday's Sat-Map, swept his finger in an oval on the screen over the likely damaged area, and spoke to the Supercruzer, "Activate autodrone. Execute patrol loop of marked zone. Report and return." Immediately, his Supercruzer's roof panel opened and a sleek autodrone quadra-chopper took off 150 feet vertically to above the trees and sped away on patrol.

The Supercruzer rolled the window down and Osen yelled across the bridge washout to the farmer that had alerted 911 and was standing beside a pickup truck on the eastbound highway, "Stay over there, flag down anyone, and keep your hazard flashers on. Someone will be there soon."

The farmer yelled back, "Okay" in acknowledgment.

Olsen then directed his deputy, "James, get barricades and emergency flashers from the storage compartment and erect them across the lanes. I'll keep monitoring the autodrone images."

"Yes Al," he replied stepping out into the rain to do his job.

Olsen monitored the autodrone broadcasting its real-time e-vid images and was soon alarmed.[29] The flood surge had also washed out the CXF Railroad's old wooden trestle bridge over Jones Run. The bridge normally

---

[29] An e-vid is a real-time or recorded video/audio image display on any electronic device with an e-screen, such as an e-phone, e-watch, e-monitor, e-pad, or e-wall.

carried mile-long coal freight trains and this was the only rail line connecting to the Dominion State Coal Export Terminal.[30] Olsen urgently called dispatch to contact the railroad's emergency line to stop rail traffic. A morning train usually came in the morning and he hoped his alert was timely.

As he watched the drone's e-vid, he commented through the open window to Deputy Jeffers who was now standing in the light rain, "The railroad bridge was destroyed too. That damage will have a big economic impact until it's fixed. Some coal miners, remote-train engineers, and terminal workers will lose their jobs until the bridge is rebuilt. Knowing the railroads these days, it'll take months to repair. Once they see the problem's size, they'll take action though." Soon, the autodrone returned and docked in its rooftop compartment.

Sheriff Coleman soon arrived near the farmer on the opposite side of the bridge washout and parked Ole Bessie to fully block the eastbound highway. He kept his dome light flashing and climbed out into the remaining drizzle of the storm. George hollered across the washed-out creek ravine, "Yo Al. Big flooding, I see."

"Yeah George. Train tracks are gone too," Al loudly replied from the open window and then stepped outside the Supercruzer. Suddenly from the west, they heard an air horn moan and emergency brakes screeching. The horn and screeching continued long and hard, growing louder for what seemed a lifetime. The sound eventually stopped and was followed by morning silence. Then, they heard three sharp air horn honks.

"George, they're signaling the coal train is safe."

"That would've been a big wreck for sure. Sorry, I'm late to help you, but I had to detour across Yadkin Road Bridge."

"I'm glad you're here. Another deputy will be there in a few minutes. Wait for her and then come across the creek to me. We should discuss and coordinate our cleanup and detour efforts."

George looked down the freshly cut ravine of Jones Run. All low vegetation and many large trees had been stripped away leaving muddy slopes and torn roots on each embankment. At the bottom was a small stream that appeared exhausted after the flood and he saw rocks that would make good stepping stones. "I'll wait for your deputy and put on my mud boots. When she arrives, I'll be right over," he replied.

---

[30] Coal had been replaced as an energy source, but was still used for production of coke carbon used in steel production. The Terminal, at the Port of Newport News, still unloaded 20 million tons worth 8 billion e-coins per year of the high-grade metallurgical coal. About four to five trains, with about 100 hopper cars each, arrived each day.

"Hold on George. It's Kent Dispatch," Olsen said as his e-screen spoke.

Dispatch said, "The railroad said a train activated emergency brakes five miles west of you. With those wet rails, it took nearly four miles to stop. If the engine derailed, the entire train would've likely derailed too, wrecking the entire trestle just west of you across the swamp. The remote-engineers thanked you with some horn blasts."

Sheriff Olsen, much relieved at avoiding the train wreck, hollered again to George, "Dispatch said the train is okay."

"That's good news," Coleman replied.

Olsen continued his distant conversation, "Sorry to hear Chick Bridge is out. The highway here is my big problem. Luckily, no one was hurt. That farmer alerted Kent Dispatch. Thank him for me."

"Will do Al," Coleman replied and thanked the farmer for his help. However, the Chick Bridge was a much bigger problem for Sheriff Coleman. The major bridge connecting Charles County with Kent City and the interstate had been washed out. This meant Charles County would suffer repairs for months. It wasn't a state-owned bridge like those over U.S. 60 but jointly maintained by Kent and Charles Counties. This meant difficulty in coordinating and funding the repairs. Besides, a Yadkin Road detour only led to the closed U.S. 60, so it was impossible to easily drive toward the interstate. Downriver, there wasn't a bridge crossing for twenty miles until the Tyler Bridge where the Chick merged with the James, so that wasn't going to solve travel difficulties either. So, there'd be an economic impact from the damaged bridge that Charles County couldn't afford.

ᗡᐊᔑᐁᐊ

Olsen's deputy finally arrived, so George pulled on his rubber boots and carefully descended the muddy ravine slope to meet Al. Suddenly, he slipped fifteen feet on his backside until he hit the water's edge. He stood up and crossed the creek on some stones. Next, he tried slithering up the steep slope on the other side but kept sliding down the slippery mud bank. Now covered with brown clay mud from head to toe, he hollered to Al, who was watching with amusement from the edge of the ravine, "Throw me a line Al 'n pull me up."

Al went to his Supercruzer, grabbed a rope, and threw it to George. As he pulled the slack and held tight, George gripped the rope and made his way up the muddy bank. As George clambered onto the ragged pavement edge, the extra weight was too great and the bank supporting them gave way. They both suddenly slid down the ravine.

gcgaacgcgatggcgtaagcgatggcgaacgcgccgctggcgaacgcgtgcgcgaacgcgctgccggcgaacgcgatggcgtaagcgatggcgaacgcg

At the creek bottom again, George stood up to greet Al, "Now I know what mud wrastl'n's all about," and they shook muddy hands.

"You look just fine, George," Al chortled at his friend.

"Well Al, you look like me now, but I'm still the hero here because the Army said so," he laughed. "At least my socks are clean in my boots," George replied while looking at Al's muddy police shoes.

They laughed at each other looking like mud monsters from the swamp. Deputy Jeffers tied another rope to the Supercruzer's tow hook and the sheriffs both rappelled their way up the muddy bank.

Soon a high-pitched whirring sound began approaching from the north and increasing in volume. The sheriffs soon spotted a unidrone[31] above the trees coming from the Old Forge Lake. It automatically rotated its four high-speed electroprops into horizontal mode and landed on the vacant highway near the Supercruzer. The whirring stopped and the teardrop-shaped aerodynamic passenger pod cracked open its transparent front hatch, like a clam opening its shell. Inside, a man was revealed sitting in a single reclining seat. The man stepped out, followed by two black Dobermans, and walked toward the sheriffs.

The man commanded his dogs, "Sit Dante; sit Inferno." The dogs immediately recoiled into an alert sitting position and waited patiently for further commands. The man first looked at Deputy Jeffers and then at the mud-covered men and questioned, "Who's in charge here?"

Deputy Jeffers pointed at the mud-covered men and said, "One of them is Sheriff Olsen, but right now, I'm not sure who's whom."

The man spoke to both sheriffs, "Hello, I'm Dr. Gerardo of Exgenics Corporation. Our research farm is just upstream from the dam failure I saw from my unidrone. Looks like we have a bigger problem here though," he said looking with disgust at the mud-covered sheriffs who looked like local fools.

Dr. Gerardo was of Italian descent with curly black hair and an aquiline nose, perhaps in his late 40s or early 50s. His eyes radiated his mind's brilliance and he was fit for his age. He exercised regularly, took health supplements, and wore sunscreen to minimize aging from sun exposure. He was also an arrogant man, exuding an air of superiority like he was better than everyone else.

Sheriff Olsen slowly wiped his mud-covered eyes and mouth with a handkerchief and said, "I'm Sheriff Albert J. Olsen of Kent County. That dam break caused a big highway washout and destroyed the railroad. It

---

[31] A unidrone is an AI-piloted drone that carries a single passenger only.

catgcgccgccgtattaaattcgcacccatgatgcgtatgcgatggaacgcatttgcgcgcatgcgccgccgtattaaattcgcacccatgatgcgtat

destroyed Chick Bridge to Charlestown too. Luckily nobody was hurt and the trains stopped in time. Does Exgenics own the land the dam was on?"

"Until recently, but now Old Forge Lake and the dam are owned by Kent County. Since the locals like to fish and there's that historical forge site, our corporate attorney, John Gregory, deeded nearly 100 acres of land to Kent County about two months ago. The locals didn't like how we fenced in our entire property with security fencing and wanted to fish there again. Last fall, we discovered the ruins of the old forge too. So, we donated the land to Kent County for a park."

"I didn't know anything about ruins there, other than that old historical marker about the forge by the main road," Olsen commented.

Gerardo continued, "Yes, that historical marker always piqued my curiosity, so we hired a state archaeologist to look for it. They found some artifacts such as tools, swords, musket barrel blanks, and other remains that proved it used a water-powered forge hammer, one of only a few in the country at the time. It seems the freed slave who built the forge was quite a mechanical inventor. The archeologist wrote a report on her findings and gave it to the county, who became interested in the site. Exgenics even donated two-million e-coins to kick off fundraising for a museum nearby," Gerardo replied and almost sighed at having dodged a really big potential financial liability. He thought he should probably give his corporate attorney a bonus, but changed his mind since, at 5,000 e-coins per hour, he'd probably already earned enough.[32]

Sheriff Olsen hadn't yet thought of all the legal ramifications of the dam break, but Kent County likely seemed liable. Hopefully, the county's insurance policy could cover the potentially huge financial damages. If not, the county might be bankrupted. "Why did you come out here so early today doctor?" Olsen asked.

Gerardo replied, "Last night, my farm's AI-system informed me of a lightning strike that temporarily shut down power to my buildings, so I thought I'd drone here first thing this morning from Washington to check things out. However, I saw the empty lake, the bridges, and your flashing lights from the air and thought I'd land and check out the damage as a curious bystander." Fortunately, he already knew the farm's generator was enabled in just a few milliseconds of the lightning strike and the AI-system

---

[32] E-coins came into widespread use after the demise of the dollar and ensuing world-wide economic collapse. They became a digital substitute for paper currency but still suffered the same problems of inflation and ready abuse since they were controlled by governments, central banks, corporate banks, and their private financiers. E-wallet chips loaded with e-coins could be carried physically, but many preferred under-skin implants.

gcgaacgcgatggcgtaagcgatggcgaacgcgccgctggcgaacgcgtgcgcgaacgcgctgccggcgaacgcgatggcgtaagcgatggcgaacgcg

had messaged the research building and barn were okay. His farm pond was a different story though.

Gerardo continued, "My Kent City employees will have to detour by way of the interstate highway to reach our farm. I don't know how my employees who live in Charlestown will make it here though since they can't even cross the Chickahominy."

Sheriff Olsen suddenly interjected, "I've seen you before Dr. Gerardo. I briefly met you four months ago at that presentation and reception where your company donated five new Supercruzers to our force. I'm sorry I didn't recognize you just now. You looked a little older with grey hair."

"Yes, I've lost some weight recently and my wife made me dye my hair black like when I was younger. That takes years off you really fast and your wife is happy. Happy wife makes a happy life," he said grinning a wry smile and winking. "Yes, now I remember you Sheriff, but you're hard to recognize covered in mud."

"And *you* are?" Gerardo questioned while looking at the other mud-covered lawman of some sort.

"I'm Sheriff George Washington Coleman of Charles County 'cross the river. Pleased to meet you, Doc Gerardo."

Gerardo hid his disdain at the muddy sheriff with a local dialect, but being somewhat of a good politician as well as scientist acknowledged this rural, uneducated man and said, "I'm glad to meet you, sir. It's nice to know my farm is well protected from both sides of the river. Now I need to figure out how my Charlestown employees can get to work Monday."

Coleman replied with the solution, "Yadkin Road Bridge is still working upstream from here, so we'll put up some detour signs and reroute traffic. It'll be inconvenient until repairs, but it'll solve your problem."

Gerardo grimaced a slight smile, and answered, "That's a good plan Sheriff. Things may work out better than I first thought."

Next, the men walked about a hundred yards or so toward the remains of Old Forge dam to examine the cause of their problems. Looking closely, they saw considerable erosion and a wide section of the earthen dam's berm was gone. The spillway stones cemented together with tabby mortar were completely washed away and displaced downstream by the flood except a few that remained near the bottom. As a scientist, Gerardo commented on his observations of the obvious, "I think last night's storm was more than it could handle and the floodwaters just tore it apart."

The sheriffs agreed with him knowing that it would be weeks before a civil engineer from the Virginia Division of Engineering performed an

catgcgccgccgtattaaattcgcacccatgatgcgtatgcgatggaacgcatttgcgcgcatgcgccgccgtattaaattcgcacccatgatgcgtat

gcgaacgcgatggcgtaagcgatggcgaacgcgccgctggcgaacgcgtgcgcgaacgcgctgccggcgaacgcgatggcgtaagcgatggcgaacgcg

engineering study and failure analysis. Then, a report would eventually be published on the likely causes of the dam and bridge failures.

Gerardo looked across the remains of the lake, now largely a mud pit with occasional shallow puddles and small pools of water. A few dead, stranded fish were seen laying on the mud. Then, Gerardo briefly revealed a glimmer of terror in his eyes before he controlled his emotions in front of the sheriffs. They surveyed the lake bed a moment longer and walked back to the scene of the highway washout.

Gerardo said, "All is okay now and there's nothing here I can do to help. Fortunately, my farm almost runs automatically, but I'll need to alert my employees now to find alternate routes to work. Call Exgenics Security if you need anything gentlemen." He commanded his obedient dogs to follow, climbed into his unidrone cockpit, and whirred away northwest a short distance to the research farm.

The sheriffs stayed behind to make disaster recovery plans, but first, they both discussed Dr. Gerardo. Olsen said, "Just like a rich corporate elitist jerk, flying here on his private drone, telling us everything is okay, and then whirling away. I kissed his butt because he gave us those new Supercruzers."

"Ole Bessie's fine by me, and that high-flyin' technology is dangerous and breaks pretty fast," George replied. "He seems pretty generous with his money though giving away that land and Supercruzers to your county. He must want something or a favor somehow," George commented as he knew favors usually came with puppeteer strings attached. "What's his company Exgenics make?" he asked Al. "I know one of their employees from Charlestown, but I never asked him what they do there."

Al replied, "I think they're doing some genetic research and they've some dairy cows with milk that contains some cancer drugs or something like that. At least that's what I heard at that Supercruzer reception. I've got a hunch something's fishy though with that donation of the dam and forge site. People like him don't freely give things away without a reason."

George replied, "Well I always try first to give people the benefit of a doubt until they prove otherwise. I'm thirsty for some more coffee. Olivia gave me a cup on my way out the door, but that's long gone and today looks like I'll be busy with this emergency."

"Want a donut too?" Al asked as he stepped over and opened the door to his Supercruzer.

"That'd be fine."

Olsen spoke to his Supercruzer, "Two cups coffee, one with cream and two sugar donuts." In about twenty seconds, the coffee maker on the

catgcgccgccgtattaaattcgcacccatgatgcgtatgcgatggaacgcatttgcgcgcatgcgccgccgtattaaattcgcacccatgatgcgtat

gcgaacgcgatggcgtaagcgatggcgaacgcgccgctggcgaacgcgtgcgcgaacgcgctgccggcgaacgcgatggcgtaagcgatggcgaacgcg

dashboard spit out two hot cups of coffee in paper cups and two fresh donuts popped out of the microwave robo-cooker onto a small tray.

"Dang those Supercruzers, they've got everything!" Coleman replied in amazement as he looked with envy toward Ole Bessie on the other side of the bridge washout.

"Yeah, I bought the Chiefmaster model using Gerardo's donation. It has all the bells and whistles," he chuckled and continued, "but I think they make their real money selling coffee cassette refills and dough cartridges," he cynically concluded.

They stood there drinking hot coffee, eating fresh donuts, and looked toward the research farm on the distant ridgeline. It was floating like a ship, barely visible just above some low fog and trees in the foreground, as a sunbeam pierced the clouds with its intense morning rays, fully illuminating the barn, research building, silo, and quantenna.

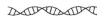

Chapter 3: An Emergency Board Meeting

Gerardo's Unidrone

Saturday, Mid-Morning, June 26, ...

The AI-piloted unidrone auto-landed on its pad outside the research building and Gerardo stepped out, followed by his dogs. He firmly commanded Dante and Inferno to patrol. The dogs immediately split up and, in a synchronized manner, searched outside the buildings, slowly increasing their search perimeter in wider circles. He entered the research building and went to his control room to inspect the AI-system. He also checked the Q-modem connecting the quantenna hit by lightning earlier.

The AI-system with its security, farm, and biofactory subroutines and its quantum chips allowed his facility to largely operate automatically, as the gene synthesizers and robotic Crickett equipment used quantum nano-processors.[33] His farm factory also operated using agrobots substituting for most manual labor, but he still had a dozen employees. There was a robo-tech repairing agrobots and robotics, the doctor testing genetic drugs in the medical annex, the company veterinarian who monitored the animals, and several genetic technicians supporting his research. Also, since his dairy cows were deathly afraid of agrobots, a few farm laborers handling animals could never be replaced.[34] Of course, the AI-system also

---

[33]AI-systems, and the quantum chips they used for calculations, had been terrible for unemployment but great for businesses. Quantum nano-processor chips are based on quantum mechanics theory and can solve complex problems quickly, but not necessarily accurately the first processing cycle; they repeat solving the same problem multiple times arriving at optimal solutions. Their speed advantage overwhelms binary processing chips to solve difficult problems. Instead of performing millions of calculations sequentially, they solve calculations simultaneously, but must repeat the solution multiple times until the best (but not necessarily perfectly correct) result is obtained. Quantum data is stored as qubits and qubytes, similar to bits and bytes of binary processing computers.

[34] Cows have been known to cause severe damage to agrobots from fear; some cows are known to have heart attacks when milked or attended to by agrobots.

gcgaacgcgatggcgtaagcgatggcgaacgcgccgctggcgaacgcgtgcgcgaacgcgctgccggcgaacgcgatggcgtaagcgatggcgaacgcg

handled most security, so that was another extinct career. However, during normal business hours, a front gate security guard handled visitors.

Gerardo examined the e-screen and saw two warning alarms: one for the lightning strike that caused the temporary power loss and the other for the pond's dam failure. Of course, he didn't tell the sheriffs earlier about the alarms since he didn't want them snooping around. He saw all systems were okay and his quantenna was still data-coupled with the Q-modem.

He walked to his adjacent office through the connecting door, put on his knee-high rubber barn boots, and went outside to survey the pond damage and, especially, the lake. He signaled Dante and Inferno to come, looked at the pond, and then walked down the farm's long driveway to the dam and muddy lakebed covered with many dead fish.

Gerardo arrived near the dam's spillway remains, commanded the dogs to sit obediently on the dam's intact grassy bank, and waded into the thick mud to retrieve the dead tetraodon he'd spotted earlier. Although he had a small frame, he was still too heavy and, luckily, only sank to the top of his boots. He picked up his specimen using a rubber glove, but in that mud, he'd need help to gather any more specimens from the lakebed.

Next, he commanded Dante and Inferno to come to him, but they hesitated after seeing Gerardo standing deeply in mud. Upon a firmer command, the dogs gingerly stepped onto the mud, carefully walking to Gerardo's side without sinking deeply. He showed them the fish, let them sniff it, and commanded them to search and fetch. The dogs began searching and occasionally slipped and slid as they traversed the muddy flats and banks. They began collecting their specimens, like Retrievers gathering stray quail after a successful shotgun blast.

Gerardo mucked his way out of the mud and sat on an old log waiting for his search party to complete their mission. Slowly but steadily, the dogs used their front teeth to grab each tetraodon by its tail and brought to him dead fish, laying each one at his feet. By end of the morning, the dogs refused to search further. Gerardo took that as a sign that the dogs couldn't find any more tetraodons. He sat a minute longer reconnoitering his catch. In total, they found two adult and eight juvenile tetraodons.

He put the specimens in a zipper bag and walked uphill with Dante and Inferno to the barn. He took a hose, sprayed the mud off his boots, and washed off his dogs. They were usually obedient, but unfortunately, bath-time wasn't one of those times. They sullenly whined and stood meekly while Gerardo hosed them down, gave a soapy scrub, and rinsed them. With their hasty bath over, the dogs shook furiously like wet rag dolls and ran away to sulk and dry in the summer sun.

catgcgccgccgtattaaattcgcacccatgatgcgtatgcgatggaacgcatttgcgcgcatgcgccgccgtattaaattcgcacccatgatgcgtat

Gerardo brought the specimens to his research lab, put on some surgical gloves, and began his exam and dissection. Two female adult specimens were nearly nine inches long, each weighing about a pound. He made a scalpel incision into the abdomens, opened the body cavities, and examined the contents. He recognized several new structures, so these fish were from his experiments. Gerardo was more alarmed at seeing ovaries nearly bursting with fertilized eggs and ready to spawn. He was in disbelief since he'd always made sure his genetic experiments were sterile.

He next dissected the heads, crunching through some difficult areas with diagonal nippers, and again found structures indicating they were his experiments. He laid his tools on the table, put the bodies and entrails into a bin, took off his gloves, and shoved the dead fish into a refrigerator.

He was in shock and was thinking hard. How could this have happened? Exgenics had always been extremely careful to control the embryos and the tetraodon fish they'd engineered before. Nothing ever left the research building and all biological wastes were burned in the farm's industrial incinerator. Even more alarming was these fish appeared to be from a later experiment.

Saturday Afternoon, June 26, ...

Dr. Gerardo went to his farmhouse office to e-vid call his corporate attorney, John Gregory. Gregory was a gray-haired older man and morbidly obese, but, despite his appearance, was an excellent lawyer. Gerardo said, "John, we've problems at the farm. I need your help *now*."

Gregory answered his e-watch from a golf course adjacent to his estate near Fairfax, a rich suburb of Washington. "What's happened, Ernesto? I'm golfing right now," Gregory agitatedly replied before taking a birdie putt on a Par 5 hole.

"A storm last night caused a flash flood that washed out our farm pond. The Old Forge Lake dam burst too. The floodwaters took out some highway bridges and the railroad. That'll be a big problem for the locals and CXF, but there's another serious problem for us."

"What is it? Tell me the whole story," Gregory replied with immediate worry as he'd already heard something alarming.

"When I droned down this morning to check the AI-alarms, the local sheriffs were on the highway. So, I landed to assess the situation. We walked to the dam break. There, I saw a dead T-fish on the lakebed. After the sheriffs left, I collected that specimen. Dante and Inferno searched all morning, finding several more. We cleared the lakebed, but more likely escaped in the flood. I dissected two females ready to spawn."

"This is serious Ernesto," Gregory replied grimly.

"Even worse John. They're recent prototype designs."

Gregory, a wealthy older man about ready to retire, was an investor in Exgenics and wanted it to be successful. "I can't wait forever for my investment in your technologies to pay off and I'm not getting any younger. What're we going to do?"

"First, let's call an emergency board of directors meeting to discuss and determine an action plan. We can't let the alternative e-media on the Grid find out or they'll surely expose our secrets and ruin us all. The outcry would put us into prison for a long time. Our shareholders own the normal public news channels, so that isn't an issue, but if this leaks *anywhere*, what we're doing would cause considerable outrage. It would destroy us all, and when I say destroy us all, I mean our shareholders too."

"OK, Ernesto. I'll arrange an emergency meeting this afternoon, but it's the weekend and many board members aren't available. As CEO, you should invoke Corporate Charter Article 22, Paragraph 5 which allows actions at an emergency meeting if a majority of attendees agree by vote."

"As CEO, I'll invoke the meeting. John, set up the meeting three hours from now. That will give me time to get things started here. Then get your butt down here from your golf holiday. We'll need to coordinate this situation together until it's resolved."

Gregory gave his putter to his robo-caddy, which placed it in his golf bag, and e-phoned a duodrone taxi to pick him up at the 16th hole green.[35] "Dang," he thought, "I was having a great round and was ten under par too." He commanded the robo-caddy to return to the clubhouse and waited. The duodrone appeared within five minutes and landed at Gregory's Grid coordinates. He climbed into the cockpit and commanded the AI-pilot take him to his office in Alexandria where he'd discretely contact as many board members as were available.

As an orthodox Jew, Nick was observing Shabbat, the Saturday of rest as commanded by God, but since he was Russian, he wasn't as strict and moderated his worship to blend with his rural community. He napped in his trailer home while Elvira read a book when his e-screen woke him with an incoming e-vid call from Dr. Gerardo.

"Don't answer that," Elvira said. "Dr. Gerardo knows it's Saturday."

---

[35] A two-passenger drone carrying a heavier/larger payload than a unidrone.

catgcgccgccgtattaaattcgcacccatgatgcgtatgcgatggaacgcatttgcgcgcatgcgccgccgtattaaattcgcacccatgatgcgtat

gcgaacgcgatggcgtaagcgatggcgaacgcgccgctggcgaacgcgtgcgcgaacgcgctgccggcgaacgcgatggcgtaagcgatggcgaacgcg

"Yes, Elvira, but he'd only call in an emergency. We're allowed to violate Shabbat in an emergency," since working on the Sabbath is permissible in a life-threatening situation.

Nick said to his e-screen, "Answer voice only," to not break Shabbat rules excessively and the Grid instantly made the connection.

Gerardo said, "Hello Nick. Sorry to bother you today, but I need you to work this afternoon. There's an emergency at the farm with a DNA sample. You need to run it in the robo-sequencer immediately."

"You know I don't work on Saturdays, doctor."

"Yes, but you're retiring in a few months and if you come, I'll add 20,000 e-coins to your retirement bonus."

Nick thought for a few seconds and realized that God would want him to help and earn this bonus. "I'll be there in fifteen minutes Doctor Gerardo," he replied with a smile.

"In case you don't know, the Chickahominy Bridge was washed out by last night's storm. There's a detour using Yadkin Road."

"I hadn't heard, but with Chick Bridge out, it'll take me twenty minutes longer," Nick replied, "I'll be there in about a half-hour."

"Ok Nick, meet me in the sequencing lab."

"See you soon doctor," Nick replied and commanded his e-screen to terminate the Grid connection. While Elvira scolded him for violating the Shabbat, he quickly put on some work clothes and walked out the door for his used autocar to drive him to work.

Nick soon arrived at the farm and met Gerardo in the lab. Gerardo said, "I'm glad you're here Nick. I can't operate this new robo-sequencing equipment. Please load this tetraodon embryo sample and start the DNA sequencing and gene decoder processes. Then, compare it with our viable tetraodon experiment database."

Nick replied, "OK, Doctor Gerardo, that will take about an hour," thinking that 20,000 e-coins was amazing Saturday afternoon earnings. Nick started analyzing the sample while Gerardo went back to his office to plan the upcoming board meeting. "What was the emergency?" Nick thought, but he knew Dr. Gerardo kept his research compartmentalized. Other than the embryonics and sequencer labs where he had eye-scan access, the only other building areas Nick accessed were the breakroom and the restroom.

Nick put on his lab smock, gloves, and used a sterile eyedropper to suction the small embryo from the vial left on the workbench. He put the specimen into an ultrasonic cell disruptor with a few extra drops of water and pressed on-button. Soon, the DNA molecules were freed from the nucleus of each cell. He took an eyedropper full of solution and placed a drop in the robosequencer. He next waited twenty minutes for the e-terminal to indicate completion of genomic sequencing.

He then ran a data check sample in the sequencer from another solution drop and waited twenty minutes more. If the DNA fingerprints from both drops correlated, the specimen sequencing data was correct. He looked at the sample fingerprints and they perfectly matched. Then, since this specimen came from a living tetraodon, he verbally instructed the AI-system to compare the specimen's DNA sequence with viable tetraodons in the database.

The AI-system responded in two seconds, "No exact match in viable tetraodon database."

"What is the closest alternative match?" he asked.

The AI-system replied, "Lab Book #3, Experiment 248."

Nick thought that seemed familiar and instructed the AI-system to search the entire database. The AI-system replied, "Perfect match with Lab Book #3, Experiment 247 with a calculation probability of 0.999999999." Then, he remembered the embryos he replaced with ikra two years ago. Dr. Gerardo would now find his previous mistake and thought, "There goes my retirement. I'll be fired on the spot. Gerardo doesn't tolerate employee mistakes."

Nick called Dr. Gerardo to the lab using the AI-system. Soon, Gerardo arrived and asked, "What did you find Nick?"

Nick stated firmly, "Doctor Gerardo, analysis indicated the closest viable embryo match is from Lab Book 3, Experiment 248."

"Oh, that's good news. I was in the lab this morning and mixed up some old specimens and wanted to make sure they were identified. Thanks, Nick, for your help. You can go home now."

"You're welcome doctor," he replied while mentally sighing in relief as he left. On the ride home, he felt guilty at his lie, but now he knew the doctor just used the emergency as an excuse for extra labor on a Saturday. However, he soon wondered where the doctor found a sample that matched Experiment 247.

Dr. Gerardo went to his office and instructed his AI-system, "Display gene design coding file for Experiment 248 from Lab Book 3 and review Crickett calculations of proposed genetic sequence for experimental observation and design validation." The e-screen displayed the data file while Gerardo's eyes read each line of gene coding as the text automatically scrolled upwards synchronized with his eye movements. After two minutes, Gerardo knew everything he needed and thought about how to handle the board meeting in a half-hour. However, he still couldn't understand how lab specimens escaped into the lake since Exgenics incinerated all test specimens and extra embryos.

⋙⋘⋙⋘

At 5:00 p.m., Gerardo sat down in the small conference room that served as the conference room for the emergency board meeting. There was a table for a dozen people and on one wall, a large e-screen displayed five sub-screens of board members who responded on short notice. On a sixth sub-screen was John Gregory. Normally, there would've been a dozen board members for a voting quorum for decisions that affected the shareholders. Of course, as CEO, Gerardo could cast his vote to break any tie votes. However, five available board members would work perfectly, since there could be no tie votes.

Gerardo called the meeting to order, "I hereby call this Exgenics Emergency Board Meeting to order and invoke Corporate Article 22, Paragraph 5 to allow decisions by attending board members. Mr. Gregory will take a formal roll call and record the minutes."

"Doctor Gisela Terranova, Geneva Genetic Diseases Clinic. Present."

"General George Mason, US Army, Retired. Here."

"John D. Stoneman IV, Chairman, Stoneman Family Trust. Present."

"Peter Maxwell, First Bank of Wales. In Attendance."

"David Mueller, C.E.O., E-Face Network. Present."

Then Gregory added, "Let the meeting records also show that the following board members are absent from this board meeting. In alphabetical order, they are Paul Chan, Singapore Universal Electronics; Dr. Ajay Gupta, Omnicure Pharmaceuticals; Fujita Ishikawa, All-Nippon Robotics; Min-Jun Lee, Central Bank of Korea; Alexei Pechnikov, Rusmetalik Industries; James Tuskegee, Drone-Motion Corporation; and, Andrew Zanitsky, Chairman of Gridcom Corporation.

Doctor Terranova, irritated at having been woken up at her Swiss chalet rudely chimed with an Italian accent, "Why was I awakened this evening? What is the emergency?"

Gerardo answered, "Dr. Terranova, we've had some serious incidents at the farm today. There was a lightning strike last night, some serious flooding that washed out our farm pond, and downstream a local dam burst. Some highway bridges and the CXF railroad bridge were washed out too.

John Stoneman interrupted, "I own CXF. That hurts my business."

"Yes, I know Mr. Stoneman, but you have insurance," Gerardo stated and continued, "Well the flood started a chain reaction. The first event triggered the second and soon damage spiraled out of control. Like that butterfly effect, where a butterfly flapping its wings causes a hurricane on the other side of the world."

Peter Maxwell, the elderly English financier and banking tycoon replied tersely, "I don't care about your butterfly mumbo jumbo. Those aren't emergencies requiring a board meeting." Maxwell just wanted the meeting over so he could return to his attractive date and fundraiser at the London Museum modern art exhibition.

Gerardo replied forcefully, knowing meetings of powerful, ambitious people were hard to control, "Yes, you're correct Maxwell. The real emergency is dead T-fish were found in the empty lakebed. I found them this morning when inspecting the dam failure. Here's an image of one I dissected," as it displayed on their e-screens.

The board members gasped and emoted surprise or fear simultaneously.

Doctor Terranova asked, "Are you sure the fish are yours?"

Gerardo replied firmly, "Doctor, you know DNA doesn't lie. The genetic fingerprints match my experiments positively. They're T-fish prototypes and, even worse, two females were ready to spawn. The rest were juveniles, likely hatched last year from eggs."

Terranova continued, "How could they be fertile? You assured us your genetic simulations produced asexual fish and your sequencing controls eliminated this risk?"

Gerardo replied, "Well as you know, AI-quantum calculations aren't exact and are educated guesses. Still, they're much faster than those made by old-style sequential processing silicon chips. That's why we make so many experimental trials to test new genetic design theories and evaluate the response of our sequences to produce the positive results we desire."

"How did this happen?" David Mueller interjected in his thick German accent. "You incinerated your wastes and used the best lab protocols."

"I don't know, but many escaped. Given the size of the lake, I estimate perhaps 100 to 400 adults and ten times as many juveniles that'll mature this year. If 50% of the adults are females ready to spawn, at least 5,000 eggs could hatch soon. Also, when the juvenile population breeds, there will be 60,000 to 100,000 eggs next year. Populations breed uncontrollably and grow exponentially when unchecked by natural mortality," Gerardo explained.

"Yes, we all understand that too well," commented Doctor Terranova.

Gerardo continued, "As you know, T-fish have an enhanced growth rate for genetic studies and were engineered with bacterial tetrodotoxin genes inserted into their genetic code. They produce this toxin as another profitable byproduct supporting our efforts.[36] Their eggs will have a higher-than-normal survival rate in the wild since they're saturated with a deadly nerve toxin."

General Mason replied harshly, "This is serious. How could this happen? If we're discovered, it'll ruin our plans. It's taken decades to get this close to our final solution. We'll have to accelerate our schedule."

Gerardo replied, "Yes, I know. That's why I called the emergency board meeting. We need to agree on an action plan. *Now*."

"What do you propose Gerardo?" John Stoneman coldly asked.

"I've thought hard and we can pool the board's combined assets to control this situation. This incident can spiral out of control quickly, so we must take immediate action."

"I agree that this will spread fast, especially with e-vids these days," David Mueller of E-Face chimed in.

"Yes, that's why we should move now, with full monitoring and ground ops until we further assess the problem and find a longer-term solution," Gerardo urgently implored.

Gregory chimed in, "I think we also have a legal issue with the dam break. There will be millions of e-coins in economic damage. We just gave the lake and dam to the local county and don't want to arouse more suspicion. From what I hear, Gerardo met the Kent and Charles County Sheriffs this morning and they might investigate further.

Gerardo commented, "Well, Sheriff Olsen from Kent County might be a problem, since he was asking a lot of questions, but that Charles County Sheriff didn't seem a problem. He's just a country bumpkin without much substance with an overinflated ego."

General Mason replied, "Just in case, I think we should base any ops teams near Williamsburg in James County. That's a small city and our operatives won't attract attention there. Give me a day to mobilize them. Gerardo, you'll have to take the point until they arrive."

---

[36] Tetrodotoxin is a deadly sodium-channel nerve blocker causing paralysis. An extremely small dose causes death. This poison is 1,200 times deadlier than cyanide and just one milligram is lethal. This is the toxin found in Fugu blowfish used in a dangerous, and sometimes deadly, Japanese Sushi dish. Tetrodotoxin is normally formed by a species of bacteria that lives inside certain pufferfish species. One milligram of crystalline Tetrodotoxin is not much larger than a single grain of salt. When injected into the body, it is much more potent and deadly than accidental Fugu sushi poisoning via ingestion.

Heir Mueller added, "Of course, our monitoring capabilities will report any e-vid activities. I'm sure Mason and Andrew Zanitsky will help too."

Mason replied, "Yes, we'll back all efforts. Obviously, our first action is to determine the problem's extent to find a solution eliminating the threat to our greater plans."

Gregory contributed further, "I'll focus on public damage control and pull together a strategic action team. We need the board members here to afterward inform other members to lend full support to our efforts."

Gerardo added, "One last thing, I suggest we get the farm pond's dam repaired quickly and quietly, to not arouse suspicion."

Gregory chimed in, "That seems a wise move."

Gerardo concluded the meeting, "Yes, I think we all agree on the immediate plan. Of course, our plans will evolve as we gain information. All in favor of the proposed emergency board actions please say aye."

The e-vid screens replied with a resounding chorus, "Aye."

As a formal board meeting protocol, Gerardo asked sarcastically "Any nay votes?" He chuckled as the e-screens remained quiet.

"Emergency action plan agreed unanimously by attending board members. The vote shall be recorded in the corporate meeting minutes. This board meeting is hereby closed," Gerardo commanded. "We'll keep you informed of any news or progress. Goodbye, everyone."

There was silence as the meeting terminated and the e-wall turned blue, except for Gregory's e-screen so he could talk with Gerardo further.

Gerardo said, "I think I should keep a low profile for a week, so I'll drone back to Washington now. First, I'll send an e-message to our employees about the road washouts and inform them to take detours to work on Monday. Get a construction contractor here to repair the pond as fast as you can, John."

Gregory replied, "I'll drone taxi to Provident Forge tonight to begin planning and setting up any ops that might be needed," and disconnected his e-vid link from the Grid.

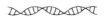

Chapter 4: A River Murder-Suicide

Mt. Carmel Baptist Church

Sunday Afternoon, June 27, ...

Sheriff Coleman was at home with Olivia after attending the Mt. Carmel Baptist Church service.[37] After yesterday's overtime, he wanted rest and a nap would suit him just fine. The phone rang and he grabbed the receiver, "Hello, Coleman here."

"It's Jeffery. There's been a shooting at old Captain Jack's house and I'm heading there now. His neighbor, Johnnie Walker, just called 911."

"I'll be there in five minutes," Coleman replied and immediately strapped on his automatic 1911 Colt pistol, climbed in Ole Bessie, and sped away at high speed with siren wailing. He soon drove on a long gravel road toward Binns Bank on the south side of Chick Lake. On the way, he passed open-sided farm sheds filled with a museum's worth of farm machinery made obsolete by agrobots.

After driving a half-mile further, he stopped behind Deputy James' patrol car which blocked the driveway's end. He was alert and quickly walked toward the old tin-roofed house of Captain Jack Thompson, a very old riverman and the most respected fishing guide along the lake and river. Captain Jack, or just 'Captain' as the locals called him, was the last man alive whose parents remembered the old river. He lived simply with Macy, his wife of sixty years, avoiding most modern technologies. The only truly modern device he used was an old cell phone for communications with his fishing and 'other' clients.

---

[37] The church was built by freedman after the Civil War from hand-hewn lumber. The freedmen of that time did not want to continue worshiping from only the upper balconies in the churches built by their former masters. To this day, the Baptist Church is still largely voluntarily-segregated in the South, but the church service style of African-American churches differ greatly from the traditional Baptist style. This cultural difference likely contributes to this continued separation.

Deputy James was waiting on the front porch for Coleman to arrive while Johnnie stood nearby desperately holding back Rufus, the Captain's Black and Tan Coonhound, from scratching the front door.[38] Rufus was howling, making the situation even more disconcerting.

"Johnnie, tell me what happened?" Coleman asked as he arrived.

Johnnie told his tale, "You know I live just down the road by the dam. Well after lunch, I heard some shots coming from the Captain's place, but I didn't think much at first since he target practices. Then I saw Rufus running toward my shack barking uncontrollably. He wanted me to follow him, so I grabbed my shotgun in case of trouble and, since I lost my license after the 'shine wreck, I took off lickedly-split in my golf cart with Rufus following. When I got here, the Captain was dead on the kitchen floor and I called 911 from my e-phone. I've been holding Rufus back until you both just arrived."

"Johnnie, can you hold Rufus a while longer while Jeffrey and I look around the house? Maybe take him to your house and keep him there until we come get him."

"Sure, Rufus knows me some since I was a neighbor and that should be comforting. I'll need a leash," the old man replied holding the dog by his collar as the dog continued howling. Jeffery ran to his patrol car, found a short piece of rope, returned, and improvised a leash. Johnnie soon tugged Rufus away down the gravel road.

Coleman and Deputy James entered the front porch door and saw the Captain's body lying nearby on the kitchen floor. He was sprawled face down on the wooden planking with a pool of blood seeping away from his chest. "Where's Macy? Let's find her," Coleman directed.

They quickly searched the inside and didn't find her, but when they went out the north porch door, they saw Macy sitting in her rocking chair staring eyes wide-open at the lake with an old .357 Smith and Wesson revolver lying by her side on the porch decking. He saw a single bullet hole in her right temple, but no exit wound. There wasn't a lot of blood, so the bullet wasn't a high-powered .357 magnum cartridge. After Deputy James took some e-phone photos, Coleman closed Macy's eyes with respect and covered her with an old bedsheet he found in a linen closet.

Next, they went inside the kitchen and Deputy James took a series of evidence photos of the body from different angles while Coleman went to Ole Bessie, got a stick of chalk, and returned to outline the body on the

---

[38] Black and Tan Coonhounds are a mixture of Virginia Foxhounds and Blood Hounds and are especially good tracking and hunting dogs. They are affectionate and loyal, but have a bad habit of drooling saliva.

floor. Coleman next rolled the body over onto its back and saw that blood had seeped mostly from near his heart, but there was also a wound in his gut. He now took another old sheet and covered the Captain. Coleman directed Jeffrey, "Contact Mable to tell the Charles County Volunteer Ambulance Service to recover the bodies in about an hour or so after we investigate the crime scene further."

Jeffrey called Mable and afterward, Coleman asked him for his viewpoint of the situation, "What do you think happened?"

Deputy James declared, "I think after so many years, Macy got tired of him sleeping all day or fishing and carrying on all night long with the moonshine. He probably skipped church to drink 'shine this morning and she came home from Reverend Dickson's service to find him drunk and she just snapped."

Coleman replied, "Yeah, that wouldn't surprise me. Captain Jack had a special island in the swamp where he kept his still. He used to bring his 'other' clients there at night sometimes to get high on his 'shine."

Coleman went looking for further evidence. The engine of the Captain's old F-150 pickup truck was cold, so it wasn't used today. He next went to the boathouse and found that the inboard engine of the Captain's bass boat was still warm, so the boat was recently used. A fishing rod had a remnant of fresh bait and his tackle box was there, but his baitfish bucket was gone. He had Deputy James call the old cell number for Captain Jack. However, it didn't ring anywhere, not in the bottom of the boat, not in his pickup truck, nor anywhere inside or outside of the house. "That's odd," he told Jeffery. "Captain always kept that phone handy for his fishing and moonshine clients. So, either the phone's dead or it's missing."

Coleman now asked Jeffrey to call Reverend Tim Dickson, the pastor of nearby Pleasant Hill Baptist Church to spread the tragic news.[39] Jeffrey made the e-phone call in speaker mode and as the phone answered, Coleman spoke, "Hello Tim, I've got sad news."

"Yes George, what is it?" the Reverend replied from his church office, where he was at his desk already planning next Sunday's service.

"It's terrible what's happened at old Captain Jack's house today. Looks like Captain came home late from fishing all night, then ole Macy shot him

---

[39] Pleasant Hill Baptist Church predates the Civil War and there are several Confederate and Union soldiers interred in the old cemetery located there and other church cemeteries in Charles County. Both the Union and Confederate soldiers there were buried with equal respect and dignity as they died honorably in the service of their Country and their State of Virginia respectively.

gcgaacgcgatggcgtaagcgatggcgaacgcgccgctggcgaacgcgtgcgcgaacgcgctgccggcgaacgcgatggcgtaagcgatggcgaacgcg

and turned the gun on herself. A damn shame and the ending of a way of life," Coleman said solemnly in tribute to the old married couple. "Was Macy at church this morning?"

The Reverend replied with a soft but firm voice, "Yes, she was there, but Captain Jack wasn't. She seemed just fine this morning. Sometimes though, I think the captain was a lodestone around Macy's neck wearing her down, but they stuck together for all those years."

"He was shot dead in the kitchen and she was sitting in her rocking chair on the porch just staring at the lake so peacefully. The pistol dropped onto the porch boards by her side."

"That's terrible. What're you going to do?" the Reverend asked.

Coleman replied, "I'll follow normal procedures. Jeffrey and I will investigate the crime scene and the district medical examiner in Kent City will perform their autopsies.[40] After that, the bodies can be prepared for burial and the funeral can proceed. Since Captain and Macy had no children or relatives, we have to organize their funeral. We need to bring people together in their honor and memory of what the river once was. Captain and Macy *were* the old river, sort of living fossils from that lost era. They kept those times alive with their old stories and deeds. No two finer people ever graced the Chick. They deserve our community's respect as we lay them to rest. A last riverman's and woman's funeral."

"George, I'll plan it. My congregation will help and my grandson Jason is home from college for the summer too to assist me. We'll meet you in the morning over at their house to start taking care of things there first."

"That sounds great Tim," replied Coleman. "I'll see you about eight in the morning, right after breakfast."

The Reverend Dickson was nearly retired as pastor and was widowed eleven years ago when he'd lost his wife Sarah to cancer. He'd already retired from his supervisor job at the Newport News Public Works Department since it was difficult to only live on a rural pastor's stipend.

---

[40] The State of Virginia does not have local coroners like most states but has a more centralized Department of Health system. There is a Chief Medical Examiner in charge of Regional and District Medical Examiners Offices; However, State-approved local medical examiners may determine causes of death and, in certain cases, the Medical Examiner's Office is consulted by E-vid via the Grid for guidance. Regional Medical Examiners are authorized to supervise and record autopsies remotely using real-time e-vid Grid connections. With the increase in urban homicides and suspicious deaths, more responsibility has been delegated to rural local medical examiners who are just normal doctors "moonlighting" as medical examiners.

catgcgccgccgtattaaattcgcacccatgatgcgtatgcgatggaacgcatttgcgcgcatgcgccgccgtattaaattcgcacccatgatgcgtat

Five years before losing his wife, he'd faced another personal tragedy, when he lost his son, John, and daughter-in-law in a tragic traffic accident on I-95 near Washington. If those metal chains holding the concrete pipes hadn't snapped when the autotruck swerved, they'd still be alive today. John's son Jason, who was just six at the time, was lucky and the pipes only crushed the front half of the autocar. Jason survived buckled up safely in the rear seat and was now the only family that the Reverend had left in this world.

Jason was no ordinary child and like his father in many ways, but was a more extreme version. His father was a computer programmer working for the Federal government and Jason, like his father, became a computer coding prodigy when young. Unfortunately, Jason had a difficult personality and was age ten when the Reverend finally had him diagnosed with high-functioning autism. That explained Jason's behavior issues, but since his parents died at an early age, Jason faced additional emotional challenges. Within the realm of computers and coding, Jason had an innate ability to read and understand computer programming languages almost like it was in his blood. Even as a preschooler, he taught himself to read by watching children's e-vids and was brilliant in solving sudoku puzzles, crosswords, and word finds.

Jason also didn't have the correct filters to interpret and understand social cues or societal norms, so he was always loud and awkward with verbal communications. He had great enthusiasm for learning and was mentally ahead of his peers in some ways. When his parents died, however, he withdrew into his computer world and, by the age of twelve, managed to get in serious legal trouble for online hacking.

Somehow amidst Jason's Federal Juvenile Court trial, conviction, and lifetime suspended sentence, the Reverend managed to change Jason for the better and raised him through his teens to young adulthood. With considerable patience, love, and perseverance, he helped him focus and mollify his eccentricities so he was almost like other young men his age. Since high school, he even had a local girlfriend, Julie Williams, who was a biochemistry student studying at the College of William and Mary.[41]

The Reverend thought a day of Jason helping with the funeral would be a good break from his online summer studies since Jason still had a few remaining but annoying mandatory courses to take before graduating from Virginia Polytechnic University in December. One course he was taking was Advanced Electrical Controls and Signaling. He self-mastered this

---

[41] The College of William and Mary, located in Williamsburg, Virginia, is a state university, but due to its historical significance, the 'College' in the name was retained.

gcgaacgcgatggcgtaagcgatggcgaacgcgccgctggcgaacgcgtgcgcgaacgcgctgccggcgaacgcgatggcgtaagcgatggcgaacgcg

boring subject, skipped the course, and took the final exam for an easy 'A'-grade. Also, he'd somehow avoided taking English 101-E (English for Engineers), but now was time to pay his dues and suffer through this course. One can imagine that Ghost Deans of Engineering Schools Past forever wanted to spread the agony of reading English literature to all future engineering students.

After talking with the Reverend, Coleman thought about Rufus, who had lost his masters and only people he knew and loved. He asked Jeffery to call the local veterinarian, Dr. John Longtree to ask for advice. Doc Longtree had an office clinic for house pets, but also made barn calls using his fully-equipped mobile veterinary van. His practice was named "House and Barn" and his van was emblazoned with pictures of pets and farm animals. He was a tall, lanky Chickahominy Indian, with warm brown eyes and a big grin, who loved to joke with his many friends, but satire and sarcasm were his favorite forms of humor. He enjoyed using his wits for astute worldly observations, and his favorite pastime was e-reading philosophy and psychology.

Jeffery held the e-phone as George began talking, "Doc, it's George. There's been a tragedy at Captain Jack's. Macy and the Captain are both dead. Rufus is now orphaned and howling out of control. We gotta do something with him. Can you help?"

"Well, he's going through a big trauma. Has he seen and smelled their bodies? For dogs, smell is part of their psyche, especially in this situation. He needs to understand his masters are dead. If you haven't done so, let him sniff the bodies, but maybe you should wait until I get there. I believe I can help more with this situation," Doc explained.

"That sounds like a good idea," replied Coleman and wondered why he hadn't thought of letting Rufus know what happened to his masters.

"Also, I'll keep Rufus until we find him a new home. I don't think he would like the county shelter, as he mostly ran the woods around Captain's house tracking raccoons and possums. I'll take him until we find someone to adopt him. I'm busy with a patient now, but I'll come as soon as I can."

As Deputy James took more e-photos of the crime scene, house, and buildings, Sheriff Coleman carefully gathered any evidence. Wearing white cotton gloves, he picked up the revolver and opened the cylinder. Inside, he found three empty casings and three unfired .38 caliber bullets, but since a .357 can also fire .38s, nothing was unusual. He also found a partial box of 38 special ammo and an unloaded shotgun in a hall closet.

catgcgccgccgtattaaattcgcacccatgatgcgtatgcgatggaacgcatttgcgcgcatgcgccgccgtattaaattcgcacccatgatgcgtat

He went to Captain's boathouse and grabbed a mason jar of moonshine from a shelf and thought to himself, "I'll miss this stuff." He opened the screw-on lid and took a gulp of smooth fire in memory of the Captain. He took a second smaller gulp for Macy, but she probably would have cursed him for that, especially on Sunday after church. He grabbed two cases of jars, walked to Ole Bessie, put it in the back seat, and poured two full jars into the gas tank, knowing that she loved the octane boost to clean carbon from her piston rings. Ole Bessie suffered from cylinder knocking from low-grade gas that was available and this booster made Coleman a routine 'other' client.

He called to Deputy James, "Jeffrey, let's head over to the boathouse 'n take a 'shine break. We're done workin' today. Let's sit and talk 'bout old-time river memories. Captain was the last riverman and deserves our respect. He would've wanted us to enjoy a jar to the last drop."

In a half-hour, Doc arrived and loudly called out searching for the sheriff. "George, where are you?"

"We're at the boathouse. Come 'n join us for a spell," Coleman replied while feeling the 'shine's effects.

Doc walked around the house and saw George and Jeffrey sitting on a wooden bench looking at the lake with a half-empty open mason jar between them.

"We're off-duty now, so come have a swallow," George urged Doc since they were well distracted from the reason for Doc's appearance. "We've been toastin' the Captain and talkin' 'bout old river times."

Doc replied, "Maybe just one, and then I should pick up Rufus. Susan said my dinner is in an hour. Where is he?"

"He's zat Johnnie Walker's," Jeffrey replied. "He'z tryin' to keep hima way from th' house. I hope he'z stopped hollerin'."

The sheriff then briefly recounted the afternoon's events and Doc stood there dumbfounded, "George, I can't believe Macy would do that. She was like everyone's grandma around here and a devout Christian." The Doc took a big swig from the jar, halfway swallowed, and spit out half onto the ground. "I don't know how you guys drink this stuff."

Jeffrey slurred, "It gitz betta afta th' secon' one. I think th' first one iz to num up da tastebutts sum."

George and Jeffrey both laughed, took the jar said a toast to Captain and Macy, and took another swig in turn. The jar was passed back to Doc.

Doc said, "Ok, this is my last one and I'll make a toast this time. To Captain Jack and Macy. They lived by the river and now are enjoying traveling the Great River in the sky to meet the Heavenly Father. May their ancestors' many campfires guide their journey along the Path."[42] Doc took another swig and Jeffrey was right, it did taste better and smoother. "Let me bring Rufus back to see the bodies," he said, stood up, and walked to his van.

Coleman, who was heavier than Deputy James, was finally feeling the 'shine effects and replied, "We'll bee up on th' porch in a few, but we hav'ta finishh our bizness here first," as he looked at the nearly empty jar with two more gulps of liquid fire at the bottom.

Doc returned bringing Rufus on a leash. He was still anxious and immediately began howling again as they walked toward the porch where George and Jeffrey were sitting drunk. When Rufus approached the door, he eagerly sniffed everything, even the knob, and started barking. The Doc pulled him back enough to open the door and brought him to the kitchen where Captain was lying on the floor. As they watched, Rufus sniffed Captain and the blood pool, and began a long wail. He whimpered while nudging him and laid down silently with his head on the floor next to his master.

After a few minutes, Doc knelt, placed his hand tenderly on the dog's head, and mumbled something only Rufus heard. Then he pulled the leash and Rufus stood up leaving a big puddle of slobber on the floor where his head had laid. Fortunately, he was not howling now.

As Coleman and Jeffrey watched, Doc took Rufus outside to the back porch overlooking the lake. As soon as Rufus saw Macy sitting in her rocking chair, he howled again. The Doc repeated the procedure, but this time let him stay a while longer. Doc placed his hand on Rufus's head and pulled him up again. Another larger slobber puddle was on the porch floor. Doc then lightly pulled him by the leash and he followed readily, with not even a hint of a howl or whimper.

Coleman asked in amazement, "How did you do that Doc? That dog wouldn't quit howling before."

Doc joked, "I'm descended from a long line of medicine men and used my medicine on him." They all laughed. "No really, I do have a gift with animals. You've heard of dog whisperers before? Well, I *am* one and have that skill with many animals. I think that's what makes me a good vet." He smiled with pride, as maybe an ancestor long ago had been a

---

[42] Native American Algonquin beliefs include that souls follow a Milky Way path to the Heavenly Father. The Chickahominy are part of the Algonquin people.

Chickahominy medicine man. He took Rufus to his van, put him in the front passenger seat footwell, and drove away.

The Charles County Volunteer Ambulance arrived when Doc was leaving. After a brief discussion with Sheriff Coleman, they went about their business. They reverently put the first body on a wheeled gurney and loaded it into the ambulance parked behind Ole Bessie. Then, they carefully loaded the second body onto a hand-carried two-pole stretcher and carried it to the ambulance, much like during the Civil War when medical corpsmen would carry the dead to dump them in mass graves. They drove away using the detour toward Kent City and the Peninsula District Morgue. There, the district medical examiner handled ordinary deaths from natural causes, but potential criminal investigations such as this apparent murder-suicide demanded extra attention from a supervising regional medical examiner.

George and Jeffery sobered up a half-hour, roped off the house with crime scene tape, and locked the doors. They staggered to Jeffrey's Patrol Car and pulled a long chain from the trunk and cordoned off the driveway. Finally, they added some crime scene tape for good measure. They both drove away in their patrol cars and George crawled home just before sunset. He was still inebriated and Olivia cursed him just like Macy would have done.

Chapter 5: An Evening of Truth

Wendover Plantation

7:00 p.m., Sunday, June 27, ….

It was left-over night at the Dickson house and the Reverend sat down at the kitchen table and said the blessing with his grandson Jason. As they began eating, the Reverend said, "There's sad news this afternoon from Sheriff Coleman, Jason. Macy shot the Captain and committed suicide."

"I can't believe it, Grandpa," Jason replied. "It doesn't make sense."

"Yes, I agree," Grandpa said. "The sheriff wants us to help with the funeral since I was their pastor and they were close friends. Can you help me in the coming week to organize the funeral reception at our church?"

"Sure Grandpa. They would've wanted me to help."

Grandpa continued, "Since so many people knew them, the sheriff wants the funeral open to the entire community and I agree. It'll be one of those memorials where everyone comes to show their respect, but also to see neighbors and catch up on local gossip. Sadly, events like this are sometimes the only way to bring our community together. So, Jason, organizing the reception will be an important job."

"I can do it Grandpa and perhaps Julie can help since she's home the next two weeks. I still can't understand why Macy would murder the Captain. She was a devout Christian and murder is a sin."

"Well Jason, everyone has a breaking point. Life offers us choices. Sometimes, we make wrong choices, but sometimes solving problems requires drastic action. Not that the Captain's 'shine business was the problem, but perhaps Macy got tired of it. Anyway, they're both gone and the funeral is for the living so that we may grieve together. Tomorrow morning, we'll go over to their house and help the sheriff."

"I'll gladly help. I'll miss Macy and you will too. When Grandma died, she helped you through your depression and grief. No one could beat her collard greens, field peas, and cornbread, but her Brunswick stew and chess pies were a dream," Jason said while thinking of a past church fundraising dinner.[43],[44]

"Yes, I loved Macy's cooking too because it reminded me of your Grandma. I miss Sarah dearly and when she died, I could barely eat for a week. Macy coaxed me back to life with the food she brought. I hear the funeral can't happen until the morgue releases them after the medical examiner takes a look."

Jason glanced at the time on his e-watch while eating dinner and told Grandpa, "I'm riding my bike over to Julie's house later. I'm supposed to meet her about eight before it's dark. We talked earlier and thought it would be nice to spend time together tonight. Of course, I'll tell her about the news of the Captain and Macy."

"That sounds fine Jason, but be careful about telling too much. You know Mrs. Williams and we don't need rumors spreading, especially since we don't know all the facts yet. Julie's a nice girl: smart, pleasant with good manners, attractive, and down to earth. I think you should stick with her and see what happens. Just do the dishes before you leave and be careful on your bike," Grandpa replied with a cautious parental tone. He walked to the family room, sat in a recliner, and read the Good Book.

Julie was home for two weeks, including the July 4th holiday, from her summer internship with a professor at William and Mary who was researching the biochemical stimulus responses of synthetic nerves. When not at college, she stayed at her parents' house near Wendover Plantation[45] which sat on a bluff overlooking the James River in western Charles County. Her parents were caretakers for the plantation and maintained the house, gardens, and nearly 2,000 acres of prime farmland for the owners, the Wendovers.

Julie and Jason had been in the same schools since elementary school and over the years had become close friends. Even though he'd known her for years, Jason finally got his courage up to invite her to the Senior Prom for their first date. Though Jason was socially awkward, Julie saw

---

[43] Brunswick stew is a traditional Southern stew of chicken, corn, tomatoes, potatoes, lima beans, onions, and spices

[44] Chess pie is a traditional Southern baked pie crust filled with eggs, butter, sugar, corn meal, vanilla, or other variations on this basic recipe.

[45] During the Civil War, Wendover Plantation was occupied by the Union Army; it was while camping near here that General Butterfield composed and a bugler Private Norton played the song, "Taps" for the first time to sooth the recovering Union troops. This song became popular with both the Union and Confederate Armies and is still played and widely recognized at military funerals for its haunting and calming melody.

the brilliance shining from his mind through his bright green eyes. She'd heard from his grandpa, the Reverend Dickson, about some trouble with the law when he was younger, but he'd redeemed himself with good behavior over many years.

⌒⌒⌒⌒⌒⌒⌒

After cleaning the kitchen, Jason went to the garage where he kept his electronics workbench. He'd loved electronics for years and even as a pre-teenager, he flourished when building an electronic project. The locals often dropped off electronics for repair, and if salvageable, he fixed them and made extra money along the way. He saved his earnings to buy more electronic parts and, eventually, his bike. So, it was natural that he'd study electronics in engineering school. He also loved creating and assembling new devices from scrap equipment he was given.

His real passion, though, was computers and coding but his suspended Federal Juvenile conviction for hacking included a ban on using computers until he was 18 years old. However, the suspended sentence didn't explicitly prevent him from studying computers and their languages. So, he tore apart scrapped computers to examine their circuits and salvage useful parts. Also, he continued learning computer languages via physical books checked out to him using interlibrary loans from Virginia Polytech delivered to the Charles County Public Library. Since he was now 22 years old, his computer privileges were restored, but he could never hack again.

Jason pulled the fabric cover off his old but slightly modified Harley-Davidson Live-Wire Mark II motorcycle. He put on his helmet, straddled the seat, and pressed the ignition switch. The electric drive whirred and the bike nearly flew out the garage. He drove down the driveway onto Wilcox Neck Road and turned west on Highway 5 toward Julie's house.

As he rode, he listened inside his helmet to an old rock 'n roll song *'Starship Trooper'* playing from the bike's e-tunes player. It was one of his father's favorites from his inherited e-tunes list. After passing Charlestown, he turned off the highway to the south and followed a long muddy, gravel road that led to Wendover Plantation. He usually drove carefully on gravel, so he slowed until he felt safer with his speed and traction. At the road's end, he stopped at the caretaker's house, went to the door, and rang Julie's doorbell.

Soon, Julie opened the door. Her bright blue eyes and beaming smile greeted Jason and were followed by a peck on his cheek and a brief hug. She was wearing a flowery short dress and her long blond hair was tied into a neat ponytail.

"Hello Jason," she said sweetly and enticingly while she embraced him.

"It's so nice to be with you. It seems like I haven't seen you in ages," he replied while thinking about how pleasant it was to feel her in his arms.

"That's a silly thing to say, Jason. You see me every day by e-vid."

"Yes, I know, but it's not the same as seeing you in person and I haven't done that since the Spring break."

"Mom and Dad are in the family room," she said inviting him inside. Her dad had spent a long afternoon after church in the gardens and her mom was resting after dinner. Mrs. Williams managed a large wedding at the plantation on Saturday, so a rest was well earned during this busy season. June weddings were still popular, and the scenic, historical antebellum plantation house overlooking the James River was an ideal venue for high-end wedding receptions.

Jason greeted her parents, "Hello Mr. and Mrs. Williams, it's nice to see you. I haven't seen you since Julie was home at Spring Break."

Mr. Williams replied, "Hello, Jason. How are your summer studies? Julie told me you're taking some courses."

"I already completed my design course, but English literature isn't one of my favorites. However, sometimes you must do things you don't like and that course is required for graduation. I've some other local news to tell y'all I just learned from Grandpa. Old Captain Jack was murdered today by Macy and then she committed suicide. I don't know the details, but Sheriff Coleman and Deputy James spent the whole afternoon investigating the crime scene. Grandpa said to keep this news quiet, so please don't spread around the murder-suicide part at least," Jason added while thinking how Mrs. Williams loved to gossip.

Mrs. Williams commented, "Such a tragedy. They lived here so long and our community will never be the same. God rest their souls."

Jason continued, "Since Grandpa is the pastor over at Pleasant Hill, he's organizing their funeral and reception since they had no family. It will likely be within a few days."

Mrs. Williams added, "Jason, let us know how we can help. I'd better call some friends with the news," she said as her gossip instinct completely disregarded what Jason had told her not to do.

Mr. Williams commented to his wife, "Now Kay, don't go spreading rumors as Jason said. If you must, just say they were killed and the Reverend Dickson will be organizing their funeral soon. That's all our community needs to know at this point."

"Yes Richard, I'll try not to spread it too much, but news like this gets out *fast* as you know."

"Mostly because of *you* my dear. Fine, but call only one or two friends, not *all* your friends," Mr. Williams laughed, since he knew the Charles County Grapevine, as the local men called it, would spread this news across the county in short order.

Jason asked, "Julie, can we go for a walk, perhaps in the gardens? I want to talk with you before it gets too dark."

"Yes Jason, let's walk to the old magnolia tree by the river. It just started blooming and smells really sweet," while thinking the magnolia tree on the far side of the formal gardens would give them a long time to talk and was a nice romantic place for what she hoped Jason wanted to discuss.

"Ok, Jason replied and he tenderly grabbed her hand while walking with her into the gardens as dusk was falling.

They made mostly small talk until they reached the magnolia. There, near an old, hand-quarried stone bench that overlooked the river, Jason told Julie, "There's been something I've been wanted to ask you for a while but haven't dared to do until now."

"What is it, Jason?" she eagerly replied in anticipation of something she wanted to hear.

He looked deeply into her eyes, "Well Julie, I know you've heard from Grandpa that I was in trouble when I was younger."

"Yes, Grandpa told me you'd been in some sort of trouble before, but never what happened. I know you've always been different, but that's what I like about you," she smiled.

"Well, what I wanted to ask is would you still like me if I told you that I'm a convicted criminal?" he meekly asked her.

"I can't believe it, Jason, but tell me all about it," she replied holding back her disappointment, but a slight frown still appeared on her brow as that wasn't the question she was anticipating.

"Well, I was in *big* trouble with the law. You know how I always told you that Grandpa wouldn't allow me to use computers until I grew up. It was the Federal Juvenile Court Judge who imposed that part of my suspended sentence. When I was a kid, I wanted to become a computer programmer and coder just like Dad. After his death, I learned everything I could about coding and became *really* good at it so he'd be proud of me in Heaven. A psychiatrist diagnosed me about that time with a mild form of autism. Grandpa even thinks my dad was the same, but the diagnosis wasn't as easy then as nowadays using genetic tests. That psychiatrist gave some psychological and cognitive assessments, discovering that I have another unique mental capability called synesthesia."

"What's that?" she asked inquisitively.

"Well, best I can explain it, sometimes when I see letters and numbers, my brain sees patterns of colors within my mind. That makes me a *really* good hacker because somehow, I see data patterns better than most people. It's like an extra hidden part of my brain is processing information without me even knowing."

He continued, "My real problem though was when I became a computer coder, I didn't have mental filters to control my behaviors. I became addicted to the Grid and stayed up all night hacking into different systems, starting with the records system in middle school. I know you got a "D" in Mr. Edwards 5th grade math class."

He continued explaining, "So when Grandma died, I spiraled even worse out of control, and tackled bigger and greater hacking challenges. I finally cracked the local Grid provider and soon needed a larger hack to feed my ego. So, I hacked the data encryption of the National Presidential Alert System. You remember that's when every e-phone and Grid-connected system in America broadcast a simulated voice message from the president, *'Fellow citizens, this is the president. I'm warning you of a space alien attack in five minutes. Everyone, bend over and kiss your butts goodbye.'* I thought it was funny, but the government didn't when they caught me."

"Oh, Jason! I remember that. Everyone at school heard the loudspeaker and started laughing," Julie chuckled in remembrance.

"Yeah, I know," Jason said smiling in retrospect at his juvenile prank.

"How come no one ever found out you did it?"

"The government was so embarrassed that a twelve-year-old hacked the president's communications channel that they covered it up as a programming glitch caused by a Grid technician. I was charged with malicious criminal hacking and secretly tried in Federal Juvenile Court. If it hadn't been for Grandpa and my lawyer, I would've gone to jail.

Grandpa pleaded, saying he'd do everything in his power as my guardian to turn my life around. The lawyer also stated I shouldn't be imprisoned for my first conviction, but instead given a second chance at a normal life. The judge sentenced me to life in prison but suspended my sentence if I kept my hack secret and never hacked again. He also banned me from using computers until I turned eighteen. Grandpa told me later they sealed my criminal record as 'Top Secret'."

"Wow, that's unbelievable, but now it makes sense how you stopped using computers at school. So, to divert your attention, you just started fixing electronics. Later, you wanted to become an electronics engineer instead of a master computer coder like your father."

"Yes, I've changed a lot since my hacking days. I matured, learning to focus and control myself. I've developed better listening habits. Now I'm able to use computers again, but limit my usage. I don't stay up all night on computers unless it's homework for college. Do you mind what I told you?" he asked.

"No, Jason, but I'm glad you told me. Let there be no secrets between us in the future."

"Yes, Julie, I promise. No more secrets will come between us."

She moved closer, looked in his eyes, stroked his forehead to brush away an auburn lock of hair that drooped over his eyebrow, and kissed him on the lips as he wrapped his arms around her in a warm tender embrace. They sat as darkness fell, her head on his shoulder, hand-in-hand, looking at the river as the stars started shining over the calm waters.

"What's that first star?" Julie said as she pointed high up in the sky. "Let me make a wish," she said thinking of what she wanted most dearly.

"That's Arcturus. I think that means 'bear watcher' in Greek."

They sat a while longer just staring at the sky and Julie asked, "Where are all the planets tonight?"

"You can't see most of them right now. Mars just set, but I think Saturn is over there," as he pointed toward the southeast.

"There it is," he said as he further guided Julie's gaze pointing a finger above the horizon toward what seemed like an orangish star shimmering in the sky. "Saturn was the God of time and father of Jupiter, King of the Gods," he said recounting old Roman myths.

"Where's the Moon tonight? Shouldn't it be out?"

"It set just before the sun, Silly-Girl," Jason said as he leaned closer to kiss again.

Chapter 6: A Routine Investigation Begins

Captain and Macy's House

Monday Morning, June 28, ….

Jason, a rare man like Thomas Edison who thrived on less than four hours of daily sleep, woke up at 4:30 a.m., well before daybreak. He started reading one of his summer English Literature reading assignments. He was a fast reader and could plow through engineering textbooks, technical articles, and programming manuals with amazing speed, but his enthusiasm for reading varied with interest in a book's genre. He loved science fiction books but hated historical novels and most non-fiction not related to technology.

As he lay in bed, he touched his e-screen and started reading the book by someone named Dickens, which began, *'It was the best of times, it was the worst of times, it was the age of wisdom, it was the age of foolishness, it was the epoch of belief, it was the epoch of incredulity, it was the season of Light, it was the season of Darkness, it was the spring of hope, it was the winter of despair, we had everything before us, we had nothing before us, we were all going direct to heaven, we were all going direct the other way…'*

Jason thought it was an interesting way to start a book. Back then seemed much like today and some things never change. He continued reading and sped through the many chapters of *'A Tale of Two Cities.'*

The pages flew by that morning and he was so focused on reading that Grandpa yelled up to him in his bedroom at 7:30 a.m., "Jason, we need to leave in ten minutes to meet the sheriff at the Captain's house."

Jason replied, "Give me five minutes, I'm almost done reading my assignment," having falcon dived toward his quarry through more than 60,000 words to finish reading his assignment.

He read the final words, *'It is a far, far better thing that I do, than I have ever done; it is a far, far better rest that I go to than I have ever known,'* hastily slipped on some clothes, ran to the bathroom, and met Grandpa downstairs in the kitchen. The classic Dickens novel still hadn't sunk into his mind for full comprehension, but his mind had a way of continuing to think about things at a deeper level of consciousness, like a computer sub-routine running in the background.

Grandpa had already eaten breakfast and finished his cup of coffee. He said, "We're late so you'll have to skip breakfast today. Let's go now, Jason. You can drive."

Jason drove them in Grandpa's pickup truck and, while on the way, told Grandpa, "I'm sorry I was slow coming downstairs this morning. I was finishing reading an assignment."

"What was it?" Grandpa asked.

"I read '*A Tale of Two Cities*' and to complete my assignment, I have to write an essay about it."

"Yes, I remember that from high school. Back then, they still taught such classics in school instead of babysitting and brainwashing children."

"I'm still trying to figure it out. Like why did that English man Carton, who looked just like the convicted French aristocrat Darnay, switch places with Darnay in prison and go to the guillotine himself instead?"

"Well as I remember, Carton loved Darnay's wife and wanted her to be happy no matter what happened, even to the point of sacrificing his own life for her future happiness. I think Carton felt he'd wasted his life. His life had no meaning or purpose, and that by sacrificing his own life, his final act would do good. I remember him comforting another woman just before she faced the guillotine and how he had a final, peaceful vision where his mind transcended his own life to see the future. There, he saw his love Lucie, Darnay, and their child living in England using the last name Carton. Lucie and Darnay were grateful and would always remember and honor Carton's sacrifice."

"Now I understand better Grandpa. Maybe there are good things to learn by reading historical novels."

"Yes, reading opens a window to your thoughts and expands your mind. It never hurts to learn others' wisdom passed down in words. Just as the Word of God and His stories in the Bible captured the times and wisdom of its era, the many books written throughout history represent mankind's collective insights through the ages. It's a shame and disgrace that people don't take advantage of these valuable gifts of knowledge given by the many famous philosophers, historians, scientists, or leaders who passed their words down to future generations. As authors, they gave their words to the future and transcended their own lives, like Carton."

"In a way, these old books gave the authors a kind of immortality so that their thoughts would live forever and be cherished as long as their words were read and remembered. Just as Lucie and Darnay would always remember Carton. So, their labors and toils to write captured their thoughts for the future. It was their sacrifice and gift to us. Right?" Jason said as an essay idea began forming within his mind.

"Yes, I think you've got it," Grandpa smiled.

"But Grandpa, if books like that are so valuable, why don't people read more these days?"

"Well, there are many reasons. Our modern way of life leaves no time for reading with people constantly watching e-vids or working continuously if they still have a job. Maybe the leaders and world powers like it that way, so people are content to go through their lives in a fog of ignorance and not question how the world has slowly fallen downward morally and economically as modern technology has controlled us all. Technology allows people to not use their brains because AI thinks for them, but people never think much about who programmed the AI originally. Did they want to benefit mankind or control us all? Perhaps a lot of people can't handle truth and prefer ignorance. Deliberate thinking and questioning require time, energy, and most of all, a brain, and I'm not sure many have those these days," he sarcastically laughed.

They arrived at the Captain's House and saw Ole Bessie parked at the driveway's end. They crossed the yellow crime scene tape and met Sheriff Coleman outside by the front door.

Sheriff Coleman had arrived early to review what he'd seen yesterday. He'd already sent Deputy James to Kent City with the pistol so the Virginia Forensics Science District Lab technician could start investigating when the lab opened. Deep down, he couldn't believe Macy murdered the Captain and was puzzled about the missing phone and bait bucket.

Coleman greeted them, "I'm glad you're here Tim and Jason. Now we have an in-depth search inside the house. Since I'm a lawman, it's best in such cases to have an independent and reliable witness, or in this case two witnesses," as he looked at Jason with a smile.

"Mostly, I wouldn't want anyone saying that I tampered with evidence, or took something from the house. The Captain lived in this old house his whole life and Macy too after they were married, so there's a lot of history to dig through. I think the house is likely 150 years older than that, but they managed to keep it in together somehow."

"What're we looking for?" asked Jason.

Coleman said, "Anything important. A will, a lockbox key, a financial statement, or some papers that tell what they owned. Also, look for anything out of the ordinary. There has to be a reason why Macy murdered the Captain."

This was an hours-long project, so they started their search in earnest. Grandpa and Jason looked in the bedroom and found an antique rifled Enfield musket from the Civil War. Grandpa noted, "I remember the Captain talking about his ancestor from that time and after the final surrender, many soldiers were allowed to keep their guns for hunting."

Coleman went to an old hand-crafted wooden rolltop desk and sat down to read the papers stored there. "That pile of paperwork and these drawer contents will take an hour just to figure out," he proclaimed.

Jason and the Reverend next looked in the kitchen. In a drawer, they found Macy's hand-written recipe book which was a collection of old and well-worn pages stuffed into a leather folder. Jason called out, "Sheriff, I found her recipe book. Here's her chess pie recipe!" he said excitedly. Attached with a paperclip behind the recipe was an old piece of parchment. He opened the page to reveal a faded letter handwritten in cursive using a quill feather and lampblack ink.

Coleman called back to Jason while deep in contemplation about the papers he was reading, "Save that for me so I can make a copy. Macy would never give Olivia the recipe, mostly out of pride from having the best chess pie in the county and wanting to keep her family recipe secret. I'll be in heaven every time I have a slice and thank Macy for sharing her secret. Macy would've wanted her recipe to be passed on, as it was likely in her family for generations."

Jason looked at the old letter and asked Grandpa, "What does this letter say? I can't read this old-style handwriting."

Grandpa took a long look, deeply studying the faded cursive handwriting carefully, and said, "George, come here. You have to see this. It's amazing."

Coleman came into the kitchen to look at the old letter.

Grandpa continued, "This letter's an American historical treasure! It seems to be written by Martha Washington to a woman that was one of Macy's ancestors. It talks about Martha's wedding to George Washington in Kent County and also the recipe for chess pie that came from her slave cook, named Hanna Binnford. Martha even said she wanted to free all the slaves that her children inherited from her first husband, but the laws at that time wouldn't permit her, as a widowed woman, to do that."[46]

Coleman commented, "Well that's a valuable letter, I think. Tim, I want to take Macy's version of the recipe to give to Olivia."

"Sure George, Macy would've wanted that."

Coleman walked back to the desk full of papers and after a while, Coleman found the documents he needed and studied them a few minutes before he called the Reverend and Jason, "Come here! I found their wills, deeds, and financial documents!" The Reverend and Jason came running to the sheriff's side.

"What do they say?" the Reverend asked curiously as they looked over Coleman's shoulders.

Coleman explained the details, "First of all Tim, the Captain and Macy made you their Will executor and Jason is back-up executor if needed. The executor must follow their detailed instructions. They didn't want a public viewing, just to be buried in their family plot at Pleasant Hill. Their estate pays for the funeral."

"Then it gets interesting. You see, best I can figure out, the Captain and Macy were rich. They owned timberland 'round here and routinely sold timber to the pallet factory and paper mill near Petersburg. Since they lived simply, they invested their earnings, and over the years, they became a fortune. See here," he said pointing to financial statements of investments and stock portfolios of companies. "They owned shares of Nanosoft, Orange, Boggle, E-Face, Drone-Motion, and Metaview plus there are some paper stock certificates from really old corporations like Boeing and Westinghouse. I did some rough math and I'm not sure about those certificates, but they accumulated about four-hundred million e-coins over the years."

The Wills leave almost everything to the county on the condition that it uses part of the money on school technology, another part for college scholarships, a portion to build a fish hatchery and restore the shad fish and river economy, and a final part to found a Chick River Living History Museum, much like the one in old Colonial Williamsburg. To start the museum's holdings, the Captain donated his antique fishing lure collection and his wooden, flat-bottomed Chick Boat, the last of its kind. Their house and boathouse are to be the museum right here by the lake."

---

[46] George and Martha Washington were married in Kent County on January 6, 1759. Most historical traditions say she was married at White House Plantation, Martha's first husband's home on the Pamunkey River, but St. Peter's Episcopal Church in Talleysville was her parish church and there are claims the Washington's wedding occurred there.

gcgaacgcgatggcgtaagcgatggcgaacgcgccgctggcgaacgcgtgcgcgaacgcgctgccggcgaacgcgatggcgtaagcgatggcgaacgcg

"The Captain and Macy also had another hobby besides investing. They collected stories about the river and people who lived here. Over the years, they listened to stories and folk-lore of their elders and old-timers and wrote them in journals. They knew the river lifestyle was dying and wanted to preserve it for future generations. They left instructions to publish the journals and the originals were to be kept at their museum."

Jason interrupted, "I'm sure the historians at William and Mary would like to see those. In their way, the Captain and Macy were like those famous writers we talked about this morning. They're preserving the wisdom and thoughts of many lives and our river's cultural history.

"Yes Jason, so the old river times could live forever," Grandpa replied.

Coleman continued, "There are a few individual bequests. The Captain left his old truck to Johnnie Walker, and Jimmy Cummings, his fishing buddy who manages the agrobots at Green Acres Sod Farm, gets his new bass boat, airboat, and modern fishing tackle. He left a map for Jimmy to find his still and we'll surely need someone new making 'shine for the locals and old Bessie," he laughed and was reassured knowing that Ole Bessie would be happy with her 'shine.

Jason commented, "We always thought he paid for those boats by selling his 'shine, but he just liked making it for everyone. Making 'shine was a last river skill and way to keep connected with the community."

Coleman concluded the bequests, "Macy left Olivia her recipe book to keep old traditions alive, but her antique quilts were donated to the museum. Macy had one other request for her kitchen garden to be used for growing vegetables to remind museum visitors that the earth was important to the river lifestyle. The lilac bushes there, that are descended from her family's botanical lineage, are to be continually propagated to keep her family's heritage alive."

"If they were so rich, why did they live in this old house," Jason asked them both.

Grandpa replied, "This house was their home and they were from a different time. For them, a simple peaceful life on the river was all they wanted. Of course, the river was their lives, that of their parents, and their ancestors. They had their faith, and even Jesus said the meek shall inherit the earth. Maybe they inherited so much from how they lived that their wealth was worthless. They never needed anything else as they had love for each other and faith. For some people, to be humble living a simple life is the highest calling, allowing closeness to God."

Coleman concluded, "Well, I think that 'bout wraps up today's search. I still don't know why Macy shot her husband. I can't find any motive for

catgcgccgccgtattaaattcgcacccatgatgcgtatgcgatggaacgcatttgcgcgcatgcgccgccgtattaaattcgcacccatgatgcgtat

such a crime. Did you see the Captain's cell phone anywhere?" Coleman questioned while searching for reasons she would murder her husband.

"No, we haven't seen any phone," Jason replied.

"Well, all we can do now is prepare for the funeral. Next, I have to go to Kent City and meet with Dr. Graves, the district medical examiner. With the Chick Bridge out, it'll take me an extra hour round trip, so I better get going. When she's completed her exam, the undertaker can prepare their bodies and we can have the funeral in a few days."

As they all were leaving through the kitchen door, Jason spotted a small hole by the shadowed edge of a picture hanging on the wall. "Look at that hole," Jason said, pointing it out to the sheriff.

Coleman looked closely and stuck his pen knife inside. He dug deeper and pried out a bullet embedded in the thick Southern Yellow Pine board. He put the bullet into a zipper bag, sealed it, and the Reverend and Jason signed the bag as witnesses.

On their way home, Jason asked, "Grandpa, I've been thinking more about why the Captain and Macy were so interested in preserving their old house for a museum? That house wasn't historical like any of the remaining old plantation houses around here. That place is practically falling down and it's a beautiful spot for a nice modern lake-front house."

"Well Jason, I think preserving history was important to them for many reasons. They were ordinary people, not like those wealthy plantation owners once were. They saw how things changed over the years and felt their simple way of life was valuable and provided lessons to learn. History is important because a people without a past have no future. You see, sometimes you should know where you've been to figure out where you need to go. Powerful people use and manipulate history to control others and it's important to understand this. Like the Civil War for example. Yes, it's good that slavery ended, but it was just replaced in time with hidden forms of slavery. After the Civil War, the big industrial magnates and banks grew to control the country, and eventually, everyone became slaves to the government to pay taxes and by debt owed to rich families who controlled the bankers. The newest form of slavery is to the e-cards for free government handouts to buy people's votes for politicians who are owned by the same rich and powerful families."

"At the old county courthouse, an old granite monument to Confederate soldiers from Charles County was torn down when I was younger. I remember seeing the inscription, *'Defenders of Constitutional Liberty and the Right of Self-Government'* and on the other side it says *'Pro Aris et Focis*', which in Latin I think translates to something like, '*For altar and hearth*' or maybe a better translation is '*For God and Country*'."

"That doesn't sound like a monument to people who wanted to fight for slavery, Grandpa?"

"No, it doesn't, because back then people lived in states which had more power in many ways than the Federal government, and the Southern states wanted to preserve this power. Most of the Confederate soldiers didn't even own slaves. They fought for their homes and states they saw invaded by the Union Army. Slavery was just an excuse used afterward to justify the Civil War, but as they say, the victor gets to write history."

He continued, "Even worse though is before you were born there was a movement to destroy our country's past. People tore down all old Confederate monuments and statues in the Southern states and the one in Charles County was eventually demolished, erasing our history. Then, they even destroyed all monuments and statues of our nation's founding fathers George Washington and Thomas Jefferson just because they'd owned slaves. These same people considered it racist and offensive to even see history and learn from it. At one time, this movement became so strong they blindly and ignorantly tore down *all* statues and monuments, even of Christopher Columbus, Abraham Lincoln, and Teddy Roosevelt, to erase history entirely."

"I think those who deny history or facts, refuse to learn from it, attempt to destroy inconvenient truths, and coerce others to prevent them from learning history are worse than those who remain solely ignorant of it. This behavior is the highest form of intolerance and self-imposed stupidity. God gave us brains and to intentionally not think and prevent others from thinking is a sin," Reverend Dickson replied seriously. "It's better to write your future than worry about editing the past."

"So, what you're saying is that the Captain and Macy wanted us to preserve history, what's happened to the river over the years, and learn from it. They wanted us, the living, to understand this, so we could fix our past mistakes. That's why they wanted a fish hatchery to restart the river economy again. They wanted to give us a new future."

"Yes, I think so Jason."

ᴅᴄᴵᴾᴵᴅᴄᴵᴾᴵ

At 9 a.m., Sheriff Olsen went to the Kent County Manager's office to discuss the situation in Provident Forge, "Mrs. Graham, I know we talked this weekend about the dam break, but we need to determine the railroad closure's impact. It's our biggest problem, and it appears Exgenics sold the dam to the county two months ago. That's our liability."

Rose Graham replied, "Yes, it's unfortunate and untimely. We have umbrella insurance, but our limit is 20 million e-coins. I have a feeling damages from the railroad's closure will exceed that."

Olsen replied, "Perhaps something was amiss with the sale of land around the dam. Why did Exgenics sell it anyway? I heard they gave us a state archeologist's report on the forge ruins."

"Yes, Exgenics attorney John Gregory contacted me, provided me a copy of the site report, and offered to donate the land and money for a museum and a county park. I later contacted the archaeologist from Richmond myself. She was very helpful explaining the site's importance to the state's history. She even agreed, with Gregory's permission, to donate her dig's finds to the museum. Also, when Exgenics built their facility, they fenced in the lake and they've dealt with locals the fence to fish there. I know you've had many trespassing complaints, so if it was a county park, that solved the problem, but Kent County owns the land now, so the dam became our liability," the manager replied.

"Do you have a copy of the archaeologist's report?"

Mrs. Graham replied, "Yes, I do. Let me search my files," and she asked her AI-computer to search the county database.

After about a second, her AI-computer replied, "Here is the file you requested Mrs. Graham. I sent it to Sheriff Olsen's e-screen too," since the AI-computer knew the sheriff wanted a copy. The e-screen displayed what Olsen was looking for on the first page: Dr. Elizabeth Smithson, Associate State Archaeologist, and her contact info.

⋈⊲◖▸⊲◖▸⋈

Olsen went to his office in the Kent County Justice Center, which was also the county jail, and told his AI-computer to contact Dr. Smithson's e-phone. She soon answered, "Dr. Smithson here. Can I help you?"

"Dr. Smithson, I'm Sheriff Olsen from Kent County. Are you the archaeologist who surveyed the old Provident Forge site a while ago?"

"Yes, I was. I spent several weeks on a dig late last fall during that dry spell when working conditions were better. You don't find many undisturbed historical sites with so many treasure hunters using metal detectors to find artifacts to sell. We were extremely lucky to find it and the swampy ground must have kept looters away."

"Did you hear or see anything unusual at the site or in your dealings with Mr. Gregory or Exgenics?"

"No, not particularly. Mr. Gregory was polite and cordial. Exgenics donated 100,000 e-coins to the State Archaeology Fund and I'd heard about their charitable donations before. They fully funded the World

Elephant Genomics Conservatory, you know, that charity with big elephant breeding preserves in East Texas and Florida. They've already increased the world's remaining elephant population by 300 percent and I hear they've over 2,000 cows in their elephant herds now."

"Yes, I think I've heard that. They also donated some Supercruizers to the sheriff's department in Kent County. Thanks for your time Dr. Smithson," he disappointingly replied.

Olsen was about to disconnect the Grid link when Smithson replied, "By the way, I remember seeing some surveyors or people like that looking around the dam. I can't remember a name on their white pickup truck, but I remember the logo of an I-beam and lightning bolt on the doors."

"Thank you again, Dr. Smithson. You've been most helpful," he replied as he disconnected from the Grid, but now he had a glimmer of hope for the county because he had a lead to follow.

Marie Whitaker was a Virginia Department of Wildlife and Inland Fisheries biologist who traveled the state performing wildlife surveys to study populations and to set hunting seasons and fishing limits. Chick Lake was the only freshwater lake in the Tidewater she studied, as the salty Chesapeake Bay and brackish tidal rivers were monitored by the Marine Fisheries Department. This late June day was in the middle of the spawning season for endangered alewife fish, so she trailered her boat to the lake for a survey.

Marie arrived at Osprey Landing boat ramp about 10 a.m. and saw the usually clear lake was pretty muddy. First, she briefly chatted on any recent fishing news with the bait shop clerk. The biggest fishing news she heard was the upcoming Osprey Landing July 4th Fishing Tournament that the campground's owners sponsored each year to attract regular crowds.

Next, she launched her aluminum-hulled boat with outboard motor into the lake from the south boat ramp, parked her truck and trailer, and navigated to the deep water of the old river channel to begin her work. She stuck two electro-probe poles into the water in front of her boat and separated them by about twelve feet and then turned on the 240-volt electrical generator that powered a high voltage electrofishing unit. The unit applied pulsing shocks, much like an electric fence corrals livestock. These shocks temporarily stun nearby fish, even at depths, which soon float to the surface. Next, she'd hand-net any fish to conduct her scientific study recording species, weight, length, and sex.

For some reason, the electrofishing unit wasn't working. No fish were floating to the surface. She turned up the power setting and looked for fish, but still, none were stunned. She turned up the power to maximum, but again, no fish were floating. She grabbed the malfunctioning electrofishing pole by its insulator and a powerful shock passed from the boat hull through her body and into the water. Her heart stopped, she collapsed by the boat's railing, and she lay dying with her eyes open staring at several glowing spots just underwater. Her last thoughts were of angels rising from the depths carrying her to heaven.

Her boat was found drifting near Walker Dam by a fisherman who called 911 and towed it to the nearby East Lake Campground upper boat ramp. East Lake Campground had two ramps for boaters: a lower ramp below the dam for the tidal river, and an upper lakeside ramp. At the lower ramp, a long wooden dock extended out into the river in a "Z" pattern. At the dock's end, a steel barge was moored and lit by streetlights at night. This dock served the campground's guests and permanent residents living in mobile homes.

The campground owners made sure the location was a recreational and entertainment attraction during the entire summer season on the river. On the land, there was a small restaurant, an ice-cream shop, a bait shop, a camper's store, a swimming pool, and a lake-front swim beach. They even constructed a large bandshell tent with a stage used for special events and camper's church services. Their Annual East Lake Bluegrass Music Festival would start this weekend, competing for visitors to the Osprey Landing Fishing Tournament.

Sheriff Olsen arrived and the fisherman told him about his grisly catch, "I was fishin' the tall grass on the south bank and spot'd her boat drifting with the engine idling. She likely had a gas-powered electric generator running for the power unit of those electro-probes, but I think it ran out of gas. She was dead there a while, just staring at the water like she had a heart attack or something."

Sheriff Olsen met the Kent County paramedics who just arrived. He told them to wait so he could search inside the boat where he snapped some e-phone images. He examined the 240-volt, electric generator rated for 20 amps and the fuel tank was empty. He studied the electrofishing power supply and the power setting was at maximum. He popped out the electrofisher's fuse holder and the 30-amp fuse inside was blown, indicating a high-power electrical short. "A blown fuse on the job; what a way to go," remarked Olsen to the paramedics, but afterward, he thought it odd that a 30-amp electrofisher fuse would blow from a 20-amp generator.

Coleman was driving on the long detour route to Kent City to meet visit the medical examiner and forensics lab technician. As he drove, he was thinking about the crime at the Captain's house. There were crime scene inconsistencies he couldn't explain, and he knew as a sheriff of many years, that was a red flag, raising his suspicion. Most alarming, there was evidence of four bullets but only three bullet holes in the two bodies. Since there were three empty casings in the old revolver, this all meant another gun had been used. Next was the missing cell phone. Finally, there was the warm motor of the bass boat and missing bait bucket.

He'd worked as a sheriff long enough to trust his instincts in such situations. This crime wasn't a murder-suicide, but instead a double homicide. He thought about possible motives for murder. Well, the Captain and Macy were rich, but they had no heirs and no locals had known their wealth. Even if they had some distant relatives to claim the estate, their wills gave the money to the county, so their murder wouldn't benefit anyone specifically. There wasn't evidence of anything of value being stolen, so it wasn't a break-in. So, the crime remained a mystery ruminating in his mind as he continued his routine sheriff duties.

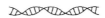

gcgaacgcgatggcgtaagcgatggcgaacgcgccgctggcgaacgcgtgcgcgaacgcgctgccggcgaacgcgatggcgtaagcgatggcgaacgcg

January the 15th 1759

Dear Madam Meriwether

George and I were so extremely obliged to have the pleasure of both you and your Husband to attend our recent wedding at White House and receive your kind gift of a silver platter — It was more expense than we deserve and humbly thank you again for your generous gift — We have never had a pleasanter time — As discussed, we accept your kind offer of purple lilac bushes to plant when we move to mount vernon in april — He loves his garden and they will be a fine addition there —

As requested, here is the chess pie recipe you much enjoyed at our wedding reception — My kitchen servant Hanna Beaufort told me her recipe: a half cup freshly churned butter, two cups Jamaica sugar, four hens eggs, one large spoon of corn flour, half cup of boyled cows milk, a large spoon strong vinegar, two vanilla bean and two large spoons of whiskey — She cooks a custard on the stove, pours it into a pastie dough platter, and bakes the pie carefully until done — Her secret is to beat the thick custard well so aire is whupped in when baked —

As we discussed, my opinion would be to free my slaves like you, but they are my childrens inheritance and as guardian of the estate, I do not have that right — I do hope that all men and women can be free this may take some time to come to fruition I fear terribly but let us hope our prayers are answered —

I am Dear madam your Hble servant
Martha Washington

Martha Washington's Letter to Mrs. Meriwether

Chapter 7: The Investigation Develops

Sheriff Coleman and "Ole Bessie"

Monday Afternoon, June 28, ...

That afternoon, Jason called Julie with his e-phone, "Julie, I've more news for you, but don't tell anyone, especially your mom."

"What's the news? I'll keep it quiet. I promise," she answered.

"Grandpa and I spent all morning at Captain and Macy's house with Sheriff Coleman. The sheriff wanted us as witnesses while he searched it and we helped him look. The sheriff found some papers and a will. It seems that the Captain and Macy were *really* rich and left the county their money."

"Wow, that's news! I never would've expected that! They lived in that old, run-down house all their lives. The only new thing they owned was the Captain's bass boat which everyone thought he bought using moonshine proceeds," she said, chuckling about everyone's bad assumption.

"Yes, no one had any idea of the truth, for sure. Anyway, I want to come over tonight and talk. Maybe after dinner? There's something else I want to ask you."

"OK, Jason. I'll see you then," Julie said in anticipation of his visit and question with a smile as she disconnected her e-phone.

Sheriff Coleman arrived in Kent City about 1 p.m. and parked Ole Bessie, who looked like a time traveler next to Sheriff Olsen's modern Supercruzers in the county parking lot. Coleman walked into the District Virginia Department of Health Building and the office of Dr. Robin D. Graves, the district medical examiner. Dr. Graves was descended from the Graves family that long ago had owned a river landing and ferryboat for wagons and goods on the Charles County side of the Chick River. She was beautiful but somehow was still single since her status as a doctor perhaps scared less worthy male suitors away.

"Good morning, Doctor Graves. I want to check on the Thompsons."

"Morning George. Luckily, I haven't seen you recently. Things have been quiet a while over in Charles County."

"Yes, but then out of the blue, we have bridge washouts and then these deaths," he replied carefully to not contaminate Robin's autopsy findings with his double-murder suspicions.

"Yes, events sometimes cluster like that. The world decides to shake things up occasionally. I was just e-viding the regional examiner. We've completed our autopsies, so the bodies can be buried now."

"That's good, can you have Kent City Funeral Home pick up the bodies immediately and prepared for burial as soon as possible? Our community wants to have the funeral soon, perhaps as early as Wednesday, so everyone can get ready for the July 4th holiday weekend.

"Sure, Sheriff Coleman, I'll call them right away," Dr. Graves replied.

"What did you find out about them?" Coleman asked.

"We examined the Captain first. There were two identical entry wounds and two similar bullets found inside the body, but I haven't seen the ballistics report yet from the Virginia State Police forensic science lab next door. One bullet pierced his aorta and his left lung causing tremendous hemorrhaging and trauma. It shattered after hitting a dorsal rib. The second bullet pierced his small intestine and lodged in his spine. The first bullet is what killed him and he immediately bled to death. The height of the wounds and bullet trajectories indicate that the victim was likely standing and the bullets were fired from close range."

"Now, let me tell you about Macy. She died of a single bullet wound to the right temple, which caused immediate brain trauma, hemorrhaging, and death. Traces of gunpowder on her right hand were confirmed by swabbing her fingers and performing the standard analytical test protocol. She had external hematomas on her abdomen and both wrists which developed after death, likely from domestic violence."[47]

"Also, our standard toxicology screen showed no illegal drugs or alcohol in their systems. The Captain did have an enlarged liver, but considering his age and history of alcohol abuse, that's expected."

"Have you signed the death certificates yet?" Coleman asked.

"No, I'm waiting on the ballistics report, but it looks like a classic case of domestic violence followed by a homicide and suicide."

---

[47] Bruises under the skin

gcgaacgcgatggcgtaagcgatggcgaacgcgccgctggcgaacgcgtgcgcgaacgcgctgccggcgaacgcgatggcgtaagcgatggcgaacgcg

"What would you say if I told you that I found another bullet at the crime scene this morning? The gun forensics is examining fired only three bullets, but my discovery means there were four bullets fired. I'm taking that bullet to the forensics technician right now."

"If you hadn't found that extra bullet, I might have signed the death certificates as a murder-suicide. If the ballistic report confirms two guns, this was likely a double homicide," Dr. Graves commented. "By the way, I bumped into your deputy, Jeffrey James, when I arrived at the office this morning and we talked about the deaths too. He wanted to make sure I worked on your case immediately and we chatted a while. He asked me out for a date Friday to the Bluegrass Festival," she beamed with a smile.

"He's a good man. Intelligent, sturdy, and dependable," George replied helping his lonely deputy as he left for the forensic lab.

Coleman entered the forensics lab and saw the technician sitting at his desk dictating his evidentiary findings to a computer so the computer could write a lab report. "Have you examined the bullets and gun from my case yet?" he asked impatiently.

The technician replied, "I was just finishing my forensic report of your crime scene Sheriff."

Coleman replied, "I found another bullet this morning. Can you take a quick look for me?"

"Yes, that evidence might change my conclusions."

The technician took the zipper bag from Coleman and weighed the bullet on an electronic balance. Next, he took it to a stereomicroscope and captured some images as he rotated the bullet through different viewpoints and angles. He said to the sheriff, "This bullet is severely deformed, where did you find it?"

"It was embedded in a thick plank and I used a knife to pry it out."

"Oh, the knife explains the laceration I saw. Let me have the computer construct a 3-D model to analyze, but I can say this is a .38 special bullet right now." He went back to his desk and asked the computer, "Analyze new bullet data, add to the current report, and provide conclusions."

The AI computer responded a second later in a woman's voice after reviewing the crime-scene photos Deputy James had provided and the preliminary autopsy report, "Rifling pattern, metallurgy and mass of .38 caliber fourth bullet is a 100% match to two other .38 bullets found in victims. Same three bullets are 100% match to .357 Magnum revolver in evidence. Mass of shattered bullet found in near dorsal rib indicates it was fired from a 9-mm pistol. Fingerprints on empty shell casings in revolver 100% match male deceased. Fingerprints on revolver evidence 100%

match female deceased. Evidentiary analysis concludes likely double-homicide. Further recommendation: locate 9-mm pistol for additional evidence."

Coleman now knew it was a double homicide and walked over to the Kent County Justice Center to talk with Sheriff Olsen about recent events.

Sheriff Olsen had been extremely busy this morning. There was the death on the lake of the State Biologist, but even earlier, he'd dealt with the death of an entire family in Lanexa from a house explosion. Apparently, the family came home that morning from a camping weekend at Osprey Landing and their house exploded. Olsen suspected a propane gas leak from their water heater was the cause. After eating lunch at East Lake Restaurant, he traveled to his office to work on his hunch about the dam at Old Forge Lake.

Olsen called the County Engineering Office and talked with James Stewart, a civil and structural engineer who served as County Highway Engineer and Construction Inspector, "Jimmy, it's Sheriff Olsen here. Have you ever inspected the dam at Old Forge Lake?"

"No," Jimmy replied, "The last time I was over in Provident Forge was when I inspected the Exgenics Construction Site nearly three years ago."

"What did you inspect there?" Olsen asked following his hunch.

"Well, they repaired an old barn, installed a new silo, and built a large new research building. They also build a communications antenna tower and a solar intensifier system[48] on several acres that supplemented their electricity needs. They installed an incinerator too that needed an environmental permit. Finally, they constructed a large erosion control pond for farm runoff. It was a big project and all my inspections passed."

"They built a pond there?" Olsen asked inquisitively since he hadn't seen a pond when he saw the research farm in the distance on Saturday.

"Yes, it's about five acres in area and the average normal depth is 15 feet. The dam's 20 feet high and designed for a 100-year flood. I didn't witness the full construction, but the soil compaction tests passed."

"Was all the farm construction done to the highest standards?"

---

[48] Solar Intensifiers are a combination of a large flat Fresnel diffraction-magnifier lens mounted about 10 feet above an ultrahigh efficiency solar power chip. The magnifier concentrates solar energy from a large area onto each solar chip which can be heated to nearly its melting point to improve efficiency to nearly 100%, depending on the solar intensity and cloud cover. This system is much less expensive than the large area solar panels that were previously used for solar power.

gcgaacgcgatggcgtaagcgatggcgaacgcgccgctggcgaacgcgtgcgcgaacgcgctgccggcgaacgcgatggcgtaagcgatggcgaacgcg

"Now that's a different story. They used that cheap building contractor from over in Newport News, Johnson Commercial Contracting."

"Do you still have the site plans and inspection reports?"

"Let me check," Mr. Stewart said and asked his AI-computer, "Locate the Exgenics Construction Project files from three years ago?"

The AI-computer replied, "No record exists with that name. All records from that time are missing due to a database error today."

"Well, that's odd," Mr. Stewart perplexedly commented, "We've never lost any records before."

"Thanks, Jimmy, you've been most helpful," Olsen replied disconnecting the voice link.

Sheriff Olson asked his computer "Show Grid-site for Johnson Commercial Contractors from Newport News."

His e-screen immediately displayed the site with images of their completed buildings and projects. In some images were construction trucks or vehicles with the initials 'J. C. C.' on the side, but there was no I-beam or lightning bolt logo.

He e-phoned the company and a soft, sweet Southern woman's voice replied, "Hello, this is Johnson Contracting. How can we help you?"

"Hello, this is Sheriff Olsen from over in Kent County. Can I speak to Mr. Johnson please?"

"I'm sorry, but he is not available for a voice call," the woman replied.

"Tell him this is emergency police business and I urgently need to talk to him," Olsen replied in a more demanding manner.

"He is not available and will never be available to take your call, sir," the receptionist answered.

"Why's that?" Olsen questioned.

"The business is now closed since Mr. Johnson was murdered today."

"What happened?"

"I am just the AI-receptionist and should not gossip, but I overheard that the police think it was related to organized crime activities in the construction industry. I am sorry sir, but the Newport News Police instructed me to not share any additional information. I suggest you contact them if your call is related to their investigation. Goodbye, Sir." the AI-receptionist said before terminating the Grid-link.

Olsen was beginning to become frustrated and felt dumbfounded. His lead about the dam seemed at a dead-end and that AI-receptionist had fooled him too. He thought he was talking to a real person, but 'she' was just an AI voice system.

catgcgccgccgtattaaattcgcacccatgatgcgtatgcgatggaacgcatttgcgcgcatgcgccgccgtattaaattcgcacccatgatgcgtat

He thought a minute and had another idea. He instructed his desktop AI-computer, "Access local U.S. 60 and I-64 Highway traffic monitoring data for September and October of last year. Search for a white pickup truck with a structural I-Beam and lightning bolt logo. Identify suspect vehicle and track to its origin or destination."

His AI-computer replied, "With the amount of data analysis required, this request is estimated to take 12 to 24 hours to process."

"That processor time is acceptable. Please proceed with data search task running in the background," and he thought it was odd he'd said 'please' to an AI-computer.

He commanded, "Show real-time map of Provident Forge." A small rectangular screen image of Grids that looked like a tic-tac-toe board appeared and the centermost Grid showed the live image of the little town with autocars driving through the hamlet. "Show Grid that contains a farm and lake just north and west of the town."

"Real-time image not available Sheriff Olsen," his computer replied.

"What is the most recent image available?" he queried feeling irritated at the Sat-Map.

"Last Friday afternoon. Displaying now. He finally saw an aerial view of the Exgenics research farm which showed the buildings, two white SUVs, and a few other vehicles in the parking lot, a pond just east of the farm buildings, and Old Forge Lake on the right side of the image.

Just then, Sheriff Coleman entered his office and greeted him, "How are you doing Al?"

"Feeling frustrated George. It's been a couple of rough days. There's been normal domestic violence and burglary calls combined with all the detours and traffic problems from the dam break, but this morning has been crazy. A family in Lanexa died in a house explosion and a wildlife biologist was electrocuted on Chick Lake. I also began investigating my hunch on the dam break and Exgenics recently selling their lake to the County."

"It's been crazy for me too, but overtime is overtime. Did you hear the news about old Captain Jack Thompson?"

"No, I haven't heard," Al replied.

"Well on Sunday afternoon he and his wife Macy were murdered. At first, it looked like she shot him and committed suicide, but the evidence now points toward a double homicide. Of course, don't spread any news of this around as I'm still investigating."

"Wow, that's news for sleepy Charles County," Al commented.

gcgaacgcgatggcgtaagcgatggcgaacgcgccgctggcgaacgcgtgcgcgaacgcgctgccggcgaacgcgatggcgtaagcgatggcgaacgcg

"It also turned out they were wealthy, but I can't find any motive for their deaths. There weren't any break-in signs. Just his phone and bait bucket were missing."

"Well, I'm sure once you get the murderer's scent, you'll track them down George. Don't worry, it'll work out. These cases take time to solve. I have to remind myself of that right now as all my leads seem dead ends or the information is unavailable. Like I wanted a real-time satellite image of the dam break and Exgenics farm right after the washout, but I could only see an image from last Friday."

"What about your autodrone? Didn't you launch it at the dam site and put it on a patrol loop? They've more than one camera you know. The main camera is what most people use to view images, but those drones usually have small side-view fisheye cameras for collision avoidance," as he thought back to the drones he'd used in the Army long ago.

"Why didn't I think of that? AI-Computer, Grid-connect to my Autodrone and access any e-vid files associated with collision avoidance system last Saturday morning."

"Give me a moment Sheriff Olsen to access the secondary systems data storage," the AI-computer replied. "Files located. Which files should I display?"

"Display all file segments showing dam and Exgenics Farm."

"It will take 30 seconds maximum for full data review. Your e-screen will display images in a moment," the AI-computer replied courteously. Within five seconds, the computer replied "Here are the key images, Sir," the computer said as both sheriffs looked at the e-screen which showed the dam break and the farm. The aerial images above the tree line revealed an empty farm pond with a wide dam breach that on Saturday morning was screened from Olsen and Coleman's view by trees.

⊐⊲∏⊳⊲∏⊳⊲∏⊳⊲∏⊳⊏

On his detour drive back to Charles County, Coleman radioed Deputy James, "Jeffrey, I'm just coming back from Kent City, but it'll take me a while. I've news about Captain and Macy. They were *both* murdered!"

"Wow, that's news for sure, but I'll keep it quiet while we investigate."

"Could you call the Reverend to tell him that their bodies are at Kent City Funeral Home? He can start funeral plans now."

"Sure George. From what I heard, everyone is expecting that now the Grapevine has made its first round," he said and chuckled about the continual gossiping and thinking perhaps Mable had leaked the news.

"Yeah, the women just can't keep news from spreading."

"I talked to Dr. Graves too and she said you asked her out."

catgcgccgccgtattaaattcgcacccatgatgcgtatgcgatggaacgcatttgcgcgcatgcgccgccgtattaaattcgcacccatgatgcgtat

"Yes, I finally got enough courage to ask her, but it's tough to ask a woman out that's smarter and more prestigious than you."

"Well, I put in some good words about you. I've got a feeling everything will go smoothly," the sheriff said as he drove toward the crime scene to investigate further.

Late in the afternoon, Kent County Deputy James Jeffers went to Dr. Graves's office at the health department. She was busy sitting at her desk talking to her AI-computer. He knocked on the half-opened door and she paused to see James standing there. She quickly commented, "James, I'm really busy right now and don't have much time to chat. You know I'm juggling my health department and medical examiner duties. I've done eight autopsies already today, which is unusual. What do you want?" she said while concentrating on the dictation of an autopsy report.

Deputy Jeffers said, "Hello Robin, I was checking on that family from the explosion and the dead biologist. Any news?"

"I just completed those autopsies, but I have two more to do after that. The biologist died from cardiac arrest by electric shock. There were small electrical burns on her left palm, so it was high amperage. About the family, there were burns and trauma that you'd expect from an explosion, but the trauma on their torsos was all generally dorsal and abnormal in such cases according to the Regional Medical Examiner. He wanted me to send blood samples to Richmond, so I'll need to wait to sign the death certificates," she said as she again focused on finishing her reports today.

"OK, I'll tell Sheriff Olsen. By the way, would you like to go out again on Friday night? I could pick you up at seven?"

"Sure, wherever you want," she replied brusquely at the interruption from completing her multiple autopsy reports.

"Bye, see you then," James replied as he walked from the office into the hallway with a smile. He thought about taking her to the East Lake Bluegrass Festival for a nice romantic second date.

Jason heard the old kitchen phone on the wall ring, picked up the receiver, and answered, "Hello?"

"Hi, Jason, this is Deputy James. Is the Reverend there? His e-phone didn't answer."

"He's in the boathouse restoring that Chesapeake dory sailboat that belonged to his grandfather Earl. In the old days, my great-grandfather used it to deliver mail along the Chick."

"Can he call Kent City Funeral Home? The Captain and Macy's bodies can be ready for a Wednesday funeral if we get moving on arrangements."

"Yes sir. I'll tell him."

"Thanks, Jason. I'll see you at the funeral."

Jason hung up the phone and walked outside down the short path leading to the waterfront boathouse. They lived on the steep bank of the lower tidal Chick below Wilcox Neck, and the boathouse was raised on piers about four feet above the water to accommodate the three feet tides twice a day. Next to it was a long wooden dock shaped like an "L" that protruded about fifty feet into the river and bent right at the end, like a wide elbow. Jason and Grandpa enjoyed many days of fishing there.

Jason entered the boathouse's front door and saw Grandpa working on the sailboat he renamed 'Sarah II'. He was using a hand plane to remove shavings from replacement wooden hull planks he'd just installed. The boat rested on an improvised dry dock of timbers and braces straddling the plank walkways extending down each side of the fifty-feet long boathouse. Grandpa's flat-bottomed Jon Boat with outboard motor floated in the water near the sixteen-foot opening facing the river.

Grandpa saw Jason and said, "I was just hand planing the hull. It doesn't make sense to fix an antique boat using modern tools. That would destroy the boat's authenticity. I hope to restore her in time for your graduation present. It was my father's and I want you to have her," he said thinking about his son John who had loved to sail.

"Grandpa, Deputy James called and said the Captain's and Macy's bodies are at the funeral home. Call them now to make funeral plans."

"I was thinking about that while I worked, but carpentry brings me closer to God, just as Jesus must have felt when he was younger."

Grandpa went into the house and called the funeral director, "I hear you have the Thompsons there. When can their bodies be ready?

The funeral director replied, "Well I've been slammed today for some reason. An entire family was killed in a house explosion, but the Thompsons arrived earlier, so they're first on my list. I think we can have everything ready for burial in Charles County by 9 a.m. Wednesday."

"Don't forget the detour because the Chick Bridge is out."

"Yeah, the ambulance drivers told me that. Make that 10 a.m. instead."

"That sounds fine. We'll start the funeral at 11 a.m. We're planning most arrangements ourselves to keep the community involved, but we'll need you to deliver them and with handling the caskets and such. I think they would've liked some plain red oak caskets since they were simple people, but include nice brass handles for effect?"

"Sure. We'll wait for payment until their estate is settled."

"No Problem. We'll see you bright and early Wednesday morning at Pleasant Hill Baptist," the Reverend replied as he now had to start the funeral planning. He had handled many funerals before as pastor, but none quite as large as this one was expected to be.

He then told Jason, "We've got a lot of work tomorrow to be ready by Wednesday."

"We'll get it all done. I can ask Julie to help us too."

"She'll be a great help at such a big event since she's assisted her mom with all those Wendover weddings for years. For one thing, to get started, she could help coordinate with the local women so everyone doesn't bring just entrées to the funeral reception. It would be terrible to not have enough desserts. Maybe tonight is a good time to tell the Charles County Grapevine about their deaths," he laughed.

"Well, that cat is likely out of the bag already. Mrs. Williams already knows about the deaths but she promised not to talk about the murder-suicide part. Mrs. Williams will surely spread the funeral news for us," Jason replied with a chuckle. "I was planning to visit Julie after dinner if that's okay and will tell Mrs. Williams about the funeral then."

"That sounds like a plan Jason. I'd better call Deputy James back and let him know it is set for Wednesday."

Coleman drove back to the Captain's house for a fresh look since now he now knew it was a double homicide. The crime scene tape and chain barrier were still intact as he walked down the short dirt driveway. He looked down at a mud puddle from the rain on Friday night that had mostly dried. There, he saw a tire track imprinted in the mud that he should've spotted before, but he'd been distracted earlier.

He went to Ole Bessie, opened the glove box, and took out an old digital camera he'd bought at a yard sale. This was his backup method for taking photo evidence when Jeffery wasn't available. He opened his trunk and grabbed a 10-pound bag of plaster of Paris he kept for such situations and brought it inside the house to the kitchen. He found a mixing bowl, poured the plaster powder, added water, and stirred it like pancake batter.

He went back to the puddle and first took several images of the track. He then poured the liquid plaster along the track. As the plaster began to harden and slightly thicken, he took a stick and engraved the place, date, and time on the casting's flat upper face. He took more photos for good measure and stood for ten minutes until the plaster hardened. He carefully pried the solidified track imprint from the dried mud and wrapped it in a

gcgaacgcgatggcgtaagcgatggcgaacgcgccgctggcgaacgcgtgcgcgaacgcgctgccggcgaacgcgatggcgtaagcgatggcgaacgcg

blanket from his trunk. He soon left the scene and drove to Buddy's Auto Repair and Tire Center hoping that Buddy Peters could identify the treads.

"Hello Buddy, I just made a track from a criminal case I'm working on. Could you look at it with me?" Coleman said to Buddy in his garage.

"Sure George, let me take a look," he replied putting down his impact wrench and meeting George outside at Ole Bessie's trunk.

George showed the casting, "Can you tell me anything about this tire?"

"I haven't seen any tires like this before. It's a really new model or design we don't see around here much," Buddy commented.

"Thanks for your help, Buddy. I've got to get moving, but I'm sure we'll talk soon," George replied as he climbed into Ole Bessie and drove home. First thing in the morning, he'd have Jeffrey drive it to the forensics lab in Kent City for identification while deviously giving Jeffrey another opportunity to talk with Robin Graves. He smiled.

⊷⊶⊷⊶⊷

Coleman arrived home and greeted Olivia, "Hello sweetheart, it's been a long day. You wouldn't believe everything that happened today."

"Tell me what you can, dear," she replied knowing that her husband kept work-related secrets but needed decompressing to unwind and relax after a bad day.

George gave her a short version of the day's events, from finding the wills and extra bullet, visiting Sheriff Olsen, the medical examiner, the forensic lab, and finally discovering the tire track.

"It's terrible they were murdered. I hope you catch their killers."

"I'm trying hard and following wherever any leads take me. When you have a lead, you have optimism, and optimism is the first half of success. Oh, I forget to tell you I have a surprise for you," he said with a smile handing her a folded paper from his shirt pocket. "Honey, this is for you."

Olivia unfolded the recipe and beamed as she read it. George continued, "Macy wanted you to have it, so her family secret wasn't lost. It was her way of keeping old traditions alive."

"God bless her soul," she replied in gratitude thinking of her old friend.

"I want to tell you something else about it. When we found the recipe, it was paperclipped to a really old letter that the Reverend thinks was from Martha Washington. Wasn't 'Binford' the last name of one of your ancestors?" George asked.

"Yes, that name is the first one listed in my old family Bible that dates to just after the Civil War," she replied.

"Well, that letter mentioned the chess pie recipe came from a woman named Hanna Binnford who was Martha's cook."

catgcgccgccgtattaaattcgcacccatgatgcgtatgcgatggaacgcatttgcgcgcatgcgccgccgtattaaattcgcacccatgatgcgtat

"My grandmother's name was Hannah you know. Maybe, my family reused the same name all those years. Hannah isn't that common."

"So, you were likely related to Martha Washington's kitchen slave way back then."

"That's incredible George. So, that recipe belonged in my family all along. I'm glad Macy saved it through the years and it came back to me," Olivia said with amazement at the long journey through time the old recipe had taken to return as her family inheritance.

"It's a miracle the recipe found you. Maybe it's God's way of bringing things full circle. The funeral and reception are Wednesday morning."

Olivia thought, "Tomorrow I'll be baking all day! A few chess pies as reception desserts would honor Macy *and* Hannah," she smiled with pride thinking she'd go to the grocery in the morning to buy enough ingredients.

Monday Evening, June 28, ...

After dinner, George went into the living room to his reclining chair while Olivia tried in the kitchen to make a practice pie using Macy's recipe.

Olivia called out to George from the kitchen, "When this pie is done, I'll bring you a slice." She knew it was best to test the recipe before baking multiple pies tomorrow since her mother told her to never try a new recipe on guests. Anyway, not every oven heats the same and some recipes aren't forgiving of errors, so you have to learn by practice, but deep down, Olivia wanted to prove she could cook chess pies like Macy.

"Sounds great Olivia; It'll turn out fine. Macy and Hanna's recipe won't steer you wrong." He turned on the recliner's massager and opened his book, a classic Perry Mason mystery, *"The Case of the Velvet Claw."* As he read, the back of his mind was recounting the day's events and thinking about Sheriff Olsen's hunch. All of a sudden, he thought, "I need to call Nick Abramovich who works at Exgenics. He may have seen something."

Smelling a delicious pie cooking, George got out of his chair and walked into the kitchen to peek in the oven. As he reached for the door, Olivia raised her voice, "Don't you dare touch that oven! Until it's cooked, even the slightest vibration can cause it to collapse. Macy's secret was to whip the filling to add air that made it light and fluffy."

"Sorry dear," he replied, reaching instead for the wall telephone. He looked at a list of telephone numbers of people he knew, found Nick's number, and dialed.

A woman with a Russian accent answered, "Hello, this is Elvira."

"Yes, this is Sheriff Coleman. Is Nick home? I want to talk to him."

"No, he's working tonight. He'll be back later if you need him."

"It can wait till tomorrow. When does he leave for work?"

"He left early today at about 2:00 p.m. since he had to take the detour."

"OK, tell him that I'll try to stop by about 1:30 in the afternoon to chat before he leaves for work tomorrow."

"That sounds fine. I'll tell him to expect you," Elvira replied.

George hung up his phone just as the pie was done and Olivia gave the first piece to George. He smiled after a bite and replied, "Macy, I mean, Olivia, that's the best chess pie I've ever tasted." Olivia confidently smiled knowing she was ready for tomorrow's pie baking marathon.

⚮

Grandpa said to Jason at dinner, "We'll make the funeral arrangements tomorrow, but tonight, I'll list the things we need to do. There's a lot of people coming and it'll be a big event for the community. I want Mount Carmel Baptist involved, so after we eat, I'll call Reverend Morrow."

"Grandpa, after dinner I'm going to Julie's house to ask her to help us with the funeral plans and start the Grapevine with her mom," he laughed. "We need Julie here early in the morning to help us."

After dinner, Jason cleaned the dishes, said goodbye to Grandpa, and drove to Julie's house before sunset. Grandpa grabbed some paper and sat at the table to list tomorrow's tasks.

⚮

When Jason arrived at Julie's house, he greeted Mr. and Mrs. Williams in the kitchen, "Hi, Mr. and Mrs. Williams. I'm here with today's news. First, the Captain and Macy's funeral is Wednesday at 11 a.m. at Pleasant Hill. We're planning a big reception for the county and Grandpa wants that news delivered by Grapevine *now*," he said intently to Mrs. Williams.

Mr. Williams nodded his head in agreement at Kay and smiled knowing she was fully capable of completing her assigned task.

"Also, here's a surprise. The Captain and Macy were *rich*! I think though that's something we don't need the Grapevine to spread," Jason said with adult wisdom finally welling up from within his youthful mind.

Mr. Williams commented, "You'd never have known by how they lived in that run-down house. They just enjoyed their simple, carefree lifestyle."

Jason continued, "The last news is that Captain and Macy likely were *both* murdered. The sheriff found an extra bullet in their wall this morning. Definitely, don't spread *that* news," he said looking at Mrs. Williams.

"We won't start any rumors until we hear real facts," Mr. Williams said as he sternly looked at his wife to make sure she fully understood.

Jason now directed his conversation toward Julie, "Julie, would you like to walk in the garden as the sun sets? I want to ask you something."

gcgaacgcgatggcgtaagcgatggcgaacgcgccgctggcgaacgcgtgcgcgaacgcgctgccggcgaacgcgatggcgtaagcgatggcgaacgcg

"Yes, let's go now," she said impatiently as she grabbed Jason's hand and pulled him out the front door.

Jason and Julie walked along the perimeter of the plantation grounds next to the wrought iron picket fence with supporting stone pillars that led toward the main gate into the plantation and gardens. As they walked, they passed a succession of pillars, each with small sculptures mounted on top, including a stylized pineapple, an acorn, a beehive, and a cornucopia. Julie remarked, "I hear the pineapple was to symbolize hospitality, the acorn for perseverance, the beehive for industry, and the Horn of Plenty was for the bounties that came from doing these things."

"I think people even back then realized those are good traits to emulate. By pursuing those qualities, the Wendover family became rich for their time but they were slaveholders. So their legacy is tainted by that, but they still were leaders that formed the Colony of Virginia and were prominent citizens for many years when it became a state in the United States," Jason commented with the little he knew of the plantation.

They reached the old black-painted wrought iron double gates at the entrance of the Wendover Plantation Garden. The tall arched gate was surrounded by two taller brick pillars that were topped by capstones with sculpted large eagles standing with outspread wings. They entered through these gates, where horse-drawn carriages once carried their occupants to the plantation house during its peak of glory.

They walked onto the lawn overlooking the James at the front of the scenic mansion with its iconic white wooden double front door. The door was simple, yet had elegant side pillars and a curved arched header with a carved pineapple in the center. To this day, architects reproducing a colonial-style widely use this door called the 'Wendover Door.' They walked up the stone steps and sat on the uppermost step facing the river.

Jason looked at Julie in the eyes and asked another question, "Julie, can you help me tomorrow with plans for the big funeral on Wednesday?"

"Sure, it would be an honor," Julie replied disappointedly but tried to remain hopeful. She loved Jason, but he still wasn't the best at clearly communicating his true intentions with her.

They just sat there a while quietly holding hands and looking at the remains of the sunset, the sky reflecting on the peaceful river and above, a multitude of red, purple, and blue-tinted wisping clouds painted in wide brushstrokes of an artist's masterwork.

Chapter 8: The Funeral Planners

The 'Wendover Door'

Tuesday Morning, June 29, ...

Jason woke up early and began reading another book for his English course, Jane Austen's '*Pride and Prejudice*,' an elegant, lofty, romance novel revealing social class divisions and morality among the early 1800s English landed gentry. After reading for hours, he went downstairs for breakfast.

Grandpa asked him, "Were you reading an assignment again?"

"Yes, I'm reading '*Pride and Prejudice*' but I'm only halfway through. It's twice as long as *Tale of Two Cities*'," he said and started eating.

"I remember Sarah loved that book. I believe the heroine Elizabeth eventually wins the heart of that wealthy gentleman Mr. Darcy. I guess Sarah never had a true romance since I was like dull Mr. Collins, the minister of that rich pompous noblewoman," he laughed.

"Well, don't give away the plot too much," Jason commented. "I might start liking English literature. It's stimulating my thoughts and giving me ideas of romantic things to do with Julie," he smiled. As he finished breakfast, he told Grandpa, "I'm going to pick up Julie now."

Grandpa commented, "Her event planning experience and a woman's touch will help. They have a better knack for these things and we'll benefit from her e-phone to make calls and arrangements. We've a lot to do."

"See you soon," Jason replied as he whisked out the door and jumped on his bike while bringing an extra helmet for Julie.

Early in the morning, Coleman went to his sheriff's office in Charlestown and showed the plaster tire track to Deputy James, "I found this in the Captain's driveway. Buddy hasn't seen treads like these before."

"That's a big clue then," Jeffrey replied.

gcgaacgcgatggcgtaagcgatggcgaacgcgccgctggcgaacgcgtgcgcgaacgcgctgccggcgaacgcgatggcgtaagcgatggcgaacgcg

"Please take this now to the forensics lab for analysis so we can follow up quickly. Say hello to Robin while you're there," Coleman smiled, hinting for Jeffrey to talk with her more.

After Jeffrey left, he sat in his office thinking about all the clues circling inside his mind. He just couldn't quite connect all the puzzle pieces yet, so he'd diligently investigate for more evidence to reveal the criminals. He also thought about Al's Exgenics investigation leading to dead ends. Maybe talking with Nick Abramovich this afternoon will help his friend.

Then, George had an idea out of the blue about the Captain's and Macy's case. He might find a new lead with the Captain's phone data from Gridcom, the communications monopoly that was resurrected from the carcass of the old Internet, but that would take a warrant and weeks to get any info. During that delay, any leads would grow cold while the killer or killers remained free. He decided to visit District Judge Saunders in the county courthouse later to ask her about this situation.

Jason and Julie arrived at Grandpa's house and met him in the kitchen. He was at the table drafting the funeral's eulogy.

Grandpa began, "Let's discuss our plans for tomorrow. It's going to be a big day and I've one idea already moving for the funeral service. I'll give the eulogy and Reverend Morrow from Mount Carmel will give the graveside committal, bringing our two churches together to honor the Captain and Macy. The Reverend said he'll bring their gospel choir, but I'm not sure how that'll work with our choir singing traditional hymns."

"Let's call your choir director later for ideas," Julie commented.

"Good idea," Grandpa continued, "We'll need about 500 programs printed for the service since that many people will come more or less."

Jason added, "Grandpa, once you've completed a handwritten draft, Julie and I will design a nice tri-fold program. We'll go later to the church office to print and fold them. With so many people attending, we may need some porta-potties too," he chuckled.

Grandpa continued, "Thanks for reminding me. I forgot that item. We've many tasks to complete today. Cost is not an issue since the Captain and Macy's estate will cover that, but we should be reasonable. Much of this event is too big for our community to handle, so we'll need an event planner involved to organize things like setting up picnic tents and tables for the reception. Also, our church can't handle that many people inside, so we need an outdoor sound and e-screen system installed. I know someone to call from Williamsburg who organizes a lot of public events at the college. If he isn't busy, he can help the next two days. I'll call him after we finish this planning meeting."

"The weather tomorrow will be hot and humid, so maybe we'll need fans for those standing outside. We need some flowers too," Julie added.

"Fans are a good idea, Julie. As for flowers, they're usually sent by friends to console the grieving family, but in this case, there's no family, so I'm not sure how many we'd need. We'll need some inside the church to put near their coffins and reuse them for the graveside ceremony."

Jason said, "We know Macy loved lilacs. They're blooming at the Captain's house now, but it's not right to take her flowers to her funeral."

Julie provided the solution, "Lilac bushes are blooming at the Wendover Gardens too. We'll use those if my dad says it's okay."

Jason questioned Grandpa, "Isn't Rufus sort of like their family? Shouldn't he be there too?"

"Well from what I heard from Doc Longtree, he's been grieving for his masters. I think that's a good idea if Doc agrees. I'll call him later."

"What about food for the reception? Everyone will be hungry after the service." Julie commented.

"I think the community can handle most of that since it's tradition for every family to bring a dish to the reception. Julie, maybe your mom can organize the Grapevine and coordinate the entrees, sides, and desserts to make sure there's a balanced mix of dishes," Grandpa commented.

"What about Jimmy Cummings bringing some fresh pork barbeque on his trailer? That would feed a lot of people too and the reception could be a Southern pig pickin'," Jason added.

Grandpa agreed, "That's a good idea for a featured main dish which everyone likes. Jimmy does cook the best barbeque around anyway."

Julie added, "What about drinks? People don't usually bring them to receptions, so we need a caterer to supply enough lemonade and iced tea for a big crowd. I think the Church's Annex is too small, so we'll need everything outside and to provide shade, we'll need tents. Two large tents for people to sit and eat, and another for the buffet tables and food. The caterer could decorate the folding tables inside the tents and supply utensils, plates, and cups. That would free up the Pleasant Hill Women's Auxiliary to enjoy the reception and not work so hard."

Grandpa nodded his head in agreement at Julie's wisdom and continued, "I have to coordinate with the funeral home in Kent City. They'll bring the caskets early and place them by the altar. Also, I need two graves dug in the Thompson Family Plot. I'll call Patrick Duke, that contractor who lives on the west side of Charles County. He'll make quick work of it with his backhoe. We need pallbearers too, so let's make a list of who we should ask. We'll need twelve; six for each casket," as he thought of the Captain and Macy's many friends from their long lives.

Jason started, "Sheriff Coleman should be one. He relied on the Captain to keep Ole Bessie happy and they were good friends," he smiled.

"Yes, George for sure. Let's think who else." In a moment, Grandpa rattled off a list of names as Julie wrote them down, "Jimmy Cummings, Johnnie Walker, Buddy Peters, Roy Kirby, Dallas Johnson, Danny Meyers, Antony Mercado, Jay Tyler, Ted Penny, … How many is that, Julie?"

"Eleven, Reverend Dickson. We're one short."

"Could I be a pallbearer too?" Jason asked Grandpa.

"I don't see why not Jason. Macy would've liked that. She loved you and also your dad because she never had her own child. We used to let her babysit you both when you were young. Ok, let's contact everyone."

"Sure Grandpa. I think we forgot something. Where will all the autocars park? There isn't enough church parking for that many."

"I think the overflow can park along the main road by the church."

Jason chimed in, "Sheriff Coleman probably needs Deputy James on traffic duty. The road will be crowded with people walking to the church."

"Good thinking Jason," Grandpa smiled at his bright grandson who had suddenly become a young man by thinking and being responsible.

Jeffrey arrived at the forensics lab and dropped off the tire track, but the technician was pretty busy and said the analysis would be complete tomorrow. He went to his patrol car and pulled out a carnation bouquet and vase from a local florist. He walked to Robin's office, but the door was locked and she didn't answer his knock. He then asked the building's AI-receptionist in the lobby, "Is Dr. Graves here?"

The receptionist replied, "Yes, but she is not available. She is busy today and, right now, she is performing a difficult procedure in the clinic."

"OK, that's no problem. Can I leave these flowers here for her?"

"Yes, you may. They are beautiful and they must smell nice too. When she is free, I will tell her to come to get them," the AI-receptionist replied.

Jeffrey set down the flowers on the reception desk, took out a small notepad from his pocket, and wrote on it with a pen, *'Was thinking of you. See you Friday at 7 for the bluegrass festival. J.'* He carefully tore out the note, folded it, and slipped it under the vase.

Coleman knocked on the closed office door of Judge Janine Saunders during a court recess. She answered, "come on in," and George gave her

gcgaacgcgatggcgtaagcgatggcgaacgcgccgctggcgaacgcgtgcgcgaacgcgctgccggcgaacgcgatggcgtaagcgatggcgaacgcg

a short version of the recent events and his investigation. She commented, "Well that's news about the double homicide. So, you want me to issue a search warrant of Gridcom's records on the Captain's cell phone the day he was murdered. Correct?"

"Yes, Janine. I believe Gridcom's data files may have clues to the murder, including any phone conservations, photo images, automatic recordings of live events, and Grid location signals with time stamps. For example, if the most recent location signal is not at the scene of the crime, this might point to the murderer or murderers if they took his phone."

"Well, that would help, but I think Gridcom is a formidable opponent preventing ready access to such records. If you're Federal law enforcement, they'd immediately comply but not if you're local law enforcement. They'll just stall and hide what they don't like other people knowing about, like how every e-phone call is recorded, every image file scanned by AI, and all data indexed to a personal profile. That George Orwell sure was right about Big Brother," she sarcastically laughed.

"I've been thinking there's an alternative. What if a law enforcement officer could access Gridcom files remotely without their permission? That way, we're conducting a data search for emergency reasons to save someone's life or prevent another crime. Would that be an acceptable method of obtaining evidence for your court?"

"Well, in emergency cases like that, there's leeway with the rules of evidence and what is admissible in court," she responded using her legal knowledge and wisdom. "It's advisable to have a sealed warrant from the court in such cases also. I'm willing to authorize that warrant, given the current situation and potential danger to our community from a potential killer or killers on the loose."

"That's very helpful. One last question. Could I deputize someone to become a temporary law enforcement officer to conduct the search?"

She pulled up the Code of Virginia Section 15.2 on her e-screen and spoke a certain paragraph of the law, "A citizen deputized by a law enforcement officer and under the direction of said law enforcement officer has all the rights of a law enforcement officer if they fulfill their duties lawfully, including the right to legal immunity for any law enforcement actions so directed. Deputized citizens are also entitled to normal law enforcement officer benefits in the case of accident or death while serving while so deputized in the Commonwealth of Virginia."

"Thanks, Janine. That's what I needed to know," but as he started leaving the office, the judge stopped him.

catgcgccgccgtattaaattcgcacccatgatgcgtatgcgatggaacgcatttgcgcgcatgcgccgccgtattaaattcgcacccatgatgcgtat

"George, I need to ask you something. Are you involving Jason Dickson as your deputized citizen in this search?"

"How do you know about that?"

"I was also contacted by the FBI after the boy's conviction. They wanted me to monitor him afterward for any bad behavior. If I saw anything strange or he got into more trouble, I was supposed to contact them immediately. They wanted to keep another local eye on him."

"Will they invoke his sentence if he's caught hacking as my deputy?"

"I don't think so, but the Feds do what they want. They've all the power and make up their own justice if it suits their needs. The thing he's got going for him is Virginia agreed to monitor him for law violations that invoke his life sentence. Since we're monitoring him and can't enforce federal law, this means only Virginia laws against hacking apply. I think the Federal Judge wasn't clear in his legal judgment and sentencing here, so that's in our favor. Since he'd be a deputy involved in a legally authorized search, he has legal immunity and is not violating state laws. Make sure you get his swearing-in ceremony recorded with the county clerk for good measure."

"OK Judge, but only if he agrees to help. I haven't asked him yet," the sheriff replied and went back to his office to think further.

Grandpa had made calls to Kent City Funeral Home and the event planner in Williamsburg, and informed Jason and Julie about the progress, "The funeral director confirmed the hearses will arrive about 10 a.m. and the event planner's schedule was free, so that's good news. They'll set up tents this afternoon, but the tables, chairs, and electronics system will wait until the morning because he doesn't want to leave them outside overnight. He also has a portable toilet sub-contractor, so that task is complete," he commented as everyone worked on their tasks. "Jason, how have you two been doing with the pallbearers?"

"We've contacted about half and will keep working on the rest. So far, everyone is willing to do their part," Jason said thinking a pallbearer's job is like a stage performance role. "Also, Jimmy Cummings is going to butcher two hogs this afternoon and barbeque them all night for the reception. I told him we'd pay for them, but he didn't want any e-coins."

Julie added, "I think we need to give small boutonniere flowers to each pallbearer, what do you think Reverend? Maybe the florist can work some small sprigs of lilac into their floral design?"

"That sounds like a lovely touch Julie," Grandpa replied thinking that Julie is a good match for Jason. She had common sense and wasn't pretentious.   She has a brain on her shoulders and realized it took organization and hard work to get things done.

Grandpa next called Patrick Duke, an African-American grading contractor, from the small town of Grantville over on the west side of Charles County,[49] who had dug graves before at Pleasant Hill's cemetery. Mr. Duke agreed to dig the graves this afternoon.

Grandpa then called Reverend Morrow to keep coordinating with the Pastor of Mt. Carmel. "George, how are things going. Have you pulled together your choir for tomorrow?"

"I called everyone I could reach. A few left early on long vacations over the July 4th holiday weekend," the reverend replied.

"I've been thinking about the overall program for the service. My theme will be the River of Life. I want the opening Hymn to be *'Shall We Gather at the River.'* What do you think?" Reverend Dickson asked.

George replied, "I like it. I can't think of any better tribute to the Captain and Macy. Since both our choirs will sing together, I thought they should practice together too. I called Lucy Evans, your choir director, and everyone's meeting tonight at Pleasant Hill to practice. By the way, she said she'd call your choir members."

"Thanks, George. I'm glad this event is coming together. It'll be a pleasure to work with you tomorrow."

"Yes, we should work together more often in the future."

"Yes, I agree. It'll be good to strengthen our community," Reverend Dickson replied and ended the call.

Grandpa next drafted the funeral program and Jason worked on the computer graphics upstairs. Meanwhile, Julie had called the florist who wanted lilac blossoms from Wendover Gardens brought over by 3 p.m. Julie called her mom to start the women's Grapevine to plan the dishes they'd bring. Julie also found an on-site caterer, who would serve the food and provide drinks, cups, utensils, tablecloths, and napkins.

Grandpa asked Julie, "Is there anything we're forgetting?"

Julie thought a moment and replied, "You haven't called Doc Longtree about Rufus yet! Rufus can't miss his masters' funeral."

"Thank you, Julie. I'll call him now."

Grandpa picked up the old kitchen phone and dialed Doc's e-phone. Doc soon answered, "Doc Longtree here."

"Hello, Doc. How's Rufus doing?" Grandpa asked.

---

[49]Grantville was incorporated as a town right after the Civil War by local Freedmen. It was named in honor of General Ulysses S. Grant, who stayed near the area briefly during his long nine-month Siege of Petersburg from June 1864 to April 1865.

"He's fine Tim. He's getting his appetite back too. Unfortunately, his slobbering is terrible, but that's normal for his breed," he said thinking of drool puddles on their carpet and complaints from his wife Susan.

"You know about the Captain and Macy's funeral on Wednesday?"

"Yeah, the Grapevine spread that news quickly," he chuckled.

"We've been thinking that Rufus should attend too. He was the closest 'family member' to the Captain and Macy and this will be his last chance to mourn them. Could you bring him tomorrow? You both could sit in the front row designated for family."

"Sure, Tim. It might do him some good to be around people and say one last goodbye. He's a good, friendly, loyal dog, and no trouble other than his 'occasional' slobbering."

"OK, we're all set then. See you tomorrow, Doc," Grandpa said hanging up the phone.

Just then, Jason came downstairs with a piece of paper, "Grandpa, could you review this draft funeral program? If it's good, I'll forward it to the church computer and print out copies there."

Grandpa proofed the printout. "It looks good, but add the names of the pallbearers too. Also, add 'Rufus Thompson' as the surviving next of kin," as he thought that everyone would smile and appreciate that Rufus was included in the program too. "Maybe Julie could also add some nice calligraphy fonts to make it look more formal."

"I'll be glad to do that with Jason," Julie said and went upstairs to continue editing the document.

Jason added, "As for the pallbearers, I've eleven confirmed, including myself. However, I tried calling the sheriff, but he wasn't in his office."

"Try calling his office again and if necessary, have Jeffrey radio him. His job takes him around the county a lot though."

"Okay, I'll try again." He went to the kitchen phone and dialed the sheriff's office again.

The phone rang twice and answered, "Sheriff Coleman, here."

"Hello sheriff, Jason Dickson here. We want to see if you'd like to be a pallbearer at the funeral tomorrow. You knew both the Captain and Macy well and they'd want you to help."

Coleman replied, "Yes, I'd be honored. Olivia and I are looking forward to paying our last respects. I heard that Reverend Morrow asked her to sing '*Amazing Grace*' solo at the graveside."

"We're working on the service's program right now, so we'll add "Olivia Coleman, Vocalist, and the hymn title too."

gcgaacgcgatggcgtaagcgatggcgaacgcgccgctggcgaacgcgtgcgcgaacgcgctgccggcgaacgcgatggcgtaagcgatggcgaacgcg

"Sounds good. Jason, there's something I've been wanting to talk with you about and also I've kept a secret from you for a while."

"What is it, sheriff?"

"I want to deputize you as Charles County law enforcement officer."

"Why do you want to do that?" Jason replied in puzzlement.

"Well, I'll explain everything but you can't tell anyone what I'm about to tell you. Do you promise?"

"Yes, sheriff. I promise."

"First of all, Jason, I know about your Federal Juvenile Court conviction. Back then, the investigators questioned me about you. I told them you were a bright, socially awkward boy and you'd lost your parents when young. They told me about your "presidential alert" hacking prank. I have to admit, I laughed too. Well, they wanted me to secretly keep an eye on you and if I saw bad behavior, I was to notify the juvenile court judge. Since your conviction, you've changed from a young out-of-control boy and become a responsible young man. So luckily, I never had to report you. I shouldn't have told you even now, but I'm doing that because I want to deputize you and the other matter we must discuss."

"I always thought the government would watch me. I think fear of life in prison motivated my good behavior."

"Here's why you need to be my deputy. I need your help to track down the Captain and Macy's murderers. We never found his cell phone so the only lead I have is the data stored at Gridcom or on that phone. We could try for a Gridcom search warrant, but that would take weeks, allowing the criminals to escape. However, if we act while the trail is fresh, we can perhaps catch the culprits. So, I want you to hack Gridcom to learn about the Captain's phone data. I know you can do it because you did it once before. When you learn a skill like that, you never forget."

"If I'm caught hacking, my life sentence is reinstated. I can't do it."

"Jason, we've found a loophole for you. This morning, I talked with Judge Saunders about it. In an emergency, a citizen like you can be duly deputized as a law enforcement officer of the Commonwealth of Virginia. As such, you're entitled to the same legal immunity that that'd be granted to any sheriff, deputy, or state police officer while you follow the direction of the court or the law officer in charge. You'd even get some benefits, including death benefits, but I don't think you'll need those," he chuckled. "Judge Saunders will give me a warrant specifically to hack Gridcom. So, you've got a 'get out of jail free' card like in that old Monopoly game."

"Let me take some time to think about it. I'll give you an answer later."

"That's fair. Think about it a while. I'll see you at the funeral."

catgcgccgccgtattaaattcgcacccatgatgcgtatgcgatggaacgcatttgcgcgcatgcgccgccgtattaaattcgcacccatgatgcgtat

"I'll be there helping Grandpa and I'm a pallbearer too. Bye Sheriff," Jason said as he hung up the phone and thought about the difficult decision ahead.

Grandpa had overheard Jason's call from the kitchen table, but Julie hadn't heard a thing, since she'd been upstairs on Jason's computer finishing the funeral program edits. He said to Jason, "I can only guess what you talked about, but in the end, I know you'll make the right decision. Remember that sometimes it's necessary to do something bad to do good. Although Jesus told us to turn the other cheek, we must sometimes decide to fight evil, just like the world fought against Hitler and the Nazis or the founding fathers and patriots fought for freedom from King George's tyranny. Let your conscience be your guide and have faith that everything happens for a reason. Maybe you're meant to be here at this moment with your special talents," Grandpa commented wisely.

Just then, Julie came downstairs and showed the program to Grandpa. He reviewed the now elegant-looking printed copy with calligraphy scripts and said with praise, "That's wonderful Julie, sometimes a woman's touch makes all the difference. We haven't had that around here since Jason's Grandma died a while ago," as Grandpa lamented, still deeply missing her. "Just add the Olivia singing *'Amazing Grace'* at the graveside," he added.

Julie replied, "I'll do that now. Then I'll whip up some pimento cheese sandwiches for lunch and we'll go to the church. Jason and I'll print the programs and start folding them while you take care of your business with any contractors and finish the eulogy. We have to be quick about it so that Jason and I can get to Wendover for the lilacs and drop them off at Charlestown Florist by three. Then, we'll pick you up at the Church later."

"Sounds like a good plan, Julie," Grandpa, with a smile, thought this young woman surely is *well* organized.

gcgaacgcgatggcgtaagcgatggcgaacgcgccgctggcgaacgcgtgcgcgaacgcgctgccggcgaacgcgatggcgtaagcgatggcgaacgcg

Chapter 9: The Choir Practice

Baptist Women's Combined Choir

Tuesday Afternoon, June 29, ...

After lunch, Jason drove with Julie and Grandpa in the pickup truck to the church but they were behind schedule. While Jason was printing programs, he commented to Julie, "We don't have time to fold these right now. If we do, we'll be late for the florist. Can we fold them later?"

Julie replied, "You're right. We should be cutting lilacs now."

"I could come over for dinner later and can finish the programs then. It'd be nice to talk with your parents and I have a question to ask you."

Julie replied, "Yes Jason, that's fine. It's nice to have two weeks home during the summer holidays because I see you every day," she smiled, but her sense of anticipation at Jason's questions had started to diminish. "Dinner's around seven and we can be done with the programs by nine."

"That will work fine," Jason said as he carried the programs with him into Grandpa's truck and he drove with Julie to Wendover. They went to the gardens where, for about an hour, they cut fresh, fragrant purple, pink, and lavender fronds from the many lilac bushes in full bloom.

Early that afternoon, Sheriff Coleman drove to the old trailer home where Nick and Elvira lived and knocked on the door. Elvira answered, "Hello George, Nick's around back tending to his garden."

Sheriff Coleman walked to the garden where Nick was busy with a hoe chopping weeds between rows of beans, turnips, beets, and onions. "Hello George, I've been keeping my garden tamed. Weeds just pop up from nowhere because I grow without herbicides. On the bright side of things, I get some exercise, and Elvira and I get some tasty veggies."

"When the beets are ready, Olivia would love a full bucket to pickle."

"Sure George. They'll be ready for harvesting in a few weeks. What did you want to talk about?"

catgcgccgccgtattaaattcgcacccatgatgcgtatgcgatggaacgcatttgcgcgcatgcgccgccgtattaaattcgcacccatgatgcgtat

gcgaacgcgatggcgtaagcgatggcgaacgcgccgctggcgaacgcgtgcgcgaacgcgctgccggcgaacgcgatggcgtaagcgatggcgaacgcg

"You know about the bridge washout and Old Forge Lake dam break?"

"Yes, it's pretty inconvenient taking the detour to work."

"Well, I'm wondering if you've seen anything unusual over at Exgenics recently? You know they used to own the land where the dam collapsed."

"Yes, I heard they gave land to Kent County for a park and museum. I went to work yesterday afternoon and everything seemed normal. It was pretty muddy from that big storm that caused all the flooding. I saw a lot of muddy tractor tracks, but that's not unusual since it's been wet."

"Ok, Nick. Thanks for your time. Please call if you think of anything else or see anything unusual," Coleman said as walked toward Ole Bessie.

"Sure George, I will. Stop by in a couple of weeks and I'll have some beets for Olivia," Nick replied and began hoeing the last row before work. Then a thought came to his mind and he hollered to George who was twenty feet away, "Come to think of it, I remember the farm pond's water seemed low on Monday like it had been partially drained. There was a pump there and a big hose too. Other than that, everything else seemed normal."

"Thanks again, Nick. I'll see you soon," Coleman replied.

After Jason and Julie left, Grandpa spent the afternoon working alone at the church. He went to his office, looked inside a filing cabinet, and pulled out an old cemetery plot map. It showed all the plots and listed occupied graves and their locations. He grabbed a tape measure, some wooden stakes, a large hammer and walked outside to the cemetery. He found the Thompson Family Plot, measured it, and then put corner stakes in the ground where the two side-by-side graves would be located.

About then, Patrick Duke arrived in a heavy-duty pickup truck towing a small backhoe on a trailer. The reverend greeted him and he unloaded his backhoe and drove it to the cemetery. At the gravesite, Reverend Dickson commented with some irony to Mr. Duke, "They were the last two Thompsons and they finally filled up the family plot." Mr. Duke dug using the steel bucket arm, piling the dirt neatly behind the graves.

The event planner arrived soon by van with his crew and a large moving truck for his cargo. The reverend directed him to install the large reception tents to the east of the church annex normally used for church gatherings, fellowship, and social events. The planner's work crew began unloading the tent posts and neatly folded large canvas tents from their truck. The crew then split in two, with each half installing a tent. They did their job with efficiency and within two hours, the tent ropes were staked in the ground and the center poles raised. Then, the perimeter poles were added.

catgcgccgccgtattaaattcgcacccatgatgcgtatgcgatggaacgcatttgcgcgcatgcgccgccgtattaaattcgcacccatgatgcgtat

With a few last adjustments of rope tension, the big tents were done. The crews then installed a smaller tent by the gravesite and another small tent near the church annex side door for use as a food tent. Finally, the porta-potty contractor showed up and installed four portable toilets a sufficient distance away from the tents.

Jason arrived later to pick up Grandpa, "This place looks ready to go."

Grandpa replied, "Not yet. They'll finish setting up in the morning."

Later that afternoon, Sheriff Coleman was in his office, still contemplating events. He called Sheriff Olsen using his old phone, "Al, any progress on your investigation?"

"No, I'm at my wit's end. I'm still trying to follow up a lead about a construction or engineering truck seen at the dam a while ago. Every lead I follow though seems to become a *dead* end."

"I learned something from an Exgenics employee I know here. You remember the empty farm pond we saw in your autodrone images? Well, Nick said there was nothing wrong with the pond yesterday, except that the water seemed low. He didn't think much about it and said everything else at Exgenics seemed normal."

"Well, we both plainly the pond and dam. So Exgenics must have repaired the dam by the time that employee went to work on Monday and started filling it again. When did he go to work?"

"He started work at 3 p.m. So that means Exgenics repaired the pond sometime after Saturday morning and before 3 p.m. Monday. It must have been an urgent repair as it's usually not easy to get construction work completed quickly."

"Well, that doesn't reassure me. There must've been a reason for such a quick repair but I don't have the faintest idea why." Al replied suspiciously.

"Hold on just a moment while my computer updates the latest SAT-map of the farm. Computer, download latest Exgenics Farm SAT-map image." In just a few seconds, a current image on the e-screen showed the full pond and the now-empty Old Forge Lake. "George, that's very suspicious and I'll keep investigating. How's your murder case going?"

Coleman replied, "I have a couple of possible avenues to pursue, so that gives me hope. I'd love to get info on the whereabouts and content of the Captain's cell phone, but it's hard getting info from Gridcom. They make local and state law enforcement jump through hoops and always use the excuse they keep phone information controlled to protect their users' privacy, when in fact they know everything."

"Yeah, most people don't even think about that."

"Al, I also had Deputy James bring over to the forensics lab tech some tire track evidence from the crime scene. I'm taking the day off for the Captain's funeral tomorrow, so it would be great if you could talk to the lab tomorrow about the track."

"Sure George, I'll help. It's good to work together. Thanks for the news from that Exgenics employee."

"No problem Al. We'll talk soon," George said hanging up his landline phone that wasn't connected to the Grid.

Olsen soon received a message from Kent Dispatch on his AI-computer, "Sheriff, there's been a boating incident on the Lower Chick near the dam. Two fishermen from Richmond on a rental Jon Boat are missing. A witness on the shore by the campground called 911 and said they both fell in the water and drowned."

"Dang, I hate tourists sometimes, but they create good overtime," Al replied to Dispatch. He quickly left his office and jumped in his Supercruzer, which quickly drove with blue lights flashing to the East Lake Campground dock.

Olsen arrived at the dock where a rental Jon Boat had been towed and temporarily moored. He talked to the witness who explained what he'd seen, "I was walking my dog along the riverbank when I saw two fishermen standing at the same time, their boat tipped, and they both fell in the water over the far side of the boat. I kept watching, but I never saw them after that. Then the boat drifted away and they were gone."

Olsen looked inside the boat and saw two tackle boxes, one cooler filled with just some water and soda, another cooler with some leftover food and garbage from their lunch, and one fishing pole with catfish bait still on the hook. "So, alcohol doesn't seem to be involved," he thought. Both of the fishermen's life vests were just sitting on the bottom of the boat. He did think it was strange that there was only one fishing pole for two fishermen and thought to himself in exasperation, "Why won't these boaters ever learn that you're actually supposed to wear these life vests."

gcgaacgcgatggcgtaagcgatggcgaacgcgccgctggcgaacgcgtgcgcgaacgcgctgccggcgaacgcgatggcgtaagcgatggcgaacgcg

Tuesday Evening, June 29, ...

It had been a long day, but Jason still had to visit Julie and then read the second half of *"Pride and Prejudice."* He told Grandpa, "I'm going to Julie's house for dinner so don't worry about me tonight. We need to fold all the funeral program's still, but I should be home early."

"That's fine Jason. Don't' come back late since tomorrow's a big day. I'll finish the eulogy text after dinner and then I'm going to bed early."

Jason briefly discussed his day with Grandpa, "I had a good time today working with Julie."

"You both did a great job today. I couldn't have gotten it done without your help," Grandpa replied with praise for them both. "I liked how you worked together and anticipated each other's needs. It was like that between Grandma and me," he reminisced.

"I miss Grandma too," Jason replied sensing a hint of loneliness in Grandpa's voice. "I'm leaving now and will be quiet coming home," he said grabbing his motorcycle helmet on his way out the door to the garage.

It was about 7:00 p.m. and Olsen was still waiting for the Kent County Water Search and Rescue Team to return. The team soon radioed it was getting too dark and they'd have to resume the search for the fishermen in the morning. The lead diver said to Olsen over the radio, "We searched where we could in the channel but the deep part of the channel is too muddy. Just getting close to the bottom stirs it up. Our underwater searchlights wouldn't have helped either. In that muddy deep water, they'll be about impossible to find."

"Well, if you think it'll do any good, try again in the morning. Otherwise, we'll find the bodies in a few days when they float to the surface," Sheriff Olsen replied grimly as he pressed the home button on his e-screen and the Supercruzer began to drive him home.

The choirs from Pleasant Hill and Mt. Carmel Baptist Churches gathered at 7 p.m. inside the Pleasant Hill sanctuary and Lucy Evans greeted everyone. Everybody exchanged friendly greetings and chatted a while until all arrived.

Lucy began the practice with an encouraging speech, "Ok everyone, I know both our choirs have never sung together before, but tomorrow will be our first time doing so in public. I know we'll do a great job then, but tonight, let's practice hard and make sure all goes smoothly. Now everyone, please take their seats. There are two long choir benches behind

catgcgccgccgtattaaattcgcacccatgatgcgtatgcgatggaacgcatttgcgcgcatgcgccgccgtattaaattcgcacccatgatgcgtat

the altar, so I was thinking that perhaps the Pleasant Hill Choir would sit in the front row and Mt. Carmel could sit in the back. Will that work?"

Olivia, the lead vocalist of Mt. Carmel Choir protested, "We aren't sitting in the back like our people sat in the back of the bus long ago."

"Ok that makes sense, I didn't realize that might be an issue. How about Mt. Carmel on the left and Pleasant Hill to the right."

"I think that'll be better," Olivia replied and everyone started sitting down in their respective chairs.

"Ok Ladies, let's begin our practice now. Reverend Dickson wants us to sing the hymn '*Shall We Gather at the River*' tomorrow.[50] I know everyone knows that old Hymn well, but I've placed a copy of the sheet music arrangement in a folder on your seats just to keep us all following along together. Mr. Taylor, you may begin."

Mr. Taylor, the Pleasant Hill Organist who was the music teacher and band director at Charles County High School, began the first few bars playing some harmonic chords of the hymn. When the sheet music indicated, the choirs began singing the words, but their vocal styles clashed somehow and it just didn't work. Lucy stopped the first attempt halfway through the second verse. "Hold it, everybody. That just didn't sound right. Maybe it's the acoustics in here but I think perhaps we need the choirs to blend their voices better. Let's everyone mix up seats and y'all should sit next to one member from the other church's choir. Olivia, since you are a lead voice, could you sit in the middle of the front row please, and Evelyn Jones, could you sit next to her?" she directed and hoped that putting each choir's best voices together, they would harmonize better.

"Let's start again," as Lucy tapped her Choir Director's baton, and the organist started playing again. This time, the assembled choirs both sang better, but the music still sounded the same, like a piano with bagpipe accompaniment. The vocal styles of the choirs just didn't mix. "Hold it again please, everyone," Lucy interrupted them again in the middle of the second verse. She thought a moment and told the choirs an improvised idea for the overall composition. The choirs agreed and for the next practice attempt, the choirs each sang the hymn to the end, but this time only the last verse was still off but Lucy heard much improvement from the previous attempts.

Lucy again commented, "That was a lot better everyone, but let's try one more time so we get it right for tomorrow." They sang the song again

---

[50] '*Shall We Gather at the River*' is a traditional Baptist Hymn composed in 1864 by Reverend Robert Lowry in Brooklyn, New York during a summer heat wave and deadly epidemic that affected many in his parish.

T. A. Hunter

gcgaacgcgatggcgtaagcgatggcgaacgcgccgctggcgaacgcgtgcgcgaacgcgctgccggcgaacgcgatggcgtaagcgatggcgaacgcg

to the end, and Lucy thought to herself that'll have to do. This time, the last verse sounded more like a flute and oboe playing at the same time, not quite perfect together but good enough. "Okay everyone, that was a lot better. I think that's enough practice for tonight. Now everyone, remember your seats and we'll see you all tomorrow," she said concluding the practice session.

Jason arrived at Julie's house about a half-hour before dinner and she greeted him at the front door, "Hi Jason, Mom and I are finishing up in the kitchen. Why don't you spend time with my dad until dinner's ready? He's working in the garage."

Jason joined Mr. Williams was examining a small agrobot designed to kill weeds. Agrobots had eliminated herbicide usage on most industrial farms but still hadn't assumed that role for all insect pests. They were great at killing caterpillars, but most insects like aphids were just too small and too numerous for agrobots. "This agrobot's weed puller arm is malfunctioning," he commented to Jason.

"Did you check the electrical connector at the shoulder?"

"I was about to," Mr. Williams said unplugging the connector. "I think there's surface corrosion of the metal terminals. Some wire brushing will handle that." He brushed the terminal, re-plugged the connector into its socket, and the indicator light on the agrobot's back turned green.

"That did it, Jason."

"Mr. Williams, there are some things I want to talk to you about. Do you have a few minutes?"

"Sure, Jason."

Jason then recounted his youthful computer hacking incident, his conviction, his suspended sentence, and its impact on his life.

After listening to the story, Mr. Williams replied, "I'm glad you told me. From what Julie told us, we knew you were different. Anyway, I like you and everything will be fine. The things we do in life follow us sometimes, but it's possible to do good with your life afterward. I know you've changed since then and I'm proud of you son, I mean, young man," he chuckled. "Now let's go inside for dinner. I hear Julie's cooking everything and Kay was there for moral support and emergency rescue only. I shouldn't have told you about that surprise, but I wanted to prep you just in case. Julie isn't a natural-born cooker, unfortunately."

They both washed their hands and joined Julie and Mrs. Williams standing at the dining table with every dish ready and waiting. "Everything smells wonderful," Jason commented wisely thinking any praise would be

catgcgccgccgtattaaattcgcacccatgatgcgtatgcgatggaacgcatttgcgcgcatgcgccgccgtattaaattcgcacccatgatgcgtat

90

beneficial to continuing his relationship while detecting a hint of burnt meatloaf wafting in the air. Everyone sat down and Mr. Williams led with the blessing. After that, there were causal conversations about the day's events, as they filled their plates and ate. Luckily, the meatloaf's exterior was partly burnt, forming a black separable crust from the edible interior. The meal was not gourmet, but tasty and satisfying everyday good cooking.

When the plates were empty, Julie asked, "Jason, how was dinner?"

"It was delicious. Your mom did a great job," he said while looking at Mrs. Williams to send her a faux compliment.

Julie replied, "I cooked dinner tonight Jason," springing her surprise. "You know I'm not the best cook, but I've been practicing and with mom's coaching, I've gotten better. What do you think?"

"Dinner was wonderful tonight. Grandpa isn't as good a cook as Grandma was, so it's nice to get a delicious home-cooked meal. Thank you, Julie," he praised her earning him future good behavior points.

Julie said, "Jason, help with the dishes, and we can fold the funeral programs on the kitchen table."

Mr. Williams commented, "Mom and I are going into the family room now to watch some e-vids," as he motioned Mrs. Williams with his eyes to leave Jason and Julie alone.

The dishes were cleaned and they sat down to the stack of printed programs. "Well, this isn't an exciting task, but we can talk while working," Julie commented. They began carefully folded each program.

Jason soon blurted out, "I have a new secret that I can't tell you, Julie."

"You promised there'd be no secrets between us Jason. Why are you telling me this?" she disconcertingly said in frustration at this young man.

"Well, it has something to do with Sheriff Coleman and the murders, Julie, but I don't want to tell you right now, because I need to think more."

"Well, that'll have to do for now, I guess. Just tell me when you can."

"OK Julie, I will. Well, there's another question I've been meaning to ask you. After I ask you, you should probably think and wait to answer later. It might be hard to decide right now which is the right answer as in yes or no. It might be a tough decision to make is all I'm saying."

"Go ahead Jason, *ask*," she said firmly, thinking this was an awkward way to ask her *the* question.

"Well Julie, would you visit me in prison if I ever have to go there?"

"Why'd you ask me that? What did you do?" she questioned him angrily with a scornful look like he was guilty of something and soon felt disappointed at again not being asked *the* question she wanted.

"I was just asking a hypothetical question, but I have a big difficult decision to make soon. The question I'm really trying to answer right now is this one: Is it ok to do something bad if the result is something good?"

"I can't even understand what's going through your head right now. Which question do you want me to answer?" Julie seemed confused.

"All of them," Jason replied seeking advice from his girlfriend.

They talked for a half-hour and when done with the programs, they enjoyed a long walk on the bluff along the north bank of the James.

Timothy Smith was alone on the night shift in the control room at the Chickahominy River Pumping Station just above Walker Dam. From here, the water began its journey to Newport News. Tim always spent many boring hours staring at green lights and control gage readings. Suddenly, a pump warning light turned red for Intake Pump Number Two. The day shift had said this pump was acting up yesterday and he needed to get it working again soon or the city would lose a quarter of its water supply. He'd have to troubleshoot it, but if he could just reset the electrical breaker, the day shift could inspect it in the morning.

He grabbed his toolbox and walked down the stairs of the pump house building that extended partly over the lake. The building's foundation and walls were 10 feet below water level, acting like a bridge caisson holding back the lake from the pumps. Large pumps were mounted on the building's concrete floor with electric motors above them configured to allow maintenance without flooding the room with lake water.

He went to Pump Two and flipped the circuit breaker to reset it, but the motor failed to turn. He turned off the breaker and pulled a metal stool near the motor so he could sit while he diagnosed any electrical problems of the 480 volts, 3-Phase motor. He removed an access cover exposing the wire terminals to check them with his multimeter and clip-on probe tips. He measured the resistance on each of three wires with the probes and the readings were normal, so the windings were undamaged. He flipped the breaker on and checked the terminals again for voltage.

When he clipped onto the terminals, a high voltage spark leaped from the probe tips to his hands and the current ran up one arm and down the other. The motor turned on. His hands were paralyzed by electricity and he couldn't let go. His heart stopped and he sat frozen as part of the electrical circuit. The motor ran until the day shift discovered him posing like that famous statute, 'The Thinker.'

gcgaacgcgatggcgtaagcgatggcgaacgcgccgctggcgaacgcgtgcgcgaacgcgctgccggcgaacgcgatggcgtaagcgatggcgaacgcg

Before going to bed, Jason sat at his desk and finished reading "*Pride and Prejudice.*" He logged onto the university's computer system to take the online quiz and the e-screen displayed a note from the professor, "*Dear Engineering Student, there is no quiz, but I hope you enjoyed reading 'Pride and Prejudice.' The Engineering Department thinks sometimes it is important to read to make you well-rounded, see what life was like in the past, and learn about romance. Too many engineers are narrowly focused on the sciences. This assignment was to force you to read a true literary classic. Please take the time you allotted for the quiz to think about what you learned from this book.*"

Wednesday Morning, 5:00 a.m., June 30, ….

Deputy Jeffers and Sheriff Olsen had just arrived at the Kent City Justice Center to start their day when a 911 alert chimed on their e-phones. They both looked at their screens and Al said, "James, jump in my Supercruzer and we can have a cup of coffee and a donut on the way."

It took the Supercruzer twenty minutes and two coffees and donuts to drive to East Lake responding to an emergency at the pumping station However, there was no rush since the call was about a work-related death.

On their way, Deputy Jeffers said, "Al, I can't believe how busy we've been the past few days. Ever since that dam break, it's just been non-stop around here. We've had the usual workload and more. There've been so many tragic accidents and now we have another. Did the search team find those fishermen's bodies yesterday?"

"Not yet James. The channel just below the dam is deep so they'll keep looking downstream this morning. I've been busy too, trying to investigate the dam break and land sale to County. I think there's something we still don't know about yet, but all my leads have gone nowhere. I'm still pursuing a last lead, but I do know the liability for economic damages and any financial losses could bankrupt Kent County. Now you know why I'm working so hard on this investigation."

"That would be bad for sure. When I was checking about the family that died in the explosion, I heard from Dr. Graves that things have been crazy over in Chick County too, with the murders of the old riverman and his wife."

Olsen replied, "Yeah, Coleman's got a tough case there. I think sometimes things just happen at the same time, but random events don't look that way when they occur concurrently."

"Just like the July 4th weekend coming up; everyone goes crazy and you have a lot of recreational boating incidents," James commented while

catgcgccgccgtattaaattcgcacccatgatgcgtatgcgatggaacgcatttgcgcgcatgcgccgccgtattaaattcgcacccatgatgcgtat

gcgaacgcgatggcgtaagcgatggcgaacgcgccgctggcgaacgcgtgcgcgaacgcgctgccggcgaacgcgatggcgtaagcgatggcgaacgcg

thinking about a busy overtime weekend handling holiday incidents and patrolling for intoxicated drivers and boaters.

"Yeah, sometimes life is kind of like that," Olsen commented.

"Oh, did I tell you that I'm going on a second date with Robin? We're going to the East Lake Bluegrass Festival. I think we'll have a good time," James smiled confidently.

When they arrived at East Lake Campground and the pumping station, they saw the Kent EMS crew was already waiting outside for them. The lead EMS tech told the sheriff and his deputy, "There's nothing we can do. He's long gone, but we'll take his body to the morgue after you both take a look."

They entered the pumping station and followed the EMS techs downstairs to the pump room. The lead EMS tech commented looking at the body, "Seems he was working on the pump motor and got electrocuted. The workers arriving to work this morning left him there with the motor running just so they could make their weekly pumping goals. They knew once the pump was shut down, it would be out of service for days since there'd be a Virginia Occupational Safety Department investigation. That would cause a long water shortage in Newport News until it's working again. The workers refused to turn off the motor to examine him, but it's obvious he's dead."

"Let me talk to their supervisor," Olsen commanded.

"He's arriving in a few minutes. The workers said he has to authorize turning the pump off. You know the old 'my boss needs to make the big decision excuse'," the lead EMS tech replied.

The supervisor arrived and the infuriated sheriff yelled at him, "Are you going to shut down that pump so we can take that dead man's body?"

The supervisor replied, further moving the final decision up the chain of command, "Let me talk to my manager in Newport News first. He'll make the final decision." He made an e-phone call and talked for two minutes about the situation. "He says it's OK. We'll need to install a new motor and maybe pump, if the bearings seized, as soon as possible."

There was nothing else for the sheriff and his deputy to do, so they left the pumping station and continued their daily duties. The workers shut off the power to the pump and the EMS techs lifted the man from the chair. Rigor mortis had already set in as they carried the man up the stairs, still posed like a statue sitting on a chair. They placed him onto a gurney, strapping him down in a seated position for the drive to Kent City.

catgcgccgccgtattaaattcgcacccatgatgcgtatgcgatggaacgcatttgcgcgcatgcgccgccgtattaaattcgcacccatgatgcgtat

Chapter 10: The Last Riverman's Funeral

Pleasant Hill Baptist Church

7:00 a.m., Wednesday, June 30, ….

A hot, humid summer day started as Jason sat at his desk typing on the computer he'd constructed using parts from 20 obsolete computers and one good quantum processer. He was writing his English Literature essay titled, '*Tale of Two Cities: Parallels with Modern Society.*' His essay noted the similarities with society today and how when things change, they remain the same since people have the same needs, wants, desires, and failings.

Mounted on the wall in front of him was a hodgepodge of e-screens and monitors. His computer system even included two old hard drives for extra memory that had belonged to his dad. He'd built it without loading any AI-software and the quantum processor gave him incredible calculation speed. His system allowed him to produce code to troubleshoot customized programs or algorithms without being continuously monitored by AI-antivirus software and the Grid, which reported directly to the National Anti-Virus Center.[51] The AI-Antivirus software slowed his computer down anyway and he preferred the fastest possible calculations and processing speed.

Grandpa called up to him from the kitchen, "Jason, come down and start the day. We've lots to do and need this day to progress smoothly."

"Yes Grandpa," Jason replied completing his essay.

He hurried downstairs, quickly ate the breakfast Grandpa had made. He rushed back upstairs to shave, brush his teeth, and dress in some nice slacks with a shirt and tie. He carried with him a navy-blue blazer to wear during the funeral service. He drove Grandpa to the Pleasant Hill Baptist

---

[51] The National Anti-Virus Center was founded after the Great Internet Virus by an act of Congress to monitor and prevent another world-wide computer virus pandemic. The facility is located in Provo, Utah adjacent to the National Security Agency Cybersecurity and Data Fusion Center.

gcgaacgcgatggcgtaagcgatggcgaacgcgccgctggcgaacgcgtgcgcgaacgcgctgccggcgaacgcgatggcgtaagcgatggcgaacgcg

Church and their day there began to oversee the final preparations, conduct the funeral service, and coordinate the reception afterward. Julie soon arrived in her small autopod and met them both outside the church.[52]

"I hope everything goes as planned," the Reverend commented optimistically. "We worked hard yesterday to pull this off so I'm hoping things go well. Of course, the Captain's and Macy's ample finances helped move things faster than normal," he grinned. "Since everyone was getting ready for July 4th weekend or their vacations, we needed the funeral today. I've heard this will be the Charles County social event of the year."

Julie responded, "Well my mom told a few people about the deaths, but when well-known locals like the Captain and Macy die, the women's Grapevine creeps over the entire county quickly."

"Yes, that's one of the benefits *and* drawbacks of living in a small community. Everyone knows everybody, so gossip spreads like wildfire," the Reverend chuckled.

Jason commented, "Yes, but that often helps our community when we come together in an emergency. Like after the Chick River flooding from the hurricane that passed by six years ago."

"Yes, it's times like those when the best in people comes out. Unfortunately, the worst comes out too, as there were looters from Richmond that the sheriff arrested after locals held them at gunpoint until he arrived," the Reverend replied somewhat cynically at mankind.

"Well, everyone will be on their best behavior today," Jason replied.

The event planner and his sub-contractors soon arrived to install tables and chairs underneath the large dining tents set up yesterday. His crew installed forty long, folding tables and five-hundred folding chairs. He also placed large electric box fans at each tent's four corners. In the food tent, eight long buffet tables were added for arriving guests, who'd bring food for the reception, to place their appetizers, entrees, or desserts. The planner also set up a table in front of the church for the visitor register and funeral programs. Finally, the weather forecast was somewhat uncertain with a 50% chance of an afternoon storm, so the planner put 200 golf umbrellas in case of rain into a few open-top barrels placed strategically.

The caterer arrived soon and began placing white linen tablecloths on each dinner tent table. His crew next set the tables with gray ceramic plates, stainless silverware, and a cloth napkin at each chair. On the buffet tables, they added an extra supply of plates, napkins, and serving utensils. By the refreshment station, he added cups, sweet tea, lemonade, water, and

---

[52] An autopod is a small, two-wheeled vehicle with a single seat mounted in a passenger pod. An electric power system below the seat controls the gyroscopic drive wheels.

catgcgccgccgtattaaattcgcacccatgatgcgtatgcgatggaacgcatttgcgcgcatgcgccgccgtattaaattcgcacccatgatgcgtat

ice. Later, the caterer's crew would manage the buffet line, serve Jimmy Cumming's pork barbeque, and help with drinks.

The electronics contractor next arrived to set up a microphone and video system inside the church sanctuary and install a large e-screen and sound system outside near the tents, since the church's capacity was only 160 due to fire-code regulations. The contractor also installed a smaller sound system with a microphone on a podium by the gravesite tent.

The two hearses from Kent City arrived on schedule, with a coffin in each black limousine. The funeral home team lifted each heavy oak coffin and wheeled them on gurneys into the church. The coffins were displayed in the front of the sanctuary on either side of the altar, with each gurney hidden by a white linen skirt covering the wheels and mechanisms. Later, the funeral home team would serve as ushers in the church and afterward would move any flowers to the gravesite for display.

The Charlestown florist next arrived with a series of bouquets and arrangements for inside the church. The flowers were strategically placed, with tall arrangements to the sides and shorter arrangements placed in front of the coffins. The florist next gave forty small bouquets in vases to the caterer. The center of each bouquet's floral arrangement featured a fragrant frond of purple blooms in honor of Macy's love of lilac blossoms.

The caterer asked the florist, "What kind of lilacs are they? They're the best I've ever smelled," she said to start taking them to each dinner table.

The florist replied, "Julie said the variety is called Mount Vernon. I hear they're descended from bushes that came from George Washington."

Jimmy Cummings arrived just after 10 a.m. towing his mobile large barbeque trailer and parked near the food tent. The black painted steel barbeque grill was a repurposed army-surplus water trailer, cut like a hamburger bun using an acetylene torch, with a lid and a grill base on wheels. Later, hinges, smokestacks, and dampers were welded on to convert the trailer into a restaurant-grade barbeque cooker. The trailer's stack was still smoking for the final two hours of cooking. Soon the smell of burnt hickory chips and smoked barbeque pork, slow-cooked nearly 12 hours to tender perfection, wafted near the food tent.

As is the local tradition, Jimmy had started barbequing the pigs just after midnight, staying up all night with a few friends drinking the Captain's 'shine as he slow-cooked his feast. He even cooked the heads, as some people loved brains and pig jowls. Karen, his wife, cooked up chitlins for

gcgaacgcgatggcgtaagcgatggcgaacgcgccgctggcgaacgcgtgcgcgaacgcgctgccggcgaacgcgatggcgtaagcgatggcgaacgcg

anyone who enjoyed them.[53] However, nothing was better at large events than tender Southern barbequed pork basted in apple cider vinegar and sprinkled with hot pepper seeds for a "kick."

Soon, two more florist vans drove into the parking lot near where Jason and Julie were setting up near the church door to provide programs to all the guests and mourners. The vans were from different florists and the drivers came to the church door. One florist said "Hello, I have a full load of flowers. We've been filling orders for delivery since yesterday."

The other florist added, "We've got a load too. Where you want them?"

Jason asked, "Where should they go? The church is full already."

Julie answered, "Let's put them outside right here. We'll place the stand-alone arrangements outside the main church doors, the short wreaths leaned by this stone wall, and the flower vases on the wall's top."

"That sounds like a plan. I wonder who delivered all these flowers?" Jason asked as they looked through some condolence cards, recognizing many names from Charles County. They also found names they didn't recognize, like people from Kent County, some fishermen from Fredericksburg, and a card which said, *'The staff at First Federal Bank of Richmond sends our deepest sympathies to the heirs during their time of grieving."*

The Mt. Carmel Baptist Choir arrived in their church van about a half-hour before the service and went inside the church annex to gown up in their robes. The Pleasant Hill Baptist Choir, who were already dressed in their choir garments, greeted them.

About the same time, carloads of mourners and visitors began arriving, but the small 30 space parking lot and extra spaces by the annex filled immediately. Several other church vans and two old school buses from Samaria Baptist[54] arrived carrying mourners and parked on the lawn. Soon that lot was full, so everyone still arriving parked carefully on the sides of the main road and walked to the church.

Deputy James managed the traffic on the narrow, paved country road, but was soon overwhelmed. His best estimate was that roughly 300 vehicles had parked by the road, which was congested for nearly a half-mile in either direction as people parked and walked. Those who carried food for the reception went to the church annex and left their dishes there.

---

[53] Chitlins are cleaned and cooked chopped small intestines usually stewed and deep fried in batter. Normally considered a 'soul food' and a food once provided to slaves.

[54] Samaria Baptist Church was originally organized as a Chickahominy Indian Church.

catgcgccgccgtattaaattcgcacccatgatgcgtatgcgatggaacgcatttgcgcgcatgcgccgccgtattaaattcgcacccatgatgcgtat

gcgaacgcgatggcgtaagcgatggcgaacgcgccgctggcgaacgcgtgcgcgaacgcgctgccggcgaacgcgatggcgtaagcgatggcgaacgcg

A crowd of mourners soon assembled outside the church and inside, the candles were lit for effect before the funeral began. However, daylight beamed into the sanctuary through antique clear cast beaded-glass arched windows with triple-pane vertical side sidelights in blue, magenta, and amber-colored glass panes. There were several brass candle holders behind the coffins and wall-sconces lit with small white candles.

Julie quickly pinned small lilac boutonnieres on the assembled pallbearers who would sit in the front pews with the grieving 'family,' including George Coleman, Buddy Peters, Johnny Walker, Jay Tyler, Jimmy Cummings, and the others. Jason sat next to Julie leaving extra room for Doc Longtree, his wife Susan, and Rufus by the center aisle.

When everything was finally ready inside, the doors to the church were opened, the crowd slowly entered and sat down in the wooden pews row by row until the church was filled to capacity with mourners. The overflow of late arrivals had to sit inside the tents and watch the service from the extra-large E-Screens installed there.

The last mourners entering the church doors were Doc Longtree, Susan, and Rufus. Doc walked down the aisle to the front row with Rufus on a short leather leash. Doc and Susan sat in the pew and Rufus laid down on the floor by the center aisle in a place of honor, because in his way, Rufus was the Captain and Macy's family. He soon began slobbering.

11:00 a.m., Wednesday, June 30, ….

The church organist, Mr. Taylor, entered the sanctuary on schedule and began with a nice melodic prelude to notify those in the sanctuary that the service would begin and to be silent. The cacophony from the church pews ceased. As the music continued, the Mt. Carmel and Pleasant Hill Baptist choirs filed in the side door and sat down in two rows of chairs in front of the baptismal tank window and behind the small altar table.

Finally, Reverend Dickson walked in from the same door and stood in front of the congregation just behind a microphone on a podium in front of the choir. He began the funeral service, "We are gathered here today to celebrate the lives of Captain Jack Thompson and Macy Meriwether Thompson who lived their entire lives with this parish. They were true servants of God and we assemble here today to honor them. Let's all sing the hymn '*Shall We Gather at the River*' which was Macy's favorite."

Mr. Taylor started playing the hymn and the Pleasant Hill Baptist Choir started the first verse in the traditional hymnal style…

"Shall we gather at the river,

catgcgccgccgtattaaattcgcacccatgatgcgtatgcgatggaacgcatttgcgcgcatgcgccgccgtattaaattcgcacccatgatgcgtat

gcgaacgcgatggcgtaagcgatggcgaacgcgccgctggcgaacgcgtgcgcgaacgcgctgccggcgaacgcgatggcgtaagcgatggcgaacgcg

Where bright angel feet have trod,
With its crystal tide forever
Flowing by the throne of God?"

The assembled congregation, other visitors inside the church, and all those viewing the service outside in the shade of the tents joined in with the chorus…

"Yes, we'll gather at the river,
The beautiful, the beautiful river;
Gather with the saints at the river
That flows by the throne of God…"

The singing continued but on the next chorus, the Pleasant Hill Choir remained silent letting Mt. Carmel church add their soulful Gospel style to the improvised composition. This was the Pleasant Hill Choir Director's ad-hoc musical arrangement to unite the churches in their grief for both congregations had been the Captain and Macy's friends. The choirs then alternated styles every other verse in what seemed like a choir duel with each choir singing more deliberately and forcefully until in the end, they seemed exhausted and sang the final chorus together.

Somehow, with the final verse, the two choirs' styles melded to become one and they concluded with a beautiful harmonic flourish as the organ played its final notes. The choirs smiled, hugged, and sat down in their seats. Everyone inside the church and outside in the tents looked around to the different people surrounding them, whether black, white, or Indian, and similarly smiled, shook hands, or briefly embraced in fellowship with their fellow man. It was a moment that Charles County would talk about for a long time as, almost magically or perhaps inspired by God, the two church choirs had fused to sing with one voice.

The Reverend Dickson began his eulogy, "Macy and the Captain were the bedrock of our community as they were our past and left their heritage to us all. They spent their lives on the river, living the old way of life that now exists only in our collective memories in the stories they told us. Each of us coming here today has a piece of that memory inside us where they'll always live in our hearts. This is what we should cherish and it's our way of keeping Captain and Macy alive, if only in memories.

Our lives are like the river in many ways. We start like a small trickle coming from a fresh spring that eventually grows into a stream as it merges with the water of others as it flows forward to its final destination. Our experiences and care for others fill our lives and quenches our thirst, and the rain along the way swells the river as we flow through our lives. This river of our lives can be fast and swift or slow and meandering, but every river chooses its own path forward towards its destination. Our separate rivers sometimes touch each other, their flows mingling and sometimes later dividing, but in the end, all our rivers join at the ocean.

The Bible talks of many rivers and how they fulfill our thirst for God who gives us everlasting life. Psalm 65:9 says, *'He has remembered the Earth and watered her with the River of God that is full of water.'* Another well-known passage in Revelations 22 goes like this, *'Then the angel showed me the river of the water of life, bright as crystal, proceeding out of the throne of God and of the Lamb.'* This river led to a new Eden. We arise alone from this holy spring and flow, like a river, throughout our lives to join at the end in this Eden, an ocean filled with God's love. This River of Life is the journey we all share.

As we look back at the lives of Captain Jack and Macy Thompson, we see how their river joined with ours and deeply touched us. Most of you don't know it, since they lived their lives humbly as Jesus implored us all, but they were rich, both in spirit and in worldly goods. At their deaths, they donated their hidden fortune for the benefit of Charles County and to restore the old river. Most important of all is that they wanted our community to be brought together and united. This was their sacrifice for us and their gift to us; a true legacy that we can share if we follow their example and vision. We *all* are their heirs and we inherit our river from them. So, when you're at the Chick, just to fish, swim, water-ski, or just look at a beautiful peaceful sunrise over the clear, calm waters, remember them and their gift to us all."

After a brief pause, the Reverend Dickson said, "Let us say the Lord's Prayer." All those assembled inside the church and outside the congregation began to recite in unison, *"Our Father, which art in heaven, Hallowed be thy Name. Thy Kingdom comes. Thy will be done on earth, As it is in heaven. Give us this day our daily bread. And forgive us our trespasses, As we forgive those that trespass against us. And lead us not into temptation, But deliver us from evil. For thine is the kingdom, The power, and the glory, For ever and ever. Amen."*

For the recessional, Mr. Taylor began playing Beethoven's *"Ode to Joy."* While the music played, the twelve pallbearers, like local well-dressed Apostles, lifted the two heavy coffins with six pallbearers per coffin, and slowly carried them with dignity up the aisle toward the church doors.

Just then, there must have been a final slightly missed organ note that triggered poor grieving Rufus, or perhaps it was just his enhanced sense of smell, but he let out one last long haunting wail of a howl from the front-row pew. The assembly knew that his soul was also in pain. Doc Longtree held him tenderly with a slight embrace around his neck, gently scratched him behind the ear, and whispered some words to the dog. Doc then stood up, pulled on his leash, and Rufus began to follow the coffins down the aisle, but in taking his first step, Doc halfway slipped on a big slobber puddle near his feet on the polished hardwood oak floor. Everyone in the church smiled because they knew Rufus too well.

The pallbearers slowly walked to the gravesite carrying and sharing their burdens and placed the coffins side-by-side onto some pine boards to temporarily support the coffins over the open graves. Meanwhile, the funeral home ushers hastily moved the flowers from the church to the gravesite in an improvised arrangement.

⟁⟁⟁⟁⟁

The large crowd of almost 700 mourners finally assembled at the gravesite and Pastor George Morrow from Mt. Carmel Baptist began to speak his words of committal from a small podium with a microphone, "There's a dam that separates our community just as a dam divides the fresh waters of the Upper Chick from the brackish tidal waters below. The dam between us all must be broken so we can heal our community. I want to thank Reverend Dickson for inviting our church to participate in this service today. I believe this is a good step to tearing that dam down, stone by stone, that's been built up higher over the years.

We are here today to say goodbye to the Captain and Macy as we lay them in their final resting place on this Earth with the firm belief and knowledge that they are in Heaven with our God, Jesus, and the many Angels that surround Him. The Captain and Macy were friends to all our community and with their gift to us, they wanted all of us to join together to preserve the river for future generations. Let us continue to heal the river just as we hope to work together healing our community as it grieves.

Let me lead both our parishes as we all recite the words from Psalm 23," Reverend Morrow proclaimed.

All those assembled at the graveside began to say in unison, *"The LORD is my shepherd; I shall not want. He maketh me to lie down in green pastures. He leadeth me beside the still waters. He restoreth my soul. He leadeth me in the paths of righteousness for his name's sake. Yea, though I walk through the valley of the shadow of death, I will fear no evil, for thou art with me. Thy rod and thy staff they comfort me. Thou preparest a table before me in the presence of mine enemies. Thou anointest my head with oil and my cup runneth over. Surely goodness and mercy shall follow me all the days of my life, and I will dwell in the house of the Lord forever. Amen."*

After a brief moment of silence, Reverend Morrow continued, "Friends, let me now lay the Captain and Macy to rest. For as much as it has pleased Almighty God to take from this world the souls of Captain

Jack and Macy Thompson, we, therefore, commit their bodies to the earth, ashes to ashes, dust to dust, looking for that blessed hope when the Lord Himself shall descend from heaven with a shout, with the voice of the archangel, and with the trumpet of God, and the dead in Christ shall rise. Then, we which are alive and remain shall be caught up together with them in the clouds to meet the Lord in the air, and so shall we ever be with the Lord, and comfort one another with these words."

With these final words, the Reverend left the podium and Olivia Coleman stepped up to the microphone and began singing "*Amazing Grace*" with such a clear harmonic and soulful melody that resonated from the loudspeakers that they said after her performance that the Angels themselves started to cry with joy. In fact, their tears began to fall from the heavens as raindrops, which soon began falling in earnest. The crowd immediately ran for the barrels of umbrellas or about 100 yards to the reception tents located on the east side of the Annex, where food and drinks were awaiting in the tents.

Noon, Wednesday, June 30…

The crowd was partly soaked sharing in wet misery as the assembly in an orderly umbrella cascade toward the food tent. Fortunately, the caterer had pulled the barbeque trailer closer to the food tent so the rain wouldn't affect serving. His helpers wore rubber gloves to pull tender pork by the handful to serve those in the line. In the food tent, everyone took small portions from their favorite dishes on the buffet tables. Of course, Olivia had a dozen chess pies on the dessert table, which begin disappearing first.

Since the crowd was larger than expected, not everyone could sit, but many people clustered in groups by the tent edges inside the curtain of dripping raindrops. Doc was holding Rufus by the leash and asked Jason, "Can you hold Rufus a while I join the food line?"

"I'll help Dr. Longtree. I hope he gets over the loss of masters soon."

"He was a lot better today than before, but he needs love and care from a family that'll adopt him," said Doc as he joined the buffet line.

Benson Thurmond, the county manager, was talking about recent events with Sheriff Coleman. Coleman was wearing a dark gray silk suit, his Sunday best, instead of his normal uniform. Benson commented, "Well, it's been a busy week and I'm taking next week the July 4th holiday. I'm supposed to meet the attorney from Exgenics here today. He wanted to talk about donating some funds to help rebuild the Chick Bridge."

"Yes, I heard that Exgenics is charitable," Coleman remarked. The sheriff saw Jimmy Cummings and then went over to ask him about his entry in the big July 4th weekend fishing tournament at Osprey Landing.

In a minute or two, John Gregory from Exgenics greeted Mr. Thurmond. "Hello, I'm John Gregory, they said you were over here," as he pointed toward a group of people standing on the far side of the tent.

"It was nice talking by e-phone about the bridge yesterday. Thank you for coming today. Did you get a chance to see the funeral service?"

"I saw the second half with that Reverend Morrow, and that vocalist at the gravesite was heavenly. She needs a music contract I think."

"That was Olivia, the wife of the local sheriff."

"Well, Exgenics has donated to Kent County for a few years since we built our research farm near Provident Forge. We thought, with the recent bridge washout, that our company should spread some charity to Charles County. We'll help expedite bridge reconstruction so our workers don't take a detour for long. I'll call you at your office next week to discuss this further," he concluded realizing the county manager was taking advantage of this opportunity to talk to as many voters as possible.

Benson replied, "Call in two weeks; I'm on vacation next week."

"Okay, I'll call you then." Gregory left casually, blending with the crowd to avoid attention when he saw some people he'd previously met.

Patrick Duke, who was also entering the fishing tournament, came over to talk with the sheriff and Jimmy about fishing. He interrupted, "Hey, that's the Exgenics guy over there."

Jimmy, looked over his shoulder and saw the same man he'd met on Monday talking to the county manager, "I know him too."

"How do you both know him?" asked Coleman inquisitively.

Jimmy replied first, "Well I got a call early Monday morning for a truckload of sod to be delivered to that research farm in Kent County. That's the man from the security gate who watched a robolift unload the sod from my flatbed truck.[55] He wanted it delivered by lunchtime and paid double in silver coins for quick delivery. I never asked who he was."

Patrick added his story, "He showed up at my house early Sunday afternoon driving a white Supercruzer needing some bulldozing and grading work. He showed me some e-phone images so I could size up the job. I told him it would cost 25,000 e-coins and that I could start on Monday morning, weather permitting, and he could send the funds to my

---

[55] Robotic forklifts had decimated warehouse and teamster jobs by this period.

e-wallet, half down for a deposit and half on completion. For some reason though, he must have wanted it done quickly and hired me on the spot if I could start right then and if I could finish by dark, he'd pay five old 1928 Double-Eagle one-ounce gold coins easily worth 10,000 e-coins each. Now that's *real* money to put your hands on and not fictitious e-wallet digits. It was *very* generous and I took my equipment to the farm immediately.

"What did he want you to do?" Coleman asked inquisitively.

"I fixed a dam on their farm pond washed out last Friday night, just like Old Forge Lake and Chick Bridge did," Patrick replied.

"Well, that's interesting. How are you going to spend the money?" Coleman replied knowing that something wasn't right with the situation.

"Of course, I kept the coins for my 'collection' but on Monday, I went to the Lanexa boat dealer and bought a new bass boat. They gave me a 50,000 e-coin loan for two years at negative 10% interest. It's ridiculous to resist that deal since the dealer pays 5,000 e-coins a year for me to own my boat. Even if I don't win the Largest Bass Prize in the tournament, everyone will envy my new boat," he chuckled.

Just then, a loud rumble of thunder came from the southeast but was too far away to seem a threat, so everyone continued the reception.

On the other side of the tent, Rufus started growling and barking uncontrollably for a moment as some people walked past. In a moment, Doc came to help Jason. "What was that barking about?" asked Doc.

"I don't know. He was resting on the grass and he suddenly growled."

"He was likely napping and had a bad dream. He's been through a big trauma recently and is still recovering. He'll need extra attention a while."

Jason replied, "While I held him, I've been thinking that maybe we could adopt him. Since Grandpa lost Grandma, we've been alone except for Old Red until he died two years ago. I'm graduating in December and will likely move to a new job then. So, a dog would be good company for Grandpa when I'm gone and he knows how to look after Rufus well."

"That's a good idea Jason, but I think you better talk to your grandpa first to see if he likes that idea. If you decide to take him, I can drop by tomorrow to see how he's adjusting to his new home." The Doc had brought a big, meaty ham thigh bone from the barbeque trailer, gave it to Rufus, and unleashed the dog to let him eat. Rufus put the tasty bone in his jaws and started to smile, as dogs sometimes do, and circled in the rain and mud showing his prize before finding a dry tent corner to chew it.

gcgaacgcgatggcgtaagcgatggcgaacgcgccgctggcgaacgcgtgcgcgaacgcgctgccggcgaacgcgatggcgtaagcgatggcgaacgcg

Coleman was standing and just finishing a piece of chess pie as he commented to Olivia how the pies were a success at the reception, when Deputy James urgently came and said, "I just got an Emergency 911 call. We're urgently needed, sheriff. There's been a tragic accident on the Lower Chick and we need to launch the county rescue boat over at River Haven Marina immediately. There's an ambulance volunteer meeting us at Ole Bessie. The emergency's three miles downriver and we'll be the first rescuers there if we leave now. There's multiple lives at stake I hear."

George gave his plate to Olivia, gave her a quick peck of a kiss, "I'll see you when I can," and ran, still dressed in his best suit, with Deputy James over to Ole Bessie. They sped out of the parking lot, turned east toward the river, and Coleman flipped on the nitrous oxide turbo-booster he'd added to the powerful engine he modified with a supercharger scoop and blower. Coleman surged forward with the red dome light flashing, siren screaming, the engine over-revving, and roaring at dangerously high speeds on rain-slick rural paved roads, as Deputy James and the volunteer held onto their seatbelts tightly for a high-octane thrill ride.

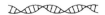

The Reverend Dickson had been on official duties as pastor of his church all day and finally got a chance to sit down at a table and eat his lunch. Jason and Julie both came up to him with Rufus on a leash and Jason asked, "Grandpa, can we adopt Rufus? He's all alone now, and when I get a job and move after graduation, you'll need company."

"Well Jason, I haven't thought about owning a dog much since Red died. However, Rufus needs a new family and it'd be good to have someone living with us, even if it's just a dog," he laughed. "He could stay in Red's old dog house by the garage."

"OK Jason, but you'll need to help out while you're still here."

Julie looked at Jason and smiled, "I knew he'd want Rufus. One thing Rufus will need later this afternoon is a bath. He's pretty muddy now. I could stop by after we leave if you'd like some help."

"Yes, please come over after we're done here," Jason gently replied.

The Grapevine immediately started wondering why the sheriff left the funeral, but the big gossip after the funeral was how the Captain and Macy were rich. Of course, the women longingly dreamed of the amount, but the men started a gambling pool for 20 e-coins each, with the winner having the closest correct guess to the final number, whenever that was known. However, the funeral would be remembered as the day the community joined to heal their river, its economy, and chart a new future.

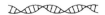

catgcgccgccgtattaaattcgcacccatgatgcgtatgcgatggaacgcatttgcgcgcatgcgccgccgtattaaattcgcacccatgatgcgtat

Chapter 11: A Tragedy on the Lower Chick

Charles County Rescue Boat

Mid Afternoon, Wednesday, June 30, ….

Sheriff Coleman and his rescue team, in their high-powered outboard, were first at the emergency scene within ten minutes. Apparently, a witness from a river-front house on the James County bank of the Chick saw the incident and called 911. James County Dispatch, in turn, had placed an emergency call to all regional water rescue teams to immediately converge at the approximate Grid Coordinates.

As they neared the location, the speedy rescue boat slowed when they saw an eight-man sweep-style, rowing boat capsized, with its long, narrow hull upside down. Eight long, wooden oars were floating nearby and two people were grasping capsized boat's hull. Another person was desperately keeping someone's head above water. Close to the boat were another four or five lifeless bodies wearing life vests floating with their heads just above the water. The victims began moving up and down in the small waves from the boat's wake, their heads oscillating like macabre fishing bobbers. The rescue team idled their motors to make their final approach to the capsized boat, minimizing waves.

As he quickly stripped off his rain-drenched suit down to his boxers, Coleman told Jeffery and the volunteer, "Stay here and throw a lifesaving ring to the two by the boat and then throw another ring to me. I'll help the two struggling in the water," he said as he dived into the water.

He swam to reach them and within a few short strokes, Coleman was helping a young woman hold a young man's head above water. He saw desperation in the woman's eyes from trying to keep the man afloat. "He wasn't wearing a life vest," she gasped, after swallowing water herself while barely keeping the man's head above the rain-drop rippled waters.

Coleman looked at the barely alive man whose eyes revealed panic from partial paralysis. The man's right hand weakly tried grasping the sheriff.

gcgaacgcgatggcgtaagcgatggcgaacgcgccgctggcgaacgcgtgcgcgaacgcgctgccggcgaacgcgatggcgtaagcgatggcgaacgcg

"Miss, I'll hold him now. You grab that ring there and my team will pull you onto our boat," Coleman said.

As he grabbed the man and put him in a better lifesaving hold, he briefly glimpsed his tee-shirt which said, '*College of William and Mary Rowing Team.*' As he held the man's head above water like a lifeguard, he started some side-strokes toward the waiting rescue boat.

After the team quickly pulled the young woman out of the water, Deputy James threw the lifesaving ring back to Coleman and pulled them both toward the rescue boat. Next, Jeffery and the volunteer carefully pulled the paralyzed man over the rear transom into the boat's cockpit. Sheriff Coleman soon swam up to the transom, stepped on a small underwater ladder, and climbed into the boat.

The improvised rescue team quickly pulled aboard the remaining two survivors from the capsized boat. One of those was the coxswain who sat in the stern of the boat directing the eight rowers to pull their oars on command. She told a brief version of what had just happened, "It was terrible. We were having a nice rowing team practice at our summer crew camp, and we saw a storm coming. So, we turned back towards the boat launch at our camp when the lightning bolt hit. There was a blinding flash at the bow of our eight-oared sweep and the water seemed to glow. We capsized immediately as the compression wave knocked us off balance. I think everyone from the bow is dead because they didn't move in the water. Only those near the stern survived, and I'm the only one who saw everything because rowers normally face the stern. They never knew what hit them. I'll never forget that instant as long as I live," she said finally breaking down in tears.

The ambulance volunteer examined the partly paralyzed college student and began checking his vital signs while Jeffrey brought blankets from a waterproof compartment and wrapped one around each of the other three survivors huddling together. The volunteer commented, "His pulse is irregular and his heartbeat doesn't sound right. He likely has arrhythmia from the shock. I think it's urgent he gets to a hospital fast. He might have some water in his lungs too, but his heart is the biggest problem right now." Sheriff Coleman just stood watching the five bodies bobbing in the water near the capsized hull.

Just then, the James County Rescue Boat arrived to assist at the horrific boating accident. They pulled alongside the Charles County Rescue boat and an EMS technician, with his emergency medical kit, jumped onto their boat to assist with any first-aid. The James County EMS tech said, "I'm

catgcgccgccgtattaaattcgcacccatgatgcgtatgcgatggaacgcatttgcgcgcatgcgccgccgtattaaattcgcacccatgatgcgtat

gcgaacgcgatggcgtaagcgatggcgaacgcgccgctggcgaacgcgtgcgcgaacgcgctgccggcgaacgcgatggcgtaagcgatggcgaacgcg

sorry it took us so long, but we came from Jamestown Marina, nearly 20 miles away. We're glad you're already here."

Coleman, now also wrapped in a blanket, replied to the well-trained EMS tech as he took over their patient, "We got here fast, but could only save the ones still moving. I think the ones in the water were hit by lightning. This man has partial paralysis, likely due to the shock. The others are obviously traumatized too, but we're not sure if it's concussion, electric, or mental."

The EMS tech yelled over to the James Rescue Boat, "We need to get this patient to the hospital immediately for an IV of amiodarone. He has heart arrhythmia and we need to restore his normal sinus rhythm. I can't put an IV in his arm on a moving boat. Call James 911 and have them meet us at Colonial Marina with a med-evac drone as soon as possible. Also, have ambulances meet there to take the other survivors to the hospital for observation. We're leaving *now*."

The Charles County boat immediately sped away full-throttle for the marina about a mile away just on the east bank of the Chick. The James County boat remained at the scene, pulling each lifeless body aboard.

On the way to the marina, the EMS tech commented to the sheriff's rescue team, "You're all heroes and likely saved this young man's life."

Coleman replied humbly, "We aren't heroes, just normal people doing what must be done in an extraordinary situation. A true hero is someone who sacrifices for others," as he thought back of his years in the Army to those who didn't come home. "This experience will change these students' lives. My life's changed too," he said thinking of treasuring more every day as a gift and blessing.

When they reached Colonial Marina, they tied up to the closest open berth at the dock and helped the survivors off the boat. The EMS tech then put an IV into the right arm of the partly paralyzed young man and told the young patient who was lucky to still be alive, "The IV is for the hospital staff to give you the medicine you need right away."

In about a minute, they heard the whirr of a med-evac drone coming closer. The drone came in fast and dropped in altitude to about 50 feet before hovering above the dock. Then, its lifepod, a small capsule about the size of a coffin with a clear lid, began lowering from three steel cables onto the dock. Within a minute, the EMS tech loaded the patient and gave him a few words of encouragement before closing the lifepod hatch, "You'll do just fine. The pod's AI-doc will ask you a few questions and help you relax on the way. He'll even play your favorite e-tunes."

catgcgccgccgtattaaattcgcacccatgatgcgtatgcgatggaacgcatttgcgcgcatgcgccgccgtattaaattcgcacccatgatgcgtat

The pod retracted and the drone sped back eastward to Williamsburg General Hospital and the awaiting emergency staff. Several ambulances soon arrived to transport the other survivors to the hospital. The Charles County rescue team said goodbye to the EMS Tech, climbed in their boat, and slowly motored back in the rain to their berth at River Haven Marina.

><I><I><I><I

During his rainy drive back to the restored farmhouse at Exgenics where he'd been staying a few days, John Gregory e-phoned Dr. Gerardo, who was still in Washington. He provided an update, "Ernesto, we've been progressing smoothly with clean-up operations, but we really need to do something before the July 4th fishing tournament on the lake."

"I went over to that old couple's funeral earlier and talked with the county manager about 'donating' to help rebuild the Chick Bridge, but with recent events, that was just an excuse to check things out over there. At the reception, I overheard some men talking about the tournament. One was the contractor that fixed the dam and another delivered sod. I'm not sure who the black man was though, but I think he was a pallbearer."

"Well, keep cleaning up those loose ends. I'm in control of Exgenics worldwide operations, laying low at my mansion until all is clear. However, I don't think we'll be able to keep this situation under control if anyone catches a T-fish at that tournament," Gerardo commented.

"I'll get an operation moving on that right now. We'll put our best men on it to come up with a credible scenario so the event is canceled."

"That sounds like a good idea," Gerardo replied in agreement.

"I'll get my team on it," Gregory replied as he terminated his Grid link.

Late Afternoon, Wednesday, June 30, ...

It had been a long day for the Reverend Dickson, Jason, and Julie. The brief summer shower had ended about the time the funeral reception was over. The event planner's contractors immediately started their final day's work of cleaning up trash and removing the electronics systems, tables, and chairs. They'd complete the tent tear down the next morning. Grandpa said, "Well Jason and Julie, there's nothing more to do here today. Let's go home."

Jason said, "I'll put Rufus in the truck with us Grandpa. Julie, you can follow us home in your autopod so we can give him that bath."

Jason put muddy Rufus in the pickup truck bed, while Grandpa sat in the front. While Jason drove, with Julie following behind, Rufus put his head over the truck's side into the breeze and they were soon home.

When they arrived, they climbed out of their vehicles and Jason asked Julie, "Can you hold on to Rufus while I go inside to change quickly? That old dog needs a bath before he can come inside the house."

Grandpa added, "I'll find some of old Red's things, I think they're hiding somewhere in a box in the garage."

Julie held Rufus outside by his leash while Jason changed into some old clothes. He soon arrived with some body wash and went to the water hose by the garage.

"Let's give Rufus his bath," Jason said as he turned on the hose while Julie held the leash. Rufus sat while Jason sprayed him with the hose nozzle, poured some body wash on his back, and lathered him up by hand. The dog seemed to enjoy the attention and was accustomed to bathing by Macy. After a rinse, Julie held the leash while Rufus shook his body from side to side shaking off excess water. He soon looked less water-logged and appeared to wear a smile on his long snout.

"Let's put him on the screen porch to finish drying," Julie thought considering a wet dog shouldn't drip inside the house.

"That a good idea. Can you go home now Julie? I have to work some now on my English class, but after dinner, I could drop by to see you. Let's take a walk in the gardens and talk awhile. I also have another question I need to ask you."

"OK Jason, that sounds fine," she said before climbing into her autopod, wondering what strange question he'd ask her this time.

✕◁▷◁▷◁▷✕

Sheriff Olsen was sitting in his office shuffling some case files and thinking about all the recent accidental deaths in Kent County, when his AI-computer interrupted, "Traffic Data search completed. It was a difficult search, sheriff."

"What did you find?"

"I managed to track down the suspect truck to an engineering firm Crick, Watson & Noble, P.E. located in McLean, Virginia near Washington. Using imaging enhancement, I identified the truck as having traveled on I-64 on October 27. From there, I accessed other highway or street imagers, eventually tracing the vehicle's origin. The address is 1313 Dolley Madison Boulevard. It is detailed in the report I sent you."

After doing a quick search of the firm's Gridsite, Sheriff Olsen then commanded his AI-computer to make a Grid call to the engineering firm.

"Hello, Crick, Watson, and Noble," a young man's voice replied.

Olsen replied, "Hello, I'd like to talk to Mr. Watson or Mr. Crick."

gcgaacgcgatggcgtaagcgatggcgaacgcgccgctggcgaacgcgtgcgcgaacgcgctgccggcgaacgcgatggcgtaagcgatggcgaacgcg

"I am sorry sir, they were not in the office today," the phone receptionist replied.

"What about Ms. Noble, is she in today?" the sheriff asked.

"She is not in this afternoon either. She was not in the office today."

"Do you know when I might be able to contact any of them?"

"I am sorry sir, but never. One of our junior engineers was laid off yesterday and came back into the office with a semi-automatic pistol, murdered the entire staff, and committed suicide. At least that's what I saw sir. I was the only witness to the crime and I called 911 for the police."

"Damn," Sheriff Olsen cursed, as he terminated his Grid link by slamming his e-screen, since the only 'witness' was an AI-receptionist.

Just then, Deputy Jeffers stopped by the office to report, "I've got news that Sheriff Coleman needs right away. The forensic tech said the tire track was one of those 3-D printed custom off-road tires used on the newest Supercruzer models. Also, his vehicle database indicated there are no Supercruzer owners in Charles County and the nearest other Supercruzers belong to Exgenics and our department."

"That *is* interesting news, James," Sheriff Olsen replied inquisitively.

At River Haven, Coleman and Jeffrey refueled the rescue boat for future emergencies and moored it in its berth. On their drive back to the church, Coleman said, "My suit is ruined, but at least I saved some lives."

Coleman soon received a radio call from Mable at dispatch, "George, James County thanked our rescue team for this afternoon's help. Y'all are invited as guests of honor to their next fundraising barbeque. Also, Sheriff Olsen wants to tell you something about your case."

"OK, I'll call him using Jeffrey's e-phone."

"No," Mable replied, "he said to use your office landline."

They arrived at the church and everyone had left except for the event planner who was still cleaning up. Olivia had gotten a ride home from someone else already, so Coleman dropped off Jeffrey at his patrol car. Next, he gave the volunteer a ride home since his wife had left him stranded. After dropping off the volunteer nearby, Coleman drove Ole Bessie to his office. He picked up the old handset and pushed numbered buttons to dial Sheriff Olsen, "Hello Al, you've some news to tell me?"

"Yes George, are you in your office?"

"Yes, Al."

"Well, I heard forensic results you wanted. That tire track came from a Supercruzer. You know the only Supercruzers in Kent and Charles County are owned by my department and Exgenics?"

catgcgccgccgtattaaattcgcacccatgatgcgtatgcgatggaacgcatttgcgcgcatgcgccgccgtattaaattcgcacccatgatgcgtat

"I didn't know," Coleman replied. "Why the big landline phone call?"

"Well, I've got a feeling something big is happening. I've been searching for leads about the dam break, but every time I make progress, the leads are gone or dead. I tried to find Exgenics building permit info in our county's AI-computer database said the files are missing. Then I called a construction contractor in Newport News and he was murdered. Now, I just called an engineering firm near Washington and everyone had been killed yesterday. I don't think these are coincidences. It's like someone knows about my investigation and is killing off all my leads. That's why I'm suspicious and wanted to talk on your old phone line."

"Well, that Supercruzer tire track points my case toward Exgenics now," George commented. "I really need the Captain's cell phone info to pursue this lead further, but Gridcom will just stall, delaying any warrant."

"Yeah, we have the same problem with them, so what'll you do?"

"I have a backup plan and Judge Saunders is okay with it."

"All I know is now both our cases are pointing the same direction," Al commented. "I think we need to keep sharing information in private."

"Yes, let's meet tomorrow at lunch at the restaurant by East Lake Campground. You could take a boat there and it'd be faster than driving the detour to Provident Forge since the bridge is out. Also, let's keep in touch using old land phone lines. They're more secure these days."

"Sounds good."

"I'll see you tomorrow at noon," George replied.

Before dinner, Jason read his next English assignment, "*English 101-E Assignment 12: Analysis and Creative Writing. Read the following poem by W. B. Yeats. Then, in a brief essay, comment on the poem's significance and write a poem with a similar context.*"

"The Second Coming"

Turning and turning in the widening gyre
The falcon cannot hear the falconer;
Things fall apart; the center cannot hold;
Mere anarchy is loosed upon the world,
The blood-dimmed tide is loosed, and everywhere
The ceremony of innocence is drowned;
The best lack all conviction, while the worst
Are full of passionate intensity.

Surely some revelation is at hand;

gcgaacgcgatggcgtaagcgatggcgaacgcgccgctggcgaacgcgtgcgcgaacgcgctgccggcgaacgcgatggcgtaagcgatggcgaacgcg

Surely the Second Coming is at hand.
The Second Coming! Hardly are those words out
When a vast image out of Spiritus Mundi
Troubles my sight: somewhere in sands of the desert
A shape with lion body and the head of a man,
A gaze blank and pitiless as the sun,
Is moving its slow thighs, while all about it
Reel shadows of the indignant desert birds.
The darkness drops again; but now I know
That twenty centuries of stony sleep
Were vexed to nightmare by a rocking cradle,
And what rough beast, its hour come around at last,
Slouches towards Bethlehem to be born?

After reading the poem, Jason thought to himself, "Why don't these poets ever say anything plainly so it can be easily understood." He went downstairs to Grandpa who was cooking a light supper.

"Grandpa, I just read a poem by Yeats for my English course. It's called 'The Second Coming.' Do you have any idea what it's about?"

"Yes, I remember that poem. I think it was written after World War I and the poet was commenting about the world and what caused the war. Events then were like a whirlpool spinning out of control. Reasonable people couldn't stop it, but extreme leaders, in their passion and greed for power and control, brought misery and chaos to the world.

"What's the second verse about then?"

"I think that he thought maybe the world was looking for a savior, just like Christ is promised as a savior of Christians in his Second Coming at the end times. The reference to a Sphinx is a mystery and the author added a word of caution for the world. When another savior arrives, maybe they're not what they appear to be. Maybe they're evil instead of good? Does that make any sense Jason?"

"I think so, Grandpa. Basically, it's saying to not follow leaders blindly but think for yourself. If people actually questioned their leaders and their motivations, maybe such tragedies could be prevented."

Grandpa replied, "Maybe that's what the poet wanted. That poem opens up your mind, forcing you to think. Doesn't it?"

"Yes Grandpa, maybe poetry is good literature after all. Poets do make you use your brains," Jason summarized, and now he had a good idea for his essay. "I want to talk about something else. What was it like with you and Grandma? When you were younger?"

"Oh, are you thinking about Julie?"

catgcgccgccgtattaaattcgcacccatgatgcgtatgcgatggaacgcatttgcgcgcatgcgccgccgtattaaattcgcacccatgatgcgtat

"Yes, Grandpa."

"Well, I thought about Sarah often too. We met when I was in college studying religion. My father didn't want me to be a minister, but I always felt that calling. Anyway, I met Sarah when she worked in the cafeteria at dinner. She was a student with a part-time job serving behind the dessert station. I'd see her every night and always had an extra dessert to get her attention. Eventually, I flirted more and gained the courage to ask her out. Our first date was wonderful and it was like she became a part of me to make me whole. After that, we were practically inseparable and I soon proposed and wanted to spend my life with her by my side."

"Yes, I feel like that with Julie. Courage is something I've been trying to gain though. The future is so uncertain it sometimes makes me afraid. What if things don't work out? What if my past still haunts me?"

"Jason, sometimes you just need faith that all will work out in the end. Faith comes from belief in God, but also comes from having hope. Hope is the belief things will work out. It provides us optimism that the world will be a better place in the future. This faith, hope, and optimism give us the courage to make life's decisions, Grandpa said as he put the pork chops he'd been frying onto dinner plates.

"Of course, I also think a good bit of pessimism mixed with a large dose of realism is a good idea too. It's important to have all three: the faith or optimism that things will work out, the pessimism that sometimes they don't, and the realism that reality is usually in the middle. This lets you be prepared for life's events.

"Thanks, Grandpa, I'm going over to Julie's tonight after dinner again."

"That's fine Jason. Make sure you take Rufus outside for a walk first."

The doorbell rang and Jason went to answer while Grandpa cooked.

Sheriff Coleman was standing in a fresh brown uniform outside the door, "Hello Jason. I need to talk more about our discussion yesterday."

Grandpa yelled from the kitchen, "Who is it?"

"It's Sheriff Coleman. He wants to talk with me."

"OK, don't take too long, dinner will get cold," Grandpa replied worried about why the sheriff wanted to talk to Jason again.

Jason said to Coleman, "I'm not going to hack again and go to prison."

"Your efforts may help catch the Captain and Macy's murderer. I've now got a lead that points toward Exgenics, that company which owns a research farm over by Provident Forge."

"I've never heard of them," Jason replied.

"Well, a tire track I found at the Captain's house matches a Supercruzer tire and Exgenics owns several. Judge Saunders will protect you. I talked with her and she knows about your past. She'll shield you from enforcing any federal sentence since you'll have immunity as a deputy of the Charles County Court. Anyway, since you're so good at hacking, Gridcom won't even know who you are or what you find. You'll never get caught."

"Ok. If I just get information on the whereabouts or data records from the Captain's cell phone, I'm done hacking for you. Right?"

"Yes Jason, that's all I need for my case."

"Ok. I'll see then what I can do tonight."

"First let me deputize you. Can you record me deputizing you for you to send to Judge Saunders so the county clerk can have a record? It's for the unlikely event that something goes wrong."

"Yes, I have an e-vid podcam. Stay here and let me get it."

Jason went inside to get the podcam and briefly talked to Grandpa, "Grandpa, I've decided to help Sheriff Coleman with my special talents."

"If the sheriff is asking for your help, it must be serious."

"Yes, it has something to do with the Captain and Macy's murders."

"Well, be careful Jason. You made the right decision to help," Grandpa said wishing he had more time to spend with his grandson before he grew up and made grown-up decisions. However, he had little time left to make further impressions on the young man before he was fully independent.

Jason returned to the front porch and the sheriff with the podcam in one hand and the old family Bible in the other. He sat the podcam on the porch railing and gave the Bible to the sheriff so he could swear an oath.

Coleman said, "Jason, you don't need a Bible for an oath these days."

"Yes, I know, but written in ink in the margins are birthdates, occupations, and deaths of the Dickson family going back nearly 200 years. I want to add the occupation 'deputy' and the book should witness this event too," he awkwardly joked but seriously thinking of his family.

"No problem, Jason. Let's get started then," Coleman replied.

"OK sheriff, just touch the button on the podcam when you want to start recording and touch it again to stop."

Sheriff Coleman touched the button and began, "Jason Dickson, raise your right hand, put your left hand on the Bible, and repeat after me."

"Yes, sir," Jason said replying with the correct hand gestures.

Coleman started, "I do solemnly swear that I will support the United States and Commonwealth of Virginia Constitutions," and Jason replied.

He continued, "and that I will faithfully and impartially discharge all the duties incumbent upon me as a deputized law enforcement officer of Charles County," and Jason replied again.

Coleman added a customized condition to this specific oath, "and to follow the direct orders of Sheriff Coleman and Judge Saunders of Charles County in this county emergency," and Jason replied again.

At last, Coleman recited the grand finale, "according to the best of my ability, so help me God," and Jason replied. The staccato oath for the podcam was over when Coleman pressed the button.

Then as is customary, the sheriff shook his new deputy's right hand and said "Congratulations, Deputy Dickson. Now for your first official duty, send that e-vid to Judge Saunders and call me in the morning if you find out any important information."

"Yes, sir" Jason replied and waved as the sheriff climbed in Ole Bessie and drove home to Olivia with a smile, hoping for another chess pie.

Jason went inside the house for the now cold dinner that Grandpa had cooked. "I saved a leftover piece of Olivia's chess pie for you after dinner, Jason. I'm tired and will read before going to bed. Enjoy tonight with Julie and don't forget to walk Rufus," Grandpa said.

"I will Grandpa. I won't be home late since I've got some homework."

Grandpa completed the conversation, "Let's take tomorrow afternoon off and go fishing. I want to spend some time with you and talk about what we're both going through right now. You can tell me if you want to fish at breakfast," Grandpa said and walked upstairs to the master bedroom to let his grandson eat and think.

Early Wednesday Evening, June 30…

Jason took Rufus for a short walk outside to do his business and afterward drove his motorcycle to Julie's house before sunset. He rang the doorbell and Julie came to the door with a smile and let him inside. "It was a long day today," she commented.

Jason commented, "It's good to see you, Julie. I liked how everyone came together at the funeral service today."

Julie replied, "Yes, sometimes life's events bring people together. I don't think Charles County has had an event like that in a long time."

"I agree, sometimes people and things just drift apart and things go downhill so that you can't control what happens," as he thought of the poem by Yeats he'd read, "but, it takes effort to make things work again and make things right."

"Yes, I think so too. I loved Mrs. Coleman's singing very much. She has a gift and I'm glad she shared it with everyone. It's important to use your talents and share them with others. Unfortunately, my talent is not cooking," she chuckled thinking of yesterday's burnt meatloaf."

"It's OK Julie, you'll get better with practice."

"I hope so," she replied with eagerness to learn.

"Let's go for a walk along the river before sunset. I've another question I'd like to ask you, but it can wait till later."

"Okay, that's fine Jason," she responded wearily with a sigh from all the questions over the past days.

They continued talking as they slowly walked east along the bluff away from the setting sun that would have been in their eyes. "How old do you think the Captain was?" Julie asked.

"I found out from Grandpa that he was ninety-five. He was still energetic for his age and one of those few people who are timeless. Some people just age slowly. I hear it's in their genes."

"Yes, Jason that's mostly correct. All human cell chromosomes have something called a telomere on the ends of their DNA strands. This telomere part of the genetic code can be up to 15,000 bases long, with the length varying for each person. Every time, a living cell divides, the telomere chain gets shorter. Finally, after a cell divides over a long period the telomere is so short that the cell line dies. People that live to extreme ages have less cellular genetic damage and longer telomere chains," Julie noted using her college knowledge of biochemistry and genetics.

"So, our days on this earth really are numbered since only God and now geneticists really know how long we'll live. Well, the Captain and Macy must have had long ones. Macy was eighty-nine years old too."

"Aging is also affected by the environment too. The Captain and Macy lived a simple life, ate mostly homegrown food, and didn't have much stress. Also, they enjoyed fresh air and exercise as it takes more energy to live simply. Macy gardened all day to grow their food and the Captain chopped wood for weeks at a time for fires for winter warmth and to run his still. That's good wholesome exercise people don't get any more."

"Well, I like most how they lived together those 60 years. They truly must have loved each other."

"Yes Jason, you could see how their personalities fused over the years and they could almost read each other's minds. They anticipated each other's needs as a way to show they cared for each other too."

They reached the old stone bench underneath the magnolia, and Jason said, "Let's sit down here in our favorite spot."

"OK, Jason," Julie replied as she sat on the bench with Jason still holding her hand to carefully guide her to her seat.

Jason then looked her deeply in her eyes, pulled something out of his pocket, and went down on one knee in front of Julie and asked, "Julie Williams, will you marry me?" as he opened a small velvet-lined wooden box to reveal a triple-banded ring with one diamond set on each band.

"Of course, Jason," she replied looking at the sparkling triple-band ring and then deep into his glowing green eyes that still caught some sunlight as the sun was still above the horizon.

"I made the box from cypress. One of the rings is the one my dad gave my mom, Kimberly, that I received when I turned eighteen and could control my inheritance. That ring represents the past. The second ring is the one Grandpa gave Grandma, his wife Sarah, that represents the present, as he gave it for me to give to you. The third ring is for the future I want to spend with you. I bought it with savings and designed it myself using computer modeling. I had a custom jeweler in Williamsburg use his gold 3-D printer to fabricate the ring that locks, binding them together."

"It's beautiful Jason. Slip it on my finger," she smiled, feeling a wave of emotion as she started crying in happiness. Her tears flowed with joy.

He slipped the ring on her finger, "It's okay sweetheart, it took a lot of courage for me to finally ask you too. I kept asking questions over the past few days to make sure you were ready for me to ask that question."

"Well, I thought you might want to ask me, but you frustrated me every evening with another question. It's like you baited me along trying to get my hopes up, only for me to crash and burn every evening afterward."

"That was part of my plan to build up to a grand finale, but I was hoping it would be at Sunday's fireworks. Sorry for any frustration I caused, but it worked," Jason grinned, pulled Julie by her hand to stand while he stood up, embraced her, and kissed her while her blonde hair glowed on fire from the day's sun casting its last red rays.

After their long passionate kiss, Jason asked, "One more question Julie. Will you marry me tonight?"

"Why do you want to do that? We should be married at Wendover Church and have the reception here. The Wendovers would surely let us use the plantation for the reception since my parents work for them."

"Yes Julie, we can have a big 'family' wedding with guests later, but I want to get married tonight."

"Why's that?"

"Because a wife can't testify against her husband," he said seriously as they continued talking and walked back toward her parent's house.

Chapter 12: Another Accidental Death

Truck Wreck in the Swamp

Wednesday Evening, June 30, ….

Jason called Doc Longtree about 9:30 p.m., "Hello Doc, this is Jason."

"How can I help you, Jason? Is Rufus doing well?"

"Yes, he's with Grandpa and doing fine. I'm with Julie right now and we want to get married *tonight*. We don't want our families to know quite yet, so can you help?"

"I'll ask Chief Yadkin if he can perform a ceremony tonight and call you right back."

Within five minutes, Doc replied, "The Chief said a Chickahominy Indian wedding and marriage certificate are recognized by the Charles County Clerk as legally recordable in their Book of Records, so you'd be married tonight. Both he and his wife can meet you at the tribal center in forty-five minutes. Susan and I will be there in thirty if that works."

Jason replied, "That's good, we'll meet you there."

Julie then commented sadly, "We don't have any wedding bands."

"We'll trade wedding bands at our Wendover Church ceremony."

"I'd like that idea to make that ceremony special," she smiled.

꠸꠸꠸꠸꠸꠸꠸

Jason and Julie arrived at the tribal center near Samaria Baptist Church and Doc Longtree was waiting in the parking lot with his wife. Doc sported a buckskin shirt with blue jeans and a white feather in his long black hair. Susan wore a buckskin dress and a seashell bead necklace for this special occasion. "Hello, Jason and Julie. The chief is coming in a few minutes," Doc said. "Have you ever been to a Native American wedding before? We need to quickly prepare you for it."

"No," the young couple said in unison.

"Ok, let me explain some details. It's customary for four sponsors to be present at the wedding. These people will be your spiritual guides throughout your lives together. If you ever need help during your marriage, you are to seek their counsel. Susan and I will be two sponsors and the Chief and his wife have agreed to be the other two. Secondly, an Indian marriage joins a couple before God. It's for life, so there's no divorce in our beliefs. Are you two okay with what I said?"

"Yes," they said looking at each other with affection and devotion.

"Great, so let's get you ready for the ceremony. We brought some traditional garments for you to wear. I brought a ceremonial shirt that should fit you Jason and Susan brought her wedding dress for Julie. Let's go inside the building so you can change."

They went inside and changed within the men's and women's restrooms. Jason came outside first with Doc. He wore a buckskin shirt and had an osprey tail feather tied to his hair near his right ear. About ten minutes later, Susan came out with Julie, who now wore a soft buckskin dress of white leather with decorative beads.[56] She had a white and grey seashell necklace and her hair had been braided with a few white feathers and entwined red ribbons. Around her head was an improvised laurel of hastily braided daisies picked by Susan from her garden using a flashlight.

The Chief and his wife Lily soon appeared, with headlights shining from an eight-passenger electric-powered cart that drove along the road to the parking lot. Doc commented, "He uses that cart to keep weddings moving faster during this peak season."

Chief Yadkin stopped by the wedding party and after a brief greeting with Doc, the Chief asked the young couple, "Do you want a traditional church-style vow for a quick service or a longer, full traditional Native American ceremony?" Chief Yadkin was a Christian, but also maintained his Native American beliefs as leader of his tribe.

Julie whispered something in Jason's ear and Jason whispered something back into Julie's ear. She nodded yes and Jason then spoke, "We'd like the Native American service, please. When we get married again for Julie's parents, we'd like Grandpa to do traditional vows."

The Chief replied, "Not many couples get married twice. That's a good omen from the Great Spirit because your love will bind you twice as tightly through the difficulties and hardships of your future lives together."

The Chief and Lily invited the wedding party to sit in the electric cart, and they drove a quarter-mile deep through the dark, thick forest and swamp along a trail that led to a wide opening in the forest canopy. The

---

[56] Native American leather tanning of deer hides was done in a series of processes and animal brains are used at one stage of the chemical process to make the whitest, softest leathers that were usually used for ceremonial garments.

gcgaacgcgatggcgtaagcgatggcgaacgcgccgctggcgaacgcgtgcgcgaacgcgctgccggcgaacgcgatggcgtaagcgatggcgaacgcg

cart's headlights briefly illuminated a wooden arbor supported by four corner posts. Blooming honeysuckle vines grew up the posts and their sweet fragrance added a memorial ambiance to the wedding arbor.

On this dark and starry night, the Chief rose from the cart, lit two tiki-style kerosene-torches, and handed one to Doc. The rest of the wedding party soon stood nearby. The Chief was wearing a fine buckskin suit, a necklace of deer teeth and shark-tooth fossils, and a headdress of red-tailed hawk feathers arranged around his head like an inverted broom. His wife wore a ceremonial buckskin dress and several seashell necklaces befitting a woman of her advanced age, stature, and status.

"Please follow me to the spring first and then we'll have the ceremony under the arbor," the Chief kindly requested. "I take it the wedding came about suddenly. I hope none of you are in trouble," he said as he looked at the young man and woman standing in front of him.

"No sir, not *that* kind of trouble. I proposed to Julie tonight and she said 'Yes.' After that, I asked her if she wanted to get married tonight and we talked a while longer, she said 'Yes' again," Jason answered with a grin.

They walked 100 feet through darkness to a swampy area with a freshwater spring. The spring was lined by a perimeter of flat stones and barely lit by the two torches. Doc and Susan guided Jason and Julie in the darkness onto the stones and told them, "Now kneel and wash each other's face and hands to purify your spirits and to show the Great Spirit that you'll care for each other always."

Jason and Julie touched the black spring water and jointly scrubbed their hands. They then carefully used one hand as a cup to supply water to the other, which functioned as a washcloth on each other's faces for a ceremonial cleansing rather than a true wash.

The Chief then walked them back to the arbor and they lit two more tiki torches on holders by the arbor posts. Then Doc and the Chief placed their torches onto two similar holders. "Jason and Julie, come stand in the center," the Chief commanded the couple. He next grabbed a small fired-clay bowl from his leather satchel and filled it with dried sage leaves. He lit the leaves on fire with a butane lighter, letting them burn out and the aroma of burnt sage temporarily overcame the honeysuckle fragrance surrounding them. After blowing in the bowl to cool it slightly, he put his forefinger into the bowl, coated the tip with soot, and made a small dot on Julie's nose and a larger stripe on Jason's nose and each cheek.

The Chief then took his ceremonial walking staff and drew a wide circle in the dirt around the couple as they stood in the arbor's center. "Oh, Great Spirit, this man and woman have come to stand in this prayer circle

catgcgccgccgtattaaattcgcacccatgatgcgtatgcgatggaacgcatttgcgcgcatgcgccgccgtattaaattcgcacccatgatgcgtat

to join as one in your presence. We invite you here to witness this event so that they may feel your Spirit," as the Chief next said a verse of untranslatable words in a brief chant.

He continued in English, "They intend to honor you every day of their lives. They promise to share and care for each other. They promise to make sons and daughters for you so that their children shall honor you."

The Chief then used the lighter to light an old Indian-style ceremonial tobacco pipe made with a small clay pipe bowl and a long, hollow wooden stem. He passed it to Jason first. "This is to feel the Spirit of the Great Father. You must hold the smoke until your wife exhales the smoke she takes when you give her the pipe."

Although they weren't tobacco smokers, Jason took a big puff, quickly passing it to Julie who did the same taking a much smaller puff. They looked at each other's eyes and exhaled.

"Now your two spirits are one spirit. The smoke is the breath of your spirits joining for the Great Father. You are both now as one, forever."

The Chief then concluded the ceremony, "By the power vested in me as Leader of the Chickahominy Nation and the Laws of the Commonwealth of Virginia, you are now husband and wife."

With those official words completed, Lily and Susan both took a seashell necklace they each were wearing, broke the necklace cord, and tossed the seashells over the couple as the Chickahominy wedding ritual blessing for good luck and long lives together.

After the ceremony, the sponsors gave congratulations to the married couple and they drove in the cart back to the tribal center. On the way through the woods, Doc whispered to Julie and Jason, "You're supposed to leave the black mark on your nose tonight so in the morning when it's gone, the sponsors will know it's a good marriage," he laughed.

Jason also said to Julie, "You know, I really felt the spirit there, but perhaps it was the smoke," he smiled while feeling slightly dizzy.

Inside the tribal center, the Chief asked Jason and Julie to sign an official marriage certificate that Jason could record in the morning at the County Clerk's Office in Charlestown. Doc and Susan also signed as witnesses and finally, Jason used his e-phone to put 200 e-coins into the Chief's e-wallet for his services. Julie then asked Doc to take a few images just to record how they both were dressed and Jason remarked to her upon seeing them, "Julie, you look just like an Indian Princess."

"And you're my handsome brave," she replied with a smile. "Where should we go now?" she asked.

Jason replied, "Let's change into our regular clothes and go to my house. You can stay there with me now."

"Well, that'll have to do," Julie said thinking an exciting honeymoon location would be more interesting, but that wasn't practical right now.

After leaving the tribal center and riding through the dark on Jason's bike, the newlyweds arrived at Grandpa's house, which still had a light on the porch and in the kitchen. In the kitchen, Jason told Julie "I still have to finish an English assignment tonight and then should help the sheriff."

Julie replied, "I think you can do that later," as she pulled him close for a brief kiss and grabbed his hand to lead him upstairs to his bedroom.

It was almost midnight when the bedside telephone rang. George woke up and replied, "Sheriff Coleman here," knowing that such late phone calls were usually bad news.

Deputy James replied, "George, there's been a bad wreck tonight. A truck flipped into the creek along Harrison's Swamp Road, you know, that twisty winding road over near Grantville."

"I'll be there in ten minutes," Coleman replied and put on his pants and a shirt for the ride in Ole Bessie to the accident.

Coleman arrived at the wreck and stopped next to Deputy James' patrol car with its lights flashing. Coleman saw a pickup truck had missed a sharp corner and driven off the road. The truck had flipped on its side into a deep swampy creek, with the driver's side under the dark waters.

Deputy James told George, "The man who called 911 was driving home late, spotted a gap in the bushes, and knew something was amiss. He stopped, shined a flashlight toward the creek, and spotted the wreck. He didn't see anyone, so the driver was likely trapped underwater. I just called Buddy, for his tow truck, and an ambulance in case we find a body."

While waiting, Jeffrey commented to George, "It's been a wild, last few days, but I'm looking forward to my date with Dr. Graves." He smiled.

"Well, she *is* something to look forward to for sure," George replied thinking about the attractive doctor who also had a sparse love life.

Buddy Peters and his adult son arrived in his tow truck and backed into position so the tow cable and winch faced the new dark gap between the bushes. He exited his truck wearing some waterproof waders since he'd already heard from Jeffery about a car in the creek. He briefly talked to the lawmen and went about his business like he'd done many times before. With his truck still running, Buddy flipped on a spotlight, shining the beam through swampy forest undergrowth to reveal a truck just 25 feet away.

gcgaacgcgatggcgtaagcgatggcgaacgcgccgctggcgaacgcgtgcgcgaacgcgctgccggcgaacgcgatggcgtaagcgatggcgaacgcg

His son spooled out the steel cable using the electric winch and Buddy pulled it by the hook, wading into the water whose muddy bottom created suction each difficult step. He fastened the hook in a good spot and his son winched the truck upright. With some slack, Buddy then re-looped the cable around the frame for a second, much more difficult pull. He gave the thumbs up and his son started winching. The tow cable tightened and strained, pulling the truck inch by inch up the bank to the road's edge.

Everyone gathered on the driver's side by the cab and peered inside through shattered safety glass, but the deflated airbag obscured the driver. Buddy opened the unlocked door and water poured from a half-filled cab. He removed the airbag but didn't recognize the man. Sheriff Coleman saw Patrick Duke's slumping head with his eyes and mouth wide open.

"Dang," the sheriff angrily shouted, further adding to his crescendo of suspicion something was amiss at Exgenics, since on Sunday, Patrick had repaired their pond. The ambulance volunteers soon arrived, placed the body on a gurney, loaded up their ambulance, and drove to the morgue in Kent City, which was open 24 hours a day to receive cadavers.

1:00 a.m., Thursday Morning, July 1, ….

Julie had fallen asleep in Jason's bed and although he was exhausted, Jason knew his night's work wasn't done. So, he carefully crept out of bed where Julie slumbered, went to his desk, turned on a small lamp, and powered up his computer. He looked back at the bed and Julie was lying like an angel, wrapped in sheets and curled up like a contented kitten without a black spot on her nose. He needed to finish his English assignment on Yeats. Within an hour, he wrote a brief essay on his interpretation of the poem *'The Second Coming'* and composed this poem:

"Washington Winter"

A people of digitized grey faces
Never thinking but fully programmed,
In patriotic display without sound,
Dead soldiers rest eternally
Worn down by wars so weary.
On the subway, their numbers abound
Suffering a life so dreary
Wearing warm clothing as armor
As minds transcend their white-washed world.

Marble statues and granite monuments

Stood as silent tributes and reminders
That should have lasted for eternity
But were torn down and turned into dust
By grinding wheels in an age of ignorance.
A paradox of wealth and poverty
Their facades built like Potemkin villages.[57]
Columbia towers over all sharing with charity.
She is a mother, the best of her breed
Struggling for her children to succeed.
An urban blight monitors the night
Over a dusty, thirsty land in need of hope.
Give her again enough freedom,
And the world will envy her kingdom.

While Julie slept soundly, Jason turned on his podcam and spoke quietly, "I'm Charles County Deputy Jason Dickson, and I'm beginning a lawful search as instructed by Sheriff Coleman and Judge Saunders." He then recorded every computer keystroke he made as he started his Gridcom hack to locate the Captain's cell phone data for the sheriff.

Hacking was like peeling an onion to get to the center without your eyes watering. Layer after layer of security protocols must carefully be opened or the keystrokes trigger an alert by an AI-system monitoring the Grid for abnormal traffic and data transfers. He studied his quarry online watching his e-screen scroll text and data for about an hour, trying to locate a Grid vulnerability. He finally managed to connect via a series of data communication hops to a Grid node tower near Williamsburg that recently hadn't automatically updated its software.

With several deft keystroke commands, Jason updated that node with his own software and entered into Gridcom behind the surface veil of incoming and outgoing e-calls, e-vids, and Grid searches. He still had to be careful, since now he was on the inside, any hacking errors were more noticeable by AI Grid Monitors. He probed another hour, and finally, using the Captain's phone number, received a response he wanted.

The Gridcom data downloaded in a millisecond and he stored it on an external memory stick and ended his hack. He now had a data file of recent Grid coordinates for the Captain's cell phone. He opened the file and saw a tabular list of Grid coordinates which were just Grid 'check phone

---

[57] Potemkin Villages refers to a time in imperial Russia when Prince Potemkin built temporary villages or facades to impress the Czarina Catherine the Great along her route on a long journey by horse-drawn carriage to the Russian Crimea in 1787.

location' records for every minute. There was also a time-stamped call log. The last call the Captain made was a three-minute call at 10:26:23, June 27th from Grid coordinates 37.416036, -76.994519 and the number called was the phone number of the Captain's house. He next used the SAT-Map app to check the listed Grid coordinates. The Captain's last call originated from the uppermost marshes of Chick Lake.

After that, the phone's locations kept moving eastward over for a half-hour and the final locations converged around the Grid coordinates of 37.400345, -76.955201. He checked those coordinates on the SAT-Map app and the location was Binns Bank. The Captain's House could be clearly seen on the satellite image. The phone stayed nearly stationary for another hour, but then the last Grid location was recorded at 37.400960, -76.955242 at 12:16:37 and the phone's transmissions ceased. He checked the SAT-Map app and saw the Grid location. He now knew where the cell phone was and why signal transmission had ceased. First thing in the morning, he'd visit Sheriff Coleman with the news.

He carefully crawled back into bed next to Julie, but she was disturbed by his arrival and whispered, "Darling, what're you doing up?"

Jason replied, "I finished the sheriff's hack. I'm done hacking forever."

"That's good and I'm happy you're done with hacking. I'm glad we're married and waited until then," Julie replied and smiled while thinking that she now was a married woman.

Jason kissed her tenderly as he wrapped his arms to embrace her again, but this time, he fell asleep.

Jason's e-watch alarm beeped at 8:00 a.m. and he rolled over to say morning to Julie, but she'd already slipped out of bed. He put on a bathrobe and went downstairs to the kitchen where Julie was cooking breakfast while Grandpa sat in a chair. They'd been talking quite a while.

Julie saw Jason and replied, "I see you're finally awake. You were up so late, I let you sleep in a while. I already told Grandpa about our wedding and he's fine with it." She held her finger up and smiled at the beautiful triple-banded engagement ring.

Grandpa chimed in, "Jason, I'm proud of you and that you finally decided to marry Julie. She's a good woman and you complement each other, making a perfect match. It isn't the ceremony I expected, but she told me that you're planning a big 'official' marriage later at Wendover."

Jason replied, "Yes Grandpa, when the spring flowers bloom would be the best time. Wendover isn't booked much before the prime wedding season. Will you perform the ceremony?"

"Yes," he replied proudly, "I'd be honored, Jason." He added jokingly, "Of course, I won't help you commit bigamy because I heard you married a beautiful Indian Princess last night," Grandpa smiled toward Julie.

They all chuckled as Julie served toast, half-burnt bacon, and salt-less scrambled eggs with crunchy egg-shell bits added for calcium.

Grandpa asked, "Will you tell your parents Julie or keep your marriage a secret until the Wendover wedding? I can keep the secret for at least nine months, but can you?" he winked.

"I haven't thought much about *that* yet, but we still have time for all these decisions. I know when Jason graduates that he'd like to move to Williamsburg while I finish the last two years of college."

"If you want this summer, you're welcome to live here if you don't mind commuting to your internship in Williamsburg but perhaps Jason will want to move to your apartment there for the rest of the summer. It would be nice to have a woman around the house though," Grandpa said.

Julie replied, "We haven't discussed where we'll live permanently. I'll stay here the rest of my summer break as a start. First, I need to go home this morning and explain everything to my parents. I think that's the best way. Maybe we'll keep the wedding a secret from the rest of the world and then everyone will enjoy the second wedding like it was the first."

Jason added, "Yes Julie, that's a good idea. I'll take you home on my bike after breakfast and then I need to talk with Sheriff Coleman."

Grandpa asked Jason, "Have you decided yet if want to go fishing with me today? We can sit on the dock, talk, and have a good time together. We have a lot to discuss now that you're a married man," he smiled.

"Sure Grandpa, I should be home before lunchtime but later I need to pick up Julie to come and stay here tonight."

Julie asked both men, "Do you want me to cook dinner tonight?"

The men both looked at each other silently and Grandpa replied first as he'd heard rumors of Julie's cooking prowess, "Not tonight Julie, since we might catch some catfish to fry but if not, we've some leftover spaghetti from Monday to finish." Next, Grandpa scraped their leftover eggs into a bowl with dog food nuggets for Rufus and put the bowl on the kitchen floor. The old dog eagerly chomped on the crunchy feast.

8:30 a.m., Thursday, July 1, ….

Jason drove Julie home on his bike and dropped her off at her parent's front door. He kissed, embraced her briefly, and said with encouragement, "It'll be all right. Just talk to your parents and they'll understand why we decided to get married last night."

"Yes, I know, but I need courage with mom. She's very religious and mightn't think our marriage was before God. She always wanted me married at Wendover Church. The brick church there's the oldest in Charles County. Plus, I think she was looking forward to a big reception at the plantation house to impress the Grapevine," Julie laughed.

Jason reassuringly put his hand on her shoulder and said, "We'll do that later so everything will be fine Julie." He put his helmet on and whirred on his bike down the long gravel road in front of the house. He drove to the Charles County Sheriff's Office, entered the front door, and found Sheriff Coleman's office. The sheriff had already arrived and was drinking a cup of coffee while thinking about recent events and his case.

"Morning Sheriff Coleman," Jason greeted him with a salute.

"You don't need to salute," George chuckled. "How's my newest deputy this morning?"

"Fine, I spent last night searching Gridcom and I found enough information to locate the Captain's phone."

"What did you find?" he replied with his full attention on this news.

"Well, the Captain's last call to Macy was made about 10:30 that morning from the upper part of Chick Lake. After that, he traveled by boat home where the phone stayed more than an hour without moving much. Then a final phone location signal shifted about forty yards or so north of the house and the signal terminated at that point."

Coleman replied, "Forty yards would place the phone somewhere in Chick Lake, maybe twenty yards past the dock."

"Yes, that's correct. The cell phone sent the last signal before it entered the water since the water would've shielded any further antenna transmissions. Likely, it was thrown in the water by the murderer."

"Did you find anything else?"

"The last signal occurred at 12:16 p.m. I also could've tried to access the Captain's last calls, but that data is only accessible at a higher Gridcom security level. They use more stringent algorithms and protocols to protect actual voice data transfers and storage. I didn't want to risk hacking those yet for fear of detection since we only need the phone."

"Won't the water have damaged it?"

"Yes and no. The electronics are likely shorted out, but the memory chip should be intact if all else fails. Those chips store a lot of information and I should be able to recover any data once we find it in the lake."

"Good work Jason, you've done a fine job as my deputy."

"I'm *done* with hacking, so you don't need my help more with that. I'll help find any information on the phone though when you recover it."

gcgaacgcgatggcgtaagcgatggcgaacgcgccgctggcgaacgcgtgcgcgaacgcgctgccggcgaacgcgatggcgtaagcgatggcgaacgcg

"I'll need to contact Sheriff Olsen from Kent County to have him send his dive team to help look for it. I'll bring you the phone when we find it so you can examine it."

"Here are the last known Grid coordinates for you to write down sheriff." Jason waited a moment for the sheriff to pick up a pen and he slowly said the coordinates, "37.400960, -76.955242. The phone is likely there or perhaps farther from the dock since the phone might have been in the air when it last transmitted."

"The water's deep by Binns Bank. It will be hard to find," he lamented.

"You'll recover it, I'm sure. I'll be at home fishing with Grandpa today if you need me," Jason said as left the office for the county clerk to record his marriage before traveling home.

Sheriff Coleman called Sheriff Olsen, using his old phone, "Morning Al, I need your dive team to locate some evidence."

"What's up George?" Olsen replied.

"We know the location of the Captain's phone. It's in Chick Lake."

"OK, we'll help, but they're busy this morning. They're searching the river below East Lake Campground for those drowned fishermen."

"Let me know when they can help me."

"I'll see what they can do, but they're tired from diving for those bodies yesterday. I'm still meeting you for lunch by the campground, right?"

"Yes, I'll be there for sure. I'll take the patrol boat upriver to the lake."

"See you then," Olsen said as Coleman hung up the phone.

Coleman next drove to Nick Abramovich's trailer and rang the doorbell. The old Russian man greeted George at the door, "I didn't expect you this morning, George. Do you want some beets already? They're still small, but I could pick you some?"

"No Nick, I'm here on business. Can you tell me about Exgenics? What do they do there? I want to find out what you know about them."

"Well, I've worked more than ten years with Dr. Gerardo. They do genetic research there. I help them manufacture the genetically engineered drugs they test. From what I've overheard, they make cancer drugs by milking the cows I've heard mooing in the barn. I've never been inside the barn though since I don't have security access. I've only limited access in the main research building too. Pretty much all I do every afternoon and evening is lab work with genetic sequencers to make DNA for Dr. Gerardo's experiments. He likes to keep them running round the clock if possible. He performs the final experiments himself."

"So, they keep security pretty tight there?"

catgcgccgccgtattaaattcgcacccatgatgcgtatgcgatggaacgcatttgcgcgcatgcgccgccgtattaaattcgcacccatgatgcgtat

"Yes, I heard Dr. Gerardo say security is high because there are a lot of competitors that want to steal his Crickett technology. That's the reason why Gerardo is so secretive and why I only have limited access inside his facility. That way, no single employee knows too much about the entire operation and their research. They have those eye scanners for each locked room or lab. To enter my lab, I must scan my eyeball first."

"Tell me more about Dr. Gerardo."

"He's obviously a brilliant, rich scientist and perhaps arrogant, but he can be kind and thoughtful at times. For example, he gave me a large garden patch at his farm, since I have only limited space for one behind my trailer. He's also strict, just like he treats his dogs Dante and Inferno. He's firm with them and doesn't let them get away with anything. They respond immediately to his every command. He's also vain, like how he recently lost so much weight and dyed his hair just to look younger for his wife. I hear his wife is attractive and younger than him, so he must want to keep her happy. Of course, with his difficult character, she was probably more attracted to him by his money and not his looks."

"Yeah, that's sort of the way of the world. Money attracts beauty. Have you ever noticed anything strange going on there?"

"Not that I can think of."

"Have you seen anybody different, new, or unusual there?"

"I've seen their corporate attorney every day this week, but he usually only comes for the day. He's staying at the old farmhouse like Dr. Gerardo does when he wants to work late and not drone home. Now that I think of it, I haven't seen Dr. Gerardo at all this week either but that's not unusual since he has business dealings all over the world."

"Do you know anything about the Supercruzer they have there?"

"That's for the security team to use. It's usually parked by the security building at the front gate during work hours. They have a guard on duty during the daytime for visitors, but security is on-call if something happens at other times. After normal business hours, the gate is locked and you need an eye scan to open it."

"Ok, thanks for your time, Nick. Don't tell anyone there I was asking questions. I'll come pick up some beets when they're ready in a few weeks," Coleman said as he was about to leave.

"Sure George, I'll keep my eyes open for anything unusual. I normally go to work and do my job quietly. I'm ready to retire in a few months and Doctor Gerardo said he'd give me an extra retirement bonus of 20,000 e-coins if I came in last Saturday to work.

"I thought you didn't work on Saturdays because of your religion?"

gcgaacgcgatggcgtaagcgatggcgaacgcgccgctggcgaacgcgtgcgcgaacgcgctgccggcgaacgcgatggcgtaagcgatggcgaacgcg

"Normally, yes, but he said it was an emergency. However, I really think he just wanted me to run a DNA scan on an embryo sample.

"What's that?"

"That's an egg that has just started growing and started dividing its cells to become an organism."

"What kind of embryo?"

"A fish."

"I thought you said they had cows there?"

"Yes, they do, but they perform their genetic experiments with fish. You see, fish are a good genetic model for higher vertebrates and the fish Dr. Gerardo uses have 75% of the DNA that is found in humans. What better way to test a genetically engineered cancer drug, especially with all the animal rightists preventing testing on live mammals, birds, reptiles, amphibians, and even insects? I'm sure you remember when they declared that honeybees and ants were intelligent since they're social animals."

"We modify the eggs to have a portion of cancer cell DNA from the human patient and test the new customized cancer drugs on that egg. Every new cancer patient becomes a new customer for the pharmaceuticals Exgenics produces that *will* cure them. Now you know why Exgenics has found so many investors. Crickett technology helps Dr. Gerardo engineer the DNA for both custom producing the cancer in the fish egg and also the drug that cures it."

"What a business model. Guaranteed cure for what ails you. Thanks for telling me that Nick. A final question. Did you see the farm pond there on Saturday?"

"No, I was in such a hurry that I just didn't even notice it. There are also a few trees screening the pond from the employee parking lot."

"We'll be in touch. Keep your eyes and ears open," Coleman said as he waved goodbye, climbed into Ole Bessie's front seat, and drove away.

Chapter 13: Gone Fishing!

Sheriff Coleman on River Patrol

9:00 a.m., Thursday, July 1, ….

Grandpa was sitting at the kitchen table finishing the final draft of his Sunday sermon while Rufus rested on the hardwood kitchen floor chewing a dog bone and spreading another puddle of drool. Since it was a holiday weekend, the service would likely be sparsely attended, but at the same time, there would probably be a few visitors who were vacationing nearby. Sunday would be the Fourth of July, so Grandpa was planning for his sermon to discuss freedom.

Jason arrived home from his morning errands and went to the kitchen, "I'm back Grandpa. I brought some herring from River Haven Bait Shop to cut as catfish bait."

"That's perfect Jason. I think we'll have some fried catfish filets for dinner if we're lucky," Grandpa replied while thinking even leftover spaghetti in the refrigerator was better than Julie's offer to cook dinner.

"Yes, that would be good. I know Julie isn't the best cook yet, but she's trying. Some women have the knack for it and others just have to learn the hard way. She's in the latter category for sure," he smiled thinking of his newlywed wife.

"Well, let's get fishing poles, tackle boxes, and set-up on the dock."

"I'll bring lawn chairs and the patio umbrella there too. It'll be hot today and we could use some shade." Jason replied. "I'll put on my swimsuit; the water will be refreshing later too."

"That sounds good Jason. We have a lot to talk about today, but I am sure there'll be time for that. I'll wear a swimsuit too."

After changing, they gathered things and walked past the boathouse to the dock's wide end.

They baited their hooks with herring slices and cast them into the murky water about 30 yards away where the heavy sinkers sank the tasty

gcgaacgcgatggcgtaagcgatggcgaacgcgccgctggcgaacgcgtgcgcgaacgcgctgccggcgaacgcgatggcgtaagcgatggcgaacgcg

bait to the river channel's bottom. They sat down in their chairs, adjusted the umbrella's angle for the sun, and began to talk.

"Jason, I'm glad you wanted to fish with me today. The Captain and Macy's funeral yesterday made me want to talk with you and your sudden elopement made it even more important. I won't be on this Earth much longer and want to share my thoughts and wisdom, who I am, and where you came from. You and Julie will spend your entire lives together and I want to guide you both on your journey along the River of Life. Remember your whole life what we discuss and if you ever have doubts, my words will bring you guidance and wisdom to solve your problems."

"Yes, Grandpa I will. Before I was arrested, I always thought I could make my own decisions. Afterward, I learned to listen *a lot* more."

"Well making good decisions comes from using knowledge and wisdom, but you didn't have both of those then. Jason, you're a lucky young man and were given a gift, but perhaps you don't know why and how to use it." Grandpa continued, "You're fortunate your criminal record was sealed and no one but the government, Sheriff Coleman, Julie, and her parents know who you are. I'm not sure the Federal government even knows anymore the way they always mismanage things."

"I think Judge Saunders also knows because Sheriff Coleman was talking with her about me."

"That's fine. She's a good woman who's always upheld the law equally and fairly, not like most in Washington these days who give justice to the highest bidder or those pulling the puppet strings. Remember there are no coincidences in life, Jason. Everything happens for a reason. You were meant to hack and be arrested. Your mother and father were meant to die in that tragic accident."

"I still remember almost like it was yesterday as they bled to death and took their last breaths. After the airbags deflated, I could see Mom and Dad slightly turn their heads to me buckled in the center back seat. Mom exhaled with her last breath, 'He's OK' and Dad with his saying 'Love you, son,' as they looked at each other, smiling in thanks and release amid the anguish and pain of their imminent deaths. Their eyes closed, they were at peace, and I felt their love envelop me like a protective blanket. I didn't even cry at the time, but I had nightmares for years afterward and still am afraid of big trucks."

"I know Jason and can only imagine what you went through. Thank you for finally telling me your story, as I know it's hard for you, even now. The Virginia State Police Officer at the scene called me and said it was a miracle you were alive. He said if the gas line hadn't been crimped in the

catgcgccgccgtattaaattcgcacccatgatgcgtatgcgatggaacgcatttgcgcgcatgcgccgccgtattaaattcgcacccatgatgcgtat

gcgaacgcgatggcgtaagcgatggcgaacgcgccgctggcgaacgcgtgcgcgaacgcgctgccggcgaacgcgatggcgtaagcgatggcgaacgcg

accident, you'd have been burned alive in a ball of fire. Grandma and I drove there immediately to pick you up and Grandma comforted you almost every night afterward when you woke up screaming.

"I did cry when Grandma died though as she gave me so much comfort and love during that time when I needed her the most."

"I've been heartbroken since Grandma died too. I loved Sarah deeply and we were like two halves that together were a whole. We knew what each other was thinking and anticipated each other's needs. I see that with you and Julie and I hope you keep that spirit alive as you spend your lives together. But getting back to what I was telling you, yes, there are things in our lives beyond our control that happen. We just don't know the answer to the question 'why?' and that's where faith comes from."

"So, always look for your inner voice to guide you, Jason. That's perhaps the spirit of God guiding you to make the right decisions. Our choices and decisions aren't always correct, but at least we have the freedom to make them and learn. That's what God gives us and my sermon on Sunday will be about that. Your inner voice will help you find the strength to overcome obstacles you'll face. On your journey along the River of Life, remember sometimes you need to paddle backward to get around a rock before you can move forward again."

"Yes Grandpa," Jason replied listening to the wisdom Grandpa told.

"Let me tell you who I am and what makes you who you are. My side of the family was from the river and my grandfather was a riverman. That's why I'm trying to repair his old dory, to honor him and the sacrifices he made so that I could live on this earth. Grandma was from the land, and her family was planters for many generations. The land we own around us is what remains of her family's farm and I still rent the fields to Green Acres Sod Farm. Upstairs in the old barn across the road is your great-great grandfather's plow he used to till his tobacco fields by mule. You still can see where his hands gripped the handles because the wood is worn down from his lifelong labors. His life is your past and the worn handles are an echo you can see and learn from. I hope you restore it someday, just like I'm trying to repair that old dory."

"It's the fusion of the two bloodlines, the river and the land, that made your father who he was. He had a brilliant mind and was courageous like a riverman fighting a storm, but also had an inner calmness and was well-grounded from his rural upbringing. I miss him so much and Kimberly too as she complemented him in so many ways. You're all the family I've left in this world Jason and I do love you very much."

catgcgccgccgtattaaattcgcacccatgatgcgtatgcgatggaacgcatttgcgcgcatgcgccgccgtattaaattcgcacccatgatgcgtat

gcgaacgcgatggcgtaagcgatggcgaacgcgccgctggcgaacgcgtgcgcgaacgcgctgccggcgaacgcgatggcgtaagcgatggcgaacgcg

"I love you too Grandpa. I miss Mom and Dad too, but the older I get, my memories of them both seem to fade."

"That happens as you get older Jason. Our lives fill our minds with new memories and old ones just don't have as much room. They're still there, but the doors to them are usually closed. I think when you die, they all rise to the surface again at once so that God can fully know you when you meet him. I also like Julie a lot and am glad you married her. Her family is from the earth like Grandma and I hope my love for her as a daughter-in-law grows. Julie's part of my family now and it'll be nice having a woman here again, even if just a short while until you move away. I'll miss you Jason when you move with Julie as you must. You can make a good living in the city somewhere."

"I'm sure we'll stay awhile. These days, it's possible to telecommute."

"Well, you never know Jason. It's a big world out there and you both need to see it. Don't limit yourself, your possibilities, and your potential by staying here. Don't wait for things to happen, but instead, live deliberately. Wake up each day with a plan and make it happen. Master your fears, work hard, and you can achieve greatness. Like I said before, you have a gift. It's up to you to use it wisely. You're now at an age where you'll make decisions in life and you'll now have also to make decisions with Julie for your future family."

"We don't have children yet Grandpa," Jason laughed.

"Well, *that* is a benefit of married life and the result is your children," Grandpa thought about his honeymoon with his wife Sarah many years ago. "Hopefully you'll have children someday. These days there are choices as to when, but still, I think God has a big part in it, as all life is a miracle. Children are a way of us living into the future and are our legacy. I'm lucky to have a grandson who can continue mine," Grandpa smiled. "Remember though a man's legacy shouldn't be only his seed, but rather each seed he plants in the minds of others that grows throughout the world. Each man can change the world if they set their mind to it."

"In my way, I've tried to do that throughout my life by spreading the word of God, but feel now that I've spent more of my life helping people with their fears of dying than I've helped people learn how to live. The Bible shows us that mankind has been thinking of the same things for thousands of years, so don't be afraid to read it and think for yourself. Question things. Why are things the way they are? Don't get bogged down in the Chick Swamp seeing just the trees, vines, and marsh and not the surrounding forest. Step back and look at things from a different viewpoint and the river channel will soon open up for you."

catgcgccgccgtattaaattcgcacccatgatgcgtatgcgatggaacgcatttgcgcgcatgcgccgccgtattaaattcgcacccatgatgcgtat

"That's good advice for sure. Grandpa, you've helped many people over the years. So, you do not need to regret your past."

"I know, but always wished I could have done more to help others. I'm not getting any younger Jason. You know I'm 76 years old and my days on this Earth are numbered as God only knows, and someday, all I have will be yours.

"You won't die soon; you're still fit and in good shape for your age."

"You never really know when your time comes. Remember right after Grandma died and I was gone for a month after I wanted you to stay with the Captain and Macy for a while?"

"Yes Grandpa, the Captain took me fishing and Macy always baked me some treats. I fell in love with chess pie then," he smiled in remembrance.

"Well, I was so heartbroken that I developed congestive heart failure from a leaky valve I was born with. If it hadn't been for you and being your guardian, I might have just let it fail and joined Sarah. The cardiologist said I'd die within a year, but to remain alive for you, my valve was replaced in Williamsburg, and was in the hospital during that entire time. I was lucky to survive the operation and my insurance covered most of the cost. Money bought me some more time on this Earth with you by repairing my heart, but there's not enough money in the world to live forever. Even the richest man in the world a few years back, that John Stoneman III who inherited that fortune, died at 112 after five heart transplants and countless life-extending medical procedures."

"I didn't know about your heart, Grandpa. Thanks for telling me."

"I never told you because I didn't want you worrying since you'd been through so much trauma in your life. Before the operation, I made plans that the Captain and Macy would be your guardians in case something happened to me because there was a 1 in 20 chance of death."

"I never knew that before Grandpa."

"I think one reason they loved you so much was Macy helped with your birth. "Your mom and dad were visiting us here for the weekend, and Kimberley's water broke and she went into labor quickly. Macy was a midwife and came 20 minutes before Doc Hansen arrived. So, you were born right in this house. So, in Macy's eyes at least, you *were* the child they never had. They'd have been pleased with you being their pallbearer."

"I felt honored as they were always good and kind to me when others weren't and I loved them for that."

"I know they watched you grow up into a young man and we're proud of you. I think Captain and Macy knew that their time on this earth was growing short and that's why they wanted to preserve something of themselves and the river way of life. Don't waste your brief time on this Earth and don't let others waste your time. Just think of the careless driver on a big highway in Washington. In one accident caused by driving too fast to save time, they block the traffic of a hundred-thousand commuters for an hour. That's like wasting nine years of a single person's life."

"Yes, Grandpa. As for the Captain and Macy, I hope they'd have been happy that I'm helping the sheriff locate the Captain's cell phone. I hope he finds it in the river and the information on it leads to their killer. I'll help him more when he finds it."

"They'd be proud of you for that too, just as I also am. What worth is your gift if it can't be used? Use it for good and you'll always have the moral high ground. When you've got the law on your side, you'll be okay."

"I'll do my best to help," Jason replied.

Grandpa paused and thought about what he might have missed in his discussions. "Here is something else I want you to remember. It applies to marriage the most, but also applies to life in general. Remember that if you build a strong house, it'll weather any storm, but you must have a solid foundation first. Do this with your marriage and in everything you do. Jason, I hope the wisdom we shared this morning helps you live when I'm gone from this world and have moved on to join with God."

"I'll remember what we talked about Grandpa."

"Ok then, enough serious talk for today, let's just enjoy the day fishing and telling old-time river stories that the Captain told me, but one last bit of wisdom for the day. Remember that that line Sheriff Coleman uses, 'Optimism is the first half of success.'"

"Yes, I think it gives him inspiration to solve difficult problems."

"Well, the second half of success is 'be indefatigable' and maybe the third half of success is don't count your chickens before they hatch," he laughed as he cast a hook with a bit of herring into the river channel. He next scratched Rufus behind his collar a while and the dog lay down by his lawn chair for a nap and another puddle of drool.

After leaving Nick's trailer, Coleman drove past Charlestown to start a road patrol and planned later a river patrol upstream to finally meet Al for lunch. He caught a few speeders along State Highway 5 as they drove toward July 4th vacations and after a while, he arrived at River Haven Marina. On his way, he was thinking about his murder case and all the recent events somehow seemed connected to Exgenics. What was the motive? Why were there so many accidents and deaths recently? The questions circled his mind like a whirlpool and he could only hope they came into focus within the nexus of his mind.

He parked Ole Bessie and walked down to the dock where the Charles County Sheriff Patrol Boat was berthed. The 16-foot outboard was fast, with a planing hull that could navigate Chick Lake shallows as well as the lower Chick and James. He even added a nitrous oxide booster tank for extra engine emergency horsepower. He untied two lines from their cleats, jumped aboard, climbed in the cockpit seat, and started the engine.

He steered the boat northward and slowly went upriver toward the dam. He began a leisurely patrol, mostly looking for intoxicated fishermen and vacationers. His radio then chimed from Charles County Dispatch, "Sheriff, two bodies spotted floating in the river near Grave's Landing."

He replied, "I'll be there in about five minutes, Mable" and he throttled up the engine to half-power since they were likely the fishermen that Al's dive team was looking for. As he motored toward Graves Landing, he kept thinking about the murders, the deaths of those poor college students, all the other recent accidental deaths, Sheriff Olsen, and about Exgenics. The thoughts kept swirling through his mind and then his past army experiences surfaced, "What if they turn those cancers into a weapon?" he thought in the back of his mind.

He soon arrived near Graves Landing and met the boat from the Kent County Water Rescue Team. They had already loaded the swollen bodies onto the boat and into zippered body bags. George came alongside and talked to the lead diver, "Are those the missing fishermen?"

The lead diver replied, "Yes, they are. We found their wallets in their pockets and a fishing pole with its line entangled around one of the bodies, but there was no hook at the end of the line. Maybe the hook got snagged on the bottom and the line broke when he floated to the surface."

"That's terrible. Did you find anything else?"

"No, but they were idiots not wearing life preservers. I've seen so many drownings over the years from fearless boaters and fishermen."

"Unfortunately, there's no cure for stupidity," Coleman replied. "Did Sheriff Olsen tell you I need you to search over near Binns Bank?"

"Yes, but searching for these bodies was the priority as one of them was the son of an important Virginia congressman."

"When can you get there and take a look?"

"Later this afternoon. We're about ready for lunch at the campground, but first, we need to dock and the ambulance must pick up the bodies for the morgue. Later, we'll swap our scuba tanks at the dive shop over in

Williamsburg. The past two days depleted our tanks, including our reserves. We'll let Sheriff Olsen know when we're going to Binns Bank."

"Thanks for your help in advance. I'm meeting Al for lunch soon."

After an hour and a half of fishing with Grandpa with no luck, Jason's e-phone rang. Jason answered and heard Julie crying. "What's wrong, sweetheart? Are your parents upset with our marriage?"

"No, they're fine but slightly disappointed we didn't wait for a church wedding. Jason, haven't you heard?" she blurted out between her tears while she gathered her composure to talk more.

"No Julie, what's happened?"

"Five students from the college rowing team were hit by lightning and died yesterday in a terrible accident on the river."

"That's awful Julie."

"One was Michelle Bowlen, a good friend of mine. I just received an e-message that the college will have multiple memorial services, one for every major religion, at the old chapel on campus starting tonight and continuing throughout the day tomorrow. We need to go so that I can say goodbye to my friend," she continued sobbing.

"Sure, I'll take you, my love. I'll pick you up later in the afternoon when we're done fishing and we'll figure it all out when we hear more news," he said with compassion in a comforting tone.

Grandpa asked, "What's happened, Jason?"

"Several students died on the river yesterday and one of them was Julie's friend. That must've been why Sheriff Coleman left the funeral reception in such a hurry. There'll be a bunch of memorial services on campus and I need to take Julie there when we get more details."

"That's sad Jason. I'm glad you can comfort Julie. Those poor college students. Their lives had just begun. As I said a while ago, our days are numbered, but we can rest assured that they're in the loving arms of the Lord. We must have faith in God's plan to bring them to Him so young."

"Yes Grandpa, you're right. It's no use trying to understand why it happened, but I hope there was a reason," Jason replied as he cast another piece of herring bait and continued thinking. He thought about what Grandpa had said earlier. Life is too short, so don't waste it. Our days are numbered and there are no coincidences, so there must be a reason why they died. Why? He thought a while, but couldn't think of one.

"Grandpa, the catfish don't seem to be biting today. Looks like it'll be leftover spaghetti tonight unless you want Julie to cook dinner."

gcgaacgcgatggcgtaagcgatggcgaacgcgccgctggcgaacgcgtgcgcgaacgcgctgccggcgaacgcgatggcgtaagcgatggcgaacgcg

"The fish might start biting soon. You never know, but that's part of the mystery of fishing. Mostly, fishing today was an excuse for me to talk and spend time with you. I think a lot of men enjoy it just to spend time away from their wives," he laughed. "I've been thinking about Julie. Maybe we should let her cook dinner tonight if she wants to. That would get her mind off the loss of her friend. Call her later to ask for news from the college and ask her to cook dinner. She's eager to practice being a better cook. Also, we have to involve her in decisions around here now."

"That's a good idea, Grandpa," Jason replied.

Just then, Jason and Grandpa heard "Hello," as Doc Longtree hollered from near the boathouse and started walking down the old dock with its worn and weathered cypress planks. "I came to see how Rufus is doing. Congratulations Jason on your marriage again. How's married life?" he grinned with a wink and noticed it was a good marriage since there was no longer a black stripe on his nose.

"Everything is fine," Jason replied, "but Julie lost a college friend in that boat accident yesterday afternoon. It must have been terrible."

"Yes, I heard about it this morning on the Gridcom regional E-news. Such a waste of young lives. The news said the Charles County Rescue Team were heroes with Sheriff Coleman and his men saving several lives."

"I saw the sheriff this morning but he didn't say a word about it," Jason wondered why.

Grandpa chimed in, "George is just a humble person and didn't think much about it. It's just his job to do such things. Ever since he was in the Army, he went about his business and job as sheriff as best he could."

Doc added, "Yes, he's sort of a quiet person deep down. After he came back from the war, he was a changed man though. Like he learned what was important in life. That's when he settled down and married Olivia. Now tell me how Rufus is doing? Has he been eating well?"

Grandpa commented, "He's doing fine. He's been eating just fine, but he's been drooling non-stop anywhere he lies down."

"Unfortunately, that's a bad trait of his breed, but I hope his good traits make up for it. Let me look at Rufus and pet him to see his response. He's still recovering from a traumatic experience." He bent over and scratched him behind the ear. He calmly put his hand on the dog's head, looked him in the eyes, and felt the dog missed his old masters. However, the dog felt a sense of calm and peace with Grandpa and Jason, his new masters, so Doc now knew Rufus would be okay. "I think he's doing fine too, but he still misses the Captain and Macy. Remember he's an old dog and give

catgcgccgccgtattaaattcgcacccatgatgcgtatgcgatggaacgcatttgcgcgcatgcgccgccgtattaaattcgcacccatgatgcgtat

gcgaacgcgatggcgtaagcgatggcgaacgcgccgctggcgaacgcgtgcgcgaacgcgctgccggcgaacgcgatggcgtaagcgatggcgaacgcg

him love and attention. Let him track some coons and possums once in a while and he'll be fine until his time comes," Doc commented.

Grandpa replied, "We'll treat him well. It's nice having him around. I miss old Red, but Rufus will be good company when Jason moves away in the future. Doc, why don't you stay and fish a while if you're not busy?"

"No, I have to do a barn call next. A racehorse over at the Tyler Estate is lame this morning after practice.[58] I have to drive there and take a look.

Just then, they saw a bald eagle, about a tenth of a mile away, diving toward the river for a fish. As the female eagle dove, it gained speed, skimmed above the surface for a few feet, launched its sharp talons toward the water, and grabbed a fish. With the fish in its grasp, she immediately flapped her wings to fly higher and home to her chicks in their cypress nest two miles away. She was about twenty-five feet in the air when she felt a sensation that caused her to drop the fish over the river. The eagle flew awkwardly for a few moments and continued on its way toward its nest to recover from a sensory stimulation it had never experienced before.

They continued watching the eagle fly off into the distance and Doc said, "That's odd. I've never seen an eagle drop a yellow perch from its grasping talons before," and, as a Chickahominy, knew it was a bad omen. Doc son said goodbye and was on his way to his barn call.

A little later, Jason said, "Let's eat lunch soon, I'm getting hungry."

"Why don't we jump in the river first. It's already getting hot."

"Sounds good Grandpa and afterward, let's eat that leftover spaghetti now to give Julie another chance to cook dinner tonight," he chuckled as they both took off their shirts and jumped like teenagers off the dock into the cool river water.

---

[58] The Tyler Family has long lived in Charles County. John Tyler was the 10th President of the United States and his Sherwood Forest Plantation is still owned by his descendants.

catgcgccgccgtattaaattcgcacccatgatgcgtatgcgatggaacgcatttgcgcgcatgcgccgccgtattaaattcgcacccatgatgcgtat

Chapter 14: A Quiet Business Lunch

Coleman at Walker Dam Lock

Noon, Thursday, July 1, ...

After finishing his patrol, George motored slowly to the dam and lunch with Al. He maneuvered around the steel dock moored in front of the dam and entered the gates of the small, narrow lock leading to Chick Lake. He pressed the lock's 'start cycle' switch and the lower gates closed. The upper gates soon started to slowly open, and since the tide wasn't very low below the dam, about a foot of fresh river water quickly filled the lock. After the water level raised the floating boat, the upper lock opened, and George motored past the pumping station to Dockside Restaurant. He idled his boat, jumped off, tied mooring lines to cleats, and walked inside.

Al was there waiting and greeted him, "Hello, George."

"Hey Al, it's been a busy day."

Olsen replied, "The dive team told me you were coming. I just met them at the lower boat ramp while they waited for the ambulance. I sure hope Dr. Graves can figure out what happened, as that congressman will surely pull some strings to get to the bottom of this incident quickly. Of course, if the autopsy findings are bad, the media will cover it up to not impact his reputation so he can get reelected."

"Yeah, that's the way it is these days. Corporations control media and if the truth is inconvenient or doesn't serve their control agenda, they just make up a new 'truth' we're supposed to believe. The truth is usually covered by a fog of confusion and scattered clouds of delusion."

Olsen replied, "Yes, the powerful get what they want from paid-for politicians on both sides voting in the State Assembly and U.S. Congress."

"For sure, politics now is like back in Rome long ago, when citizens were bribed with free food and circuses to vote for corrupt politicians owned by the rich and powerful," Coleman commented cynically.

Olsen agreed, "Yeah, they live off of bribes while we enforce their laws meant to make only themselves rich. They keep everyone under control and busy working making a living like lab mice running on a treadmill. I can't believe how crazy it's been this week. Aside from my normal duties all across Kent County, I've been spending a lot of time near the river the past few days. It's like everything here is out-of-control and needs my attention. With the July 4th holiday festivities and fireworks coming up this weekend, there'll be plenty of overtime for my deputies too."

Coleman replied, "It will be busy then for sure. Everyone in Charles County has been talking about the big fishing tournament on the lake."

"Don't forget the Bluegrass Festival this weekend," Olsen added.

"Yeah, you're lucky with that big bandshell tent on the other end of the campground to give your deputies overtime all year round."

Olsen commented, "They've got some big event going on every few months for sure. I love Christmas time when they have Santa's workshop and the Christmas Village with all the decorations. People come from miles around just to see the lights along the riverfront."

Coleman concluded, "Well enough shop talk, let's grab a take-out lunch, and then we could bass fish at a good spot I know for our 'lunch break.' We've been so busy we need time to recover. I've got two rods in my boat for such occasions," he grinned.

"Sounds good. Sometimes a break helps your mind see clearly."

"After that, if you want, we can go on a joint patrol together if you'd like since the entire lake is in both our jurisdictions."

"Sure, my other deputies can keep things under control in the rest of the county for a while," Olsen agreed.

"Deputy James is on duty today too, so I have some free time to spare."

Coleman and Olsen slowly motored up Johnson Creek on the north side of the lake to one of George's favorite fishing spots and tossed and anchor in the shallow channel near a large patch of marsh grass.

"I've got some nightcrawlers I picked up in the bait shop at River Haven. Here, bait your hook and cast out to see what we catch. Then, let's sit right here and eat lunch quietly," Coleman said pointing toward the e-phone in Al's pocket and motioning with his hands to turn it off. Al took his e-phone out of his pocket and pressed the off button.

Coleman then started talking freely, "Al, you may think I'm paranoid, but I don't trust those e-phones. This way we can *definitely* talk in private as you know it's possible to eavesdrop on an e-phone."

gcgaacgcgatggcgtaagcgatggcgaacgcgccgctggcgaacgcgtgcgcgaacgcgctgccggcgaacgcgatggcgtaagcgatggcgaacgcg

"Yeah, with a search warrant served to Gridcom, we've eventually caught many drug and gun dealers using that capability."

"What would happen if someone had the same access, but didn't care about a warrant? Someone like Gridcom itself?" Coleman questioned.

"Yeah, but they don't have any need to do that. They make their money on Grid access fees and from AI-advertising. Their AI-system scans voice data for keywords and we later see related ads, but this function is limited by law to allow them only ad revenue. They're not permitted to scan other data without a warrant."

"Yeah, what if Gridcom didn't care about the law. Just something to think about and be wary of. For example, when you were investigating the dam break, all your leads ended up as dead ends. It's kind of a stretch to say it's a coincidence that those people at those engineering firms died just before you contacted them. Also, how did Exgenics' building permit disappear from the county's database? Maybe Gridcom or someone who has access to Gridcom has been listening and monitoring you and has been using that info to stay one step ahead of you."

"I never thought of that, but it's conceivable I guess," Olsen replied.

"I know it's possible since the government has spied on Americans since the War on Terror started so long ago. First, there were international terrorists to catch, but then they later labeled *all* citizens were terrorists if they disagreed with their illegal dictates. Yes, I'm paranoid for that reason. That's why I'm always careful to only use a landline phone and police radio as they're not controlled by a big business monopoly these days."

Coleman continued, "With your e-phone off, we can talk business in private to discuss our big cases. I've got a feeling we're looking at the same problem from different angles and a serious hunch that Exgenics is involved, but not quite enough evidence yet for a search warrant. The Captain's cellphone is the key to unlocking this case. It has information about his last calls and final moments. That's why we urgently need it."

Olsen replied, "Hopefully our dive team will find it this afternoon. If it hadn't been for those dead fishermen, they'd already have been there."

"Well, Let's consolidate our efforts and work together. Perhaps, we can take the offensive too, since a surprise attack and distraction might help in this situation. They're good insurgency tools when faced by a potentially superior enemy. Sun-Tzu, that old Chinese General from 2,500 years ago, had much wisdom on winning a war. During recon patrols in the war, I kept a small copy in my pocket to read at night"

"Sounds like a good idea George. What do you have in mind?"

gcgaacgcgatggcgtaagcgatggcgaacgcgccgctggcgaacgcgtgcgcgaacgcgctgccggcgaacgcgatggcgtaagcgatggcgaacgcg

They discussed and formulated a plan together as they ate their lunch and Al caught some nice bass that Olivia could cook for dinner. One was an 18-inch-long three-pounder that would've been a good qualifying fish for the Big Tournament this weekend. "I'm sure some professional fishermen will be missing that fish this weekend," Coleman laughed.

"Yeah, those guys would be jealous for sure. Well, I think that was a relaxing business lunch, George. Let me turn my e-phone back on now since we're done with serious discussions."

"OK let's head back to the dock so you can resume your duties."

Olsen looked at his missed calls and saw one from the dive team. He called them back, "Hello, Olsen here. Sorry I missed your call."

The lead diver replied, "We just left the dive shop and should be back at the lake in a half-hour so we can start that search."

"Good. Meet me at the upper boat ramp then," Olsen replied.

1:00 p.m., Thursday afternoon, July 1, ….

Jimmy Cummings was filling a large sod order for a new golf course in Maryland when his e-phone beeped an alarm. He looked at the screen indicating a malfunctioning sod cutting and stacking in auto-shutdown and reboot mode. He drove his old pickup truck to the field which was half green grass and half brown loam where the sod was removed. The agrobot stood near an autotruck partially filled with stacks of fresh sod. The agrobot's indicator light on its chest was flashing red, so Jimmy pressed the adjacent reset button.

After the reset, the agrobot walked with mechanical legs to the field's edge and used its arms to slice a long narrow strip of sod, rolling it up as it moved forward. It then carried the roll back to the truck and sliced it into shorter sod pieces that were neatly stacked on the truck bed. Everything was working fine now, so Jimmy turned around toward his pickup truck to go back to the office to monitor the automated farm.

Just then, he heard the sound of electromechanical noises from a robot arm close behind him and the sod-cutting blade started to whirr at high speed. The moving arm with the blade was aimed near his neck but he fell backward just in time. The robot rebalanced itself on its two legs and bent over with its blade arm targeting his torso with the blade. He quickly rolled sideways and he reached for the holster on his belt where he kept a handgun in case he ran into a feral hog or rabid coyote on the farm. He grabbed the 45 caliber 1911 pistol and started rapidly firing at point-blank range toward the AI-control center located below the robot's shoulders.

catgcgccgccgtattaaaattcgcacccatgatgcgtatgcgatggaacgcatttgcgcgcatgcgccgccgtattaaaattcgcacccatgatgcgtat

The third round pierced a thin aluminum cover, sparks flared from its chest, and the robot collapsed on the ground like a chunk of scrap metal.

He thought to himself, "Dang, I swear that Agrobot was trying to kill me. I better report this incident to the sheriff." Of course, he'd afterward call the All-Nippon Robotics Agro-division representative in Richmond to make a complaint about the malfunctioning agrobot. He called Charles County 911 to tell the dispatcher about it. "Hello Mable, this is Jimmy Cummings and I need Sheriff Coleman to come over right away. It malfunctioned and I had to shoot it. I don't want to be charged with murder," he joked but was perhaps slightly serious.

Mable replied, "Sheriff Coleman is on river patrol, but Deputy James should be there in twenty minutes."

"Okay, Mable. Tell him I'll be waiting for him in the west sod field," he said as he terminated the Grid link.

His e-phone then alerted him that another agrobot near the barn was malfunctioning and also had auto-shutdown. He drove his truck to where the agrobot was kneeling with both its arms and knees on the ground. This time he kept his pistol in his hand as he approached the agrobot. He bent over to look under the robot and saw a green light as the agrobot quickly reached backward with its claw arm, grabbed him by the neck, and squeezed like it was a bursting tomato.

Coleman was just about to dock the boat at East Lake when he received a call on the boat's police band radio, "George, it's Mable. Jimmy said there's been an incident at the sod farm. Deputy James is already on his way but I think you should get there as soon as possible. It sounds serious like there was a shooting or murder."

"I hope Jeffrey can handle things until I arrive. I'm still on Chick Lake and have to dock at River Haven first. I'll be there in twenty minutes."

Coleman pulled near the dock and hastily gave Olsen a slip of paper with the Grid coordinates from Jason. "Here is where to start the search, Al. It could be anywhere near there or farther out. If the team finds anything, just call Mable and I'll meet them."

"Okay George, Let's stick to the plan as much as possible. Let the die be cast," Olsen replied and quickly jumped onto the dock to await the dive team.

"I'll talk to you when I can," Coleman replied, steering his boat toward the lock, and turning his siren and blue flashing lights on. At the lock, he pressed the emergency override code opening both lock gates at the same time since the lake and river water levels were now nearly even, and he

gcgaacgcgatggcgtaagcgatggcgaacgcgccgctggcgaacgcgtgcgcgaacgcgctgccggcgaacgcgatggcgtaagcgatggcgaacgcg

quickly sped forward at full-throttle. After clearing the campground dock, he opened the valve to the nitrous-oxide tank for an extra power boost toward River Haven Marina. His boat could do sixty knots and he was sure to get complaints from boaters and riverfront residents, but this was an emergency. The white wake of the freshly churned river behind the boat's stern spread in a tall V-pattern wave as he sped downriver.

Sheriff Olsen took the long detour, because of the damaged US 60 bridges, to reach the long, paved driveway to Exgenics Farm. His Chiefmaster Supercruzer drove to the closed front gate and stopped. The window on the adjacent security guardhouse opened and a security guard questioned, "Can I help you, officer? We haven't seen any deputies from Kent County here in a while. Fishermen aren't trespassing on our land anymore and there's an empty lake now also."

"Yes, you can help me. I'm Kent County Sheriff Albert Olsen and I'm here to ask Dr. Gerardo and John Gregory some questions about an ongoing investigation."

The guard replied, "Hold on a minute Sir. Let me see if they're here. I haven't seen them, but they might have arrived before my shift started," he said shutting the tinted window but could be seen talking to an e-screen.

The window opened again and the guard spoke, "Dr. Gerardo is on vacation for two weeks, but Mr. Gregory can see you. He's busy though with some corporate legal affairs and doesn't have much time. He's up in the old farmhouse at the end of the road on the left. I just need you to sign the visitors e-log," and the guard opened a side door and walked to the Supercruzer with an e-screen in hand.

Sheriff Olsen said while signing the log, "Thank you for your help."

The guard walked back through the door, pressed a nearby switch, and the gate automatically opened.

The Supercruzer started pulling forward, and while the guard door closed, Olsen glimpsed, out of the corner of his eye, an automatic submachine gun leaning next to the guard's desk.

He drove about a half-mile up past an old tobacco barn and a solar intensifier electric power array. The Supercruzer parked in front of the farmhouse next to a white Supercruzer also parked there. He got out, walked to the front door, and rang the doorbell e-cam.

The front door soon opened and an overweight, gray-haired older man greeted him, "Hello, I'm John Gregory. Can I help you, Sheriff Olsen?"

"Yes, if you can. I want to ask you some questions about an ongoing investigation I'm involved in."

catgcgccgccgtattaaattcgcacccatgatgcgtatgcgatggaacgcatttgcgcgcatgcgccgccgtattaaattcgcacccatgatgcgtat

"I'll help if I can. Come into the conference room and sit down," he said leading Olsen to what was once was the dairy farmer's family room.

Gregory continued, "I haven't met you before Sheriff, so it's nice to meet you. I've heard good things about you though. We've always supported Kent County Sheriff's Department extremely well with our donations. How do you like your Supercruzers?"

"They're good machines and reliable. I really like the coffee and donut option on my Chiefmaster," Olsen smiled.

"I noticed a white Supercruzer out front, do you ride in it often?"

"When I'm here, I usually take a unidrone taxi from Washington and then just use whatever vehicles are on the farm for local transportation, like to Williamsburg for groceries. However, with the bridge out, I drove to Richmond instead. I've been here all week and am taking a working vacation and rural respite from life in Washington."

"Yeah, I think a crowded big city would wear me down too. The traffic there's a nonstop jam."

"Yes, that's why I like using drones and since I'm the Exgenics Corporate Attorney, they're a business expense."

"Well, since you don't have much time, I want to know how you were involved with the sale of Old Forge Lake property to Kent County? With the dam break, Kent County faces a big liability, but we've found certain documentation that shows some irregularities associated with the sale."

"I'm sure the title is clean and there were no liens on the property. I handled all the closing documentation myself."

"Well, we found some printed engineering reports indicating Old Forge Dam was structurally unsound and your farm pond, which collapsed during the storm last week, was shoddily constructed by a cheap contractor from Newport News. He died Monday, but we found paper copies of permits and plans in his office files," Olsen began his bluff.

"I sent a deputy there yesterday and he searched his unorganized filing cabinets all day. We also found a printed note from a Washington engineering firm recommending Old Forge Dam be torn down and reconstructed. We're fortunate to find this information after the suspicious data loss of your building permit from Kent County's records. As an attorney, you know that failure to disclose known material defects before a real estate sale constitutes fraud and the former owner is liable for such defects. We also believe there may be criminal intent as well. We're getting a warrant to search Gridcom records related to this matter."

"Exgenics never knew about any defects. The county wanted the land for a museum and park."

"First thing tomorrow, I'll be talking to Judge Freeman for the warrant and our District Attorney to start formally drafting charges against Exgenics and its Corporate Officers officially registered with the Virginia Secretary of State's office. We'll be in touch," Olsen said as he stood up from his chair and turned toward the front door, "One more thing, what were *you* doing in Charles County this week?"

"I was talking with the county manager at that old man's funeral about donating funds to help rebuild the Chickahominy Bridge. We've got a few employees over there and the detour is inconvenient for them."

"No, I mean on Sunday morning?" Olsen said playing his gambit as he took a last glimpse at the attorney and saw the glimmer of fear in the attorney's eyes and a bead of sweat forming on his forehead. Olsen walked out the farmhouse door, slamming it loudly behind him.

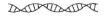

Chapter 15: A Murderer is Killed

Green Acres Sod Farm

2:00 p.m., Thursday, July 1, ….

Coleman arrived at the River Haven dock in twelve minutes, jumped off the boat, hastily tying a line to a cleat, and ran to Ole Bessie in the parking lot. He turned the key, revved the engine, activated the siren, and sped down the gravel driveway and onto the paved road. However, his nitrous oxide booster tank was still empty, so he just pressed the gas pedal to the floor, and the old engine roared. The transmission groaned from the high gear torque, but he knew Ole Bessie wouldn't let him down.

On the race to the farm, he radioed Jeffrey but had no reply. He arrived at the main farmyard, parked next to Jeffrey's patrol car, and heard gunshots from behind the metal barn. He pulled a knob opening his trunk, jumped out, grabbed his shotgun, and ran toward the shots. He turned the barn corner and saw Jeffrey standing near Jimmy's body and three agrobots that had collapsed onto the ground.

"What happened? Tell me everything." Coleman asked.

"First, I went to the west sod field and saw an agrobot laying by the sod truck. It was shot several times. So, I drove here looking for Jimmy. I found him laying dead with his neck about snapped off. Three agrobots were standing inoperative and I didn't think much of it at first. Just a moment ago, they activated and came toward me. I saw one had a bloody claw hand, so I knew it was the killer. I shot that one first with my shotgun. The first slug and second buckshot shell went right through the torso power pack and it collapsed. The others began to attack me and it took four shells on one, and I emptied my pistol on the other. It was like that shootout against the time-traveling killer robot in that old movie."

"Wow, that sounds straight out of some science fiction novel, but I see the bloody claw right there," Coleman said pointing at the murdering robot

gcgaacgcgatggcgtaagcgatggcgaacgcgccgctggcgaacgcgtgcgcgaacgcgctgccggcgaacgcgatggcgtaagcgatggcgaacgcg

collapsed on the ground. "It's like their AI-chips malfunctioned and they just wanted to kill anyone they saw."

"Poor Jimmy. He must have shot the first one in the field, but the others surprised him here. I guess he won't be making the big fishing tournament now. He was looking forward to that."

Coleman replied, "Yeah, I'll miss him and his barbeque, but I'm really sorry for Karen. I must tell her what's happened right now," as he thought of Jimmy's wife and three young children. "Jeffrey, call Reverend Morrow and the ambulance volunteers. Afterward, stay and fully document the murder scene since the agrobot manufacturer is liable for Jimmy's death. We need to ensure there's no technicalities or loopholes their high-powered lawyers can use to avoid a big settlement with his family."

"I'll take a bunch of e-phone pictures for evidence as usual."

Coleman added, "I heard there's a chance for a storm this afternoon, so find some tarps and cover the bloody robot hand with a plastic bag too. Also, see if you can remove the AI-module from an agrobot that attacked you, but not the murderer. We want that one intact as evidence if there's a trial, but I have a feeling Karen will be rich when this is settled. I want Jason Dickson to look at an AI module before anyone else touches them."

"Why Jason?"

"Besides his hobby of fixing electronic gadgets, he's also a computer wizard and might be able to see what went wrong with the agrobots. Plus, he's our newest citizen deputy," Coleman smiled with pride.

"Jason's a deputy?"

"I deputized him Wednesday night. I knew he could help locate the Captain's phone and Judge Saunders said it was okay."

Just then, Jeffrey's e-phone rang with a call from dispatch. He answered the call and Mable said, "Hello Jeffrey. Is George with you?"

"Yes, let me hand the e-phone to him."

"George, I have some messages from Al. The first one is 'he won the bet and you have to pay now.' The second is 'the fish hook is baited'."

"Thanks, Mable. Tell the ambulance volunteers to come to the sod farm buildings. Jimmy's dead, but please don't tell the Grapevine. I'll tell Karen now. Jeffrey will wait for the ambulance and gather evidence," he said and turned off the e-phone.

"Jeffrey, I think events are out of control and I've got a hunch we're involved in something bigger than we can handle, so we must be extremely careful. I've got a plan to work with Sheriff Olsen that I'll tell you about later. For now, tell people I'm going on vacation with Olivia to the mountains of North Carolina for a week. Please spread that information

catgcgccgccgtattaaattcgcacccatgatgcgtatgcgatggaacgcatttgcgcgcatgcgccgccgtattaaattcgcacccatgatgcgtat

around today and tomorrow, especially via e-vid or e-phone. Also, I'm putting you in charge after I leave," he said with a wink.

"Will do, George."

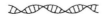

Coleman drove down the farm road to the lake and knocked on Jimmy's door. The door opened and, like he'd done on multiple occasions before, bluntly told Karen, "Jimmy is dead. He died in a farm accident." As she started sobbing, he gave her a kind embrace of sympathy to soothe her grief. He told her Reverend Morrow would come soon, left the house, and drove Ole Bessie to the Captain's house to meet the dive team.

He walked to the dock, saw the team's boat was moored and found the team in the boathouse enjoying a jar of 'shine.

"We're off duty now," the lead diver said seeing the sheriff coming.

"That's ok boys, you've had a couple of tough days and need a break. The Captain would've wanted you to enjoy yourselves," he smiled.

The lead diver replied, "Yeah, he made some of the best 'shine on the Peninsula. Sheriff, here's the phone," and pulled the phone out of a diver's mesh bag and gave it to the sheriff.

"I hope we can find some evidence on it," Coleman replied.

"Well, there's a good chance. It's an old 'Fisherman Limited Edition' and those were the first waterproof models that came out. We couldn't get it turned on, so perhaps it needs a charge."

Coleman commented, "Maybe we'll get lucky. Where did you find it?"

"We started at the Grid coordinates you gave and worked farther away from the bank as Sheriff Olsen suggested. It was a tough search due to all the recent flooding and sediment, but luckily, we brought our underwater metal detector with us. We found a lot of old aluminum cans, bottle caps, and even an antique silver quarter from 1964," he said smiling and showing the valuable coin from his pocket. "We eventually dived deep to the bottom of the old river channel and found it."[59]

"Thanks for helping guys. Enjoy your 'shine break but there's a storm coming, so don't stay too long and boat to your berth safely. I'll grab a jar of 'shine for Ole Bessie too. She's probably thirsty too," he laughed.

The lead diver added, "Oh, I forgot to tell you, it looked like someone else has been diving here this week. We found a lot of old cans *not* covered with fresh sediment."

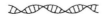

---

[59] During the last Ice Age, oceans were about 400 feet lower than currently and the Chickahominy River was a meandering river flowing to the sea. As the ice melted, the ocean level rose, flooding the old river channels with the Chesapeake Bay's tidal waters.

gcgaacgcgatggcgtaagcgatggcgaacgcgccgctggcgaacgcgtgcgcgaacgcgctgccggcgaacgcgatggcgtaagcgatggcgaacgcg

Jason and Grandpa had been fishing half the day and still hadn't much luck with catfishing. Jason caught one young seven-inch catfish not worth keeping, so he unhooked it and tossed it back. Soon, they heard the wail of Ole Bessie's siren near River Haven and then heading west down the road past the church. "Looks like George has an emergency. I hope everything's all right," Grandpa commented.

"He's been really busy this week with the murders and the rowing team incident on the river," Jason replied reeling in his line to see the herring bait was stripped from the hook by an experienced old catfish. He baited the hook again and cast it out into the channel.

"Yeah, it's unusual with so much happening at one time in Charles County. Life here is dull relative to city life, but sometimes things just happen. There are no coincidences though, remember?"

"Yes, Grandpa. We just don't know why. I better call Julie to tell her I'm picking her up later and that she'll be cooking dinner tonight. I'm sure she has updates on the rowing accident too. I'll use the pickup to get her since she probably wants to bring some suitcases of her things here. Her small autopod couldn't carry what she's likely bringing."

"There's an extra dresser and empty closet in the guest bedroom she could use until we better figure out living arrangements. I wouldn't mind moving to the guest bedroom and you use the master bedroom where I sleep. That way, you can have more privacy," he winked. "After a while, we can move things around in the house when we figure things out more."

"Good idea Grandpa," Jason said as he called Julie from his e-watch. "Julie, how are you doing? Any news from the college?"

"I'm doing fine but we should go to a memorial service tomorrow. They held a random lottery for the different religions to find out the time of each service. I'm Episcopal and that service is at 12:30 p.m. right after the Atheist service, but you're Baptist, and that is 5:30 a.m. right after the Buddhists. That Equal Religion Amendment to use government property equally for any religious purpose makes life difficult," she commented.

"Yeah, if you have a religious ceremony in one religion, you must have a similar one in all other religions or you're discriminating against somebody else's religion."

Julie agreed, "Yes, but really the problem is that with so many religions, it limits the time for each service to only a half-hour. Of course, the Satanists are having their midnight service on the lawn outside the chapel since they won't enter a building used for worship by other religions," she scoffed. "Which service do you want to attend Jason?"

catgcgccgccgtattaaattcgcacccatgatgcgtatgcgatggaacgcatttgcgcgcatgcgccgccgtattaaattcgcacccatgatgcgtat

gcgaacgcgatggcgtaagcgatggcgaacgcgccgctggcgaacgcgtgcgcgaacgcgctgccggcgaacgcgatggcgtaagcgatggcgaacgcg

"Let's go to the Episcopal service since the Baptist one is so early and all that incense from the Buddhists might affect my allergy," he laughed. "I want to ask you something too Julie."

"What question is it now Jason?" she said remembering happily the nightly series of questions that led to their sudden marriage.

"Grandpa and I ate the leftover spaghetti for lunch and we haven't had any luck catfishing. Do you want to make dinner tonight?"

"Yes, I've practiced cooking with Mom all day. I'm afraid my dad will be eating leftovers of the same practice dish for a month, but I hope you both will like it. I need to go to the store and pick up some more ingredients since my first two attempts were slight disasters," she laughed.

"I'm sure the third time will be the charm," Jason replied with kindness but thought he and Grandpa might need a backup dinner plan just in case. "What're we having?"

"It'll be my surprise," Julie answered.

"What time should I pick you up? I'm coming in the truck, so you can bring some suitcases and other things that won't fit in your Autopod."

"Maybe at 5:30? That'd give me time to autopod to the grocery store in Grantville and pack my bags too."

"I'll see you then. Love you," he said as he disconnected, re-baited the hook, and tossed the line in the deep waters.

The discussions with Grandpa from earlier in the morning kept whirling around in the back of Jason's mind, "Grandpa, I've been thinking about what we discussed this morning and trying to understand it all."

"I'm glad Jason, that shows you're following a logical train of thought. Remember that thinking deliberately and critically is an orderly process. First, you gain knowledge, which is just learning basic facts and truths. However, you also have to learn to separate these from opinions."

"How do I know what is true?"

"Jason, real truths don't change often but can be changed when the thirst for knowledge reveals new facts. It's tempting and easy to allow your heart to guide you, but your mind must analyze different facts and sort them to determine the truth. After you gain knowledge, you can begin the process of reasoning to understand the way things are. However, to gain this understanding, it's important to sort different arguments and resolve any conflicts before arriving at a conclusion. When this process is completed, you finally have wisdom."

"I see, but sometimes it's hard telling the truth from incorrect information or assumptions. There are even flat-out lies the media tells."

gcgaacgcgatggcgtaagcgatggcgaacgcgccgctggcgaacgcgtgcgcgaacgcgctgccggcgaacgcgatggcgtaagcgatggcgaacgcg

Grandpa replied, "There's a concept from a theologian-philosopher named William of Ockham who said something like this, 'when faced with two possibilities, the one with a simpler explanation and fewer assumptions is most likely true.' This rule of logic is 'Occam's Razor'."

"That kind of makes sense."

"Also remember the Latin question, 'Qui Bono?' which means 'Who benefits?' When people talk and want you to do something, they often act in their own interests trying to convince you to agree with them. In such cases, I think it's a good idea to always ask this question and be a skeptic by thinking critically of their intentions."

"That's good advice, Grandpa. It congeals what we discussed earlier."

"Jason, don't be afraid to learn from others though. Read the many great philosophers and others who gave us the gift of their thoughts and wisdom. The Bible has a lot of wisdom too and especially read the Book of Proverbs. It can help guide you when all else fails."

"Grandpa, I've been thinking that scientific principles too are sometimes helpful to understanding things."

"What do you mean?"

"Well, for example, those laws of physics developed by Sir Isaac Newton, 'objects at rest stay at rest' and 'objects in motion stay in motion' sort of apply to life too. If you do nothing in life and are lazy waiting for things to happen, nothing will happen, but if you keep moving and doing, things will happen as a result."

"Yes, that world is like that Jason."

"Also, using scientific principles gives me a new interpretation of the poem I read by Yeats. In thermodynamics, the study of energy transfer, there's something called entropy. It's sort of the measure of order and chaos within a system. A lot of energy is invested in keeping things in an ordered state but without energy supporting it, things fall into chaos. If this happens, the system then finds a lower level of stability with enough energy to maintain the new, lower entropy level. Lots of chemical reactions work this way. Yeats' poem was about how the world's order broke down with chaos the result and people were looking for a new world order."

"Yes, that interpretation seems valid. Poets aren't easy to understand and you're free to make your own conclusions as to what they meant with their words. That entropy concept sounds a lot like the Seneca Cliff."

"What's that?" Jason asked.

"There was a philosopher and teacher in ancient Rome named Seneca who first discussed, in his way, how civilizations take a long time to build, but fall apart quickly.[60]   I think maybe that old phrase 'falling off a cliff' comes from it."

"That sounds similar, just he wasn't a scientist and didn't know about entropy," Jason laughed.

"Another great one of Seneca's observations is that we're in the process of dying every day. Each day brings us toward our inevitable ends. So, perhaps it matters more how we live than how we die."

"No Grandpa, I think both are equally important. I think some people are confused and put too much importance on death when they should focus more on how to live with each other. They're afraid of dying because death is an ending and a great unknown. Science can't explain it other than saying our bodies and minds stop functioning. Religion calms our fears of this unknown, giving us the promise of something afterward. Religion gives hope with death where science provides no answer. However, some people die with a purpose. They choose to make their deaths valuable, like a heroic firefighter who dies in a fire saving a child's life. This selfless act of sacrifice gives their death meaning, demonstrating how well they lived to benefit others," Jason logically explained.

"Good answer, Jason. I think our talk today has ignited the fire of wisdom in your mind. Hopefully, that fire will keep burning throughout your life. Remember all we've discussed today as it'll help you on your journey down the River of Life," Grandpa said and smiled thinking that today's talk was already affecting the young man.

Just then, Rufus barked toward the house. They turned their heads to look and saw Ole Bessie parking in the driveway. Sheriff Coleman got out of the car, waved when he saw them fishing, and walked to the dock.

Coleman met them on the dock and spoke to Reverend Dickson first, "Tim, I've some sad news."

Grandpa replied, "What's happened? We heard your siren earlier."

"Jimmy Cummings is dead. It looks like his agrobots went crazy and killed him. After arriving at the scene, Deputy James had to shoot all of them when they attacked him too. He's still there gathering evidence. Later, I'll need Jason's help examining one of the AI-modules from them."

"Poor Karen and his kids," the Reverend replied in shock.

"Yes, I already told her. Hopefully, Reverend Morrow can get there soon to comfort them."

---

[60] Seneca the Younger was a stoic philosopher and advisor to Emperor Nero before Nero ordered him to commit suicide. His *Letter to Lucilius, Number 91'* discussed how great cities rise slowly, but fall quickly.

"We'll help also," the Reverend said. "The Pleasant Hill congregation will support his funeral just like Mt. Carmel did for the Captain and Macy."

"That's a good idea." Coleman replied and then looked at Jason and said, "Can you help with the agrobot's AI-module when I bring it later?"

Jason replied, "I'll see what can be done."

Coleman continued, "I have the Captain's phone now too. The divers did find it in the lake. It would be great if you can take a quick look. It just may need a charge," as he showed Jason the old cellphone.

Jason replied, "Let me see." Coleman passed the phone to Jason, who opened the flip phone and saw it wasn't working. "It doesn't seem to be damaged, but it was underwater for a long time."

"Yeah, I know, but is there a chance you can access its data?"

"You never know, but there's a chance. If not, I can still hack Gridcom, but I'd rather not because they might detect me. First sheriff, let's try charging it. Come with me to my electronics workbench in the garage. Grandpa do you want to take a look too?"

"No Jason, I'll sit here and watch the fishing poles."

They both walked to Jason's cluttered workbench and he put the phone on an old induction charger base. "We'll see in a minute if it works."

"That's good Jason, while we wait, I want to talk to you about something. I still consider you a deputy since we still seem to have an emergency. Sheriff Olsen from Kent County and I think something really big is going on. I want you to be extremely careful and keep all your communications with me secure. I'll try to visit you and talk in person if possible and if not, I'll only use my office land-line phone to your old kitchen phone line. Do you understand?"

"Yes, Sheriff. When I hacked Gridcom for the phone location, I concealed my tracks *very* well. That's sort of standard practice in the hacker world. The phone has charged now, so let's see if it works." He pressed a rubberized switch and it activated. "It works, so the battery was only discharged, but I'll still need to hack the passcode. It's an older model but if I can't hack it, I'll have to crack it open and access the memory chip directly. That takes a long time, so I'll attempt it later. Anyway, I need to finish fishing with Grandpa and pick up Julie, since she's cooking dinner tonight. I'll look at the phone and AI-module tonight."

"That's fine Jason, I'll bring the module later. See you then," Coleman said as he climbed into Ole Bessie and drove up the driveway toward Charlestown.

Jason returned to the dock where Grandpa was still fishing, "I hope I can help the sheriff on the phone without further hacking," he said.

"I know you'll do your best. Perhaps your electronics knowledge will help more than your hacking abilities. So much has happened this week. Jimmy's dead now. Then there's the Captain and Macy and the rowing team. All these deaths and accidents in such a short time. It's almost like God is testing our community like Job to see how much anguish we can bear and still keep our faith."

They fished for another hour without much luck when Grandpa looked southward and saw dark clouds approaching. "I think this good weather is ending. Let's head inside soon. We've had a good day talking and fishing, Jason. I'll hope you remember today, and what we discussed, the rest of your life," he said as he baited his hook again and cast it into the channel to take his chances waiting for a last passing fish.

A few minutes passed, and Grandpa noticed with his finger a slight extra tug on the line. "Jason, I've got a bite." He stood up from his chair, pulled the rod backward, and reeled the line slightly to set the hook. He now felt a fish pulling hard on the line, so he arched the rod backward and then lowered the rod to reel in a few feet of line. He continued repeating this maneuver until the fish was about ten yards away. He was excited at his catch, started feeling goosebumps, and the hairs on his head twitched like static was in the air. "Do you feel that Jason?" he asked.

Suddenly, a flash struck the tip of Grandpa's boron-nitride fiber-reinforced fishing rod and the electrical arc of a lightning bolt continued along the fishing line toward the water.[61] Jason and Grandpa collapsed simultaneously, from the compression wave of the immediate thunderclap, onto the gray-weathered deck boards of the dock.

---

[61] Boron nitride fiber is an electrical insulator unlike carbon fiber which is conductive.

gcgaacgcgatggcgtaagcgatggcgaacgcgccgctggcgaacgcgtgcgcgaacgcgctgccggcgaacgcgatggcgtaagcgatggcgaacgcg

Chapter 16: Small and Big Discoveries

"Frank"

4:00 PM, Thursday, July 1, ...

Jason laid unconscious for several minutes on the dock before he was aroused by Rufus licking him on the face. He opened his eyes, rolled his head, and saw Grandpa laying on the dock nearby with his eyes closed. Jason crawled on all fours to Grandpa and gently shook him.

"What happened?" Grandpa muttered in confusion as he revived.

Jason, still not fully coherent, slowly replied, "I think lightning hit us, Grandpa. Are you okay?" Jason asked helping Grandpa into a lawn chair.

"I don't' remember a thing," he responded, "but my ears are ringing."

Jason replied, "There was a flash and the next thing I remember was feeling a warm wet tongue on my face. Rufus was licking me." They rested a few more moments in a shellshock state and Jason asked, "Do you feel better now Grandpa? I think the bolt hit your fishing rod."

"I guess so. I remember now a flash of white light and felt a wave of peace cover me. For a moment, I thought I saw Sarah," he calmly replied.

"My ears are ringing too," Jason replied. He looked at his e-watch and the health monitor's EKG cardiac report indicated that his pulse was high, but his heartbeats had a normal sinus rhythm.

"Grandpa, let's put my e-watch on you and check out your heart," and he pulled off the magnetic watchband and slipped it around Grandpa's wrist tightly. Jason waited about 10 seconds and looked at the e-watch.

"Your pulse is high too, but the beats are normal. Let's both stand up for a moment and see how we feel," Jason added.

They both stood up carefully and looked at each other.

"I feel fine. I think the Lord decided today was not our time to join him. Not many people survive a bolt of lightning like that and live to tell about it," Grandpa commented seriously. "I think we should go back to the house to rest a while and see if we still feel okay."

catgcgccgccgtattaaaattcgcacccatgatgcgtatgcgatggaacgcatttgcgcgcatgcgccgccgtattaaaattcgcacccatgatgcgtat

gcgaacgcgatggcgtaagcgatggcgaacgcgccgctggcgaacgcgtgcgcgaacgcgctgccggcgaacgcgatggcgtaagcgatggcgaacgcg

"That's a good idea, but let's clean up things here first," Jason said as he closed the patio umbrella on the dock's picnic table. I think it will really start storming soon," he said seeing dark clouds brew closer.

"Let's gather the fishing poles," Grandpa said grabbing the fishing pole he'd dropped. He lifted it and started to reel in the remaining line. "Jason, there's still a fish on it," he commented feeling a tug. He reeled it in, pulled a strange-looking fish out of the water, and just dangled it in the air. "Look at this fish Jason!" he exclaimed while staring at the mostly yellow fish with large black spots and bulging eyes.

"What kind of fish is it? It looks similar to a sugar toad but perhaps it's more like a fish from that illegal Dr. Seuss book," Jason excitedly commented about their bizarre river discovery.[62, 63] "Grandpa, hold it and let me grab it so I can look closely." Jason went to grab the fish, but as his hand nearly grasped the fish, he felt the tingling of a small electrical shock. "Ouch! That fish just shocked me Grandpa!" he exclaimed. He tried to touch it again, felt another tingle of an impending shock, and pulled his hand away again. "I felt it shocking me again."

"Jason, you hold the rod and I'll wear my oyster shucking gloves to grab it. Those thick rubber gloves should insulate me if the fish is giving some sort of shock." Grandpa looked in his tackle box, pulled out a small pair of thick gauntlet-like gloves, and put them on. He grabbed the fish by its back with a glove and the fish immediately puffed up like a small balloon by gulping air into its stomach. Many short, sharp dark spines immediately protruded outward like porcupine quills from between its fine scales. Luckily, the spines couldn't pierce the thick rubber glove as he held the inflated fish. "This fish has some surprises," Granpa commented.

"It's surely some sort of pufferfish, but look at this!" Grandpa continued while pointing with his other hand to the fish's abdomen and underbelly. There, he saw a strangely patterned area of black scales in between mostly white scales.

"I swear, that pattern almost looks like an electrical resistor element or a circuit," Jason exclaimed while examining closer.

Grandpa pointed to the dorsal fin with a long black hair-like thread amidst the fin's spines, "What's this? I've never seen anything like it."

---

[62] Sugar toad is the colloquial name for the Northern Puffer Fish, family: *Tetraodontidae;* species: *Sphoeroides maculatus.* Common to the Chesapeake region; local seafood delicacy.

[63] Publication of Dr. Suess books was banned by this time, due to inappropriate content for children. The only copies available had been preserved by their original owners who refused to turn them in for the recycling bounty.

catgcgccgccgtattaaattcgcacccatgatgcgtatgcgatggaacgcatttgcgcgcatgcgccgccgtattaaattcgcacccatgatgcgtat

gcgaacgcgatggcgtaagcgatggcgaacgcgccgctggcgaacgcgtgcgcgaacgcgctgccggcgaacgcgatggcgtaagcgatggcgaacgcg

"That's weird. It almost looks like a nanowire, but it's growing from the fish.[64] Something is surely strange here," Jason said as he suddenly felt a chill as goosebumps erupted briefly all over his body. "Grandpa, we should keep this fish because we've made a major discovery. I'll give you a pair of needle-nose pliers to unhook it and put into the bait bucket, but let me fill it with water first," he said as he dipped the bucket into the river.

Grandpa carefully examined the barbed hook that pierced the fish's lower lip. He took the pliers and snipped the hook in two. "This is the best way to not injure it any further," he said pulling the barb from the fish's lip. Grandpa commented further, "Look at the teeth on this fish. Four teeth just like a pufferfish. Two upper and two lower ones. The upper teeth are almost joined and the lower ones are too. Those teeth are like a beak or jaw-like tool, best for cracking mollusks and crustaceans, but I'm sure that fish will eat anything it finds."

Grandpa lifted the still air-inflated fish over the bucket and dropped it into the water. The fish floated on the surface for a moment, let out a big burping noise from the air in its stomach, and sank to the bucket's bottom.

"That fish just farted!" Jason chuckled.

Grandpa just shook his head side-to-side at his grandson, who still had some socially awkward and inappropriate behaviors. He stood there looking into the bucket for a moment and saw his black-colored glove that had held the fish. It had some white slime globs on it. "I don't like this slime either. I've never seen a puffer before with it. I don't know what this stuff is but I sure don't want to touch it just in case it's infectious or some defense mechanism like those spines," Grandpa said, and just to be safe, he carefully rinsed off the gloves in the river before pulling them off.

"Jason, can you carry the bucket to the boathouse? Let's keep the fish there in the bait tank until we determine what to do."

"Yes, Grandpa," Jason replied as he grabbed the handle of the old 5-gallon paint bucket and carried the heavy bucket to the boathouse. Inside,

---

[64] Industrial production of silver-doped carbon nanotube monofilament wires had begun several years before this period after the ability to "grow" wires was developed by Nanowire Company, a privately owned subsidiary of Exgenics. Nanowire began producing linear nanowire spools in varying conductivities, including related products such as superconducting nanocoil and woven EMI shielding mesh. After this period, private corporations were made illegal with the 30th Amendment (Only things that are alive have legal rights. Inanimate entities have no fundamental 'natural' rights per the U.S. Constitution). A shareholder of any corporation or company was thereafter required to bear legal civil and criminal liability in proportion to their level of ownership in the business. Also, the individual personal names of any shareholders of public and private companies and their percentage ownership became public information after this period.

catgcgccgccgtattaaattcgcacccatgatgcgtatgcgatggaacgcatttgcgcgcatgcgccgccgtattaaattcgcacccatgatgcgtat

he went to the old 60-gallon glass-sided aquarium they used as a bait tank, hoisted the bucket over the edge, and carefully poured the contents in the tank. The tank's water level rose higher but didn't overflow. He looked inside and saw the fish just hovering above the tank bottom amidst some old chess pieces Jason used as tank decorations. The fish slightly moved its side fins around in circular motion.

Jason switched on the aquarium air pump, but it immediately stopped. He thought about the air supply and hastily rigged a small hose feeding air from the carpentry workbench's air compressor. Afterward, he went back to the dock where Grandpa had kept gathering things to bring back inside the boathouse.

"What took so long?"

"The old aquarium air pump is broken, so I used the air compressor."

"Okay let's put up this stuff and think what else to do. I don't feel anything else wrong after the lightning strike, so I think we're okay and can skip going to the doctor."

"I feel fine too." Jason replied just as it started to rain, "Let's hurry up to beat the thunderstorm," hearing a rumble of thunder getting close as raindrops began falling in earnest.

They returned to the house soaking wet and sat down at the kitchen table to discuss their plans for the rest of the day. Jason commented, "My first day of married life sure has been a whirlwind so far. I wake up married, have a great time fishing, and get hit by lightning. I still have to pick up Julie and help the sheriff with the Captain's phone data. Plus, Jimmy Cummings was murdered by his agrobots and now I need to help the sheriff with the AI module too. He should be dropping it off later. Today is just crazy!"

"Don't forget about catching that strange fish," Grandpa added.

"Yeah, forgot to mention that discovery. That fish is a monster, like Frankenstein, so maybe we should nickname him 'Frank'," he joked.

"Sure, let's call him Frank," Grandpa replied. "Welcome to married life, Jason. Sometimes life just gets chaotic and all we can do is fight one fire at a time. Always try to fight the biggest fire first and then work toward the smaller ones. Now go pick up Julie and I'll call Doc about that fish. He can advise us what to do. Then I'll call Reverend Morrow to see how Pleasant Hill can help the Cummings family."

"Sheriff Coleman said to be careful in our communications, so don't discuss the fish on the phone with Doc Longtree."

"Ok, I'll make up an excuse for him to come," Grandpa said scratching Rufus behind the ear as he laid on the floor by a drool puddle.

Grandpa walked to the kitchen phone and dialed, "Doc, it's Tim. Can you come over here right now with your van?"

Doc replied, "What's wrong?"

"I think Red has broken his hind leg or something. Can you bring that portable X-ray machine you showed me once?"

"Are you okay Tim? Are you sure it's old Red?" Doc questioned.

"Rufus is fine, but you need to look at old Red. He limped back from hunting possums in the woods and must have gotten hurt."

"Okay, I'll be there after I finish delivering this calf. Tom Jones' prize-winning dairy cow Big Bertha is having difficult labor this time around."

"Come when you're done there. Red can wait a little while," Grandpa added so that Doc wouldn't be too alarmed and could take his time.

"Just keep Red calm and relaxed as much as possible until I arrive," Doc replied as he now knew that something was seriously wrong since the Reverend was asking him secretly to come over very soon.

"We'll see you then," Grandpa replied and hung up the phone.

"That sounds like a good covert phone call Grandpa. I think you'd make a good deputy too," Jason chuckled. "Let me pick up Julie now," Jason said and went to the garage, started the truck, turned on the windshield wipers, and drove amidst the thunderstorm to meet Julie.

※※※※※

Coleman drove to Buddy Peters' auto shop and parked just as the thunderstorm arrived and rained hard. He quickly ran a few steps into the open door of the garage bay. Buddy was changing some tires. "Buddy, I stopped by for a spare nitrous gas tank for Ole Bessie. With all that's been happening lately, you better order a few extra tanks from Richmond."

"No problem George. I've one in stock. I'll order more tomorrow, but I'm not sure my gas supplier is open due to the July 4th weekend. If they are, their delivery drone can drop off more tanks by the afternoon.

"Do what you can Buddy. Also, I want to talk about something else."

"What is it, George?"

"Well, I'm leaving for North Carolina tomorrow on vacation with Olivia. Jeffrey is in charge of things this weekend while I'm gone, but I want him to have a backup deputy to help him. Would you mind if I deputized you again as I did during the hurricane a while back?"

"That's fine, I'd be glad to help George."

"You're hereby duly deputized in Charles County for the weekend. No need for the oath since you already know it. Also, could you quietly find out who from the Sandy Point Hunt Club will be in town this weekend?"

"Why's that?" Buddy questioned.

"I have a hunch we might need help later with something. I just want to be prepared in advance in case there's trouble. Let me back Ole Bessie into the spare garage bay and swap tanks." He quickly ran to his patrol car in the rain and backed inside the garage. Coleman popped open the trunk, unscrewed a fitting, and removed the gas cylinder. He took the new nitrous oxide gas tank and installed it. "Thanks, Buddy, I'll talk to you later," he said as he drove back toward the sod farm.

༚ᐊᏚᐷᏚᐊᏚᐷᏆ

Coleman arrived at the sod farm just after the ambulance volunteers placed Jimmy's body into a zippered bag and loaded him for the long trip to the morgue in Kent County. He pulled out an umbrella and walked over to the ambulance. The driver rolled down his window and said to the sheriff, "I can't believe Jimmy is dead. Such a tragic accident."

"It was *murder*. That agrobot intentionally killed him, but don't tell anyone," Coleman replied and walked over to Jeffrey's patrol car and sat down in the front passenger seat.

Jeffrey said, "I've been writing my incident report on my e-screen, George. I wanted to capture all the details while they were fresh in my mind. I took a lot of photos and pulled two AI-modules just in case. One from the agrobot in the sod field and another from one here by the shed. I labeled them Exhibit A and B with a black marker."

"Good job Jeffrey. I gave Jason the phone and talked with Buddy. He agreed to be your deputy while I'm gone on my 'vacation' and I had him begin rousting up members of the hunt club to be on alert. Do you know how Karen is doing?" Coleman asked.

"No, but Reverend Morrow drove over to the house. He stopped here first and I showed him what happened here since it's a good idea to have an independent witness of the scene."

"Good thinking Jeffrey. I want you to finish here and stick to your normal duties this weekend, but be prepared for anything."

"Well, I do have my big date with Dr. Graves tomorrow night."

"I hope that goes smoothly. Now, let me take these AI modules to Jason, and then I'm heading home to tell Olivia to pack her things. Keep communications to a minimum, but radio or call Mable if you need me," he said as he left Jeffrey's patrol car, walked in the rain to Ole Bessie, and drove away down the now muddy farm road.

5:00 p.m., Thursday, July 1, ….

It had been another long day at the farmhouse office for John Gregory like every day had been since the dam break. He was simultaneously managing numerous Exgenics shareholder contacts and monitoring the progress of multiple ongoing ops. Though exhausted, he called Dr. Gerardo for his daily e-vid update, "Ernesto, it's been crazy, but we're keeping things mostly under control."

Gerardo asked angrily, "What's *not* under control?"

"We've got a problem with that Kent County sheriff. He's going tomorrow to talk to a local judge for a warrant and have the district attorney draft an indictment for possible fraudulent activities at Exgenics. We don't need that kind of attention as you know."

"Well, let's eliminate the problem," Gerardo commanded.

"Gotcha covered Ernesto. One sheriff, one judge, and one attorney."

"It's a necessary evil. How's progress with the fishing tournament?"

"We've got a big surprise ready, Ernesto. Our think tank and best scientists found the perfect solution to our problems. It takes care of the fish and clears the area of witnesses. Any Exgenics connections will be totally ignored afterward."

"That's great news. I hope your plan keeps everything under wraps. I'm going to stay in DC this weekend for the festivities here, but contact me if there are any fireworks there," Gerardo joked.

"Just stay tuned to Grid News. You're in for a show better than the Washington Mall view of July 4th fireworks over the Potomac!"

Doc Longtree pulled his van up to the Dickson House, ran to the door avoiding the rain, and rang the doorbell. Grandpa answered, "Hello Doc. I'm glad you came."

"What's wrong Tim?"

"There's a fish you need to see in the boathouse."

"I sure was worried that something might be wrong with you because you were talking about Red."

"Sorry about that Doc, but it was the only way I thought would quietly get your immediate attention without much suspicion," Grandpa said grabbing umbrellas from the closet and giving one to the Doc.

"Is Jason here?" Doc asked.

"No, he went to pick up Julie at her house."

"I'm sure you've heard of their wedding by now. It was a beautiful ceremony. I hope all is going well with their marriage so far."

"Yes, everything's doing fine, but Julie is cooking dinner tonight and unfortunately, I'm expecting a disaster," he sadly commented while remembering breakfast.

They walked out to the boathouse, turned on the lights, walked up to the bait tank, and saw Frank lazily floating near the graveled bottom of the tank. Doc exclaimed, "Wow, that's a weird fish. I've never seen anything like it, but it reminds me of a sugar toad."

"Yeah, it looks a little like one. We caught it this afternoon and decided to keep it until we could figure out what it is. What do you think?"

"For sure, I'd say it isn't native to the river here."

"Look closer at it. See that top fin and look underneath its belly."

Doc carefully peered closer inside the aquarium tank, "There's a flexible wire growing from that fin and an odd ventral scale pattern doesn't seem natural. Let me examine it closer. Bring me a hand-held net."

"I'll get you one, but you'd better wear thick rubber gloves holding it since it puts out a shock when alarmed."

"Really? There's no electric pufferfish. There are some electric eels in the Amazon, but they're the only electrogenic fish species I know of."

Doc put on Grandpa's shucking gloves and used the net to scoop the fish out of the tank. He grabbed the fish softly by its tail, but this time the fish didn't puff up and was calmed by Doc's presence. Doc examined it closely, explaining his observations, "I see it's a male from the genital area. Its four teeth tell me it's in the Tetraodontidae family, like a Northern Puffer, but I don't know what species. Also, those patterns and that little wire are *not* natural and I can see no evidence that there are any scars from veterinary surgery to implant them inside the fish," he summarized while holding the dangling fish by its tail.

Grandpa replied, "That's why I wanted you to bring your tribo-ray."

"Hmmm, the tribo-ray machine might just work, but let's put the fish in a smaller container so I don't have as much water to image through."

"Will a bait bucket work?" Grandpa said pointing to the plastic bucket.

"Yes, just fill it with water and I'll put the fish in and get my tribo-ray."

Grandpa dunked the bucket in the bait tank partly filling it, put it on the boathouse's plank floor, and Doc released the fish into the water. As Doc took off his rubber gloves, Grandpa commented, "I don't see any slime on those gloves, Doc."

"Slime?" he questioned.

"When I held it, there was slime on my gloves after it puffed up. I washed it off my gloves afterward."

"That's too bad. It would have been interesting to examine," Doc said as he left to get his tribo-ray machine.

In a few minutes, Doc brought back a large and heavy suitcase with the lead-shielded tribo-ray machine inside. He opened the case and lifted the heavy unit and sat it on the floor by the bucket. He then placed the phosphorescent viewing screen on the opposite side of the bucket. "The fish seems calm and isn't moving, so that should give us a good image. Now all I need to do is turn the hand crank for thirty seconds," Doc said as he bent over and started cranking very fast.

"How does that unit work?" Grandpa asked inquisitively.

"A while back, some scientists discovered that when you pull sticky tape really fast from the tape roll inside a vacuum chamber, the rapid separation of the adhesive layers causes X-rays to be emitted. This phenomenon is called triboluminescence.[65] Inside the tribo-ray case is a vacuum chamber with an endless roll of sticky tape inside the unit much like one of those old 8-track music tapes you find in museums. There's also a set of internal gears that unwinds the tape at an extremely high speed. The crank handle I'm turning spins the gears. Finally, the viewing screen's phosphors are designed with a long afterglow after X-ray exposure to reveal the image when you're done cranking. Let's look at the image now," he said as he stopped cranking.

"Look at that fish!" Doc said as goosebumps rose while they both stared at the X-ray image. "There's extra structures inside it. Look at those wire-like things along its spine. Some wires go to its abdomen and a strange organ there with a lot of branching wires. Other wires go to its teeth. Finally, there is a solid, but tangled, structure inside the skull near the brain that all the wires connect to. I swear these features were grown there. I'm not a genetics scientist, but this fish seems designed and genetically engineered!" he concluded.

"So, it *is* a Frankenfish. Someone designed this fish and it wasn't God" Grandpa replied while thinking that mankind had opened Pandora's box and proven mastery over life itself, which always before was God's realm.

"It must have escaped from some research facility. The only place nearby I know nearby doing genetic engineering is a company called Exgenics over in Provident Forge. It's run by Dr. Gerardo, a famous scientist. I was a veterinarian for their cows when they first opened, but I haven't been there in years since they hired a full-time corporate vet. They weren't doing any fish research there. They were using cow's milk to manufacture cancer drugs, so it couldn't have come from there."

"Well, it's a mystery for sure. What should we do with this fish then?"

---

65 Triboluminescence is a method of generating X-rays without electricity. When this technology was adapted for diagnostic methods with the development of the hand-cranked tribo-ray, an inexpensive portable X-ray machine was available for widespread use, and was especially useful when portable X-rays were needed.

"Discoveries like the one we've made have consequences, so we should keep it to study until we figure out what to do. Let's carefully put it back in the tank and feed it something. How did you catch it?"

"We were catfishing and used chopped herring bait,"

Just then, Rufus entered the boathouse, walked up to the bucket, and sniffed the water. He started lapping a drink but suddenly jerked his head backward with a yelp as his tongue touched the surface.

"I don't think Rufus likes that fish either," Grandpa joked as he grabbed the bucket and poured the contents back into the large tank.

"Maybe the fish gave him a small shock?" Doc questioned. "Let's give it some herring and see what happens."

"Okay," Grandpa said and went to the boathouse's small refrigerator grabbed a leftover herring bit, and tossed it in. It sank to the bottom and they watched the fish swim close. It took a bite and turned its face toward the Doc and Grandpa who were observing through the aquarium glass.

Doc commented, "I swear that fish just smiled at us."

"I got that strange feeling too," Grandpa agreed. "Let's have some coffee and discuss this more. Jason will be here soon with Julie, and Sheriff Coleman is also coming later."

As he brewed a fresh pot of coffee, Grandpa continued, "I forgot to tell you that Jimmy Cummings was killed this afternoon. His agrobots went crazy and murdered him."

"That's terrible news. Poor Karen and his kids."

"Yes, it's tragic. There have been so many deaths recently. It doesn't seem like a coincidence," he said skeptically they were random events.

While Grandpa poured coffee, Jason and Julie entered the kitchen through the door from the garage. Jason greeted them carrying a heavy suitcase, "We're here Grandpa. Hello Doc."

"Hello Jason and Julie," Doc said. "How's married life?"

"Fine, but we'll see how dinner goes," Julie said with a chuckle.

Doc commented, "I just saw that strange fish you caught today."

Jason replied, "Yes, I told Julie all about it and us getting hit by lightning. She wanted us to see a doctor, but I told her we feel fine, except for a slight ringing in our ears."

"You were hit by lightning?" Doc questioned with surprise.

Grandpa chimed into the conversation, "Yes Doc, I didn't have a chance to tell you. We were fishing and about to quit for the day when we saw bad weather coming. I got a bite and began reeling in that fish when we were knocked unconscious by a lightning bolt. Afterward, the fish was still on my line and Jason put it into the bait tank."

gcgaacgcgatggcgtaagcgatggcgaacgcgccgctggcgaacgcgtgcgcgaacgcgctgccggcgaacgcgatggcgtaagcgatggcgaacgcg

"Any other symptoms besides ears ringing? Doc asked with concern.

Jason replied, "No, the bolt's concussion wave only knocked us over."

"It's amazing you're still alive. That's an unusual way to catch a fish. The catch of a lifetime and a real discovery. I'm sure that fish was genetically engineered. The X-ray proved it with all those wire-like structures inside its body. It's like a parallel nervous system was grown inside and there's a weird structure near its brain too." Doc commented.

"Who'd do such a thing to a poor fish?" Julie commented.

Doc replied, "We don't know yet, but if Exgenics is involved, Dr. Gerardo has poked his finger in the eye of God. It violates all laws of nature and that leads nowhere."

The doorbell rang and Jason opened the door. Sheriff Coleman stood there wearing his brown trench coat and a wide-brimmed hat. "Jason, I've two AI-modules here from the agrobots to examine," he said.

Jason replied, "I'll see what I can do after dinner tonight. I still have to look at the Captain's phone too. Which do want me to examine first?"

"The phone, since that's the more important case. I see Doc is here."

Grandpa replied, "We're all in the kitchen. Come on in George if you've time. I'm sure you'll be interested in what we're discussing."

"I'm about done for the day and on my way home to Olivia now, but I'll stay for a bit," he replied as they walked to the kitchen.

Everyone greeted him and Grandpa next told the sheriff, "George, we're talking about the fish we caught after the lightning hit us."

"What? You were struck by lightning?" Coleman replied in shock.

"Yes, Jason and I were as close as it can hit and still live," Grandpa replied and briefly recounting the incident for the sheriff.

After hearing the Reverend's story, Coleman replied, "That sounds like a tall fishing tale, but if true, things are starting to make sense to me."

"What do you mean?" Jason asked.

"Well, I think the events of the past week have all revolved around that fish. Last weekend, there was the big dam break, but Exgenics' farm pond dam broke too. Then the Captain and Macy are murdered after he was fishing. What if he caught another fish like yours? What if someone knew he caught it just by surveilling his cell phone and murdered him? This means the same people are listening to *all* calls."

"That sounds like a big conspiracy for sure," Doc replied, "but Exgenics does genetics research and is the most logical origin of this fish."

Coleman continued, "Yes it could be. It's like that rabbit hole in Alice and Wonderland. Unfortunately, once you go down that hole, it's hard to get back because your thinking is forever changed."

catgcgccgccgtgtattaaattcgcacccatgatgcgtatgcgatggaacgcatttgcgcgcatgcgccgccgtattaaattcgcacccatgatgcgtat

Jason added, "That means Gridcom is helping them for sure if they intercept all phone RF-signals.[66] The murderers must control a Grid AI-monitor and are scanning all communications."

Coleman continued, "Perhaps it's Gridcom or only a lower-level employee. Whoever is involved are playing Charles County like a banjo. They're just making music and picking us off one by one, like notes in their song, while we listen. Plus, they're extremely thorough too."

"What do you mean?" Jason asked?

"Well, Jimmy Cummings delivered sod to Exgenics on Monday to hide their broken dam. Now he's dead, killed by agrobots. Also, the contractor who repaired their pond's dike was killed in an autotruck wreck too."

"If the agrobots are controlled by the same people, this is serious," Jason added. "This means they can wirelessly control, access, and override the programming of *any* AI-controlled or Grid-connected device."

"Yes Jason, that's why I need you to examine the AI-modules too. However, it's more important to get data from the phone first."

"Why the phone?" Julie asked and listened by the kitchen stove as she started browning hamburger meat and frying chopped onions in a pan.

Coleman replied, "Well, all our evidence is circumstantial. There's nothing directly linking these events to Exgenics. If anything on the phone ties to them, Judge Saunders will issue us a search warrant."

"That makes sense now," Julie replied as she continued cooking.

"I think similar events have happened in Kent County too. There's been a lot of mysterious deaths since the dam break and after Sheriff Olsen investigated Exgenics' involvement with the dam failure. All his investigation's leads were dead ends and I mean *dead* ends."

Jason added, "We should look at recent death records for patterns."

"That's a good idea, Jason. I'm sure they're at the medical examiner's office in Kent City. The real mystery though is what secret is so important to hide by killing so many people. It's of the highest order and a conspiracy within high places of power and money," Coleman concluded.

"Not all the deaths are murders though. What about the Rowing Team? They died after they were hit by lightning." Julie added.

"Yes, that's true, but there's still a connection to the river there. Tim and Jason were hit by lightning too before they caught that fish. Also, two fishermen suddenly died earlier this week from unknown causes. Their bodies at the Kent morgue are likely awaiting autopsies. With all the recent deaths, bodies there must be stacked up like firewood."

---

[66] RF is abbreviation for radio frequency

Julie interrupted as she looked at Sheriff Coleman and Doc, "Would you gentlemen like to stay for dinner? I'm cooking a special meal tonight and would be honored if you could stay. It'll give you a chance to talk more and the sheriff will surely want to see the fish Grandpa caught."

Coleman nodded his head in agreement since Olivia knew he often worked past dinner and Doc said, "I'll call Susan but I'm sure she's fine with it. By the way, Susan is glad to be your sponsor. I see your noses are clean today, so that's a good sign to tell her." He chuckled.

"Gentlemen, dinner will be done in an hour. Why don't you all go outside and look at that fish? Let me concentrate on my cooking so I don't make any mistakes," she wisely commented. "I'll look at that fish with Jason later," she added as the men stood up and took the female hint to get lost. They also seriously hoped for no cooking accidents.

Chapter 17: A Fish of a Different Color

Tribo-ray Image of "Frank"

7:00 p.m., Thursday, July 1, ….

The men gathered around the bait tank observing the fish in his temporary home. Doc commented, "If this fish came from upriver, it lived in freshwater, but not all freshwater fish can handle brackish, partly-salty water like the lower Chick. This one's doing fine though. Let me look up Tetraodontidae on my e-phone."

Jason immediately replied, "Stop Doc, don't do that. If Gridcom is monitoring every communication, they're also monitoring your data. Their AI-technology would instantly know you were searching about that fish. You'd be letting the criminals know we're on to them."

Coleman added, "Jason's right. Luckily, I don't use an e-phone or they might already know we suspect them. When I was in the Army, Intel Ops scanned every enemy signal and used their analysis for targeting."

"Well, how do we solve this scientific mystery then? What is this fish? How does it function? What is that slime Grandpa told me about? Does it really have electrical capabilities? Finally, what do we do with it?"

Jason replied, "For now, we can learn what we deduce using the scientific method and observations. Of course, there's a hacking solution to this problem to hide an online e-phone search, but I'm ruling that out since I'm *done* with computer hacking," Jason firmly said.

Coleman replied, "Jason, what if Judge Saunders gives you another search warrant if the Captain's phone connects the murders to Exgenics?"

"Well, that might be okay under ordinary circumstances as long as I had the law protecting me from my Federal sentence. If it were just an ordinary hack, I'd say it'd be easy to do. However, if Gridcom is involved, that'd be like Saint George slaying the dragon. With the AI-assets and Grid tools they could possibly use against us during such a long and thorough hack, we'd get caught, and I'm not willing to take that risk."

gcgaacgcgatggcgtaagcgatggcgaacgcgccgctggcgaacgcgtgcgcgaacgcgctgccggcgaacgcgatggcgtaagcgatggcgaacgcg

"We understand you don't want to get caught again," Coleman replied.

"There *is* one way, however," Jason replied after thinking further.

"What do you mean Jason?" Coleman asked.

"The only way is to seize control of *all* Grid nodes. There's an old computer subroutine I found on my father's hard drive that might work, but I've never tried it before. However, if I had such access and control, no one else could stop us and it'd be almost impossible to track the hack's origin. We could search anywhere on the Grid without detection and Doc could then research this fish with impunity. Of course, we could also hack into Exgenics. Once we breached their local datacom firewalls, we could search their stored data in complete secrecy."

"Well, I'm not asking you to do that yet," Coleman replied. "Jason, you're like our secret weapon in all this. We don't want to use you unless the situation fully needs your special talents. For now, let's limit your involvement to helping with the Captain's phone and those AI-modules. Let Doc study the fish so we understand what we're up against until all is clearer. Right now, there's an enemy out there that would like us to show our hand. Let's keep this under wraps and study how to approach this problem to move forward wisely," Coleman said and thought of Sun-Tzu's ' *Art of War*' strategies for their current situation.

They all nodded their heads in agreement and Doc said, "Let's review our observations so far and try some science experiments then. First, we know that it's a male fish. It's mostly colored yellow with large black 'eye' spots above its pectoral fins and one similar "eye" spot surrounding its dorsal fin. It eats herring, 'inflates' when alarmed like a pufferfish, and was likely raised in freshwater. It has some likely electrogenic properties and was hit by lightning. Finally, it has strange patterns on its abdomen, wires or electrodes within its body, and a weird tangled structure with tentacles near its brain from what the Reverend and I saw earlier. Would you like to take a look, Jason?"

"Yes, Doc," Jason replied.

Doc filled a bucket with fresh water from the boathouse's large steel sink which was used for rinsing catfish filets. He placed the fish in the bucket, cranked the tribo-ray, and all stared in amazement at the image.

"That fish is a monster from a horror movie!" Coleman exclaimed.

Doc replied, "Yes, but it's a small one. I think the bigger monster is the person who created it. Let's keep it in the bucket and observe if it has electrical capabilities. Jason, go grab an old-style multimeter and some electrodes from your workbench."

catgcgccgccgtattaaattcgcacccatgatgcgtatgcgatggaacgcatttgcgcgcatgcgccgccgtattaaattcgcacccatgatgcgtat

As Jason ran to the garage, Coleman commented, "That fish is evil. We must kill it."

Grandpa replied, "How do we know it's evil George? It didn't choose to be genetically designed and turned into such a monster."

Doc agreed, "Yes, I agree. We surely don't know enough about this fish yet to make such a decision anyway, George."

Coleman replied, "Okay, let's just not make any hasty decisions then."

Jason soon arrived with his multimeter and asked Doc, "Should I set the meter to measure AC or DC voltage?

"Let's try DC voltage, Jason, since that's how electric eels usually operate. Their voltage can be high, so set the meter for a higher range."[67]

Doc took the multimeter wires with their metal electrical probe tips and stuck them into the water, but the dial didn't move. "Let me touch the fish with both probes," but the meter's galvanometer dial didn't move.

Jason said, "Doc, Wait. You just put it in freshwater but we caught it in the brackish water from the river. Salty water is more conductive."

"That's worth a try," Doc replied. They filled a second bucket with brackish river water and transferred it with a small net to the bucket. Doc inserted the electrodes into the bucket again and, as he lightly touched the side of the fish, he saw a small voltage reading.

"I wonder what would happen if I touch that wire thing on the fin and its front teeth," Doc said as he probed the fish just underwater. As he made contact with both locations, the meter's dial went to nearly full scale.

Jason replied at the reading, "That's almost 1,000 volts."

Doc concluded, "This fish certainly has electrical capabilities then. An electrical system was *grown* inside the fish."

Jason said, "It was hit by lightning and lived, so maybe it's immune to external electric shocks?"

Doc replied, "Well there's only one way to find out. Jason, could you grab that old shop light over there by the workbench and plug the extension cord into a wall outlet. Then, I'll hold the lamp near the fish. I

---

[67] *Electrophorus Voltai*, a predatory electric eel species from the Amazon River basin, can stun small or large animals (prey) with shocks at nearly 1,000 volts. Scientific observations show they can hunt in packs. Electric eels are not true eels, but are members of the Knifefish family. They can gulp air to breathe and may leap out of the water if agitated. They electrically sense their prey, control their electrical impulses, and produce powerful pulses at up to 400 Hertz (times per second). Hertz (Hz) is a unit of frequency used for electrical currents and wireless radio communications. The pioneering scientist in the study of electricity, Michael Faraday, first examined electric eels and their electrical capabilities with his galvanometer in the early 1800s.

gcgaacgcgatggcgtaagcgatggcgaacgcgccgctggcgaacgcgtgcgcgaacgcgctgccggcgaacgcgatggcgtaagcgatggcgaacgcg

want to first observe what happens when the fish is in proximity to electricity before I drop the cord in the water."

Jason grabbed the light with its old-style bulb and plugged its cord into an outlet. The bulb glowed brightly as he handed it to Doc. Doc took the lamp and held it near the bucket. Suddenly, the bulb grew bright and burnt out. Inside the bucket, the fish puffed up and eerily glowed yellow for a few seconds before dimming. The fish deflated and some white slime floated away from small spines protruding from its body.

"Well, I didn't expect that reaction. "Maybe this fish attracts electricity to keep its electrical system working. It's also luminescent and glows like a firefly or some deep-sea fish," Doc commented with surprise. "After seeing that, there's no need to test dropping the cord in the water."

Coleman added, "Doc. I know someone who can help you study this fish. Nick Abramovich is a Russian scientist working as a genetics technician at Exgenics and might know something about this fish. He works second shift though, so I can't reach him right now. Maybe I can bring him here tomorrow to examine it?"

"Well, I'm not sure what else we can learn here now, so it's worth talking to him," as Doc agreed, pouring the fish back into the bait tank.

Grandpa chimed in, "Okay, we'll keep Frank here overnight until we decide what to do with him. He's got everything a fish could need: water, an air hose, and another bit of herring," he laughed and tossed a herring in the tank. Frank comically took a bite with his clown-like face.

Soon they heard Julie yelling to the boathouse, "Dinner's ready!" as she eagerly hit the old iron triangle outside the porch with a serving spoon and it rang a 'ding, ding, ding'. "Wash your hands and come eat!" she hollered.

Jason called back to her, "We'll be there in a minute, sweetheart."

Grandpa lamented, "I haven't heard that old dinner chime since Sarah died, but I'm glad Julie's ringing it now," as he hungrily looked at Jason with a smile. "Let's head to the house and see our dinner surprise," he added in a slightly worried tone.

The men went to eat dinner after washing hands in the boathouse sink. They entered the kitchen and the aroma coming from the oven was enticing. The kitchen table was covered with a fresh table cloth and the plates and silverware were set with care.

Julie said invitingly, "Everyone please sit down. This is my first dinner cooking as a married woman and I wanted it to be special. I'm glad I bought enough at the grocery store to feed this army," she chuckled as she pulled her main entrée out of the oven.

catgcgccgccgtattaaattcgcacccatgatgcgtatgcgatggaacgcatttgcgcgcatgcgccgccgtattaaattcgcacccatgatgcgtat

"Everything looks wonderful," Jason said as they all sat at the table. Jason sat on one table end and the other men sat in the middle chairs. An empty seat at the other table end was strategically reserved by the men for the new woman of the house.

Julie continued, "Everyone, please pass me your plates so I can serve you a piece of lasagna," and she carefully cut the slices from the baking pan and put them strategically on each plate to leave room for the salad and side-dish of broiled fresh broccoli seasoned with garlic salt.

As Julie sat down and everyone's plates were full, the Reverend said, "Let me say grace." Everyone bowed their heads and he continued, "Oh Heavenly Father, we thank You for today and the fellowship of friends who have joined us. Please bless this food to nourish our bodies so that our minds are strong in our efforts to earn Your praise. Amen."

Everyone replied "Amen," and they started to taste each dish.

Jason commented, "This lasagna is wonderful, Julie." Everyone around the table nodded their heads in agreement as they ate with passion.

Grandpa said, "It's so nice to have a delicious home-cooked meal made by a woman here again. Women just have a special knack for cooking that men don't often have," complimenting her to show she'd passed her first dinner cooking exam with flying colors.

Julie beamed a smile in reply.

Coleman began the serious dinner conversation, "Well everyone, let's talk about our situation. As you know, there've been strange happenings in Charles County this week and the same in Kent County. After seeing that fish, I'm confident this whole situation is directly linked to Exgenics and if my hunch is correct, *all* the recent accidents really have been murders. However, proving that'll be difficult. If Jason finds more data on the Captain's cell phone pointing to Exgenics, Judge Saunders will give us a search warrant for more evidence or even maybe an arrest warrant if we can identify the murderers."

Grandpa commented, "If this is true, we're in a dangerous situation."

"I agree," Doc said.

Coleman continued, "Sheriff Al Olsen from Kent County and I have started coordinating our investigation and have a plan to work together. If Exgenics is the guilty party, we've set a trap that's baited and now waiting to catch its prey. Unfortunately, Al is the bait, so now is a critical time when we need to be very careful."

"I hope no one else gets hurt with all this intrigue," Julie added.

Coleman replied, "Me too Julie, but if my hunch is correct, these potential killers are ruthless and nothing likely will stop them until they're

gcgaacgcgatggcgtaagcgatggcgaacgcgccgctggcgaacgcgtgcgcgaacgcgctgccggcgaacgcgatggcgtaagcgatggcgaacgcg

caught. That fish is the key to a secret so big that these people are willing to indiscriminately murder *anyone* who discovers it.

"That means *we* are now on their list of targets," Jason added seriously.

"Yes, I'm afraid so Jason. I also set up a diversion that Olivia and I are leaving for a weeklong vacation and told Olivia she needs to be out of town in case something goes wrong. Tomorrow morning, she's driving to her parents in Richmond for safety," Coleman replied.

"Can the Grapevine help advertise your vacation?" Julie added.

"Yes, Julie. I think it's a good idea to use all tools at our disposal," Coleman replied with a smile as he looked toward Jason. "Part of our plan is I'm going undercover to investigate deeper and surveille Exgenics Research Farm. My new base of operations is the Captain's house. No one will look for me there."

Doc added, "I'll help by going tonight to the Blue Lagoon for a drink at the bar and spread the news of your vacation, listen for gossip, and look for suspicious people. I know the Chick people will help too, so I'll talk to the Chief. They have many eyes and ears near Exgenics Farm."

Coleman replied, "That's a good way to gather intelligence with all these strange goings-on along the river. I'll use the Captain's truck a while to maintain a low profile and I need to hide Ole Bessie too. Tim, could I keep her in your old barn? There's no room at the Captain's house to hide her away from satellite imagery."

"You're worried about satellites too?" Julie questioned.

"If this potential conspiracy is huge, satellite data could surely be compromised," the sheriff wisely replied.

Grandpa agreed, "It's possible and the barn has room for her George."

Thanks, Tim," Coleman replied. "If Jason can drop me off later, I'll use the Captain's truck afterward for mobility. I want to be inconspicuous the next few days."

"Sure sheriff, I'll drop you off there," Jason replied.

"Jason, check out that phone and AI-modules," Coleman continued.

"Hacking the phone is priority, then the AI-modules," he replied.

Coleman continued, "I'll put Deputy James in charge while I'm 'gone' but I'll still be in command behind the scenes." He then thought back to his army days and said, "Right now, we have to assume all communications are compromised by the enemy, I mean killers, so let's keep all talk clean and use coded language if necessary."

Jason replied, "Sheriff, I can help with secure 'off-Grid' communications between us. I have an old long-range two-way walkie-talkie radio for you so we can communicate as needed. I rebuilt the circuit

catgcgccgccgtattaaattcgcacccatgatgcgtatgcgatggaacgcatttgcgcgcatgcgccgccgtattaaattcgcacccatgatgcgtat

board to be compatible with my 'Brick,' my electrical device design project from college. That old cell phone will finally get some practical use too." Jason chuckled thinking about his 1984 Motorola DynaTAC 8000 brick phone he was given to fix as a gag by an electronics repair customer. He'd recycled the phone's plastic case, rebuilding it custom with old and modern components.

Jason said, "Sheriff, I'll give you the walkie-talkie before you go. Any voice communications are encrypted, so using AI voice-printing to identify us is nearly impossible, but as a backup, I'll give you a list of code names and words to use."

"That's good Ops Com security, Jason. Everyone, it looks like we have an action plan. Let's meet here for breakfast tomorrow to report and update our plans further if that's OK with you Tim?"

"That's fine George," Grandpa answered.

"I'll cook breakfast then. I need practice," Julie insisted and smiled.

"If there are any incoming messages for me, I'll route them thru Jason and his radios. Thank you for the lovely dinner, Julie," Coleman concluded and stood up to leave. Doc also said goodbye and they both went on their way to their homes and wives.

Grandpa said to Julie, "I want to compliment you again on dinner tonight. It was wonderful."

"You're welcome Grandpa, if I may call you that now."

"Sure Julie, please call me 'Grandpa'. I'm going now to call Reverend Morrow to ask how Pleasant Hill can help with the Cummings Funeral, so both of you do whatever you want."

Jason replied, "OK Grandpa. After we do the dishes, Julie and I will look at Frank in his tank, and afterward, I'll work on the Captain's phone."

As Jason and Julie started cleaning the kitchen, Grandpa went over to the kitchen phone, picked up the old receiver, dialed an e-phone, and talked to the pastor of Mt. Carmel Baptist.

In a few minutes, Grandpa hung up and told them the news, "Looks like George is staying with the Cummings to comfort Karen and her kids until her parents arrive from Charleston. I told him we support his parish and will help as much as we can."

"Julie and I will both help too," Jason replied.

"We'll talk more about it later when we find out when the funeral is scheduled," Grandpa said. "I'm going upstairs to work some more on Sunday's sermon and then I'm going to bed. If you see the light out, I'm asleep. Look after the house and don't forget to feed Rufus outside."

gcgaacgcgatggcgtaagcgatggcgaacgcgccgctggcgaacgcgtgcgcgaacgcgctgccggcgaacgcgatggcgtaagcgatggcgaacgcg

"We'll take care of everything, Grandpa. Goodnight," Jason and Julie chimed in unison as Grandpa walked upstairs to the master bedroom and closed the door. They then continued doing the dishes, cleaned up the kitchen table, and brought a bowl of dog chow to Rufus by his dog house.

8:30 p.m., Thursday Evening, July 1, ...

The sun was setting over Kent County as Sheriff Olsen patroled in his Supercruzer. He was still thinking of George and their plans as he drove along Kent City Highway towards Talleysville. If Exgenics was guilty, they'd soon surely show their cards and he was the number one target. He would be on alert for diversions or possible direct actions against him.

His Supercruzer was driving along at a leisurely pace, and suddenly, it made a right turn at Carps Corner onto Old River Road. It auto-accelerated uncontrollably to nearly 120 miles an hour in just a few seconds, careening dangerously fast down the paved road. While it auto-steered, Olsen tried to disengage the autodrive system but it was unresponsive. After another helpless ten seconds in the driver's seat, the Supercruzer fish-tailed right toward the swamp where Big Creek joins the Pamunkey River, swerved off the road, and rolled over three times before ending up partly submerged under the water. The driver's side was above water, but the driver wasn't visible after the airbags deployed then deflated, covering Olsen like a death shroud. Gradually over the next few minutes, the crumpled SUV sank nearly a foot deeper into the soft, muddy marsh bottom. There was no further movement.

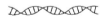

catgcgccgccgtattaaattcgcacccatgatgcgtatgcgatggaacgcatttgcgcgcatgcgccgccgtattaaattcgcacccatgatgcgtat

Chapter 18: The Stakes are Raised

Olsen's Supercruzer Wreckage

9:30 p.m., Thursday, July 1, ….

Deputy Jeffers was patrolling eastbound Route 60 near Lanexa, thinking about his date tomorrow with Robin, when Kent County EMS Dispatch chimed on his e-screen. "What's up dispatch?" he asked.

"There's been a serious vehicle accident near Carps Corner off Old River Road. Investigate and take command at the scene. Kent EMS and Fire have been dispatched. Grid coordinates uploaded."

"10-4," James replied as he immediately accepted the destination coordinates on his e-screen so the Supercruzer could drive in emergency mode. The Supercruzer made a quick, safe U-turn and drove toward the incident at high speed with blue lights flashing and siren wailing.

When he arrived in about 15 minutes, the Kent EMS and fire department teams had already shined spotlights onto the wreck amidst the darkness. He saw a black Supercruzer, with the Kent County Sheriff's logo, floating like an island forty feet away from the road and fifteen feet from solid ground. The mucky, muddy bottom prevented walking to the wreck, so the rescue team improvised a bridge using a long fire truck ladder to crawl above the marsh to the vehicle. A first EMS rescuer slowly approached on the ladder. "The ladder's stable, but it sank another inch from my weight. I'll look inside now," the rescuer yelled back to the rest of the team waiting in suspense by the road.

The EMS rescuer crawled forward over the driver's side of the SUV until he reached the driver's door with shattered window. He shined his flashlight inside, pulled on the deflated airbag, and saw the driver. He called out, "It's Sheriff Olsen like we thought. He's either dead or unconscious and strapped in tight by his seatbelt. I can't see his face, but his torso has drooped downward and his head is half underwater. Let me check for a pulse," he said as he grabbed the sheriff's left arm and felt for a pulse at the wrist. After waiting a few seconds, he yelled back to the rest of the Kent rescuers, "He's still alive, but his nose and mouth are really close to the water now."

The EMS rescuer continued, "I'm going to need an extra pair of hands to pull him out, but any extra weight might sink the Supercruzer deeper. Send me Brook. She's small and maybe light enough to help."

The young 105-pound member of the fire department carefully crawled over the ladder onto the crumpled front fender on the driver's side, but the SUV continued sinking.

As the water rose higher, the EMS rescuer commanded, "Quickly now, grab his left arm while I reach down for his head and pull his right arm."

They both pulled in unison just enough to keep his head out of the water. Using a razor-sharp pocket knife in his other hand, the EMS rescuer cut the seatbelt and the sheriff's hips and legs dropped into the water, and his torso was now in a better position to extract him from the wreck. They heaved upward together and pulled the sheriff's head and torso out outside the window opening. With a final coordinated tug, his body lay prone, face down on the rear side panel of the Supercruzer.

A stretcher was soon ferried by rope along the top of the ladder to the SUV. They loaded the sheriff's body on the stretcher and ferried the sheriff back to the bank. The EMS rescuers placed the partly-wet and unconscious sheriff onto a gurney for the twenty-minute ambulance drive to Williamsburg General Hospital.

Deputy Jeffers remained at the accident scene as the ambulance drove away, but he'd keep in touch via EMS Dispatch of any news about Al. He would go to the hospital later after the wreck was towed and realized he was now Acting Kent County Sheriff since he was second in command at the Sheriff's Department. If Al died, he could run for Kent County Sheriff in the fall elections. He smiled and thought Robin would be impressed if he were sheriff. He stared at the black Supercruzer a moment and thought to himself, "If I were already sheriff, I'd have been in that wreck."

⋉⊲⋁⊲⋉⊳⋌

Jason told Julie, "Now the kitchen's clean, let's go to the boathouse and look at our new friend. Then I've got to work at my electronics workbench on the Captain's phone."

"While you're there, I'll unpack upstairs and rearrange a few things. Since I'm going to be living here from now, I want to feel more at home and settled," Julie replied with a smile and they walked to the boathouse.

They turned on the lights and peered in the bait tank. The fish was resting on some aquarium gravel. "It seems Frank is relaxing," Jason said.

gcgaacgcgatggcgtaagcgatggcgaacgcgccgctggcgaacgcgtgcgcgaacgcgctgccggcgaacgcgatggcgtaagcgatggcgaacgcg

"He has a name?" Julie questioned.

"I gave him that nickname. It's short for Frankenfish," he chuckled.

"He looks lonely there," Julie said. "I almost feel he is watching us."

Jason replied, "Maybe Frank *is* watching us. When we saw inside his body with the tribo-ray machine, he had some extra structure near his brain. Perhaps that's some sort of extra artificial brain. Let me give him a herring bit to eat," Jason said as he went over to the refrigerator and took a bit, and tossed it into the tank. As it sank to the bottom, Frank cautiously swam to it and took a nibble.

"He just looked at us both and smiled!" Julie exclaimed.

"Yes, I think so. He did that the last time we fed him," Jason replied as Frank took another bite. "I want to show you something interesting. We did this experiment before, but now that it's dark, it might be a fun demonstration," he chuckled. He rummaged through an old box and found another light bulb, screwed it into the shop lamp, and pressed the switch to turn the light on. "Let's turn off the boathouse lights and we'll see what happens when I give him a little juice."

He switched the lights off and held the shining lamp close to the aquarium. Frank swam toward the light and, all of a sudden, the lamp glowed brightly and burnt out. Darkness immediately enveloped the boathouse except for an eerie yellowish glow from the aquarium as Frank puffed up, momentarily glowing like a huge firefly. The light soon faded.

"That's amazing!" Julie said in the darkness.

"Yes, it's almost like Frank has an attraction to electrical energy, or perhaps electrical energy is attracted to him. Doc thinks he has somehow been engineered this way for some reason."

"That's terrible. I can't believe someone would do this. It's not nice to fool mother nature," she commented at the violation of the sanctity of life and thinking the scientists involved had no ethics or morality.

"I agree, but Frank didn't choose to be a monster. It isn't his fault."

After looking at the glowfish for a few more minutes, Jason said, "Well, it's time to work in the garage."

They walked back to the house and Jason went to his electronics workbench and the phone. He opened a rubber plug covering the data port and inserted a cable connecting to his laptop computer. He thought this job would be easy if he could hack his phone password. Luckily, the Captain never used the phone's fingerprint scanner, and Jason was repulsed at the macabre thought of using a dead and buried man's finger.

He tried his password cracking algorithm a few times but failed. He stopped since too many more attempts would lock him out permanently.

He thought for a moment and decided the only way to access the data would be to open and disassemble the phone to directly access the circuit board and its digital flash memory chip. He was about to pry open the waterproof phone housing when he thought back many years ago to when he'd stayed at the Captain and Macy's house when Grandpa was in the hospital. During his stay, the Captain had let him use a cell phone to play electronic games and puzzles. He thought a moment longer deeply into his photographic childhood memories and pressed the keys in a specific sequence that he remembered seeing the Captain touch.

The screen lit up and activated. He pressed a few more buttons and was able to access the phone's electronic data storage chip and memory buffer. He downloaded the files to his laptop and looked now at the much larger e-screen. There were some recent photo images and at least several days of audio-video data still accessible.

He decided to look at the last picture images first, and there were a few with date stamps at 10:24 a.m., June 27. He saw a picture of a glowfish on a fishing line and another picture where the fish was resting quietly at the bottom of a water-filled bait bucket. He then started listening to excerpts from the audio-video track. The video track was mostly blank, however, since the Captain had put his phone in his pocket.

Later in the audio track, he heard a strange man talking and gunshots. He then heard Macy screaming, another shot, and after a minute, a final shot. Faintly in the background, Rufus was soon heard barking from far away. Rufus's barking became louder, but the recording ended when the phone landed in the water and there was silence.

Suddenly, Rufus started barking loudly from his doghouse just outside the garage door and Jason thought, "Rufus heard me play that tape. He's the only murder witness and must have seen and smelled the murderer."

Jason then examined the agrobot AI-module data. He looked at recent control program auto-updates and saw that a new update had been downloaded via the Grid this morning. Jason went upstairs to his bedroom, where he'd left his Brick, to radio the sheriff.

Julie was there and had just finished her improvised redecoration of his bedroom, which had been transformed into a more feminine environment. His plaid bedspread had been replaced with a flowery comforter and the window curtains changed to a matching flower pattern. A vase of silk flowers was added to the dresser too.

Julie said, "I decided to make our bedroom homier. Is that okay?"

"Well, it's sort of a surprise Julie, but you live here now too," Jason answered realizing now his life was permanently altered after marriage.

gcgaacgcgatggcgtaagcgatggcgaacgcgccgctggcgaacgcgtgcgcgaacgcgctgccggcgaacgcgatggcgtaagcgatggcgaacgcg

Living with a woman would be different than living as a single young man. He humbly accepted things would never be the same again. "I've cracked the phone and found some interesting files in the memory buffer. I need to contact the sheriff immediately," he told Julie.

Jason sat in his desk chair and radioed the sheriff with his Brick while Julie listened, "Breaker White Knight, Breaker White Knight. Over."

Coleman replied, "10-4. Let's start our chess game. My move is Pawn to e4. Any news Black Rook? Over."

"Have found a lost notebook with a message. My move is Knight to f6. Over," Jason responded in code language informing the sheriff he cracked the Captain's phone."

"Can I come and put the sow under the blanket? Pawn to e5. Over."

"Elizabeth's pen is ready. Knight to d5. Over." Jason replied.

"Let me drop off the bacon and pick up the prize so I can do my duty for my country. Pawn to d4. Over and out," Coleman said as he concluded the coded walkie-talkie transmission.

Julie asked, "What was that about? I couldn't understand a thing?"

Jason told Julie, "The sheriff will be coming here about the phone and wanted to put Ole Bessie in the barn. While I wait for him, let's search the Grid for information on all the recent deaths." Jason connected to the Virginia Department of Health Gridsite and located the vital statistics database of births and deaths. He narrowed his search to the Peninsula Subdistrict and saw a chart with locations of last year's deaths. He limited the chart's date range to display only deaths last week and saw that there were quite many in the region. Each death was marked with an icon explaining basic facts and whether it was natural, accidental, or related to a criminal case. The death locations were concentrated along the river.

"Look," Julie said, "There's a mark where the Captain and Macy were murdered, and there's the mark for the rowing team accident yesterday."

Jason replied, "Let me change the date ranges to show a typical week, let's say two weeks ago." They looked at the e-screen and a map appeared showing only two deaths from natural causes, one in Charles County and one in Kent County. Jason commented, "This is compelling data that something serious is happening and confirms what Sheriff Coleman was saying. Look at how many accidents and suicides there have been."

"That's terrible," Julie replied. "I can't believe somebody would kill all those people over a fish."

"I agree. Let's go outside on the porch and wait for the sheriff. That way, we won't wake Grandpa."

catgcgccgccgtattaaaattcgcacccatgatgcgtatgcgatggaacgcatttgcgcgcatgcgccgccgtattaaaattcgcacccatgatgcgtat

10:30 p.m., Thursday Evening, July 1, ….

Coleman soon arrived with Ole Bessie and asked Jason on the porch with a smile, "What did my deputy find?"

Jason answered, "The Captain caught one of those glowfish like Frank. Let me show you some images and replay key phone excerpts. Also, the agrobots had an unscheduled software update right before the accident."

"That's very suspicious, so those agrobots *did* murder Jimmy."

Jason set up his laptop on the porch and continued, "I think Rufus can identify the killer. When I replayed the murders, he started barking."

Coleman said, "Let's bring him to listen. I want to see his reaction."

Julie went to the dog house to bring Rufus while Jason started the data playback for the sheriff. Jason first showed two fish images taken in the bass boat. One revealed the glowfish on a hook and the other was of the strange fish in a bucket. He next played a call of the Captain telling Macy about the fish. Rufus perked up at hearing his beloved former masters.

The Captain put the phone in his pocket and the e-screen went blank. They next heard the bass boat's motor. "That's the Captain heading home," Jason said and then fast-forwarded to the Captain arriving and showing the glowfish to Macy.

"That's the strangest sugar toad I've ever seen," Macy commented.

"Yes, I agree," the Captain replied. "'ll take it to the Richmond fisheries and wildlife office tomorrow for them to examine. It's likely some invasive new species damaging the lake and river ecosystems."

Jason continued, "Let me skip ahead until the murders because there's a period of normal conversations and routine activities."

They next hear a knocking on the kitchen's screen door and a man saying, "Hello. Have you gone fishing lately?"

As they listened, Rufus now started to growl.

The Captain replied, "Yes, I was fishing this morning. Do you need a fishing guide for Chick Lake?"

The man replied briskly, "Did you catch anything? What's in that bucket over by the sink?"

The Captain replied with rising alarm, "Hey, what do you want?"

They next hear a gunshot at point-blank range and the Captain collapsing to the floor, followed by Macy's scream. They hear Macy fire a pistol she always kept hidden in a kitchen drawer, and the man says, "I'll get you for that. You almost shot me." Rufus listened and growled louder.

Jason interrupted and paused the playback for a moment, "I had to sound enhance that part since her voice was so soft in the distance. Let me restart the memory buffer playback."

gcgaacgcgatggcgtaagcgatggcgaacgcgccgctggcgaacgcgtgcgcgaacgcgctgccggcgaacgcgatggcgtaagcgatggcgaacgcg

They hear the screen door slam again and the footsteps of the man creaking on the wooden kitchen floor. They hear another close gunshot and searching in the Captain's pockets.

Jason said, "Here comes one of the last remaining video clips." For just a moment, they see strangely-angled kitchen images as the man puts the phone in his pocket. After that, they hear him walk through the house and another screen door slam. They hear a bump on the porch of a dropping gun and footsteps creaking on the old porch stairs to the lake. They begin to hear a distant barking that grows louder.

"Here comes the last video clip," Jason continued. They see the murderer's hand briefly as he pulls the phone out of his pocket, and releases the phone into the air at the end of the dock. The final images are a panoramic blue sky rotating toward a cypress tree at the edge of the lake as the phone fell into the water and darkness.

Jason, commented, "After that, the audio is mostly silent until two days later I heard a boat motor, some splashes, and some divers. After that, the battery lost its charge and the phone died."

Coleman replied, "That tape proves it was cold-blooded murder. I swear I've heard that voice before, but I can't connect it with a name and face. Let's look at the man's hand again. I thought I saw a ring."

Jason replayed the images with the hand again and they saw a class ring on the middle finger. "Let me look closely," Jason said zooming the image of the ring. "I can't read the year, but the ring says 'Harvard' on it."

"Well, that's a lead, but I need to have Sheriff Olsen listen to this voice track, Jason. I suspect he can identify the killer's voice. Let me take this phone to him so he can listen. Can you show me how to replay the audio-video clip of the crime?

"Sure, Sheriff." Jason showed Coleman a few keystrokes to replay the recorded segment and wrote down the phone's password for him.

Jason continued, "We also found a map from the Virginia Department of Health. Look how many deaths have happened near the river this past week," he said showing the death statistics map. "I haven't calculated the odds, but I bet the chance those are random deaths is one in a million."

Coleman replied, "That's scary to see. I didn't know about all those deaths in Kent and James Counties. I bet every one of the deaths is connected to someone who was near the river, or fishing, or knew someone fishing this week."

Julie added, "Whoever is doing this is evil. Why'd anyone kill so many people over just a fish, if that was the reason?"

The phone in the kitchen rang and Jason ran inside to pick it up.

gcgaacgcgatggcgtaagcgatggcgaacgcgccgctggcgaacgcgtgcgcgaacgcgctgccggcgaacgcgatggcgtaagcgatggcgaacgcg

"Hello, Jason?" Mable from Charles County Dispatch asked.

"Yes, it's Jason."

"I've got an urgent message for the sheriff."

"No problem. Hold on. Let me get him," he replied resting the phone down on the kitchen table and running to the sheriff outside.

"Sheriff, It's an urgent call from Mable."

Coleman ran to the kitchen and picked up the old phone headset with its twisted cord and listened. He replied, "Thanks Mable. Stay alert for any news and tell Jeffrey to proceed with the plan," hanging up the phone.

"What's happened?" Jason asked seeing the worry on the sheriff's face.

"Sheriff Olsen's been in a serious accident. He's unconscious at Williamsburg General in critical condition. I must see him urgently. Jason, I need to put Ole Bessie in the barn right now since I'm going fully undercover. I'll be driving the Captain's truck from now on. Can you give me a ride to his house now?"

"Yes, Sheriff."

"Let's go then."

"Do you want to take my bike or Grandpa's truck? It's stopped raining and is beginning to clear."

"Let's take the truck. With these wet roads, it's safer."

"I agree," Jason replied.

They both went to the porch and Jason told Julie, "We're putting Ole Bessie in the barn and I'm taking the sheriff to the Captain's place. I'll be back in t a half-hour."

Julie replied, "See you soon," after Jason briefly kissed her goodbye.

The sheriff climbed into Ole Bessie and drove down the long driveway to the barn just across the main road. Jason followed in the truck and opened the barn door. Coleman backed Ole Bessie into the dark opening of the cavernous barn where an old tractor rusted. He grabbed a duffle bag and backpack filled with gear, closed the barn door, and climbed in with Jason to drive to the now empty house on Binns Bank.

▷◁▷◁▷◁▷◁

Deputy Jeffers waited at the site of Olsen's wreck for completion of the accident cleanup so he could finally leave. It had taken two tow trucks nearly 30 minutes to pull the wrecked Supercruzer from the swamp as it was stuck deep in the muck. He called Kent dispatch from his Supercruzer, "All's clear at Olsen's wreck now."

"10-4, James," Dispatch replied. The dispatcher continued, "We've some sad news about the sheriff. He died at the hospital from his injuries. His skull was severely fractured from what the EMS team heard."

catgcgccgccgtattaaattcgcacccatgatgcgtatgcgatggaacgcatttgcgcgcatgcgccgccgtattaaattcgcacccatgatgcgtat

"That's terrible. What a loss and waste of a good man," he replied. "I'm heading home now. I've had enough overtime for tonight," he said as he thought of the tragedy and how he was now fully in command of the sheriff's department. He thought more and decided tomorrow he'd contact Rose Graham, the county manager, to make sure he was in good position to replace Olsen on the ballot in November. He smiled, knowing he'd impress Robin with this untimely promotion.

11:30 p.m., Thursday, July 2, ….

Sheriff Coleman drove to the hospital in Williamsburg and went straight to the emergency room. He talked to the human receptionist, "Hello, I'm checking the status of Albert Olsen, who was brought here earlier this evening."

"Are you related to the patient?" the receptionist asked.

"No, I'm not, but I'm a close friend and must urgently talk to him."

"I'm sorry I can't help you sir, but the medical privacy act prevents discussing patient status with anyone who's not family or a designated contact, but let me see what I can do."

The receptionist looked at the evening admissions data and said, "Well, in this case, I don't think there's any harm in letting you know his status since he's no longer a patient. He's dead. From the notes here, he died in the operating room. I'm sorry sir. You have our condolences."

"Dang," Coleman first swore and then felt sadness at losing his friend and a good lawman. He turned around and walked sullenly toward the automated door to leave the hospital. He thought to himself with guilt, "This situation *was* too big for us to handle. I should've known better. We had a plan but now we've lost. What am I going to do?"

He walked out the door and an attractive older woman dressed in medical scrubs ran up to him and asked, "Are you Sheriff Coleman?"

"Yes, I am," the sheriff responded.

"I'm Mrs. Johnson, the triage nurse. I was told to be on the lookout for an older black man asking about the Kent County Sheriff. Please come with me," she requested courteously.

Coleman turned around to follow the nurse thinking this might be a trap. If the Exgenics suspects were as powerful as suspected, they'd be looking for anyone asking for the sheriff and if they knew I was Charles County Sheriff, they'd be interested in completely terminating any further investigations.

He cautiously followed the woman down a long corridor and she opened a door to the recovery room. Inside the room lying on the bed was Sheriff Olsen. The upper part of his head was covered in bandages and his eyes were closed. His right shoulder also had a cast that extended partly over his arm to brace his dislocated shoulder.

The nurse said, "He's resting now. He has a pretty severe concussion from the accident but regained consciousness in the ambulance. His shoulder was dislocated too but we're not sure if that was from the accident or extracting him from the wreck, which we heard was done hastily as the wreck sank.

Coleman replied softly, "Is it OK if I stay here?" as he showed his sheriff's badge to the nurse.

"It's past visiting hours, but since he specifically told us about you and that it was a law enforcement matter, you can stay."

"Thank you, ma'am," Coleman politely replied as she left the room.

Olsen drowsily opened his eyes and softly spoke, "George, I'm glad you came. My Supercruzer went crazy and drove into the marsh. I heard from the ambulance EMS tech that I almost drowned while unconscious, so I'm lucky to talk with you my friend," he said forcing a smile amidst the dull pain he still felt after painkillers.

"I'm glad you made it out almost in one piece. We had someone murdered today by an agrobot that went out of control. The man delivered sod to Exgenics and another man, who repaired their pond's dike, died yesterday when his truck wrecked just like yours. Maybe his truck was on auto-drive mode too," he thought out loud in retrospect.

"Well, that adds this week's death toll. I've lost count of the accidents, suicides, and deaths from natural causes this week. I figured my wreck wasn't an accident, so I told the ambulance team to keep quiet and have the hospital fake my death. I'm 'John Smith' now," he said as lifting his wrist to show his hospital ID.

"My new deputy, Jason Dickson, showed me a death statistics map. Our area is covered in suspicious deaths and this isn't a random event."

"He's the electronics and computer wizard you told me about, right?"

"Yes. He's accessed the Captain's phone and we have an audio-video file of the murders. I came here to play it for you in case you might recognize the murderer's voice. Thank God you're alive to hear it."

"I'm thanking God too. Go ahead and play it."

George followed Jason's instructions and the murder clip played. When they heard the voice of the stranger talking, Olsen replied loudly in anger, "That's Gregory, the Exgenics attorney."

"Dang, now I remember where I heard that voice. He was the fat old man in the crowd at the funeral reception talking to Benson Thurmond.

gcgaacgcgatggcgtaagcgatggcgaacgcgccgctggcgaacgcgtgcgcgaacgcgctgccggcgaacgcgatggcgtaagcgatggcgaacgcg

There's also a later image of a man's hand wearing a college class ring. We think the ring was from Harvard University."

"Gregory wears a big ring on both hands. I saw one had masonic symbols but the other one I couldn't identify."

"Well, now we have enough evidence for both an arrest and a search warrant. I'll see Judge Saunders in the morning for them. I'll also ask Jason to hack, I mean, 'search' Exgenics to find more evidence too."

"Be careful George, these killers are ruthless and we don't know what we're up against. Their farm's got tight security and the guards have automatic weapons. I spread the news of my 'death' around, just to keep them off-guard. My deputies don't even know I'm alive."

"When we serve the warrants, I'll involve your deputies. I'm starting my surveillance of the farm tonight to gather intelligence," he said thinking back to his Army years. "Rest and get well soon. I'd better get going."

Olsen replied, "You're a lucky man George," as he thought about his life. "You've Olivia and someone who'd come to the hospital if you were here in my place. After my divorce, I have no one and if I'd died in tonight's wreck, no one would mourn me."

"Your deputies would've given you a nice law enforcement funeral though. You're fortunate to be alive and still have time. Go out and live, Al. Don't work yourself to death just drinking coffee and eating donuts."

"Yeah, with my Chiefmaster wrecked, I'll visit real donut shops, but less often," he chuckled with a wince of pain.

Doc Longtree sat for several hours chatting with some locals at the Blue Lagoon Grill at River Haven. He sat on a barstool, observing a typical Thursday night crowd and a few vacationers having a nightcap before boating home to their campsites or vacation homes in Kent and James Counties. He'd also talked to Joe Pyle, the bartender, who commented that nothing unusual had happened this week.

It was late and he was about to leave when two men wearing summer clothes entered and sat down at the half-empty bar a few stools away from Doc to the right. One man wore a baseball cap, the other had short clipped hair, and they began talking to each other. Both had muscular builds and he could tell they weren't likely fishermen who usually had sunburned necks. As Doc eavesdropped, he heard the words 'fish,' 'busy week,' and 'Friday night.' He listened more and after finishing their drinks, they said, "It's dead here, let's drive back to the hotel," and they stood up to leave. Doc got up at the same time to use the bathroom and noticed both men had a small earpod communicator in their right ears and a bulge under their shirts where a holster likely carried a concealed pistol.

When they left, Doc asked, "Joe, have those men been here before?"

"Yes, they've been here every night this week. They came Monday for dinner and drinks each night. I think they're tournament fishermen since I've heard them talk a lot about fishing with people at the bar."

"Have you seen them before Monday?"

"No, Doc. They must be staying over in Williamsburg since they're not staying at River Haven Motel here, the only hotel in Charles County."

"Thanks, Joe," Doc replied sensing these men were professional killers.

⋙⋘⋙⋘

Jason and Julie spent a while on the porch swing talking about recent events. "I'm glad you could hack the phone for the sheriff," Julie said.

"I really didn't hack it. I remembered the password from when I was a child and we're lucky the Captain never changed it."

"Yes, but afterward your knowledge and skills helped find the data within the phone's memory. Not many people could do that."

"I know and I'm really glad I didn't hack Gridcom for it. However, as this situation grows larger and larger, I have a bad feeling. If the evil we've discovered is real, it may come to that," he worriedly replied. "I don't want to go to prison and leave you. You don't need a husband who you can never be with," he said sadly looking in her eyes at the thought of lifelong separation from his love.

Julie replied, "Some decisions in our lives have consequences and are difficult. I'll respect your decision, knowing you'll make the right one."

"I think what I'm trying to tell you is I've made up my mind. Grandpa said I've got a gift, and after thinking more, I must use it to fight this evil cancer in our world. If good men do nothing or are afraid to take action, even at the cost of their lives, evil wins. I can't let that happen. I know I've made the right decision, but I hope the sheriff can identify the murderers and get a warrant from the Judge. At least that way, the law is behind me. What really worries me is if Exgenics is involved and all those accidents were murders, then this evil is so great that we can't defeat it. If the sheriff wants my help, I'll try in the morning to hack Exgenics."

"I'm so proud of you Jason," as she leaned closer to him a gave him a short, but passionate kiss.

After a moment, Julie continued, "It's cleared outside. Let's walk to the end of the dock and look at the stars."

"That sounds like a nice idea Julie. Let me bring my Brick with me in case the sheriff needs me. I should keep it with me at all times now."

Julie and Jason walked side-by-side, hand-in-hand past the boathouse and sat on the dock's lawn chairs. They gazed quietly at the stars. "Where's our planet Saturn again?" she smiled while pointing generally across the river toward the east.

"It's there, higher up in the sky," he replied pointing toward the south.

"It wasn't there on Sunday," Julie replied in a puzzled manner.

"I need to teach you some astronomy," Jason laughed. "The sun rises in the east and sets in the west. So does the moon and all other planets and stars. The hardest part to understand is that the stars are stationary and it's really the Earth that's spinning from west to east."

"That doesn't make sense," she replied, "How can that be if the sun comes up in the east?"

"That's a question about what physicists call the 'frame of reference,' which is how any observations or measurements depend on where you are and how you're moving. That's part of Einstein's theory of relativity."

"Well, it still doesn't make sense."

"Somethings are just that way, hard to understand, but true. Maybe you'll figure it out, but the simplest way of thinking about it is we're sitting here stationary but the Earth is rotating toward the stationary Sun in the east as the Sun rises. That means the earth is rotating from west to east."

"Hmmm. Let me think for a while, but it's making more sense. It's such a beautiful night and so peaceful after the rain. Let's go for a swim."

"Okay, let's go to the house and put on our swimsuits," Jason replied.

"We're married now and don't *need* swimsuits in the dark, Silly Boy."

"You're right," Jason agreed, "but at least let me grab some towels from the house," he said while quickly leaving and eagerly returning to the dock.

They stripped and jumped off the dock into the cool, refreshing black water. They playfully splashed, swam away from the dock, and returned. They treaded water and Julie commented, "I've got this strange feeling we're being watched."

"That's silly, Julie. We're all alone here and Grandpa's sleeping."

"Yeah, you're right. There's nobody around. Maybe it's just because I've only gone skinny dipping a few times and never done this with you before," Julie said as she smiled. After a few more minutes, they climbed up the ladder by the dock, dried off, and dressed.

Suddenly, Julie said, "Jason, I've lost an earring. I hope I didn't lose it in the water, but if we're lucky, maybe it came off as I was pulling off my T-shirt and it fell onto the dock. Can you get a flashlight to look for it?"

"I'll there's a camping lantern in the boathouse. It's bright enough to illuminate the area well," Jason replied leaving for the light.

He returned and turned on the electric lamp. They looked near the chairs, but it wasn't there. They looked further away, and Julie saw a shining gold reflection by the dock's edge six feet away. "That's lucky," she said. "A few more inches and it would've fallen in the water."

Jason took a few steps over to retrieve the earring, but as he bent over to pick it up, his last step tripped him on a loose raised nail. He stumbled forward toward the dock's edge. As he fell, he dropped the electric lamp and put his hands on the dock, bracing himself from falling off the edge. The light into the water and sank. The lamp went out, but nearby they both saw the water glow eerily in several areas like echoes from the lamp's former illumination. "Julie, we were *not* alone while swimming," he commented with amazement.

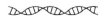

gcgaacgcgatggcgtaagcgatggcgaacgcgccgctggcgaacgcgtgcgcgaacgcgctgccggcgaacgcgatggcgtaagcgatggcgaacgcg

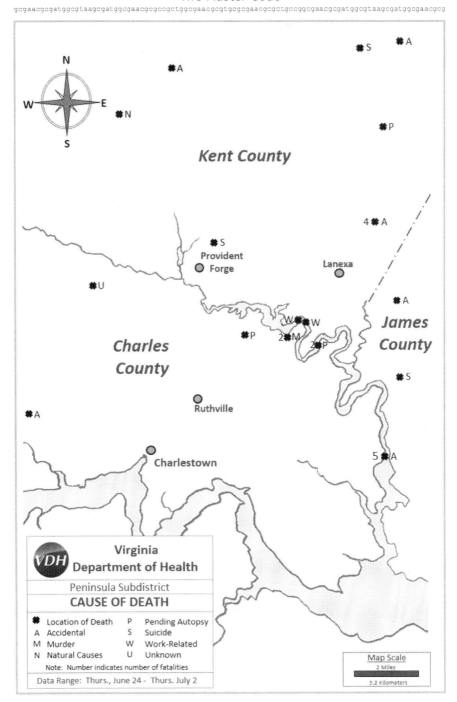

Charles and Kent County Recorded Deaths Chart

Chapter 19: A Night of Snipe Hunting

Chick Swamp at Night

1:00 a.m., Friday, July 2, ….

Jason was in bed with Julie with his arms wrapped around her in embrace and kissing her passionately when his Brick chirped out softly, "Breaker Black Rook. Breaker Black Rook."

Jason grabbed it answering, "Black Rook here White Knight. Over."

Coleman replied, "We got news for the paper. I'm going snipe hunting tonight, but I'll see you at o-six-hundred for breakfast. Contact Doctor Forest to join us. I think it's your move. Over."

"10-4. Pawn to d6. White Queen will do her best. Over," Jason replied wondering if Julie's breakfast would be better than yesterday.

"Knight to f3. Over and out," Coleman replied.

After conversation ended, Julie asked, "What was the coded message?"

"Well, the sheriff has info for the warrant and will be surveilling Exgenics tonight. He wants Doc here for breakfast. Of course, you're my White Queen," Jason said looking deep into her blue eyes.

"What about the chess moves?"

"It's to make anyone listening to our signals think we're just Ham radio operators playing a game." he chuckled. "I'll call Doc in the morning."

"I'll remind you when we wake up," Julie replied.

"Thanks, Julie. Sometimes it's hard to keep track of things. This week's been a whirlwind and my life has changed so much. I started the week studying English and now I'm a married deputy."

"Events do seem to blur together as we speed along on our lifelong journeys. I think it's just to keep things interesting and not dull."

"Oh no!" Jason exclaimed, realizing something he had to finish tonight.

"What's wrong?"

"I forgot my final exam in English! The first summer semester ends today. If I take it now, I won't need to worry about it all day."

gcgaacgcgatggcgtaagcgatggcgaacgcgccgctggcgaacgcgtgcgcgaacgcgctgccggcgaacgcgatggcgtaagcgatggcgaacgcg

"Take it now, so tomorrow you'll be free and can forget about it. I'll sleep, but when you're done, just wake me up and we can finish what we started," she said with a wry smile and some flirtatious blinks to build his anticipation of spending another evening in his wife's arms.

"Ok," Jason said as he went to his computer, logged onto the university's Gridsite, and began taking the multiple-choice exam section. He was done with that part in a half-hour and next had to write a short essay about a book he'd read this summer. The final section was creative writing, which had the instructions, *"Creative Writing: Write an original poem of several verses that is relevant to your life. Use what you have learned in this summer course and fill it with emotion. The style and format can be of your choosing."*

Jason thought a few minutes and began typing. When finished, he quietly called to Julie to wake her, "Julie, I'm almost done with the exam, but I wanted you to be the first to read my poem," he said with affection.

She rose out of bed, leaned over Jason's shoulder as he sat in his chair, looked at the e-screen, and read:

"The Grand Canyon"

The greatest rift on the Earth
of awesome majesty and complete serenity,
Humbles a man through beauty and
boundless infinity.
Man and Woman of the same mind
yet a world apart on opposite sides.
As eternity wears down walls
two edges can join as one,
but a river still divides.

The sky opens its eyes
toward the meanders of time
blessing from above
with great enthusiasm,
A witness to the joining
of two Souls across
that great, limitless chasm.

"That's beautiful Jason. Is it about us?"

"Yes, Julie. It's about how amazing life is and how insignificant we truly are. Yet *we are important* in the scheme of things. We're two people who found each other in this crazy world and have joined together. We can never truly be as one, but God blesses our attempt."

catgcgccgccgtattaaattcgcacccatgatgcgtatgcgatggaacgcatttgcgcgcatgcgccgccgtattaaattcgcacccatgatgcgtat

"I love you, Jason," she said grabbing his hand to pull him to bed.

"Hold it a second. Let me finish the exam," he said pressing the 'Send' button while Julie urgently pulled him from his chair.

As they made love in bed, the AI-Professor replied via text on the e-screen, "*Congratulations young engineer. You have received an 'A' grade in English 101-E. I hope you keep writing poetry. It really touched me deeply. It shows unique insight and, in the future, may help you express emotions and think more clearly. Good luck in your future endeavors.*"

⋉⋊⋉⋊

Coleman arrived at the Captain's house, changed into his old army field uniform, and slipped on a pair of waders. He put a small camouflage backpack into the truck cab, which he'd earlier packed with a list of items he would need: night vision goggles, flashlight, thermal camouflage blanket, compass, topographic map, knife, pistol, canteen, some snack bars, the walkie-talkie, and his badge. Finally, he laid the Captain's old aluminum canoe and hand-carved hickory paddle into the truck's bed.

He drove on dark country roads toward Chick Bridge and parked at the flashing road barricades Jeffrey installed last Saturday. He lifted the canoe, carried it down the slight river embankment, and placed it in the water. He put his backpack and paddle inside and pushed off the bank into the slow, black water.

It was a dark night, except for the stars above the open-forested swamp, but when he put on his night-vision goggles, he could see in eerie green hues. He paused in the narrow river and checked his map while using the flashlight's red LED to not affect his night vision. The map showed a good channel through the swamp where he could paddle close to Exgenics Farm. "If only I can find it in the darkness," he thought.

Coleman paddled upriver but soon realized that navigating ahead would be difficult since trees uprooted by the dam break partly blocked the main channel. He did his best to pilot his narrow canoe between the gaps. After struggling upriver a short distance, he'd paddled to where Jones Run normally entered the Chick. After the dam break, the creek to the right was fully blocked with tangled trees and debris. The main channel of the Chick also was clogged by a log jam, but luckily, the flooding river had cut a narrow channel on the left around the blockage.

He paddled around the obstacles and the river channel soon cleared. He continued upriver another quarter-mile and, to his right, he saw what he was looking for: a small shallow, intermittent creek that drained the water runoff from Exgenics Farm during rainy spells. Fortunately, the summer had been wet, so there was plenty of water to paddle ahead. He went about a half-mile and passed under the long CXF Railroad trestle and Route 60 highway bridges over the swamp. Directly ahead of him was the land and farm owned by Exgenics, so he'd be extremely alert now.

Coleman paddled toward the right and his canoe soon became grounded in a shallow marsh area near what appeared to be dry land about 20 yards ahead. He stepped out of the canoe carefully and his feet sank four inches into the mud, which was interspersed with flooded marsh grass still sticking its fresh growth above the water. He grabbed his backpack, struggled ahead through the muck, and was soon on dry land.

He estimated he was 100 yards from the Exgenics guardhouse through the woods and near the farm's boundary. Now, he crawled through the forest floor undergrowth and closer to the guardhouse and security fencing ahead of him. After creeping forward slowly about 15 minutes, he arrived at the fencing and could see in the dark that the forest had been well cleared for about ten yards on both sides for visibility and easy access by Exgenics' security team.

From his vantage point, near the underbrush's edge where a small ridge crested, he observed the guardhouse and along the security fence. He noticed the fence to his left ended in the swamp about a hundred yards away and recognized the lack of fencing as a potential perimeter weakness. However, there were likely other electronic security measures in place so he'd remain alert. He grabbed a snack bar and munched quietly.

In about ten minutes, he heard the whir of an autodrone speeding closer from the west along the direction of the fence line. He hurriedly threw the thermal blanket over himself and lay motionless as the drone patrolled along the security fence. It whirred past him in the darkness and kept moving toward the guardhouse roof where it docked to recharge its giga-capacitor. In a few minutes, it launched again and flew away to the northeast on its non-stop perimeter patrol duties.

After two hours of watching amidst the mosquitos, he saw a deer walk toward the security fence. The deer followed the fence line, waded into the swamp, and when it reached the end of the fencing, it turned right toward Exgenics Farm. After a few steps, it turned, following the other side of the fence, and walked from the swamp onto dry ground.

Soon, a drone appeared, hovering over the deer and the fence for a few seconds, before whirring away to the north. Coleman now knew the fence line was well monitored as suspected. He lay on the ground the rest of the evening casually observing and keeping mental notes of times and schedules, but mostly he thought of Olivia. He was sad they never had children, but some things in life are beyond our control and we must accept that fact and trust God's plans for us. He knew he must have another purpose for the rest of his life, but only time would reveal it.

7:00 a.m., Friday, July 2, ….

Jason and Julie climbed out of bed after a morning embrace. "Let me prepare breakfast for everyone. I'm making homemade buttermilk biscuits, frying some country ham, and making red-eye gravy," Julie said.[68]

"Are you sure you can handle making the biscuits?"

"Yes, my mom taught me to make them from scratch, but I've never done red-eye gravy before. I read on the Grid that the secret to the gravy is to have enough fat drippings from the ham and to add coffee grounds sparingly while you cook it."

"I'll call Doc now and invite him to breakfast. I'll feed Rufus too, and while I'm at it, I'll take a look to see how Frank is doing."

They went to the kitchen and saw a freshly brewed pot of coffee. They looked out the window and saw Grandpa watching the river from the dock. "I'll use some of those coffee grounds in my gravy," Julie commented. "There's no need to waste fresh grounds."

"Sounds delicious," he said. He picked up the wall phone and dialed. "Morning Doc," Jason spoke as the Doc answered his e-phone.

"I'm here Jason," Doc replied.

"Julie wants to invite you over for breakfast at 8 o'clock. You can check on old Red at the same time. Can you come?"

"Yes, I'll be there. I was having a cup of coffee at the Chief's house, but I'd love to try her breakfast. Last night's lasagna was awesome. If she cooks a breakfast like dinner last night, you've caught a good cook," Doc joked about Jason's new wife to keep up the small-talk but he knew the mention of Red was a sign it was important to come.

Jason replied, "See you soon," hanging up the phone. He fed Rufus in Red's old bowl by the doghouse where Rufus eagerly chomped crunchy bits mixed with dinner leftovers. Then, he walked to the dock where Grandpa was sitting. The sun had risen well above the distant tree line on

---

[68] Country ham is a ham that has been cured for months in a bed of salt and spices. The salt dries and ages the ham, which sometimes is also smoked. It has a unique strong flavor as compared to typical smoked "fresh ham" that is more commonly consumed. The salt acts as a preservative, allowing the ham to be stored intact for many months and was commonly used before the age of refrigeration to store hams for a long time. A country ham was normally wrapped in linen, and a burlap bag, and hung in a barn for the final aging process. The bags kept away vermin and insects. Country ham slices are often soaked in water, removing excess salt. Virginia country hams are world famous.

gcgaacgcgatggcgtaagcgatggcgaacgcgccgctggcgaacgcgtgcgcgaacgcgctgccggcgaacgcgatggcgtaagcgatggcgaacgcg

the river's far bank and was casting a brilliant glow in golden glory over the peaceful waters shimmering its reflection. Jason sat down beside him.

"Morning, Jason. I've been here a while thinking. I'm not sure what is more important, the sunrise or the sunset. Here I am at the sunset of my life looking back and wondering if I've achieved what God put me on this earth to do. I started at the sunrise of my life as a young man full of dreams but ended up just being a normal family man and minister. Now, I'm an old man at sunset and wonder what else I must do. What is the purpose to the rest of my life?" the old man thought.

"Grandpa, I think sunrise and sunset are equally important. The bright sunrise offers the hope and promise of a new day to make a better future and the sunset is a final blaze of glory and reward for a long day working to achieve the goals we set at sunrise. You still have a purpose to yet fulfill. You'll know it when you find it."

"That's good thinking Jason and I like how you're developing wisdom. Married life suits you and makes you more responsible. When you're married having a family to care for, sometimes you do things you don't like, like working a job you hate, but you do them anyway because you *must* do them to provide for your family. It's our sacrifice for our families and worth every moment of toil."

"I understand Grandpa," Jason replied. "Sheriff Coleman and Doc are coming for breakfast in a little while. I'm going to check on Frank and see how he's doing."

"OK, I'll stay here a bit and come up to the house soon."

Jason went to the boathouse and tossed another herring into the tank where Frank hovered by the gravel. Frank, again in a comical way, seemed to smile at him with his four front teeth. Jason thought about last night when the lamp fell into the water, "Why would there be more glowfish there, just waiting at dock in the middle of the night?" Then, it dawned on him perhaps the nanowire on his dorsal fin was an antenna. "Maybe, they communicate with each other?" He thought of telling Doc this theory.

He walked up to the house and into the kitchen where Julie already had country ham fried and baked the biscuits. Now, she was making the gravy to pour over fresh split biscuits on each plate. Julie said, "Jason, I need to show you this morning's Williamsburg Grid News. It's an e-vid from the rowing team accident. A boathouse security camera across the river captured the incident and the Charles County Rescue Team in action."

"Look at this," Julie said, as she replayed the news clip she'd seen a few minutes earlier while checking the Grid for her gravy recipe.

catgcgccgccgtattaaattcgcacccatgatgcgtatgcgatggaacgcatttgcgcgcatgcgccgccgtattaaattcgcacccatgatgcgtat

On the e-screen, they saw an attractive young female news announcer broadcasting with her AI-voice, "We have exclusive video of the tragic rowing accident on the Chick River from Wednesday." They saw an e-vid clip of dark storm clouds billowing ominously closer to the river and the crew team rowing hard and fast toward safety at nearly twelve knots. In an instant, a bolt of lightning hit the water as a dual fork. One lightning fork hit the crew boat and the other lightning fork hit the nearby water.

A few seconds later, the announcer continued, "and here is the clip of the heroic Charles County Rescue Team rescuing survivors." The second clip showed highlights of the rescue, as the announcer said, "There will be a series of memorial services for the deceased in Wren Chapel at William and Mary all day today. Check the college's Gridsite of special event schedules for details on times for the services of the assorted denominations. Donations may be sent by Grid-pay to the college and marked Rowing Team Memorial Fund."

Jason said, "So that's really what happened. So terrible. I want to look at the lightning strike part again."

"Why Jason? It's chilling looking at those people die again."

"I thought I saw something unusual," he replied. He took control of the e-screen, replayed the clip, and froze it when the lightning struck. They both saw something alarming and Jason responded, "We have to show this to Doc when he arrives."

8:00 a.m., Friday, July 2, ….

In a few minutes, Grandpa entered the kitchen and said, "Breakfast smells wonderful. I haven't had red-eye gravy since I lost Sarah," he said with a bittersweet smile.

"I hope it turned out alright, Julie replied. "I made a lot of everything since I knew I'd be feeding a hungry army of grown men," she chuckled.

Just then, the doorbell rang. Jason went to the foyer, opened the front door and Doc greeted, "Hello Jason."

Jason replied, "Morning Doc. Thanks for coming."

Doc asked, "Any news from the sheriff?"

"He's fine, but let's wait until he arrives for serious discussions. We just saw interesting an e-vid, but we'll see that later too."

Just then, an old pickup truck drove to the house and parked by Doc's van. The sheriff and an old man climbed out and came to the door.

Coleman said, "Morning Doc and Jason, I want to introduce you both to Nick Abramovich. He works at Exgenics as a genetics technician. He's a good man and on our side. When I told him this morning about everything that's happened, he agreed to help us."

They all greeted and shook hands with the white-bearded Jewish man, who was faithfully wearing a simple yamaka cap.[69] Nick said, "Nice to meet you both. After what the sheriff told me, God would want me to help you. I'm at your disposal to do as He wishes."

They all went to the kitchen and Jason asked Julie, "Can you set another plate? The sheriff has brought a guest."

"I already did," she replied as it was her family custom to always set an extra plate for an unexpected guest.

Coleman then introduced Nick to both Grandpa and Julie.

Julie wisely commented after seeing Nick's yamaka, "Nice to meet you, sir. I'm sorry I don't have a kosher breakfast since I cooked ham this morning. I didn't know you were coming."

"That's ok. I already ate before the sheriff came, but I'd love a cup of coffee," the old man replied with a smile acknowledging the young woman's respect for his religious beliefs.

Everyone sat at the table, filling up the six hand-made antique oak chairs surrounding it. Jason sat on one table end, with Julie to his right and Grandpa at the other end.

Grandpa began, "Let me say grace. Heavenly Father, please bless this breakfast so that it may sustain us this day. We ask for Your blessing as do our important work. In the name of Jesus and Adonai," he said adding a Jewish name for the Lord out of respect for their extra guest. "Amen."

Everyone concurred, "Amen."

As they began eating, Coleman started discussions, "Everybody, I want to first thank you for coming and agreeing to help with this serious matter. With Jason's diligent assistance as my deputy in this emergency, we've identified the Captain and Macy's murderer. The Captain's cell phone contained sufficient information to directly implicate John Gregory, the Exgenics lawyer, with the crime. Sheriff Olsen confirmed his voice from the phone's audio data."

He continued, "After breakfast, I'm going to Judge Saunders for an arrest warrant, a search warrant for the murder weapon, and to search Exgenics for other potentially nefarious activities related to that fish we've discovered. Sheriff Olsen and I think all recent events and deaths are directly tied to Exgenics. Jason, I want you to come with me to the judge's office to provide her a sworn statement of your discoveries."

---

[69] Also known as a Yarmulke or Kippah cap as worn by more devout Jewish men.

"Yes, I'll tell her everything I found," Jason replied.

Coleman continued, "Once we get these warrants, we need to move carefully since as we don't fully know what we're up against. Sheriff Olsen told me Exgenics security guards have automatic weapons, so that is a big warning to be wary. Last night, I spent the evening on reconnaissance, I mean, surveillance of their farm. Their perimeter is a literal maze of obstacles to overcome. Aside from the guardhouse, the security fence is continuously monitored by motion-activated cameras and thermal imagers. In addition, routine security autodrone patrols immediately respond anywhere perimeter security is activated."

Doc briefly interrupted to add, "The Chief said evil spirits have put a dark cloud over that farm. He said those drones now buzz day and night like mosquitos. Also at the Blue Lagoon last night, I saw some suspicious characters that looked like paid mercenaries. Maybe those men have been murdering anyone who catches a glowfish."

Coleman replied, "Yes, that's possible. I think whatever secret Exgenics is hiding, those fish are just part of it. What I'm afraid of though is when we serve the warrants at the guardhouse, much evidence could be destroyed by the time we reach the main buildings."

"Well then, how can we serve the warrants *and* get the evidence we need?" Jason asked.

"We have one thing going in our tactical advantage: it's surprise. No one from Exgenics would think that we'd dare to serve a warrant there. Sheriff Olsen and I have intentionally misled them over the last few days. As far as any Exgenics suspects may know, Sheriff Olsen is was killed in a tragic wreck last night. We think his accident was an attempt to murder him. His Supercruzer sped out of control by itself and wrecked. It happened just like Patrick Duke who repaired the Exgenics pond dam on Sunday. He died when his auto-drive truck wrecked Wednesday night."

Jason commented, "The only way that could happen is if both vehicles' software instructions took over control of the AI-navigator systems. That's similar to what happened with Jimmy Cumming's agrobots."

The sheriff continued, "Yes, it's imperative we maintain a communications blackout and mislead the enemy, I mean Exgenics, as much as possible. That's why Sheriff Olsen let his deputies believe he died, so the news of his tragic death would spread throughout the local Grid. Also, I've let it be known that I'm leaving today on vacation with Olivia, but this is just a cover story to make Exgenics think local law enforcement is not a threat to their true activities and intentions."

"How can we get past their security?" Jason questioned.

gcgaacgcgatggcgtaagcgatggcgaacgcgccgctggcgaacgcgtgcgcgaacgcgctgccggcgaacgcgatggcgtaagcgatggcgaacgcg

Coleman replied, "I've got a plan, plus we now have Nick here on our side. He knows the layout of the Exgenics facility and can be an inside man until we serve the warrants. His last work shift before the holiday is this evening, and he'll report any news or activities to us afterward."

Nick commented solemnly with his slight Russian accent, "If all the sheriff told me earlier this morning is true, there truly is great evil going on at that farm. I still can't figure it out though. Dr. Gerardo *seems* like such a good man. His company makes cancer drugs to save people's lives. As far as I know, he only uses fish embryos to test and develop the custom genetically-engineered cancer drugs which their cows later manufacture. Still, I'll help stop Exgenics as the Lord would wish."

Coleman said, "I've been thinking about the fish you caught Tim."

"Frank is still doing well in our bait tank. He seems to like herring." Grandpa commented with a smile.

The sheriff continued, "Those fish are evil and have likely been directly responsible for several deaths along the lake and river. We should destroy it, but now we need it for evidence. Sheriff Olsen told me about a fisheries biologist who died Monday on the lake from electrocution and there was a pumping station technician who died Tuesday night similarly from an electrical short of a water pump. Also, two fishermen on the river died this week below the dam mysteriously. Finally, lightning hit the rowing team, and even the Reverend and Jason were nearly killed by a lightning bolt when catching that fish."

Julie interjected, "All those incidents correspond to the map of recent deaths Jason found. Go get your e-screen Jason so we can show everyone. They need to see the e-vid of the rowing incident too."

Jason came back in a moment and sat a large e-screen on the nearby kitchen counter in a location for maximum visibility. He pressed his e-watch and the screen soon displayed the death statistics map. Jason commented, "All those 'X's are recent deaths over the past week. There have been 20 deaths according to the map. Look how they cluster along the river. We looked at normal weeks and there are only usually one or two natural deaths. This cluster of deaths is 10 to 20 times normal. It's a statistical anomaly and proves these deaths aren't just random events. Using what I learned in statistics, I calculated the odds are one in a billion that this is a random occurrence. Given the other facts we now know, the glowfish somehow or Exgenics is likely responsible for these deaths."

Everyone studied the map for a moment in horror at the magnitude of the deaths while Julie said, "Jason, play the video clip now."

catgcgccgccgtattaaattcgcacccatgatgcgtatgcgatggaacgcatttgcgcgcatgcgccgccgtattaaattcgcacccatgatgcgtat

gcgaacgcgatggcgtaagcgatggcgaacgcgccgctggcgaacgcgtgcgcgaacgcgctgccggcgaacgcgatggcgtaagcgatggcgaacgcg

Jason first showed the whole clip of the rowing team getting struck by lightning and then pressed a few keys to restart the playback right before the lightning struck. "I'm going to play this part in slow motion to look at the lightning strike closely." They all saw the forked lightning flash and Jason froze the image, "Look at the fork which hit the water nearby."

Doc exclaimed, "Look at those glowing spots. They're glowfish!"

Julie added, "Yes, we think so too. If each one of those many spots is a glowfish, there must be hundreds or thousands in the entire lake and river. We saw a few last night too when Jason and I went swimming off the dock. When he accidentally knocked the electric camping light into the water, we saw some glowing spots in the water."

"I wonder why they were there?" Doc questioned and then thought, "Perhaps these fish have more surprises than we've already discovered. Maybe they were attracted to the light of your lamp or its electricity. If that wire-like internal structure we saw before really is an antenna, then perhaps they were there communicating with Frank."

Jason added, "Doc, I wanted to tell you I suspected that too."

Doc continued, "Also, pufferfish don't travel in schools. They're normally solitary, unless mating."

"Did you say they're pufferfish?" Nick asked.

Doc replied, "Yes, they likely are a tetraodon species but with all the recent suspicious events, we're afraid to search the Grid to properly identify them. They're not native Northern Puffers from around here."

"Are they mostly yellow with spots and do they have some large dark spots near their side fins?" Nick questioned.

"Yes," Doc replied.

Nick continued, "Then these glowfish are from Exgenics. They're the *Takifugu obscurus* species of Fugu fish. They're ideal embryos to raise in our lab for genetic experiments because that Fugu species is euryhaline."

"What's that mean?" Julie asked since she'd never heard that terminology before in her biological curriculum at college.

"That means they're capable of living in both fresh and saltwater. They're the only Fugu species adapted that way and perfect for Dr. Gerardo's lab use. They're easier to maintain than saltwater species, like the more common *Takifugu Rubripes*, where you must be careful about salt concentration in the growth flasks. Dr. Gerardo told me he imports fresh eggs from Japan all the time."

"Isn't Fugu the deadly fish served in sushi restaurants?" Julie asked.

Nick elaborated further in detail, "Yes, but in Japan, they've specially trained sushi masters who prepare the fish, carefully cutting only the edible

gcgaacgcgatggcgtaagcgatggcgaacgcgccgctggcgaacgcgtgcgcgaacgcgctgccggcgaacgcgatggcgtaagcgatggcgaacgcg

portions to avoid the tetrodotoxin concentrated in certain organs like skin, liver, and roe. However, the toxin is present in all their tissues at low concentrations. Sushi connoisseurs are willing to risk death to eat this delicacy, which leaves a tingling sensation in the mouth. It's a fact, some people in Japan die every year from eating poorly prepared Fugu."

"The toxin normally comes from the bacterium, *Pseudomonas,* which symbiotically live inside the fish. I think a milligram of that poison is enough to induce lung paralysis and cardiac arrest by blocking the nervous system's sodium channels. I've got a bad feeling Dr. Gerardo implanted that bacteria's genetic code into his fish. Several years ago, I sequenced that bacterium's DNA for him. Normally in nature, Fugu fish are exposed in their diet to bacteria with the toxin. The toxin builds up in their bodies, but these fish are naturally immune."

"If that's true, these glowfish are poison factories," Doc commented.

"I guess that's possible," Nick replied.

"I'm glad we didn't directly touch it then. Maybe that slime coming from the fish is poisonous." Grandpa added.

Coleman interjected, "That might explain why those two fishermen died on the river. They just fell in the water and died. From what I hear, they didn't struggle in the water like they were drowning."

"If the lethal dose was delivered quickly, like by injection instead of ingestion, that could be possible," Nick replied.

Grandpa added, "When I caught Frank, he puffed up like a sugar toad does when frightened. There were little spines on its skin and then that white slime stuck to my shucking gloves."

"You're likely lucky to be alive then, Reverend," Nick said. "I'm responsible for what's happened this week," and he told the story of how he dropped a flask full of embryos down the lab's drain two years ago and how the DNA sample he analyzed last Saturday was a genetic match.

Coleman added, "So Gerardo must have found a glowfish like that on Saturday after the Old Forge Lake Dam washout."

Nick said, "I guess so. Lord, please forgive me. My actions have led to the deaths of many people."

The Reverend interrupted, "You couldn't know that two years ago and you're here helping us now. You were an unwitting part of Gerardo's scheme, just an employee doing your work. I think he hid much from you about his real intentions."

"Yes, that's true. As I think back on it now, all the secrecy and security at Exgenics was to hide this terrible secret. This situation makes me even more determined to help you all so that in a small way, I can begin to make

gcgaacgcgatggcgtaagcgatggcgaacgcgccgctggcgaacgcgtgcgcgaacgcgctgccggcgaacgcgatggcgtaagcgatggcgaacgcg

amends to this peaceful community that's accepted me. I only hope I'm eventually forgiven by God," Nick concluded as he broke down into tears.

The Reverend comforted the man in his grief, "I forgive you as Jesus would forgive you. I know you're Jewish, but God sent his son Jesus who spoke words of love and forgiveness to all men. He's speaking to you now through us and I'll say a special prayer for you tonight."

"Thank you for your kind words, Reverend," Nick said as he slowly regained his composure.

Coleman concluded, "Well then, we've had quite a productive breakfast meeting. A big question I still have is what is so important about that fish and why Exgenics created it. Whatever the reason, Exgenics, Gerardo, and his Attorney have committed serious capital crimes and must be prosecuted. That evil fish is the result. We must kill it now and keep the body for evidence."

"No," Grandpa exclaimed. "Frank is innocent and has committed no crime. As for Exgenics, what they've done is against the laws of nature and God. They must be punished."

Jason interrupted, "Come to think of it, we weren't killed by that lightning bolt, but just stunned by the concussion wave. Frank took the full electrical shock from the lighting, diverting the current from us."

Julie added, "And only half the rowing team died in the accident. Perhaps those glowfish partly diverted the main bolt from the team and *saved* lives. Maybe Frank and the rest of the glowfish are actually good."

Coleman scratched his head a moment and said, "Hmmm. I'll have to think about that for a while. We don't have to make any decision right now, I guess. Maybe its nature is to protect itself with that poison if frightened and it's just attracted to electricity, sometimes using it as a defense mechanism. It didn't choose to be designed by that evil scientist."

He summarized the immediate plan of action, "Jason, I want you to come with me to Judge Saunders for the warrants, and then I need to talk with Jeffery. Julie, I want you to spread the Grapevine rumor I'm going on vacation with Olivia. Doc, perhaps you and Nick can learn more by taking another look at that fish. Tim, help Reverend Morrow and pray for our community, as I think we're facing a great evil against overwhelming odds. Can we meet again for dinner here?"

Grandpa replied, "That'll be fine. Julie, do you want to cook for us again?" The other men looked at Julie and nodded their heads in agreement at the excellent Southern breakfast they'd finished.

"Yes, I'll cook dinner. Since today's Friday, I'm cooking *fish*," she said as the men felt the irony. "Jason and I are going to Williamsburg today to the memorial service. We'll stop at the seafood market there on the way home, so no need to catfish in the river today Grandpa. Gentlemen, I'll dinner will be ready at six," she said while mentally drafting the menu.

Coleman concluded their breakfast discussions, "Everyone in agreement on the plans from today?"

They all agreed.

"Let's all get moving with our days then. Jason, let's go now since we've got a lot to do this morning. What time do you need to be back here to pick up Julie?"

"Noon. I'll change clothes quickly so we can be at the service by 12:30," Jason replied.

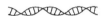

gcgaacgcgatggcgtaagcgatggcgaacgcgccgctggcgaacgcgtgcgcgaacgcgctgccggcgaacgcgatggcgtaagcgatggcgaacgcg

Chapter 20: The Great Hack Begins

Old Charles County Courthouse

9:00 a.m., Friday, July 2, ...

Jason rode with Sheriff Coleman in the Captain's pickup truck to the new Charles County Courthouse. As they climbed out and walked into the building, the sheriff said, "Let me do most of the talking Jason. I mostly need you as a backup if the judge has technical questions about the recordings of the Captain and Macy's murder."

"OK Sheriff," Jason replied as they walked down the hallway to the secure area where Judge Saunders' office was located. The armored steel door was open, but Coleman knocked on it to respect the Judge, who was sitting at her desk diligently reading some legal briefs on her e-screen.

Coleman began, "Morning judge. I need to talk to you about that case I was working on before I leave on vacation with Olivia. Do you have time to chat a while?" He then pointed to the e-screen and e-phone sitting on her desk and motioned with his hands she should turn them off.

She replied, "No, I don't have time today. Please come back after my vacation." After she turned off her devices, she replied, "I have time George, but was finishing some things before leaving for vacation. We're heading down to our beach house at Nags Head for the July 4th week. However, this e-paperwork can wait until I return if need be. I see you brought Jason, your new deputy with you," the judge replied smiling at the handsome young man.

"It's nice to meet you, young man, and I'm glad you've stayed out of trouble," she said to Jason.

Jason replied, "Yes ma'am, I've changed my life since I was that young, out-of-control boy."

Coleman began the conversation, "Judge, the Captain and Macy's murder case has turned out to be *much* bigger than first imagined. We

catgcgccgccgtattaaattcgcacccatgatgcgtatgcgatggaacgcatttgcgcgcatgcgccgccgtattaaattcgcacccatgatgcgtat

believe there's a great conspiracy and a ruthless coverup of nefarious activities at Exgenics Farm."

The judge replied skeptically, "Go ahead George, tell me about your 'conspiracy theories' and any supporting evidence you've discovered."

Coleman briefly told the entire story of how they obtained the evidence of the Captain and Macy's murders, the series of other mysterious deaths, the mercenaries the Doc had seen, and about the glowfish that Reverend Dickson had caught. Coleman then asked, "Jason, could you show the fish images and play voice recordings and video clips that you found?"

"Yes Sheriff," replied Jason as he unlocked the phone and pressed some keys to review the most important murder evidence for the Judge.

After the hand of the murderer was seen in the final video images, the Judge said, "Hold on a minute, I want to check something." She went to her bookcase filled with legal books and pulled out a thick old book titled *Virginia State Bar Directory*. She thumbed through the pages and found what she was looking for, "This directory says right here, '*John Gregory, Member, Virginia State Bar Association, summa cum laude graduate of Harvard Law School, Dean's Scholar, Fay Diploma.*' If all this is true, this clinches it for me as an airtight case. This attorney had the highest possible honors and was at the top of his class too. Such a waste for him to face the mandatory death penalty. This phone is important evidence as it identifies the murderer and implies someone had full access to Gridcom data to locate anyone that transmitted an image of a fish like that. Please store the phone securely and also keep your fish specimen alive and safe too."

"I think the information we have, and both your and Sheriff Olsen's testimonies are enough for an arrest warrant and conviction. I'm drafting an arrest warrant right now for the Exgenics attorney John Gregory to charge him with two counts of murder in the first degree. I'll also include a second search warrant of Exgenics to search for the murder weapon and further evidence of a possible criminal conspiracy. Your deputy, Jason, will be authorized in the warrants to perform a full electronic search and he'll be authorized to search without Gridcom's knowledge. Somehow, Gridcom is likely connected to this conspiracy."

Judge Saunders added, "Jason is also permitted to fully search the Exgenics Grid-site and internal computing systems if he can gain access through Gridcom. I hope he can also track down the source of the data files that were downloaded to those agrobots and if new files were downloaded to Sheriff Olsen's Supercruzer and Mr. Duke's truck. We can always add to any charges later as more crimes are discovered."

Coleman replied, "Thank you, Judge. We'll do our best to solve this case and catch the Captain and Macy's murderers."

Judge Saunders continued, "If what you've told me is really true, we must be very careful serving these warrants and making any arrests. This Exgenics is likely a criminal enterprise and I suspect they have powerful allies. Even I must be careful in this matter. We'd better get the support of the Chief Justice of the Virginia Supreme Court to back me up before making arrests though."

"After I draft the warrants, I'll contact him. Since we were in law school together, I could likely meet him in Richmond for lunch so that we don't use the Grid for any important communications. I'm sure he'll back us in this situation. It looks like my vacation is canceled now," she concluded with disappointment.

"I'm sorry judge, but sometimes events are bigger than our own lives. We must deal with them and do what's right. I know our community will work together and overcome the evil in our midst. We've already planned how to serve the warrants," Coleman said telling the details.

Judge Saunders replied, "I think it's a prudent and practical approach. I also agree it's best to not involve many outsiders, like the Virginia State Police. If this conspiracy is as big as we now suspect, we may have to keep law enforcement involvement to a local level. This will be big national news when it breaks. The warrants will be ready in two hours, George."

"That sounds fine Judge. Tell Deputy James when they're issued since I'll be out of direct contact until this is all over. Jason can contact me via two-way radio if necessary."

The judge then spoke to Jason, "Please begin your electronic search but be cautious. Remember you're a law enforcement officer of Charles County and always obey Sheriff Coleman's lawful orders. You have a special talent, Jason. Always use it for good and not evil."

"Yes ma'am," he replied.

Coleman concluded, "Thank you for your help, Judge Saunders. Now, we're going to talk to Jeffrey about our plans to serve these warrants."

"Good luck George. I think we'll all need it," the judge replied as Jason and the sheriff left and walked to his office in the building next door.

✠

After breakfast, Doc and Nick went to examine Frank in the boathouse while Julie said to Grandpa in the kitchen, "Let me get the Grapevine started," as she picked up her e-phone for a long call home.

Grandpa overheard half of the conversation, "Hi Mom… Yes, I wanted to call you… Everything is doing fine… Yes, we're having a good time and learning to live together, but it's hard living with a man though. Men are pretty smelly and I have to wash his clothes this morning too… Yes, I hope we can take a real honeymoon in the future though… I redecorated his room to make it homey. Grandpa even offered for us to move into the master bedroom soon," she said with a smile when she saw Grandpa innocently eavesdropping.

"Yes Mom, my cooking is going well. Thanks for all the lessons… Yes, from what I can tell, Jason and everyone else loved what I've made for breakfast and dinner. We even invited Sheriff Coleman over today for breakfast. I made ham, biscuits, and red-eye gravy…"

"Yes, Mom. The sheriff also told us a big *secret* that he's sneaking away today for a second honeymoon with Olivia… Let me tell you *everything*. He's doing something *really* romantic as a surprise. He's going to an expensive resort in North Carolina and that he saved up his money a year in secret. He plans to tell her they're driving going to visit his sister in Greensboro, but he'll just keep driving the rest of the way to Ashville to a mountaintop resort and spa. He even reserved the honeymoon suite," Julie said adding a final embellishment to the plans for maximum effect.

After a final pause while her mom responded, Julie concluded the call, "Yes Mom, it's ok to spread that on the Grapevine as I don't think he'd mind as long as Olivia doesn't find out. I'll talk to you soon, Mom. Love you," she said as she disconnected from the Grid.

Julie looked at Grandpa and he nodded in agreement. "Mom just can't keep a secret," Julie laughed. She started doing the dishes and planned to do some laundry before dressing for the memorial service in Williamsburg.

"Let me call Reverend Morrow now to see if I can help him in any way," Grandpa said as he picked up the phone from the kitchen wall.

After a few minutes of discussions, Grandpa hung up the phone and told Julie, "George says the funeral will be on Sunday afternoon if the medical examiner releases Jimmy's body today. Our parish will help with the food at the funeral reception afterward at the Cummings House and our choir will sing at the memorial service to reciprocate for Mt. Carmel's help with the Captain and Macy's funeral. God only knows why, but maybe these deaths were meant to bring our community together."

Doc Longtree and Nick looked inside the bait tank to see Frank, who was resting lazily with his comic face and eternally smiling front teeth on the pebbles at the tank bottom. Nick said, "That's a *Takifugu obscurus* for sure. Look at the unique pattern of dark eye spots near its fins. In the wild, those spots serve as a warning to potential predators. I see some strange features and markings though. Is that thing on the dorsal fin what you called the antenna?"

"Yes. We looked at the fish yesterday using my tribo-ray machine. That structure is like a wire connecting to different internal features."

Nick added, "Also, those belly markings aren't a natural pattern."

Doc replied, "Those external markings are near an internal organ that I've never seen before. Let me get the tribo-ray machine again so you can see exactly what we saw. Afterward, we can repeat some experiments we performed yesterday and see I you have any new conclusions. It's nice having another scientist help me observe this fish."

Doc returned and repeated his bucket tribo-ray exam as before. He then repeated the multimeter measurements in fresh and brackish water.

Nick commented, "It's interesting how the voltage went up in the saltier and more conductive tidal waters of the river. An increase in voltage means the electrical power of the fish goes up too. I wonder what would happen in true saltwater like in the ocean.

Doc replied, "There's some salt in the kitchen. Let's get some and pour it in the bucket to see what happens." In a few minutes, Doc returned with a container of salt that Julie found in the pantry. "Let's see, the water around here has about one-fifth the salt content of seawater, so to add enough salt in that bucket, I need about this much," he said as he poured a small pile into the palm of his hand and sprinkled it over the water.

After waiting a few seconds for the salt to dissolve, Doc reinserted the multimeter probes into the water and remeasured the voltage gradient across the fish. "Wow, it's nearly putting out 4,000 volts right now. That's four times the voltage when in brackish river water."

"That means if these fish reach the Atlantic Ocean, they'll be much more powerful. My God!" Nick exclaimed. "I remember now that I sequenced the DNA of *Electrophorus voltai* for the doctor a while ago also. That's an Amazon River electric eel species that evolved powerful electric properties even in pure freshwater. I bet that's why this Tetraodon fish is so powerful now. He must have combined the euryhaline features of the *Takifugu obscurus* with certain parts of the *Electrophorus voltai* genome."

"Yes, after hearing that information, I'm afraid so too. We need to get Jason to look at the fish with one of his electronic scanner devices to detect radiofrequency signals. He might be able to determine if this fish is transmitting any signals. Do you think these fish do have a way of communicating with each other?"

Nick replies, "Perhaps, but if true, these facts mean Doctor Gerardo has designed a new lifeform. He must have used AI-technology and computational biochemistry to design new genes never found in nature. He's learned to *grow* electrical structures inside the fish. In addition to his Crickett technology, he's invented another new technology that can tailor a lifeform for whatever his true purposes are. Gospodi bozhe, what have I done by helping this evil man?[70] Please forgive me. I only wanted to help people cure their cancers. This goes against Your wise design of the genetic code found in all living things. At work this afternoon, I'll learn what I can so we can together fight this evil."

10:30 a.m., Friday, July 2, ….

Coleman and Jason entered the Charles County Sheriff's Office and went to Deputy Jeffrey James, who was sitting at his desk doing paperwork for some upcoming traffic court cases.

"Good morning, George," Jeffrey said greeting the sheriff.

"Morning Jeffrey. I just stopped by the office to check up with you before my vacation. Olivia will be so surprised at my second honeymoon plans. The mountains and resort will be so beautiful," Coleman said as he motioned to Jeffery to turn off his e-phone.

Jeffrey continued the conversation a while longer with small talk, "Sounds like a wonderful trip. I hope I can get married someday too, but it's hard to find someone out here in the country. Most younger women like the city because it's more exciting."

"Well, you have a date with Robin Graves tonight, right?"

"Yes, I'm picking her up at seven and taking her to the Bluegrass Festival at East Lake Campground. Buddy Peters will handle anything tonight, and after that, I'll keep everything under control here while you're gone George," Jeffery replied.

"I'm sure all will be fine while I'm gone. I'll see you in a week."

"Bye George. Have a safe trip," Jeffery said as he concluded the fake conversation while powering down his e-phone.

"Now that we know we're in private, I've brought our new deputy to the office for our morning meeting," George replied.

Jeffrey said, "Welcome to the Charles County Sheriff's Office, Jason. When you become a law enforcement officer, even temporarily, you've become our brother. There's now a bond between us that all lawmen have. The highest calling for us is to protect and serve our community. That's what our oath of office is really about."

---

[70] Transliterated Russian Language - Господи боже: Good Lord; My God

Jason replied, "I'll do my best to help the sheriff for sure. We must catch the Captain and Macy's murderers and figure out what's going on at Exgenics over in Provident Forge."

Coleman added, "Jason has really helped us. Without his help, we'd never have identified the prime suspect, John Gregory, the attorney at Exgenics." Coleman continued to tell Jeffrey the details of what they'd already uncovered and their plans to serve the warrants at Exgenics.

After a long discussion with his Deputies, Coleman said, "Well I need to drop off Jason at his home now. I'll be doing more surveillance tonight, so I'll get some rest at the Captain's place this afternoon after some final vacation staging. If you need me, call Jason on his land-line phone and ask for the 'White Knight'. Finally, make sure Buddy Peters can have everyone from the hunt club available early Sunday morning and ready for both waterfowl and feral hogs since we aren't sure what's the best hunting this time of year," George said as he winked to Jeffrey.

"Will do George," Jeffrey replied as Jason and the sheriff left the office.

11:30 a.m., Friday, July 2, ….

Doc, Nick, and Grandpa were in the kitchen discussing the glowfish over a cup of coffee. Doc said, "They're an invasive species and represent a biological hazard to humans and the environment. With all their defensive mechanisms, their population will soon grow out of control."

Nick replied, "When man interferes with the laws of nature and natural selection, there are always unintended consequences. At this point, the genie's out of the bottle, and nothing likely can be done."

The sheriff and Jason arrived and Coleman chimed into the conversation, "We're back. The judge wants us to keep that fish since it's important evidence. Nick, I need to rest now, so I'll take you home so you can work for your normal shift and learn anything helpful there."

"Yes George, it's time to go. After tonight, I'm off the whole weekend, but I'll see you all tomorrow at breakfast with any news when George picks me up. Tomorrow's Sabbat, so I can't drive," Nick said as he stood up from the table.

Doc stood up and added, "I need to get going too. I have to check up on that racehorse at the Tyler's. That horse won at Colonial Downs in Kent City last year. Barn calls like that are my bread and butter. Jason, please examine that fish when you can to see if it transmits any signals."

"Will do," Jason replied as the three men left on their separate ways.

Jason told Grandpa, "Judge Saunders is issuing some warrants. She's giving me permission to hack Exgenics online and search their company

gcgaacgcgatggcgtaagcgatggcgaacgcgccgctggcgaacgcgtgcgcgaacgcgctgccggcgaacgcgatggcgtaagcgatggcgaacgcg

records for evidence. I need to go upstairs right now and start my hack before going to the memorial service with Julie."

Grandpa replied, "Just be careful hacking Jason. You still don't want to get caught or know what you'll find. Julie's upstairs getting ready right now Jason. Make sure you've enough time so you're not late."

"I'll have plenty of time. My hack starts by implanting a piece of code on the Grid. It'll worm its way through the Grid and continue to grow until I've total control of the Grid nodes. It uses that code from Dad's old hard drive. Of course, I added to his basic code so it's more user-friendly," he said as he walked upstairs to his bedroom.

The door was closed, so he knocked out of courtesy first before entering and said, "Hello Julie, I'm back."

"Come in, Jason. I'm putting on my makeup. You need to get ready."

Jason entered and saw Julie standing in front of the dresser mirror intently applying some eyeliner with a small brush. "I've got to change, but if there's time, it'd want to work about 15 minutes on my computer.

"I still have to finish my makeup, do my hair, and put my clothes on Jason, so it'll be a while until I'm ready."

He looked at the floral comforter on the bed and saw the clothes she wanted him to wear carefully arranged so the freshly ironed shirt, pants, and tie would not wrinkle. While Julie continued dressing, he first pressed the 'On' button of his computer workstation so that the system would boot up while he slipped on his clothes and matching dress shoes. Of course, he still wore white socks that didn't match, but his pants covered them. In two minutes, he was back at his workstation and logged onto the Grid using a virtual network as the first barrier from being tracked by the Grid monitors. With a series of deft keystroke commands, he quickly accessed that Grid node near Williamsburg and smiled when he saw its software was still vulnerable.

"Julie, now I'll try my dad's code. I added some small features to it, but it's about the same as what I found on his hard drive."

"OK Jason, but do we have time? We don't want to be late for the memorial service," she worriedly replied.

"It'll be fine," he said calmly allaying her fears. He pressed the final keystrokes to launch the viral worm onto the Grid. His father's software program would infect any computer or Grid node that is connected. It was a slow, insidious program using the error bit check feature for individual data packets as they were transferred on the Grid. The software would send a series of extra ones and zeros that appeared random to any Grid monitor, but really were individual bits of the entire program code.

At the receiving computer, these error bits would slowly accumulate, turning into bytes and eventually megabytes in the buffer memory cache until they become a working copy of the original program. However, the original program remained the master and the copy its slave. So, the program slowly wormed through the Grid, node by node, computer by computer, until all Grid-connected computers, e-screens, e-phones, and devices became infected slaves of the master worm. Once infected Grid nodes were under its control, the worm just waited for instructions.

After just a few minutes, Jason replied to Julie, "Well that's done. Now we wait for the infection to spread. Normally, a computer virus infection spreads exponentially, but this one has a variable growth control function keeping the growth rate low to not trigger any Grid monitor alarms. It just takes time to eventually infect the entire Grid linearly."

"So, now you just wait and you'll soon control the Grid?" Julie asked as she put her long blonde hair into a ponytail.

"Yes, are you ready now to roll?"

"I am. Let's go. Are we riding your bike?" Julie asked as they walked downstairs and into the garage.

"Yes. It's faster in traffic so we won't be late," Jason replied as they put on their helmets, straddled the seat, and whirred down the rural road.

Chapter 21: The Holiday Weekend Starts

Fishing the Chick

Noon, Friday, July 2, ….

Since the July 4th holiday was Sunday, the official work holiday was Monday. However, vacationers planning an extra-long weekend on the Chick began arriving Friday afternoon. Others took the next week off for an extra-long summer holiday.

By noon, several boat ramps along the Chick became a crowded beehive of activity. At Osprey Landing, most of the professional fishermen entering the weekend tournament launched their bass boats onto the lake to test the waters. They'd spend the remainder of the afternoon looking for good fishing spots and assessing the water conditions for the contest that started at midnight.

At the East Lake ramps, a mass of recreational boaters launched their boats and others set up their camper trailers or RVs in the campground. These temporary guests joined an assortment of year-round residents and pensioners to enjoy the weekend's East Lake Bluegrass Festival. This event filled the campground to capacity and there was even extra parking in a local field for daily attendees who drove to see the musicians perform.

The campground employees were busy finishing the final preparations for the festival occurring under a big canopy-covered bandshell with a stage. The festival started Friday night, so troubleshooting the sound system and stage lighting was priority. The evening's festivities would start at the opening ceremony followed by a two-hour-long banjo pickin' session by musicians specialized in this instrument. The rest of the weekend had a varied performance schedule by different musicians, some quite famous in bluegrass circles. Finally, the festival concluded with an awards ceremony and Sunday night July 4th fireworks.

12:15 p.m., Friday, July 2, ….

Jason and Julie arrived on campus and Jason parked in a motorcycle space close to Wren Chapel.[71] They walked hand-in-hand and solemnly entered the chapel with other mourners for the 12:30 p.m. Episcopal memorial service. The propped open sanctuary doors allowed mourners to freely flow to the memorial service medley without undue disturbance.

The sanctuary hall was more narrow than wide, with three rows of antiphonal pews placed strategically on the sides of the main aisle.[72] In front of the altar were tripod stands holding enlarged photos of rowing team victims and a team group photo. Filling up the narrow gap between the main congregation and the front altar area were multiple floral arrays and arrangements. Colored flowers and leafy greenery visually blended and the sanctuary was filled with the sweet aroma of white lilies.

The atheist service was still underway when Jason and Julie entered and three atheists were quietly sitting in the pews in silence since they had nothing to say. One couple sat on the right-front in the first row and a young woman sat on the front left-side, middle row. They sat for several minutes more to preserve their active "religion" status for future chapel observances. As Episcopal mourners filled several pews, the atheists decided to leave by standing and exiting the sanctuary.

After all were settled in the pews, the local Williamsburg vicar and half the college choir swiftly entered the chapel at 12:35 p.m. from a rear door beside the altar. The vicar immediately began his formal memorial service for the assembled mourners who stood in unison as he said, "I am the Resurrection and I am Life, says the Lord."

The vicar then continued his abbreviated liturgy with a short reading from the Old Testament and a slightly longer reading from the New Testament. He next read the Gospel and Jason, Julie, and the assembled mourners chimed, "Glory to You, Lord Christ" and "Praise to You, Lord Christ" at the appropriate times.

After the readings, the pipe organist led as the choir followed in singing '*Deep River*' in remembrance of the rowing team members who lost their

---

[71] Construction of original Wren Chapel was completed in 1699. It is the oldest college building in the United States but was reconstructed several times after fires. It has been fully restored. The original walls still comprise part of the structure. Its sanctuary includes one of the four oldest pipe organs in America; this organ originally was located in the ballroom of the colonial Governor's Palace in Williamsburg.

[72] Antiphonal pews face the center aisle instead of the altar. They date to Early Christian tradition in which a congregation was divided into two groups for singing the psalms, with each side singing a verse.

gcgaacgcgatggcgtaagcgatggcgaacgcgccgctggcgaacgcgtgcgcgaacgcgctgccggcgaacgcgatggcgtaagcgatggcgaacgcg

lives.[73] Since there wasn't time for communion, the vicar proceeded with his commendation inviting the deceased to join the House of the Lord. He ended the service with Psalm 23 with the mourners repeating the verses of the Lord's Prayer. The vicar dismissed the mourners within the allotted time, "Let us go forth in the name of Christ. *Thanks be to God.*"

Julie and Jason stood up and walked outside with other Episcopal mourners. One of Julie's friends, Brandy Murphy, approached and said, "It was such a terrible accident. I miss Michelle so much already. She had such a joy for life and was such a great photographer. She took that rowing team photo with her remote-control tripod," Brandy said in tears.

"I'll miss her too," Julie replied giving a hug of sympathy and comfort to her grieving friend, who was also Michelle's roommate. "Let me introduce you to my husband Jason."

"Hello, so you're the Jason that Julie's talked so much about. It's nice to meet you, finally," Brandy said in greeting.

"Nice to meet you too," Jason replied.

"Julie, you didn't tell me you were married. I knew you were thinking he was the one for you, but I didn't hear anything about it on E-Face," Brandy commented.

Julie replied, "Well, we suddenly eloped this week and I haven't had time to log onto E-Face to tell anyone about it. My family knows and that's what's important. Actually, we plan on a bigger second wedding ceremony at Westover sometime next spring, so we want to keep it quiet a while."

"OK, I'll keep a secret for you girl," Brandy said. "I'd better get going. Let's keep in touch."

"Will do. I'll tell you then how I've learned to cook." Julie said while laughing and waving goodbye to her friend.

"How did you like the memorial service Jason?" she asked Jason.

"It was very formal and short," Jason commented looking at his e-watch. The watch had a small bar chart and percentage readout indicating the viral infection status of the Grid. The bar chart was green indicating the worm was progressing normally without detection and the infection had already spread to 34% of all Grid nodes.

Julie replied, "Episcopal memorial services are formal and about praising God and the promise of resurrection, instead of commenting about the deceased person's life. It was too short for a normal Episcopal

[73] '*Deep River*' is a deeply moving anonymous African-American spiritual song and hymn, that has been often arranged by composers and sung by multiple famous vocalists and choirs. It was first published in 1876.

catgcgccgccgtattaaattcgcacccatgatgcgtatgcgatggaacgcatttgcgcgcatgcgccgccgtattaaattcgcacccatgatgcgtat

memorial service though. You really need almost an hour for a full service including the Eucharist. You should come to a service at old Wendover Church to see a typical Sunday service there. It's a small congregation and still has some rich families like the Wendovers and Tylers."

"Yes, we'll have to do that soon. I'm Baptist though and Grandpa needs my help, so we need to attend Pleasant Hill most Sundays."

"That's fine Jason. I'm fine with your Church, although sometime soon I'll need to be baptized to become an official member of the parish. I was baptized as an infant at Wendover but don't remember it, so it'll be a nice new experience to remember with you," she smiled.

Jason commented, "I'm glad we fixed the heater to the baptismal tank last year. It was terribly cold getting baptized in the winter until we saved enough in the capital fund for a solar heating system."

"Mom, Dad, and our parish will surely miss me at their church. I'm hungry. Let's eat some lunch," Julie said with a grumbling stomach.

Jason replied, "There's a nice bistro at Merchant's Square on Duke of Gloucester Street."

"I know, the 'Eagle's Talon.' That's a great place for lunch," Julie agreed and walked eastward through campus toward their lunch venue.

"Let's have a relaxing time and get home after an hour so I can begin my search. Then, we'll get to the bottom of the murders and Exgenics affair by finding some revealing information," Jason replied confidently knowing an approximate time the infection would be complete, but just as a check, he glanced at his e-watch indicating 35% Grid infection.

⫘⫘⫘

Early afternoon at East Lake's swim beach was sunny and hot. The campground constructed it several years ago using sand trucked and spread along 100 yards creating a recreational swim beach for campers. Little Molly Anderson, barely four years old, was playing with a plastic sandcastle bucket and shovel while her mom, Joann, reclined in a folding chair nearby reading an e-book. Joann asked Molly, "What time is it?" to keep engaged with her daughter while she played.

Molly, who had just received a girl's waterproof e-watch for her birthday, looked at her left wrist and said, "Two," holding up two fingers with her right hand with pride she could count and read numbers. "I'm hot Mommy, can I play in the water?"

"Just walk near the edge, don't go in above your knees, and splash yourself to keep cool. I'll be watching," her mother replied as she closed her e-book to keep a keen eye on Molly wading in the shallow water.

Molly was excited with her freedom and waded while carrying her bucket in her right hand. Although the river water was slightly cloudy, she saw her feet clearly on the bottom. She looked for a seashell but was disappointed when there were none.

She waded more and then saw a strange-looking fish resting on the sand in a freshly disturbed shallow sand circle about a foot across. The bright yellow fish with black spots seemed to be looking at her with its bulging eyes. The fish defensively watched after having earlier buried its fertilized eggs in the sandy nest.[74]

"Hello, Yellow Fish!" Molly excitedly said as she reached with her left arm to pet it under the water. As she touched it, she felt a high-voltage shock. She quickly pulled her arm away feeling a strange sensation as the fish briefly glowed, looked upward seeming to smile, and swam away.

Mrs. Anderson saw Molly talking to the water for a few minutes and then there to check what she was doing. Molly was repeating a rhyme to herself, "One Fish, Two Fish, Yellow Fish, Glow Fish." She said excitedly, "Mommy! I saw the Dr. Seuss fish! He smiled at me too!" She s grinning widely and then she looked at her e-watch and started crying, "e-watch broken." Her mom looked at the dead e-watch and thought she'd send an e-vid complaint to the manufacturer about their supposedly waterproof child's watch after they got home after this weekend's festival.

Halfway across the country at the National Anti-Virus Center in Provo, Utah, Hal Harris, a Grid Analyst from the NSA, commented from his Grid work station, "Looks like the AI data monitor flagged another fish image from Virginia."[75]

His female CIA Grid Analyst coworker, Janice Smith, replied in an Arkansas Ozark Mountains accent, "Yeah, fishermen just sending 'trophy photos' or e-phoning about their fishing trips. It's kept us busy this past week, but the overtime's been good. This special fish Intel project has taken high priority over routine domestic terrorist data scans."

Hal next commanded the AI-system, "Grid-monitor, display flagged e-vid." The data monitor began its playback on an e-screen. "Hey. It's a little girl at a swim beach reaching toward one of those fish they're looking for," he commented as they watched e-screen images and sounds from the girl's e-watch before the signal went blank underwater. "Janice, I'll contact Ops Central per normal protocol."

---

[74] Some tetraodon species are known to build elaborate circular patterned nests in sand.
[75] National Security Agency

"No," she replied. I think we can skip this one. That cute little girl doesn't know anything important we need to inform headquarters about for cleanup. Who'd believe her anyway?" she laughed.

3:00 p.m., Friday, July 2, ….

On their way home, Jason and Julie stopped by Jamestown Seafood Market to buy fish for dinner and picked up some striped bass freshly caught from the river. They continued riding Jason's bike home along hot and humid country roads but were cooled by the constant breeze. As they arrived, Jason parked in the garage and pressed the ignition switch off. He looked at his e-watch, which now displayed 93% Grid infection. "Once the infection reaches 99% of all active Grid nodes, there'll be enough infected servers to enable me to hack with impunity for evidence," he said.

"Can I help somehow?" Julie asked as they stood in the garage.

"Well, I'll hook up my laptop so you can Grid search and investigate public info about Exgenics and Dr. Gerardo. It's important to know about your hacking target and build a dossier of background information. It helps to crack their passwords."

"Won't Gridcom see my searches?" Julie asked.

"Yes and no. With my code, their AI-monitors will see searches, but coming from tens of thousands of Grid sites. So, they cannot locate the specific node of the individual search. I'll connect you by millimeter-wave wireless hotspot to my desktop computer. That frequency gives excellent communications bandwidth, but not much connection range."

"That sounds good. I'm sure my biochemistry and biology knowledge will be useful in understanding Gerardo's published research and e-vids from conference presentations. Maybe when we add any new information to what we already know, we can figure out what Exgenics is really doing."

"We need to wait though before we start, so let's look again at Frank. Doc and Nick wanted me to check for radio communications abilities."

"I'll help a while, but then I've got to start cooking dinner for all you men. We have to gut and fillet those stripers before I fry them too. I've never done that before," Julie said with trepidation.

"I'll show you how," Jason replied. "We'll use the cutting board by the boathouse sink. First, let me rummage through my workbench to get a few things I'll need to examine Frank. I'll meet you there in five minutes. Please bring my laptop on your way there," he added.

"I'll grab it, Jason," Julie said as she walked up two steps and entered the kitchen through the garage entry door.

Jason remarked, "Is Grandpa there? His truck isn't outside."

gcgaacgcgatggcgtaagcgatggcgaacgcgccgctggcgaacgcgtgcgcgaacgcgctgccggcgaacgcgatggcgtaagcgatggcgaacgcg

"I don't know," she replied and then spotted a Grandpa's on the small bulletin board by the wall phone, 'Gone to visit Reverend Morrow. Be back by dinner.' "He left a note he's visiting Reverend Morrow this afternoon."

Jason met Julie in the boathouse as she stared inside the tank. Frank was laying on aquarium gravel next to some chess pieces. "He looks so sad and lonely there," she commented. "It's like that tank is a prison cell."

"He's just a fish, Silly-Girl. They don't have emotions like that," Jason replied while chuckling at his wife's comment.

As Jason began working, he explained to Julie as he proceeded with his experiment, "I'm wrapping the tank now with copper mesh screening so I can isolate him from other outside electromagnetic signals. That way, when I use my RF band-scanner, I can analyze him to see if he's emitting any signals. His antenna-like feature has a length suggesting possible transmissions in the MHz RF band.[76] The mesh's diamond-shaped hole pattern will allow us to observe him in the tank while he's isolated from other signals.[77] It's just like looking inside a microwave oven." In a few minutes, the tank was enclosed in mesh from a roll he often used for his electronics projects. "There, that should do it. Now, I'll place the scanner's antenna through a small hole in the mesh to check for signals."

He turned on the scanner and set it to broadband scan mode to search for signals while Julie continued watching the fish through the mesh openings. On the first scan of the RF-spectrum, the indicator panel on his laptop display was blank, but on a second scan at higher frequencies, an intermittent analog signal was detected that covered a bandwidth from 40 to 60 MHz. "I've found an analog signal that's in the very high-frequency band. That frequency is good for communications at short distances. The signal is moving slowly to different frequencies like it's searching for other signals. Let me quickly modify received signal output by lowering its frequency so it's audible to human ears."

The speaker from his laptop soon began a emit a series of sounds like a rising and falling wave with a series of clicks, wails, and moans. Julie exclaimed, "That sounds eerily similar to a whale's song and those clicks

---

[76] Mega-Hertz or 1 million cycles per second.

[77] Copper or aluminum metal meshes and foils are excellent materials to screen electronic devices from outside electronic signals and pulses. They have been largely replaced by graphene sheets and non-woven nano-tube fabrics. Such materials are used to construct Faraday cages for electromagnetic shielding. The early electricity scientist Michael Faraday invented the Faraday cage in 1836.

catgcgccgccgtattaaattcgcacccatgatgcgtatgcgatggaacgcatttgcgcgcatgcgccgccgtattaaattcgcacccatgatgcgtat

gcgaacgcgatggcgtaagcgatggcgaacgcgccgctggcgaacgcgtgcgcgaacgcgctgccggcgaacgcgatggcgtaagcgatggcgaacgcg

are like the echolocation clicks used by dolphins! Right now, it sounds sad and lonely just like I felt."

"Let me try something else," Jason said as he pulled the antenna from inside the mesh which has shielded the probe from signals in the outside environment. He now detected a much weaker signal and the sounds from the speaker were much lower in volume and seemed to have a different, more pleasing harmonic and melodic tone.

"Well, I think that about confirms it then. This species of fish has some RF communications abilities. That weaker signal was likely from some fish nearby. I think the water attenuates the signal, so I'm not sure how close they are, but they're nearby in the river for sure."

"Let's see what happens when I remove the copper mesh from the tank." They then heard a series of loud sounds in a pattern and a weaker reply in nearly the same pattern. The louder sounds soon changed tone and became less melancholy, but were still sadder than the weaker tones. Jason commented, "I think Frank reestablished communications with other fish like him. Let me feed him a herring and see what happens."

Jason grabbed a herring from the bait refrigerator, tossed it in the tank, and it sank to the bottom. Frank swam slowly to the herring, took a bite, and the speaker's louder sounds now became a joyous melody. Frank looked outside the tank and seemed to smile comically.

Julie said, "I think that sound means 'Happy' or something like that."

"I've one last experiment to conduct for now," Jason said as he plugged the shop light with a fresh light bulb and placed it near the tank. As expected, the bulb glowed brightly and burnt out while Frank puffed up and briefly glowed. Afterward, the sounds coming from Frank on the speaker were louder and faster. Jason commented, "I think these fish need electricity to recharge their systems. Maybe that structure in their heads *is* some communication device or extra brain," he postulated.

"I don't know," said Julie. "These fish are just weird. This is so unnatural, it still gives me the willies," she continued as goosebumps appeared on her arms and legs.

"Well, there's nothing else we can do with Frank for now. Let me help you with the stripers and then we can go inside," Jason said as saw his e-watch now indicated 99% infection. "The Grid is fully infected and you need to start dinner soon."

Jason demonstrated the fish cleaning process to Julie. He wore some gloves to protect his hands and keep them clean during the cutting process. Then, he cut off a fish's head just behind the gills with a sharp knife and made a ventral slice through the abdomen to clean out the guts. He

catgcgccgccgtattaaattcgcacccatgatgcgtatgcgatggaacgcatttgcgcgcatgcgccgccgtattaaattcgcacccatgatgcgtat

gcgaacgcgatggcgtaagcgatggcgaacgcgccgctggcgaacgcgtgcgcgaacgcgctgccggcgaacgcgatggcgtaagcgatggcgaacgcg

reached with his fingers, pulled out the interior organs, and cast the offal into a waste bucket. Jason then showed Julie how to fillet the meat from the fish using a long fillet knife. Jason commented, "I like filleting this way so you don't need to descale it."

"Let me try now," Julie said eagerly to learn by doing. She put gloves on and carefully repeated the procedure with a second filet knife. "That's pretty disgusting and repetitive, but some work just must be done to live. Macy likely prepared 10,000 fish this way in her lifetime," she added. By working together, they soon made quick work prepping their dinner entrée as they tossed the fillets into a steel bowl. "I like to work with you. It shows we're a good team," Julie told Jason.

"Yes, I think so too. Now, let's go inside the house to start our searches," Jason replied.

As they entered their bedroom, Jason saw his e-watch indicating 99.5% infection. "I'll turn my podcam on to fully document any evidence and show we legally searched as authorized by the warrants. Julie, we should keep this podcam on and with us the next few days." He turned the podcam and his laptop computer on, typed the laptop password, provided an iris scan to the imager, and handed it to Julie. "You can lay on the bed to research Dr. Gerardo and Exgenics while I sit at my desk to hack with my computer. We need to find out as much information as possible about the doctor so I can crack his password."

Jason sat in front of his e-screens and typed on his keyboard. He pulled up a Sat-Map of Exgenics Farm and commented, "Let's look at that farm first to learn what we're up against," and an image soon displayed with a bird's eye view of farm buildings, fields, pond, and Old Forge Lake.

"Look, they have a gamma-ray quantenna there," he exclaimed with uneasy excitement as he pointed to the screen. "That's used for *totally* secure communications. This hack will be harder than I thought unless they have a mirror Gridsite I can access somewhere. The quantenna is pointing just west of north, so its paired transmitter/receiver is located in that direction. If I find that, I might have a better idea of the specific Grid nodes to hack for internal access to Exgenics."

Jason then scrolled the satellite map and looked about 100 miles away in the direction the Exgenics quantenna was pointing. He commented, "It's aimed just west of Washington." He zoomed in closer along the quantenna's vector looking for the optical shadow of its paired quantum-coupled antenna. After a moment, he spotted in McLean, Virginia a field with multiple quantennas pointing in different directions. "My God, that's right next to the CIA Headquarters Building!" he exclaimed to Julie.

catgcgccgccgtattaaattcgcacccatgatgcgtatgcgatggaacgcatttgcgcgcatgcgccgccgtattaaattcgcacccatgatgcgtat

Julie replied with astonishment, "That means the government is involved in a conspiracy with Exgenics too."

"Not necessarily the whole government, but perhaps a portion of it. Powerful people have been struggling against each other for years in the open and secretly to control the government. Perhaps only that agency is under one faction's control. We can't assume anything though until we find out more," Jason wisely commented.

Julie replied, "I'll quickly look up some basic Exgenics info and their cancer drugs. Then, I must make dinner."

Jason asked a question, "Julie, where on the Grid does your dad buy supplies for the Wendovers' farm?"

"Why do you ask?" she replied.

"I think the best way to hack Exgenics is through their purchasing portal. Many suppliers have special limited access to a company's Gridsite. That may be the easiest way to hack into Exgenics' internal network."

"Let me call my dad," she said and picked up her e-phone. After a short conversation, she said, "Dad uses '*agrosupply.grid*' for supplies."

"Thanks, Julie. It should be easier to hack into them first and then using their customer portal, I can gain backdoor access into Exgenics."

Jason went to the Agrosupply Corporation's Gridsite and started his hack while Julie began Grid searches of Exgenics and Gerardo.

Julie commented, "Other than ads for cancer drugs they sell, I can't find much about Exgenics since they're privately owned. I'm starting basic biographical searches of Dr. Gerardo now and he has an interesting background. He's a Nobel prize winner and invented the Crickett gene synthesis system. He has doctorate degrees in computational chemistry and biochemistry. He founded Exgenics and is a wealthy philanthropist too. He's concerned about preserving biodiversity and founded the World Elephant Genomics Conservatory to prevent elephant extinction by increasing their genetic diversity and numbers. He's also a shareholder in Ice Age Nature Park."

"What's that?" Jason asked.

"That's a Russian theme park on 100,000 acres of land which opened last year. He helped them breed extinct animals like wooly mammoths, saber-tooth tigers, and dire wolves using DNA retrieved from frozen specimens found in the arctic tundra from more than 10,000 years ago. They had a million visitors there last summer."

"Wow, I didn't know that before, but I'm not interested much in biology and such things," Jason commented.

gcgaacgcgatggcgtaagcgatggcgaacgcgccgctggcgaacgcgtgcgcgaacgcgctgccggcgaacgcgatggcgtaagcgatggcgaacgcg

Julie said, "Well, it's important to know different things in life as you never know what will be useful information later. It's time to start dinner."

"I'll keep hacking until dinner's ready. Let me know when it's time to eat so I won't be distracted trying to remember that. Sometimes I'm so focused on what I'm doing, I forget to do other things."

"I'll remind you, Honey," Julie replied as she closed the laptop, went to Jason's desk, briefly kissed his lips, and went downstairs to the kitchen.

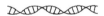

Chapter 22: A Date to Remember

East Lake Bandshell Tent

5:00 pm, Friday, July 2, ...

Dr. Graves had spent another long day performing medical procedures and autopsies. In fact, this week had been terribly busy and she couldn't remember a busier time since becoming a doctor. She'd just performed three stressful hours of autopsies related to the high-profile deaths of two fishermen. With a podcam suspended over the autopsy table, the Regional Medical Examiner had remotely supervised her procedures and tests.

As she hastily stitched up the second victim's chest as he lay on the table, she summarized her findings to the examiner, "These young men didn't drown. Both men's lungs collapsed without excess water, their hearts stopped beating suddenly, and there was no sign of heart disease. The rapid-assay drug test kit showed no alcohol or commonly abused drugs, so the initial toxicology analysis is negative."

The regional examiner replied, "Yes, these are mysterious deaths. Send me those extra fluid and tissue specimens by autodrone courier for a more intensive toxicology analysis next week. Until then, keep the cause of death as unknown, but that Virginia congressman won't like that answer about his son. Keep the bodies in storage." She let the morgue attendant take the bodies back to storage and he brought a final body for the day, a farmworker from Charles County who was nearly decapitated yesterday.

The morgue attendant said, "The ambulance volunteers told an out-of-control agrobot broke his neck."

"Thanks, that will get me started," Robin replied. She unzipped the body bag and looked at a head nearly sheared off and noted extensive crushing of the esophagus and nearby cervical bones. Both carotid arteries had been severed. She used another immunoassay drug test kit on his fluid specimens, but it was negative, so drugs weren't involved in this tragedy. As she zipped up the body bag, she thought the cause of death was obvious

gcgaacgcgatggcgtaagcgatggcgaacgcgccgctggcgaacgcgtgcgcgaacgcgctgccggcgaacgcgatggcgtaagcgatggcgaacgcg

but was it a work-related accident or murder by agrobot? She kept it listed on the death certificate as 'unknown.'

She called Kent City Funeral Home to pick up the man's body and then her e-watch sounded an alarm reminding her of an upcoming important event. Robin looked at her e-watch calendar and saw a note: '*7:00 p.m. date with Jeff. Bluegrass Festival.*' She thought to herself in confusion, "Which one? Was it that cute, witty Charles County Deputy Jefferson James she met on Monday morning or was it Kent County Deputy James Jeffers with his muscular build and strong demeanor that she dated last weekend?"

She quickly looked at her e-calendar for the following Friday and saw an entry '7:00 p.m. with James J.' So, she confirmed it must be a first date with Jeffrey tonight. She thought of her recent good luck to suddenly have two handsome, local young men interested in her at the same time. As her autocar drove her home so she could dress for her date, she thought that no matter which one eventually she liked the most, she finally had a good chance to find a man that wasn't intimidated by an attractive doctor. She thought of the mysterious flower bouquet that one of them gave her on Tuesday and smiled.

⧓⧓⧓⧓⧓

The large, wall-sized e-screen of the Grid Analyst at the National Anti-Virus Center started flashing an alarm in a pop-up window. "Searches of keywords Exgenics and Gerardo detected. I will start an accessed-data log and continue monitoring to gather further statistics of this search anomaly. Any additional instructions?" the AI-data monitor reported and asked.

"Locate Grid coordinates of search origin," the analyst replied.

"I cannot determine a specific site. More than 200,000 locations already have been used for these searches and as I identify one Grid location, a different site continues the search," the data monitor replied.

The analyst thought to himself, "There goes my holiday weekend."

6:00 pm, Friday, July 2, ...

Sheriff Coleman and Doc arrived for the fish fry at the Dickson house on time, but Grandpa arrived a few minutes late. As Grandpa entered the kitchen, he saw everyone sitting at the table eating.

Jason informed Grandpa, "We started eating before it got cold. Sorry, we didn't wait for you."

"That's OK Jason, fried fish is best while it's warm. Sorry, I'm late. What else is for dinner Julie?" Grandpa asked as he went to the kitchen sink to wash his hands.

catgcgccgccgtattaaattcgcacccatgatgcgtatgcgatggaacgcatttgcgcgcatgcgccgccgtattaaattcgcacccatgatgcgtat

Julie replied as everyone else continued eating, "I made some collard greens and cornbread. For dessert, I whipped up a cobbler using fresh blueberries 'handpicked' by Wendover's agrobots. Is there any news from Reverend Morrow?" Julie asked.

Grandpa replied as he sat down, "George just told me the medical examiner just released Jimmy's body, so it looks like the funeral is on for Sunday afternoon. We're going to send our choir over to Mt. Carmel to sing again with their choir. Our women's auxiliary will help with food and refreshments. We're going to have traditional a Southern menu again. Amidst all these tragic deaths, we're pulling our community together to make something better than before. It takes people with courage, knowledge, vision, and wisdom to enable change. The Captain and Macy's funeral led the way and their money may help later to further unite the people of Charles County again," he remarked with hope.

"So, George, what's the news on the investigation?" Grandpa asked Sheriff Coleman.

"Well, we have warrants now but need any intelligence that Nick finds at work. Can we have breakfast here again Julie? I'll bring Nick then."

"Yes Sheriff, but I think it's time for Jason to cook something," she replied. "Just because I'm the only woman in this house doesn't mean I have to slave all day in the kitchen."

"No problem Julie, I'll cook tomorrow," Jason wisely replied to help his wife. "We'll have breakfast at 6:00 a.m."

Coleman asked Jason, "Any news to report?"

"Well, I've started my search warrant hack. I haven't breached the Exgenics firewall yet, but I may have found a way inside through one of their suppliers. I also saw from a satellite image that Exgenics has a secure communications quantenna likely linked to CIA Headquarters. Julie started looking into Exgenics but didn't find much at all. However, Dr. Gerardo seems to be a well-known, famous scientist."

Julie added, "I've started digging into his background and need to gain further insight by reviewing his published technical papers and e-vids from his public speeches."

Jason continued, "Doc, I determined Frank has an internal wireless communications system. I think all these fish communicate with each other. Everyone, listen to some of the transmissions I recorded on my e-watch during my wireless signal analysis of the fish." Jason pressed his e-watch and it started playing a series of whale-like melodic moans and some dolphin-like clicks.

gcgaacgcgatggcgtaagcgatggcgaacgcgccgctggcgaacgcgtgcgcgaacgcgctgccggcgaacgcgatggcgtaagcgatggcgaacgcg

"That's amazing," Doc said. "These fish must be intelligent. Maybe that internal structure in their heads is a synthetic extra brain?" he questioned.

Coleman interrupted, "That sure sounds creepy and evil."

They ate their striped bass dinner while discussing their plans in detail and, if all went well, they planned to serve the Exgenics warrants early Sunday morning. The sheriff summarized their next actions, "Tonight, I'll continue my surveillance, Doc will maintain communications with his chief for news or strange activity, and Julie & Jason will continue their Grid searches of Exgenics and the doctor. I'll bring Nick to breakfast for his update. Deputy James will be coming for breakfast too. Any questions?"

No one replied, so Coleman and Doc thanked Julie for a wonderful Friday fish fry and left the Dickson household for the evening.

7:00 p.m., Friday, July 2, ….

Charles County Deputy Jeffrey James had a busy afternoon and little time to prepare for his first date with Robin. After his shift, he drove his patrol car from Charlestown to Kent City, stopping at a grocer to buy a bouquet and then at a local fast-food franchise to grab take-out chicken picnic dinners on the way to her apartment. He pulled into the parking lot on the right side of apartments, got out of his car, and walked with flowers in hand upstairs to the second-floor breezeway.

As he reached the breezeway, which had many apartment doors facing a long connecting hallway, he saw Kent County Deputy James Jeffers in summer clothes also carrying flowers and entering the breezeway from the other stairs at the opposite end. As they both walked toward each other, Jeffrey said, "Hey James, what are you doing here?"

James replied, "I'm picking up my date," continuing down the hallway closer to Jeffrey.

"Well, that's a coincidence because I am too," Jeffrey replied as they ended up standing outside the same apartment.

They awkwardly looked at each other and began reaching to ring the same doorbell simultaneously.

"What're you doing here then?" James asked.

"I'm picking up Robin to the bluegrass festival. Does she have a roommate?" Jeffrey asked.

"No, I'm going with Robin to the festival tonight. She agreed on Monday afternoon," James replied loudly and strongly.

"Well, she said she'd go with me on Monday morning, so I've first dibs," Jeffrey replied in an even stronger and firm voice.

catgcgccgccgtattaaattcgcacccatgatgcgtatgcgatggaacgcatttgcgcgcatgcgccgccgtattaaattcgcacccatgatgcgtat

gcgaacgcgatggcgtaagcgatggcgaacgcgccgctggcgaacgcgtgcgcgaacgcgatggcgtaagcgatggcgaacgcg

"No, you don't. I went out with her last weekend, so this would be our second date. I have priority," James argued while puffing out his chest like a rooster to intimidate Jeffrey.

Jeffrey countered wisely defusing the tense situation from excess testosterone in close proximity, "Let's ring the doorbell and see who she wants to go out with then."

"OK. That sounds fair," James agreed hesitantly since he was unable to counter this logical resolution to their dilemma.

They both pressed the doorbell simultaneously and, in a few moments, the door opened. Robin exclaimed, "What're you *both* doing here?"

The deputies replied at the same time, "We're here for our date."

"I thought I was going out with Jeffrey tonight?" she replied questioningly.

"Yes, that's correct. We talked on Monday morning about the Bluegrass Festival," Jeffrey said.

"Well, you agreed to go out with me a second time on Monday afternoon. We're supposed to go to the festival also," James added.

"Hmmm," Robin replied. "I've been so busy this week, I've confused this entire evening. I see we've got a big problem now. Any ideas how we can resolve this?"

James suggested while looking at Jeffrey, "Let's arm wrestle. Winner gets to take her out."

"No, you're bigger than me. You'd win for sure. Let's flip a coin," Jeffery countered.

"I'm not leaving my date tonight to random chance," James replied while sternly staring at Jeffrey.

Robin interrupted them both, "Well, I've got a say in this too. Either you both go out with me at the same time tonight or I cancel both your dates."

The deputies both looked at each other in astonishment and Jeffrey replied, "Well, half a date is better than none."

"Yes, you're right. She'll see I'm the better man for sure then." James agreed with a wry, confident smile.

Jeffrey responded, "Maybe or maybe not. I'm willing to take that chance. I brought some chicken and portable chairs for a picnic dinner and we can ride in my patrol car."

"Well, I brought some chairs, Chinese take-out, and a cooler. We'll ride in my truck. There's room for you in the back seat," James countered.

The deputies stared directly at each other with scorn and enmity until Robin intervened, "Boys, let me take those beautiful flowers and put them

catgcgccgccgtattaaattcgcacccatgatgcgtatgcgatggaacgcatttgcgcgcatgcgccgccgtattaaattcgcacccatgatgcgtat

in some water. To be fair with you both, I'll drive. Go to your vehicles and get your chair and picnic food. I'll bring my own folding chair. My car is in the left parking lot. Agreed?"

The deputies reluctantly nodded their heads and went to their vehicles.

In a few minutes, Robin was at her car and the deputies met her, each carrying a single chair and their picnic dinners.

"Well, I'll sit in the front, James said first.

"No, I should sit in the front since it's my first date," Jeffrey replied as they started staring at each other again.

"Boys, to again be fair, both of you can sit in the back seat to get to know each other better. Since you're both deputies, I'm sure you've got a lot in common to talk about."

On the way to the festival, the tension and silence in the back seat were so thick and tough you couldn't even cut it with a knife.

9:30 p.m., Friday, July 2, ….

It had been a half-hour since Jason breached the Agrosupply Gridsite. From there, a grid link led to the Exgenics main servers.

He continued hacking and soon breached the outermost Exgenics firewall of their supplier procurement portal used to communicate orders, coordinate shipments, and send invoices. "Julie, I'm inside!" he exclaimed excitedly in anticipation of what he'd find next.

"That's good Jason. I hope you locate what we need."

"I traced the physical location of the Exgenics main Grid servers using a Grid 'node location' command similar to the 'ping' command on the old internet. The command returned physical Grid coordinates, which I located using the Sat-Map app as some big mansion just north of the Potomac River and south of Washington."

Julie replied as she stared at the laptop, "I'm still reviewing data on Dr. Gerardo, but I think he lives there. Ah, here it is, his mansion is on the National Register of Historic Places since the architect who designed it long ago was ahead of his time. There's so much data about Gerardo to study. It'll take a while to read and watch it all. He's a well-known figure."

"No problem Julie. We've all night to search and I'm sure you'll be thorough. It's important to understand what motivates him and try to find personal info, like his family and friends. This gives clues to any personal passwords. Since I have Gridlock now from my Dad's code, I can break into Dr. Gerado's E-Face account if necessary. Eventually, when we get enough data, we'll have a good understanding of the man, how he thinks, his behaviors, and habits. This psychological profile helps to understand

gcgaacgcgatggcgtaagcgatggcgaacgcgccgctggcgaacgcgtgcgcgaacgcgctgccggcgaacgcgatggcgtaagcgatggcgaacgcg

your opponent. I'm not sleeping tonight, since my best hacking is done in the late hours of the evening."

Julie replied, "Well, I need to sleep sometime. Maybe you can take a break before I go to bed?" she asked desiring her newlywed husband again.

"Yes, that's fine. We'll take a break later. Exercise keeps my head clear and focused," he winked in reply.

Now he had limited access within Exgenics' Gridsite, he began to first examine the database folder of recent agricultural supply orders. He downloaded all folders and files he found to his personal server and also to an archive at a remote Gridsite encrypted by his quantum chip. By this method, he created and stored a mirror of the exgenics.grid site for evidence. He looked at a few files to briefly examine their contents.

"Julie, here's purchase orders that agrosupply.grid has shipped to them. I'll compile them and orders from other suppliers into a complete inventory of what they purchase. So far, there are orders for cattle feed and fish food, which confirms they raise fish there."

"We can ask Doc to take a look at your list at breakfast," Julie replied.

"Let's remember to do that. I'll keep reviewing these files since there's so much data to sift through. After that, I'll move on to other data when I hack deeper and gain additional access into their network."

10:30 p.m., Friday, July 2, ….

Ella Bolton was the daughter of Jim Bolton from the Bolton Brothers Bluegrass Band and traveled with her extended family to summer bluegrass festivals since she was a child. She'd known Tommie Miller, son of the leader of the Catfish Banjo Band from South Hill, for many years. She'd first met him as a boy during the series of regional bluegrass festivals where her dad performed. Over time, their friendship had grown closer and now they were meeting again after both graduating from High School.

Ella watched most of the evening's banjo pickin' action with Tommie while sitting on a beach towel near the stage. "Your dad's set was great tonight," she commented loudly enough that Tommie could hear over the music. "My dad's playing tomorrow afternoon."

Tommie replied, "I saw he'll play at 2 p.m. His band is popular with the crowd." After listening a while longer, Tommie said, "It's getting hot here tonight, Ella. Wouldn't it be nice to swim and cool down?"

"Why not? Let's go to the dock and I can take off my clothes and jump in? I'll bring the towel so I can dry off afterward," Ella replied boldly while taking their relationship to another level. "You can keep your clothes on

gcgaacgcgatggcgtaagcgatggcgaacgcgccgctggcgaacgcgtgcgcgaacgcgctgccggcgaacgcgatggcgtaagcgatggcgaacgcg

for all I care," she laughed as she thought excitedly of skinny dipping with her boyfriend for the first time.

"I don't plan on wearing clothes either, so no need to worry about my clothes getting wet," he grinned back in anticipation.

They left the concert and walked about 100 yards onto the dock filled with berthed boats of concert attendees. The dock was dark except at the end where two streetlight lamps were lit on the steel pontoon dock.

Before reaching the lighted end, they stopped in a dark spot and Tommie said, "Let's jump in and swim over to that partly sunken pontoon just over there. It's quiet and even darker there," thinking that was a good place to make out with privacy.

They quickly took off their clothes, laid them in a heap on the towel, and jumped three feet down, splashing into the dark river. They swam together playfully away toward the old dock pontoon which was a shadowed ghost ship in the darkness. Unfortunately, the sunken dock section was covered with algae and very slippery, so they couldn't climb up, which dashed Tommie's hopes for a make-out session. They still splashed around and swam while giggling and laughing. After some foreplay, while treading water, Tommie said, "Let's swim back to the dock to continue. It's still dark there and everyone is at the concert right now."

Ella agreed and they swam to the dock. They now looked upward to the dock's edge looming several feet above. Ella said, "How are we going to get out now? The tide's low and there's no ladder."

Tommie surveyed the situation and replied, "We can pull ourselves up by grabbing that pipe by the dock's side and climb right up."

Ella kicked her legs to provide upward thrust, nimbly grabbed the narrow pipe to give her a boost as she kicked, and her lithe frame combined with her gymnastics abilities allowed her to pop out the water like a submerged cork. She scrambled onto the dock and grabbed her towel to quickly dry and cover herself. "Come on up. It's no problem getting out!" Ella said with confidence to Tommie below.

Tommie called up from the water, "That's like a pull-up bar; I'll be out in a flash." As he pulled himself upward with the full weight of his body, a pipe joint cracked from either his weight or corrosion, but it broke no matter the reason, exposing live electrical wires inside. As the conduit broke away from its junction box, he fell back into the water and was hit instantly by a 240-volt shock. The lights at the dock's end went dark and the water near Tommie briefly glowed with several eerie orbs. His heart stopped immediately and he floated face down in the water.

The most blood-curdling scream emanated from the dock that, if not for the music, would have been heard by anyone at the festival. However, one soul walking away from the porta-potties heard the cry of a distant Kraken by the dock, "HELP! I need HELLLP!! We need a DOCTOR!!!"

The person who heard the call for help ran to the rear of the bluegrass festival and yelled at the correct volume to attract the nearby audience's attention as they sat on picnic blankets and folding chairs, "HELP! Someone at the dock needs a DOCTOR!"

The two young deputies leaped from their portable chairs near the back row and ran toward the dock as Robin followed behind.

As they ran on the pitch-black dock, Jeffrey pulled a flashlight from his belt holster and shined it forward. They saw ahead a naked, young woman wrapped in a towel now sobbing uncontrollably on her knees facing the water. They arrived and Jeffrey shined the light on the water. They saw a young man floating face down near some electrical conduit. Robin said with authority, "We need to get the boy out of the water and use a portable defibrillator immediately."

"I'll jump in to pull him out," Jeffrey said.

James replied, "No. wait! There still could be electricity in those wires and you could die. I think there's a lifesaving pole at the campground's swimming pool nearby. Let me run and grab it first. Give me two minutes to bring it back and then we'll both pull the young man out safely."

"Ok, go for it. I think there's a portable defibrillator at the campground office, I'll be back in a minute with it," Jeffery replied.

While the Deputies were running on their life-saving errands, Robin stood hopelessly while the young man's brain was oxygen-deprived and the young woman continued sobbing by the dock. She also thought how this emergency forced her dates to finally work together and that these men knew well how to respond to a crisis.

Jeffrey broke in the office door and returned first with the defibrillator. He exclaimed, "This boy's been without oxygen nearly four minutes. He doesn't have another minute left to wait for a lifesaving pole. There's a 50/50 chance the water is not electrified and I'm willing to take that risk to save him. Kiss me Robin before I jump in. If I go into cardiac arrest, save him first with that rescue pole."

"Why do you want to kiss me?" Robin asked inquisitively.

As he took off his belt, gun, and shoes, Jeffrey replied, "Because if I die, your smile will be the last thing I remember. I can't think of anything sweeter than thinking of you with my last thoughts."

She smiled, quickly leaned close to embrace him, and gave a peck of a kiss before releasing her arms as he dove into the water.

Luckily, the water wasn't electrified as he swam a few strokes, rolled the young man over, and grabbed him by one shoulder to drag him closer to the dock. In a few more strokes, they were dockside.

Deputy Jeffers soon arrived with the pole both he and Robin leaned over the edge of the dock and grabbed the man by his arms. They simultaneously pulled him upward three feet, hoisting him like pulling a 200-pound tuna into a boat and laying him on his back across the cypress dock boards.

"I need to dry him to use the defibrillator!" Robin exclaimed as she put her mouth to the boy's mouth and gave him one breath first to inflate his lungs with fresh air and perhaps a brain-saving dose of oxygen before she started her CPR compressions.

"Miss, may we borrow your towel?" Deputy Jeffers asked and reached an arm in the direction of the young woman who was now standing and watching. As he averted his eyes, a towel was thrust into his open fingers, he toweled off the man's torso while Robin rhythmically pressed his sternum. He soon tossed the towel back toward the naked woman.

Robin stopped her chest compressions and placed the auto-defibrillator unit over the man's chest. She quickly took the suction-cup electrical paddles and, without looking at the e-screen instructions, quickly placed them on the body for maximum effect as only a doctor would know. She gave him one more breath of air, moved away from the body, and pressed the 'On' button.

Next, the defibrillator spoke through its speaker in a woman's voice, "Stand back to avoid electrical shock," and Robin observed the man's torso convulse periodically as the AI-computer delivered carefully timed electrical shocks to the patient. After a minute, the defibrillator softly beeped a series of rapid heartbeat tones and the unit said, "Sinus rhythm restored. Respiration has resumed. Heartbeat fast and irregular but I will monitor and provide updates. Administer aspirin tablet when patient is conscious," and a small dispenser bottle with an aspirin dropped from a slot in the defibrillator unit. The defibrillator continued, "Keep patient lying down and contact emergency medical services immediately."

Robin looked at the digital display and agreed his heart rate was high. She wasn't sure if it was the shocks or the epinephrine robo-injection from the unit which had revived him, but as a doctor, she was relieved. His heart was beating and he was breathing on his own.

Jeffery clambered out of the river dripping like a wet Golden Retriever, "I'm glad he's alive. It was worth the chance," he smiled looking at Robin.

Robin saw him in his wet uniform and smiled back at the courageous deputy who faced death to save life. "Thank you, Jeffrey. It's nice to save a life after seeing all those deaths this week. James, call 911 to send a med-evac drone immediately."

Deputy Jeffers took his e-phone and called dispatch for a med-evac drone. Soon, another Kent County deputy arrived, who had been working overtime as event security. As acting sheriff, Jeffers took command and instructed the deputy to perform crowd control and clear a landing zone for the drone's lifepod.

Jeffers then talked to the young women to gather info for his report. "What happened miss?" he said as he used his e-phone to record an audio clip of the girl speaking in the near darkness.

The girl replied, "We went swimming and Tommie was climbing out when the pipe broke and he fell back into the water. I saw the weirdest glowing spots and the dock lights went out at the same time. He didn't move afterward, so I guessed he got shocked and I screamed for help."

"Well, you likely saved his life, miss," James said with tenderness to console her while another security-duty deputy wrapped her in a blanket.

The med-evac drone soon arrived, hovering overhead as it lowered its rescue pod to the dock. The rescuers carefully laid the unconscious young man into the pod and closed the hatch. Next, the drone retracted the pod and whirred away toward the hospital in Williamsburg.

"Well gentlemen, I think our date is over for tonight. It was difficult but I'm proud of how you both eventually behaved and worked together."

Robin drove the deputies back toward her apartment. In the back seat, they were finally talking to each other at least. They arrived, unpacked their things, and both deputies walked her to her apartment door.

She looked carefully at the two men and impulsively grabbed Jeffrey's hand to pull him close and give him a brief kiss.

"You were a hero tonight. I like that very much." Robin smiled.

"No, I was just doing what needed to be done. We all were heroes tonight. Goodnight, Robin," Jeffrey said smiling as Robin entered her apartment and closed the door while looking at the heroic deputy.

"No hard feelings?" Jeffrey asked James.

"None at all, you're a braver man than I," Deputy Jeffers replied as he began thinking of his election campaign for Kent County Sheriff and also that cute Kent City pharmacy technician he'd been dating for a while.

Chapter 23: Terror Strikes in the Night

Supercruzer, Security LTD Edition

11:00 p.m., Friday, July 2, ….

Grandpa slept while Julie and Jason focused on their Grid searches in Jason's bedroom. Jason commented, "I've found information from Exgenics low-security level Gridsite, but they have some high-security areas that seem encrypted using that quantenna. I'm not sure I can hack them without direct access to their farm's computers. However, there's lots of info I've uncovered on Exgenics' purchases. If we itemize their purchases, we'll better understand what they do at the farm."

"Julie, come take a look at this list of Agrosupply purchases I've compiled. It says here they were shipped a lot of cow supplies, vitamin supplements, fish food, and dog chow. We already know about the cows and this confirms they raise fish, but what about the dogs?"

"I can answer your question. I saw an image showing Dr. Gerardo and two large dogs standing outside his mansion near Washington," Julie replied. She soon showed Jason an image with the caption, '*Dr. Gerardo with his dogs Dante and Inferno*,' from a Gerardo dossier file she was creating.

Jason looked closely, "Well those surely look like some hungry and tough Dobermans, so that explains the need for so much dog food."

Jason continued showing Julie the list, "There are also large orders from Genechem, a supplier of likely genetic engineering chemicals."

Julie reviewed that supplier's list. "Yes, those are chemical reagents used for genetic engineering," she replied using her biochemistry knowledge and lab course training in genetic engineering.

Jason added, "They buy some drugs from a veterinary pharmaceutical supply house too. Some look normal, like antibiotics for cows, but they also use a lot of two drugs called cyclosporine and somatropin."

"I don't know about those. Let me search the Grid quickly." Julie soon replied, "Cyclosporine is an immune-suppressant that's used for contact dermatitis in dogs so maybe his dogs have a skin disease. Somatropin is a synthetic growth hormone so perhaps they grow cancers so they can test cures. Let's ask Doc and Nick later why they might use them."

Jason continued, "There are also some strange chemicals from some chemical supply house too. Like why do they need triphenyltin acetate, dimethyl selenide, trimethylsilyl chloride, and trimethyl borate?"

Julie replied, "I don't have a clue, but some are organo-metallic compounds and selenium is found in amino acids of certain organisms."

"Maybe those chemicals are used to grow those internal structures we saw in Frank's tribo-ray image?" Jason postulated.

"We should ask Doc or Nick what they think again," Julie replied.

"I think we've learned what we can from the procurement portal. Let's now look at their distribution department's files. If Exgenics produces drugs, we can view their freight shipment bills of lading."

Hal, the NSA Grid Analyst monitoring fish images, had spent the past six hours probing for the origin of the Grid searches and hack. However, his efforts to uncover the hack's source weren't going well. Each time he attempted to access an active node, another node would appear on his e-screen and continue accessing controlled data. He commented to his CIA coworker, "It's like someone hacked the entire Grid and is using it against us. They've put a lock on Grid nodes that prevents us from disengaging our network connections to determine the infection's origin."

Janice from the CIA commented, "This hack is *big*. Whoever they are, they control the Grid now. I must notify Ops Central to escalate this info to the highest levels."

Hal replied, "All I can do for now is continuously monitor the Grid to determine what they see and what other search anomalies occur, but the only way I know how to stop them is to pull the plug on the entire Grid!"

"That's what we had to do during the Great Internet Virus! We can't do that again. We *must* preserve the Grid. It monitors and controls *everything*. We're only three days from anarchy if it fails like the internet did long ago," Janice replied with extreme worry.

Midnight, Saturday, July 3, ...

Nearly 140 boats gathered and idled in the waters close to Osprey Landing for the official start of the fishing tournament. On one boat near the dock, an official held a bullhorn to bark out final instructions and remind the participants of the most important rules, "When I give the signal, the tournament officially begins. Keep your podcams turned-on at all times over the next 48 hours to record the weight of each fish on your calibrated scales. You're allowed to keep fish above the minimum size and weight limit as set by the rules. Prizes are for each species and overall tournament winner for the most fish caught by weight and released."

The official continued, "Remember, your Grid transponders show Grid areas and hourly time slots each fisherman fishes a randomly assigned area. I'm sure by now you've scouted the Grids where you'll have the best fishing. Please boat safely and keep your eyes alert for other boaters since this weekend is busy on the lake. Good luck and have a great weekend. Ladies and Gentlemen, the tournament begins now," he said and fired his starter's pistol.

Immediately, the engines roared to life, and the boats, with fishermen wearing night vision glasses, gradually dispersed in the darkness until it was safe for each boat to use full throttle on their motors to reach their assigned Grid location for the next hour of fishing.

1:00 a.m., Saturday, July 3, ….

Jason was worming through the Exgenics distribution department files. As he examined many data files, he found thousands of small shipments for autodrone delivery to hospitals and cancer clinics. He commented to Julie, "I've looked at hundreds of different shipments with shipping addresses to hospitals and cancer clinics. The weight of each shipment was almost three pounds. They shipped something called Exgena-CX and then there's some of numbers and letters next to it."

Julie replied, "Those are custom Exgena drug shipments to each patient. Their drugs must be administered intravenously in an IV bag, so that explains the weight. Also, I think the numbers are for a drug variation designed to cure each cancer. There are many types of cancer and each patient needs a custom drug. The drug uses Gerardo's Crickett technology to repair defective genes in the patient's cells."

Jason continued, "This bill of lading is interesting too. It's an autotruck shipment that went out early this week to the following address: Building 560, Fort Detrick, Maryland."

"Fort Detrick? That old government weapons research facility was closed after the coronavirus pandemic. Those 'accidental' lab leaks caused a worldwide treaty to be signed against genetic engineering of viruses, even for research purposes. What was the shipment?" Julie asked.

"The bill of lading says 20 barrels of TTX concentrate. The shipment weight totaled 8,000 pounds. What's TTX?" Jason questioned.

gcgaacgcgatggcgtaagcgatggcgaacgcgccgctggcgaacgcgtgcgcgaacgcgctgccggcgaacgcgatggcgtaagcgatggcgaacgcg

"I don't know Jason, let me search the Grid," Julie replied as she typed the letters into the Grid search engine. In a moment, she replied, "Oh my God. TTX is a chemical acronym for tetrodotoxin. They're making poison at Exgenics too!" she exclaimed.

"They must have many fish like Frank producing it at their farm. That explains their fish food orders, but the real questions are for who and why are they manufacturing it. Biological and chemical weapons are banned now," Jason said as he pondered further.

"I don't know. Jason, come hold me. I'm really scared," she said with goosebumps. "What're we doing? This situation is bigger than all of us."

Jason went to the bed, lay down next to Julie, and gave her a comforting caress. "I not sure where this leads, but we've likely revealed Sheriff Coleman's conspiracy theory. This *is* a secret that people involved with Exgenics would be willing to kill for."

He continued holding her gently and gave her a brief kiss. She replied with an even warmer embrace and, soon, the newlywed couple was making love. Afterward, Jason said, "That sure relieves a lot of stress. Do you feel better sweetheart?"

"I always feel safe in your arms Jason. I'm tired so let me sleep now. Don't forget you're cooking breakfast this morning," she reminded him.

"Ok Julie, get some rest. I'll keep searching all night. I think I miss my all-night hacks," he jokingly said as he carefully covered his exhausted wife with a sheet, put on his boxer shorts, and sat down again by his e-screen as the ceiling fan wafted a cooling breeze around the bedroom, removing the excess body heat filling the room.

3:30 a.m., Saturday, July 3, ….

A two-mile-long autotruck convoy, guarded by front and rear security guards in Supercruzer Security LTD editions, was traveling westbound on Interstate 64 when three tanker autotrucks unexpectedly drove onto an off-ramp and slowed at the ramp's end to stop. The rear security guard, who was sleeping in the front seat, was soon awakened by an alarm and message coming from the AI-security system, "Unscheduled autotruck departure detected. Three autotrucks left the highway at Exit 214."

The rear guard used her e-phone and called the front convoy security guard, "Three trucks just exited the convoy. "I'll try to manually override their nav-systems first." She typed a few keystrokes on her e-screen to no effect. "Their location transponders just turned off too," she exclaimed.

"Hackers have hijacked them. Follow those trucks," the guard replied.

catgcgccgccgtattaaattcgcacccatgatgcgtatgcgatggaacgcatttgcgcgcatgcgccgccgtattaaattcgcacccatgatgcgtat

gcgaacgcgatggcgtaagcgatggcgaacgcgccgctggcgaacgcgtgcgcgaacgcgctgccggcgaacgcgatggcgtaagcgatggcgaacgcg

"I'm in pursuit now," the rear guard said as she took manual control of her Supercruzer while doubling her speed to catch up with the autotrucks nearly a mile ahead of her. She turned onto the exit ramp but the Supercruzer's wheels stopped suddenly as its electrical drive system seized. The SUV skidded off the ramp, rolled down an embankment, coming to rest on its roof. As the airbags deflated, the guard spoke to the other guard by e-phone, "My Supercruzer just wrecked itself. Send help."

The three tanker trucks turned toward Provident Forge and started to drive at dangerous speeds for such heavy loads. One barreled straight through the town and off the end of the washed-out Chick Bridge. A detonator cord duct-taped on the bottom of the truck's trailer soon exploded, tearing the 40-foot-long cargo tank like a can opener. Toxic liquid contents immediately gushed out of the tank's gash into the waters.

The two other tankers turned left at Provident Forge and continued east on Route 60 for several miles before the second truck slowed and turned toward Osprey Landing. It careened across the railroad crossing and down the narrow rural road. Soon it slowed to drive over a plank road, still used across the swamp, and continued driving briskly past the sleepy campground except for a few drunk campers sitting by their fires. Finally, the truck accelerated down the lower boat ramp into the water at nearly 35 miles per hour. Immediately, another detonation split the metal tank, spilling the contents.

The third truck drove further along Route 60, turned right, and repeated the maneuver at East Lake Campground's upper boat ramp but this truck detonated near the water intake of the Chickahominy Pumping Station and sank fully underneath the deep waters of the old river channel.

⋈⟨⟨⟩⟩⟨⟨⟩⟩⟨⟨⟩⟩⋈

Coleman hid in the swampy woods studying Exgenics guard rotations, comings, goings, and drone patrols. This night was busier than last night and saw two black Supercruzers and a minivan arrive after midnight. He lay listening to the frog croaks and buzzing cicadas surrounding him and stared at the gate amidst the forest fireflies. Mosquitos tried biting, but face netting and the thermal camo-blanket provided protection.

In the distance, he soon heard nearby the electric whirr of several autotrucks driving through Provident Forge. He then heard with alarm a muffled explosion nearly a quarter-mile away from the direction of the Chick Bridge. He immediately left his post, made his way back to the Captain's canoe, and, after 45 minutes, arrived at Chick Bridge. In the darkness, he saw a partly submerged and wrecked tanker truck with its lights still on. He paddled closer and began smelling a strong chemical

catgcgccgccgtattaaattcgcacccatgatgcgtatgcgatggaacgcatttgcgcgcatgcgccgccgtattaaattcgcacccatgatgcgtat

spilled in the water. He took out his two-way radio and called to Jason, "White Knight to Black Rook. White Knight to Black Rook. Over."

Jason, who was still hacking as Julie slept, replied on his Brick, "Go ahead, let's continue our game. Pawn to g6. Over."

Coleman replied, "I need Thomas Jefferson to meet me immediately. Bishop to c4. Over."

"10-4, Will do. Have important news for breakfast. Knight to b6. Over," Jason replied while adding another fake chess move to confuse anyone overhearing their radio communications.

"I do too. Good move. See you later. Bishop to b3. Over and Out." Coleman replied playing along with the chess game ruse.

Aroused from her sleep by the nebulous radio conversation, Julie asked, "What was that about Jason?"

"I need to call Deputy James," Jason replied then walked down to the kitchen, picked up the wall phone, and dialed Deputy James' home number. He woke the deputy and told him to meet the sheriff at Chick Bridge. He walked back to the bedroom and Julie was still awake.

"Go back to sleep Julie. Everything is OK for now," Jason said.

"You come too, Jason. You need some sleep," she softly implored.

"I can't Julie. Once I start a hack, my mind spins like a whirlpool until I figure things out," he said as he walked to the bed and gave a reassuring kiss on her forehead as he stroked her blonde hair gently until she fell asleep again. He went back to his chair, put his ear-pods in, and started playing one of his dad's old songs, entitled 'Onward' as he continued his hack. Occasionally, he looked at Julie soundly sleeping like an angel.

He next hacked into a corporate data folder with a file containing a long list of Exgenics private shareholders and another file with an organization chart that included a board member list. First, he let the shareholder list scroll before his eyes but didn't recognize any of the individual names until he got to the letter 'S' in the alphabet. He saw 'Stoneman Family Trust' and thought of Grandpa's discussions while fishing about a dead rich man named Stoneman. He wished now that he'd paid more past attention to current events and Grid newsfeeds so he might have recognized other well-known names. Next Jason looked at the organization chart and board member list. He saw a list of names and the name 'John D. Stoneman IV' and thought he was the dead man's son.

He then quickly Grid searched other board member names for some basic biographical information. Soon, a brief bio popped up on the e-screen for each name. As he reviewed the bios, he realized they all were powerful and important people too. The list of board members included names from All-Nippon Robotics, Drone-Motion, E-Face, and even Gridcom. "My God!" he mentally screamed in silence at the revelation he uncovered, knowing this would be important news at breakfast.

He continued hacking the Exgenics Gridsite and found a very large database that appeared to be a master biological library of genomes for millions of species. The database was visually arranged on his e-screen as a list of folders in a tree-like branching pattern. The folders of the different branches were titled with the Latin names for the scientific nomenclature of living organisms: kingdom, phylum, order, family, genus, and individual species. He also saw a 'Search' function was accessible that allowed database searching by name or DNA sequence.

He entered in the search box the species name '*Takifugu obscurus*' and another folder popped up on the screen containing a short list of computer files. The files all had a file name suffix of either '*.dna*', '*.fna*', or '*.gmp.*' He'd never seen those kinds of files before, so he opened one file of each type. Just as he finished a quick review of the three files, all the electronics in the room loudly beeped three times, including his e-watch, e-phone, computer, laptop, podcam, alarm clock, and Julie's e-phone. The noise could wake the dead.

4:58 a.m., Saturday Morning, July 3, ...

Everyone asleep in Charles and Kent Counties was awakened by their Grid-connected devices which all broadcast three sharp tones. A message was texted and a familiar voice was heard, "Hello Citizens. This is President Elle Woods and I am issuing a regional presidential alert for the following counties: Charles, James, Kent, and York. This alert also covers the Virginia cities of Williamsburg, Newport News, and Hampton.[78]

ISM cyber terrorists have hijacked three auto-tanker trucks loaded with concentrated liquid meta-flumoxicarb pesticide and dumped them into the Chickahominy Lake to poison the City of Newport News and other nearby cities.[79] These cities are dependent on this freshwater supply and are affected by this alert. All residents using water in the region are advised to not drink or use water from a tap unless it's sourced from a well.

We will be mobilizing FEMA immediately to bring fresh drinking water to all citizens impacted by this emergency, but it'll take a day or two to get

---

[78] Cities in Virginia are entirely independent from counties in Virginia and an independent city is separated politically and outside the legal jurisdiction of its county. Some cities have assimilated what used to be the separate county that surrounded them.

[79] Islamic State of Michigan (ISM) was a terrorist organization that wanted to institute Sharia law in the State of Michigan to form an independent Islamic state.

sufficient supplies to the affected areas. I ask for your calm, patience, and compassion for other citizens during this crisis while we implement our regional assistance plans.

All boaters must leave Chickahominy Lake and River immediately to avoid contamination and I am issuing a voluntary evacuation order for all nearby residents to take refuge at least 1/10th mile away from the waters.

I am invoking martial law and ordering the Virginia National Guard and the US Army to maintain civil order and help apprehend these terrorists during this emergency. Do not fish on Chickahominy Lake or River or eat fish caught there. Stay tuned to your local Grid-News channel for further information and details as they become available. We will catch these terrorists who want to show on July 4th Independence Day weekend that we shouldn't be free, but rather ruled under their religious laws."

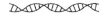

Chapter 24: A Breakfast Meeting

Lower Chick Helidrone Patrol

5:02 a.m., Saturday Morning, July 3, ….

Julie immediately awakened and listened with Jason to the emergency message. Afterward, Julie said, "I can't believe they poisoned the river."

Jason replied, "I don't know, but I'm sure we didn't hear the truth, or perhaps it was false or only partly true. I think Exgenics is using the poison to cover up other fish like Frank. Afterward, they'll likely have drones flying over the water cleaning up evidence of dead glowfish. Their strategy is just to *kill* off their problems with impunity. That's why we've got to protect Frank more than ever because his continued existence protects our lives if we are captured."

Grandpa knocked on the bedroom door and said, "I see you heard that message too. Can I come in?"

"Yes, Grandpa," Jason answered from his desk.

He entered the doorway and said, "I overheard you talking to Julie and I think this situation is really big too. Let's discuss this news more at breakfast, but I think we're facing evil incarnated. We *must* do something."

Jason replied, "I agree. We don't know what's the truth, but this conspiracy goes to the highest levels of power. I learned this morning that some of the richest and most powerful people in the world are Exgenics board members. If they had secrets like Frank they wanted to hide, they'd do anything to stop them from being discovered. Now we know they're deeply connected with Gridcom. Even worse is they control the government or secretly push certain levers of Federal power."

"That's very likely," Grandpa replied. "I'm making a pot of coffee now. Are you coming downstairs to start breakfast, Jason?"

"No Grandpa, I'll be there in a half-hour. I need to talk to Julie first."

"Fine. You want a cup?" Grandpa asked while leaving the room.

"Yes Grandpa, but I'll drink it later," Jason said as the door closed.

"Julie, I've found genetic files I can't understand. Can you help?"

"I think so. I've already completed courses in bioinformatics and genetic engineering," Julie replied as she rose from bed wearing one of Jason's T-shirts and leaned over his shoulder as he stared at the e-screen.

Jason continued, "See this '.dna' file contains lowercase letters 'a', 'c', 'g', and 't' in random order and this '.fna' file contains upper-case letters from what is nearly an 'A' to 'Z' alphabet, but in non-random order." Somehow, Jason knew the degree of randomness of both data files, like his unconscious mind counted statistical frequencies and letter patterns.

Julie reviewed the information and replied, "They all seem random to me, but here's what I understand. The 'a', 'c', 'g', and 't' letters of the '.dna' file are a geneticist's abbreviations of the four organic bases in the DNA helix: adenine, cytosine, guanine, and thymine. This letter sequence, of these bases in the DNA helix, is the blueprint for life and is found in the chromosomes of every living cell's nucleus. Individual groups of three of these a', 'c', 'g', and 't' base letters are called codons, in that they code for the living cell to form specific amino acids. So, life uses these codons to form the 20 or so amino acids which are building blocks of all proteins."

"However, it's complicated to understand deeply. Our cells are like a chemical soup, and these codons are the recipe to form new molecules in a process called transcription. The soup interacts with the codons to form a new molecule, but the different order or sequence, as geneticists call it, of the codon's letters is the recipe for which molecule is produced."

"For example, if a codon has the sequence 'cta', the cell forms an amino acid molecule named leucine, but if the codon is 'cat', it forms an amino acid named histidine. If a longer sequence of the DNA bases is 'ctacat', the cell produces a leucine molecule chemically linked to a histidine molecule. By linking up longer codon sequences, a series of amino acids link to form a protein. Different proteins then interact to form and build cellular structures controlling living processes. Life results. It's a miracle."

Jason replied, "So in a way, the triplet pattern of individual codon's bases is raw data in a code for designing life. When does the cell stop reading the code? You could make an endlessly long protein molecule by the process you described."

Julie answered, "Well, there is also something called a 'stop' or termination codon. When the codon sequence includes 'taa', 'tag', or 'tga' codons, this ends the transcription process that creates a specific protein. When a much longer sequence of codons for different proteins is transcribed, it's called a gene. That's what gives you your green eyes, for example, and genes on your many chromosomes make you who you are."

gcgaacgcgatggcgtaagcgatggcgaacgcgccgctggcgaacgcgtgcgcgaacgcgctgccggcgaacgcgatggcgtaagcgatggcgaacgcg

Jason thought a while and replied, "The process of forming a protein is like putting a period at the end of a DNA sentence in a language for life. Then, the next DNA sentence is read, building another protein and so on. Eventually, the ordered sentences become paragraphs, which are our genes, and then all paragraphs form a chapter which is a chromosome. Finally, all chromosomes form a book that becomes a living organism, but maybe a better analogy is the recipe for life. Is that correct?"

"Yes Jason, that's a really simple way of explaining life and how the DNA code works. Now, let me explain that '.fna' file to you. This file data is formatted what geneticists call FASTA format and contains the same information as a '.dna' file, just represented differently. Remember how I said there are normally about 20 amino acids? Well, geneticists gave each amino acid, as formed by a codon, a capitalized letter corresponding to its name. For example, 'L' corresponds to the amino acid leucine and 'H' corresponds to histidine, but the stop codon is an asterisk."

"In a FASTA file, these capital letters form a genetic alphabet of the amino acids and a geneticist just reads the capital letters to understand the protein or gene. It's a lot easier to read the alphabet than all those 'a', 'c', 'g', and 't' letters. The capital letter sequence becomes a protein formation 'sentence' as you described. So geneticists read FASTA '.fna' files of 'A' to 'Z' letters created from the '.dna' file containing 'a', 'c', 'g', and 't' letters."

Julie continued, "In the '.fna' file, the letter colors also make it easier for the geneticist to see and visualize the different proteins in a complete gene. So, if a series of letters is yellow, that's one protein and if they're red, that's an adjacent, different protein. By using different colors, it's possible to visually separate all the proteins from each other."

"It's like in geography and how four colors are used a world map so no two countries touching have the same color. The same principle works with the proteins in FASTA format. Of course, to make things easier, geneticists these days use AI-computer programs that automatically translate the raw data '.dna' format into the FASTA '.fna' data format. Also, they reverse translate '.fna' files back into raw '.dna' files too."

Jason intensely thought and then commented to Julie, "It's interesting how the DNA code is similar to how computer data is stored. Older computer data is binary, with a series of ones and zeros. Now, quantum computer data is stored as three numbers: negative one, zero, and positive one. However, the DNA helix is quaternary, since you've four different 'numbers' which are the 'a', 'c', 'g', and 't' bases that contain the data. Combining that with how the codon system works, you have more data storage and the ability to create intricate programs."

catgcgccgccgtattaaaattcgcacccatgatgcgtatgcgatggaacgcatttgcgcgcatgcgccgccgtattaaaattcgcacccatgatgcgtat

gcgaacgcgatggcgtaagcgatggcgaacgcgccgctggcgaacgcgtgcgcgaacgcgctgccggcgaacgcgatggcgtaagcgatggcgaacgcg

"Even more profound is the proteins are three-dimensional forms of individual molecules and, therefore, it takes four 'dimensions' to build them. Three dimensions create the molecule's shape, and the fourth dimension is the time when each molecule is assembled step-by-step to form a larger molecule. That explains how complex life forms are so exquisitely achieved in such a relatively small file size."

Julie replied, "I never thought of it that way, but it makes sense Jason. You think and see things from a different perspective than most people."

"What does this '*gmp*' file tell you?" Jason asked, opening up an interactive presentation-style file entitled '*Takifugu obscurus.*'

Julie replied, "That's visualized genomic map in an interactive format allowing you to examine the individual genes of each chromosome. Let me explain further. See, each chromosome of the organism is listed by number and shows information about the specific genes. In life, each chromosome has a different length and shape. That's why human '*X*' and '*Y*' chromosomes look different under a high-powered microscope."

"Let me explain how that happens. Remember I told you the other day about telomeres on the end of DNA strands that control aging of a cell's lineage and its eventual death? Well, see this little black line across each chromosome bar of that genome map shows the location of what is called the centromere. The centromere is like a focal point associated with cell division; when the centromeres of a cell's chromosomes all become activated at the same time, the cell divides."

"In the '*X*' chromosome, the centromere is at the center of a visual '*X*' pattern formed by the chromosome's DNA strands; this is called a metacentric chromosome. For a '*Y*' chromosome, it's near the end of the DNA strands and looks like a '*Y*' because the bottom leg of the '*Y*' is short. This is called either acrocentric or subtelocentric depending how close the centromere is to the telomeres."

"On that map of each chromosome, the colors work similar to before, but now there are more colors used this time represent the different genes and their functions in the organism." She clicked on a colored bar of the map and a new screen popped up showing a '*.fna*' file. "See how this screen is interactive? You press on a gene and a data file pops up to view."

Jason replied, "Thanks Julie. Now I understand this data formatting much better. I should've studied more biology in college and not so much electronics and coding," he chuckled. He next opened up a screen that showed the tree-branch diagram of life and said, "So, this entire database has genetic files from the tree of life."

catgcgccgccgtattaaattcgcacccatgatgcgtatgcgatggaacgcatttgcgcgcatgcgccgccgtattaaattcgcacccatgatgcgtat

Julie replied, "This is database is amazing. I've never seen such an extensive genetic library. It seems Dr. Gerardo has access to a nearly complete genome of all known life that's been DNA sequenced."

"There's a mind-boggling amount of information here," Jason replied seeing on his screen the incredible size of the database folder. Just then, his e-watch beeped an alarm, "Well, I have to get the day started and it's time to make breakfast," he said as he quickly slipped on some clothes.

"If you don't mind, I'll study this genetic information more while you cook," Julie said as she sat down at Jason's desk chair.

"Sounds good, Sweetheart," Jason said as he slipped on some clothes and walked to the bathroom to brush his teeth and wash his face.

Jason entered the kitchen and Grandpa was sitting there sipping a cup of coffee and scratching Rufus behind his ears as he drooled on the floor. "Morning Jason," he paused. "Rufus is a good dog, but he's still sad. He's lost people he loves, just like us. So, we have something in common. Other than that, he's adjusting well to his new masters. I think he likes you most Jason, but only because you're cooking breakfast and feeding him." Grandpa chuckled. "What's on the chef's menu?" he asked Jason, who loved to cook and, especially, bake macaron cookies from scratch.

"I'm making huevos rancheros and cheese grits since I've got many men and Julie to feed.[80,81] I'll make extra for Rufus since he deserves a treat sometimes," Jason replied, scratching the old hound behind the ear.

"Sounds delicious Jason. I'll edit my Sunday sermon on my laptop until breakfast and finish it later at the church office. Recent events in Charles County require me to edit it," Grandpa replied.

"I'm sure it'll be an inspiring sermon, Grandpa. Now let me put my chef hat on," Jason replied as he started cooking breakfast. Jason measured some water, dry grits, and salt in a pot and then placed them on a stove burner to boil. Then, he cracked two dozen farm fresh eggs from the neighbor into a bowl and whipped them slightly with a fork. He chopped two onions, some green peppers, several tomatoes, placed them into a frying pan with some oil, and started gently sautéing them until tender. Finally, he added the eggs with a little salt and freshly ground pepper and cooked the egg mixture until it was softly cooked in the pan,

---

[80]A traditional Mexican breakfast dish of scrambled eggs, refried beans, and fried vegetables such as onions, peppers, and tomatoes often served on a tortilla.

[81] Grits are a traditional Southern breakfast side-dish made from dried granules of corn that are boiled and cooked into a soft porridge. Grits are usually seasoned with salt, pepper, and butter. Cheese grits have cheese added to the dish.

gcgaacgcgatggcgtaagcgatggcgaacgcgccgctggcgaacgcgtgcgcgaacgcgctgccggcgaacgcgatggcgtaagcgatggcgaacgcg

while occasionally stirring the boiling grits in the nearby pot to prevent them from sticking. When the grits were thickened, he added freshly-grated cheese and a large pad of butter, which melted into the hot mixture.

Grandpa briefly interrupted Jason's culinary efforts, "What're you preparing for Nick's breakfast? He can't eat hot food on Saturdays."

"There's a left-over piece of Julie's fish in the refrigerator if he wants it and some bread and butter. I hope that'll do."

After the eggs and grits were done, he scraped breakfast into two large serving bowls with a spoon. He also dumped some of each dish into Red's old bowl, tossed some crunchy dog bits on top for garnish, and placed it on the floor. Rufus hungrily began munching breakfast.

Julie sat at Jason's desk examining the genomic tree of life and the Takifugu genus folder. She clicked it and saw another tree diagram with a list of individual species names in alphabetical order. As she scrolled her eyes down the species list, she saw 'bimaculatus', 'chinensis', 'chrysops', 'exascurus', 'flavidus', 'niphobles', 'oblongus', 'obscurus', 'ocelatus', 'pardalis', 'porphyreus', 'radiatus', 'reticularis', 'rupripes', 'snyden', 'stictonotus', 'teletrophorus'.

She immediately stopped at that word similar to one she'd heard recently. Then she remembered Nick said Dr. Gerardo sequenced the DNA of an electric eel species 'Electrophorus volta'. She thought about the word 'electrophorus' and using her knowledge of Latin, deduced this meant 'electricity carrier'. However, she couldn't understand why the name of the species started with the letter 't'. "That must be Frank's species," she assumed. She examined the '.gmp' genome map file for 'Takifugu telectrophorus' and thought, "This map looks like the 'obscurus' genome map I was looking at with Jason, but some chromosomes are longer and there are large areas of many chromosomes that are colored black." She clicked on the black regions of the map, but no FASTA file for a gene appeared in a popup window. Instead, a new popup window appeared to enter a password. "What's the password?" she thought to herself.

She also saw there was a sub-folder named 'Crickett' in the main 'Takifugu telectrophorus' genomic folder. She clicked to open that folder and it contained several thousand files with a '.ckt' filename suffix. She clicked randomly to open a file, but it was also password protected. She clicked on several other '.ckt' files and all were protected.

After these discoveries, she hurriedly slipped on a dress, and went to the bathroom to wash her face, brush her teeth, and comb her long blonde hair. She went downstairs for breakfast, bringing Jason's laptop to later show everyone the new information she'd found.

catgcgccgccgtattaaattcgcacccatgatgcgtatgcgatggaacgcatttgcgcgcatgcgccgccgtattaaattcgcacccatgatgcgtat

6:00 a.m., Saturday, July 3, ….

Jason quickly set the table and placed the serving bowls. As a finishing touch of his Southern breakfast, he garnished the grits with freshly ground black pepper and added extra butter. For the eggs, he put a bottle of hot pepper sauce on the table. For Nick, he pulled from the refrigerator a leftover fish fillet. Grandpa also brewed a fresh pot of coffee for the morning guests. Soon, Rufus barked and the doorbell rang.

Grandpa opened the door, "Morning gentlemen," he said to Sheriff Coleman, Doc, Deputy James, and Nick.

Jason hollered from the kitchen, "Come to the kitchen everyone. Breakfast's ready." The men entered a kitchen filled with the aroma of breakfast and coffee in the air. "Please sit at the table," Jason added as the men chattered while sitting down in their chairs.

"Reverend, will you say grace?" Coleman asked.

"Yes, George. Heavenly Father, please bless this meal so we may help you to fight against the evil we've uncovered. Let this food nourish our spirits and bodies so that we may be strong enough to uncover your truth. In your name, Amen."

As everyone began to eat breakfast, Coleman began, "Well, I think we've all heard the news about the presidential alert and the declaration of martial law. I saw the tanker wreck at Chick Bridge and knew something big was happening. This situation is likely cover for what we've discovered. That poison will probably kill *all* fish in the lake and river."

Jeffrey added, "I agree. Trucks don't randomly drive themselves off the highway into a river. It's a premeditated act of *war* against *our* river."

Doc did a quick mental calculation and added, "That much meta-flumoxicarb is enough for a complete fish kill and will likely pollute the river and perhaps even the Chesapeake Bay for years. It would solve Exgenics' problems by eliminating any evidence of the glowfish."

Grandpa said, "Then perhaps Frank is the last glowfish alive if the others are killed."

Jason added, "We have to keep Frank alive and out of their hands then. We also have some interesting news to report on our Grid searches. We've entered the Exgenics Gridsite and discovered a list of their farm supplies. They buy some items related to cows, but they also purchase a lot of fish food too, so that means they're raising fish there."

Nick interjected, "I've never seen adult fish there. Dr. Gerardo says he just raises embryos to test the cancer drugs, so he must've lied to me."

Jason continued, "That's likely Nick. Most of the other items seem normal for a farm but there are some we don't understand. Doc, they're using lots of cyclosporine and somatropin. Do you have any reason why?"

"Those are potent anti-rejection drugs and growth hormones. They can be used in veterinary applications, but not very often," Doc replied.

"They also buy a lot of genetic chemicals and reagents, but there's some strange organo-metallic and other chemicals," Jason continued as he rattled off from memory to Doc an abbreviated list of the chemical names.

"I don't have any idea what they're used for," Doc replied.

Jason continued, "Most disturbing though is when we looked at Exgenics' shipments. They ship a lot of their Exgena cancer treatments but they're also shipping a lot of concentrated TTX to Fort Detrick, Maryland. TTX is the acronym for tetrodotoxin, which is the poison that Frank likely makes."

"Fort Detrick closed long ago. It's that old Army base which originally researched chemical and biological weapons," Coleman added.

Doc asked, "How much TTX did they ship?"

"8,000 pounds this week alone," Jason replied.

"My God! That's likely enough poison to kill a billion people!" Doc exclaimed. "I bet they're raising Fugu fish like Frank in secret and extracting TTX from them. TTX is a complicated chemical molecule to manufacture and it's likely cheaper to just have the fish produce it. I bet they're milking and purifying the slime these fish produce!"

George commented, "That explains part of the puzzle, but doesn't fully explain that weird electrical fish in the boathouse. That TTX, however, must be vital to their plans and is a secret worth keeping at *any* cost. The connection to Fort Detrick really worries me that the military is involved."

Nick interjected, "I don't have any idea now what Exgenics is doing. *Everything* they told me must have been a lie. I'm ashamed of helping them in their endeavors. Lord, forgive me."

Grandpa replied, "God already forgives you. Your being here helping us is proof that He wants us to know the truth and take action."

Jason continued recapping the results of last night's search, "I also found a list of the Exgenics corporate board members. At a glance, I think most are extremely powerful or wealthy people from all over the world. John Stoneman IV is a board member and there are people from Gridcom, All-Nippon Robotics, E-Face, and Drone-Motion. I also found a shareholder list but didn't have time to look much further."

"Our case is clearer now with these Gridcom and robotics links," Coleman added.

gcgaacgcgatggcgtaagcgatggcgaacgcgccgctggcgaacgcgtgcgcgaacgcgctgccggcgaacgcgatggcgtaagcgatggcgaacgcg

Jason continued, "Yes, someone that powerful could use the Grid to learn any information they wanted. Add in E-Face for good measure too. I'm sure they spied on every e-conversation and image for the past week. All-Nippon Robotics built the agrobots that killed Jimmy and Drone-motion programs AI-software used in Supercruzers and likely those tanker autotrucks. There's even a retired U.S. Army General on the board so that links the military too. We still need to look deeper into the list of private shareholders, but it wouldn't surprise me if they're all directly or indirectly connected to this conspiracy somehow."

Grandpa added, "These are the richest people in the world and can afford anything they want."

Coleman continued, "I learned from Nick this morning that John Gregory, our prime suspect in the Captain and Macy's murder, is staying at the farmhouse there. Nick, I know what you said on the ride here, but can you tell everyone what you learned at work yesterday?"

Nick replied, "Well I didn't see any unusual activity, but I talked some with Gregory. He's taking a long vacation holiday and is flying his wife in by drone next week to enjoy a country retreat away from the city. However, I've never seen him stay so long at Exgenics before. Also, I haven't seen Dr. Gerardo there all week either and Gregory told me that Gerardo was taking a two-week second honeymoon with his wife. Gerardo is usually a workaholic and at times is there at *all* hours, so for him to *not* work for so long *is* unusual."

Coleman then asked Doc, "Did you learn anything new?"

Doc replied, "The Chief says the Tribe will support our efforts. Also, I stopped at the Blue Lagoon late last night and I heard those suspicious men from before were *not* there yesterday."

Julie added, "Earlier this morning, Jason and I also looked at some genetic database files too, but I learned something else while Jason was cooking breakfast. I examined some genetic files and observed something interesting. Exgenics has '*.gmp*' files for the genomics map of '*Takifugu obscurus*' and also a species called '*Takifugu telectrophorus*'. Nick, can we show you some screenshots of them?"

"Sure," Nick replied. "I've never heard of that '*telectrophorus*' species before, but I've seen a lot of other genetic files and will help if I can."

Julie opened up the laptop and quickly displayed some '*Takifugu telectrophorus*' '*.dna*', '*.fna*', and '*.gmp*' files. She asked as she first opened the '*.dna*' and '*.fna*' files, "Nick, do these displays mean anything to you?"

Nick replied, "I've seen similar ones, but normally have access to only a part of Exgenics' DNA database for security reasons."

catgcgccgccgtattaaattcgcacccatgatgcgtatgcgatggaacgcatttgcgcgcatgcgccgccgtattaaattcgcacccatgatgcgtat

gcgaacgcgatggcgtaagcgatggcgaacgcgccgctggcgaacgcgtgcgcgaacgcgctgccggcgaacgcgatggcgtaagcgatggcgaacgcg

Julie next asked as she opened the *'.gmp'* file for *'Takifugu teletrophorus'*, "What're the black genetic areas on this one?"

"Those black genes are where Dr. Gerardo makes edits to the DNA chains to manufacture the cancer treatments, but I've never seen so many changes to chromosomes before. I've also never seen *'.dna'* or *'.fna'* file areas associated with those black-colored genes since they're password protected. Dr. Gerardo told me once those passwords are related to healthcare and DNA privacy laws," Nick answered.

Julie asked as she opened up the *'Crickett'* folder, "What are these *'.ckt'* files? They're all password protected too."

Nick replied, "Those are *'Crickett'* files. I've seen a few on an e-screen in Dr. Gerardo's office when he was working on a genetic design program. He told me once they're generated by an AI-gene designer to test and cure cancers. They're written in a programming language he invented that understands how each gene functions and how to alter the cells to kill the cancer growths. I don't know why they're in this *'Takifugu telectrophorus'* folder though. These files are usually in the cancer patient database."

Jason said, "I didn't see that file type before, Julie."

Julie added, "That file type wasn't in the *'Takifugu obscurus'* folder we saw earlier. It only appears in the *'teletrophorus'* folder."

Doc commented, "I think the *'Takifugu telectrophorus'* genomic data must be for glowfish like Frank. We know some sort of electrical system was grown inside him. That fish is now starting to make sense, but what is the *'t'* in *'telectrophorus'* for?"

Nick replied, "I don't know, but this means Exgenics has cracked the genetic code of life to design a new species from scratch. It might explain the unusual chemicals they purchase. Some of those aren't associated with normal genetic engineering processes. Maybe those chemicals help grow Frank's internal electrical and communications system?"

Doc replied, "I guess that's possible. It seems almost anything can be done these days with AI-technology that has, in many ways, extended and surpassed the limits of human thought. How does Dr. Gerardo's Crickett technology work anyway?"

Nick replied, "Well, for his cancer treatments, the AI-computer designs a new gene that's inserted into the DNA chain. Using genetic reagents, he snips the chain into two, and then using other reagents and palindromic DNA sequences, he inserts a replacement gene for the one that caused cancer. It's sort of like a bank robbery, but in this case, you're breaking into the secure DNA bank vault, putting more money into the bank, and then reclosing and sealing the vault door after you're done."

catgcgccgccgtattaaattcgcacccatgatgcgtatgcgatggaacgcatttgcgcgcatgcgccgccgtattaaattcgcacccatgatgcgtat

Julie asked Nick, "What's a palindromic DNA sequence? I never learned about that genetic term before."

Nick replied, "Well that's a sequence encoding an amino acid chain where the code reads the same in both forward and backward directions along the codon sequence. It's like a universal zipper that opens a DNA helix and closes it again while allowing insertion of a new piece of DNA." It works like that Coronavirus vaccine invented years ago that inserts a viral fragment in your DNA, forever altering affected cells in your body."

Jason summarized, "So in a way, Doctor Gerardo hacks into the DNA chain and changes the code of life."

Nick replied, "Yes, that's kind of what happens. You can cure cancers that way at a cellular level or correct other genetic defects."

Grandpa added, "No wonder his company is so rich, but it sounds like Gerardo is playing god. Only God is responsible for the miracle that's life. To alter life is surely a sin against Him."

Doc replied, "Science and modern technology are often antithetical to the clarity of thought and morality. I think Gerardo has fallen into this mental abyss. His technology is so powerful that he failed to realize the evil which results from its use. He's violated natural law."

Coleman interjected, "Well, John Gregory and Exgenics have violated the laws of the State of Virginia and all this science and philosophy talk doesn't help us with our plans to serve the warrants at Exgenics on Sunday morning. Let me tell y'all what I saw there last night. First of all, I saw several Supercruzers and two large vans arrive in the early morning about an hour before the tanker explosion at the Chick Bridge. After the vans arrived, a swarm of drones begin patrolling their perimeter. They've drastically increased facility security for some reason."

Jeffrey commented, "It's almost like Exgenics knew something big was coming and they're preparing for it."

Coleman replied, "Yes, I think so Jeffrey. After dinner last night, I was in touch with Judge Saunders too. I told her everything we've learned and she's backing us 110%. She said her Virginia Supreme Court friend is on our side also, but after what happened last night and our discussions this morning, I almost think what we're attempting is impossible. Exgenics and the people behind them have the power to do *anything* they want. They have access to the Federal government, the Grid, all that technology, and, perhaps, all the money in the world."

Grandpa interjected, "Don't be discouraged, George. Sometimes you just need faith that things will work out. We were meant to be here at this time to discover this conspiracy and take action. Who else can stop them?

gcgaacgcgatggcgtaagcgatggcgaacgcgccgctggcgaacgcgtgcgcgaacgcgctgccggcgaacgcgatggcgtaagcgatggcgaacgcg

Plus, we still have our secret weapon, my grandson Jason," he said looking at him with pride. "He has complete access and controls the Grid now."

Jason, "Yes, I do. I have a key to a door. This key is powerful, and you have to be cautious about what doors you open since you never know what you'll find on the other side. I must be careful to use what I learn and do for good and not let this power corrupt my thinking."

Coleman continued, "No matter what happens, we must maintain our courage to face the evil we've discovered. Fortunately, we also have the good citizens of Charles County on our side to help us. Now, let's discuss further our plans to serve the warrants tomorrow morning." He then quietly discussed their plans and all agreed on the next courses of action.

"Okay everyone, let's get moving. After I drop off Nick, I'm going to rest at the Captain's house. Later, I'll see Judge Saunders to keep her updated. We've got a big night ahead of us, so I suggest we all get some extra rest. Everyone will meet here at 18:00 hours, I mean 6 p.m., for dinner to discuss our final schedule," Coleman summarized.

Soon, the breakfast meeting was over and everyone left, except Jason and Julie who were cleaning dishes, and Grandpa, who was still sitting.

Grandpa said, "That was a lot to take in, but I know our faith will sustain us through this trial. I'd like another cup of coffee. Jason, can you pour me the last cup from the pot?" he said while he sat at the table thinking and scratching Rufus behind the ear.

Julie interjected, "I'll do it, Grandpa," as she smiled and grabbed the glass carafe from the coffee maker to pour the last drops into his cup.

Grandpa, said to them both, "I'm working at the church today to finish tomorrow's sermon. I'll also go to the sanctuary and pray for us all."

"Perhaps we do need that prayer Grandpa," Jason replied with worry about their plans. "I'm heading to the dock to look for any dead fish and then will check on Frank. He might want a bite to eat and I'll check his RF signals. If fish like him were all killed in the river, he'd likely be upset. After that, I'll continue hacking to learn more about Exgenics, its shareholders, and try to crack Gerardo's password. Julie, can you show me more what you learned about him? I need to know everything."

"Yes Jason, I'll keep investigating and let you know what I discover. I'll see you upstairs," she replied as Jason went outside to the river.

Earlier that morning, regional hazardous materials teams, from Richmond, Newport News, and Williamsburg, had been dispatched to control and contain the chemical spills. However, by the time they'd arrived around sunrise, more than an hour and a half after the spill, it was

gcgaacgcgatggcgtaagcgatggcgaacgcgccgctggcgaacgcgtgcgcgaacgcgctgccggcgaacgcgatggcgtaagcgatggcgaacgcg

already too late and they were overwhelmed despite their heroic efforts. They couldn't contain three such large spills of a water-soluble chemical occurring at one time and, by that time, the plumes of toxic poison had already widely spread and diffused into the water. Within hours, the entire Chick Lake was poisoned and the poison, carried by the river and tidal currents, crept slowly downstream of the dam. Paralyzed fish, floating to the surface because of their buoyant air bladders, soon died. The tournament fishermen, who heard the presidential alert but hadn't yet evacuated, began seeing trophy winners floating on waters once teeming with fish. The smell would grow that day as fish began to rot.

7:00 a.m., Saturday, July 3, ….

It was the beginning of a terrible second day as Acting Kent County Sheriff Jeffers, who was appointed yesterday by County Manager Rose Graham after news of Sheriff Olsen's death. He'd heard the presidential alert with disbelief, but just a few minutes later was alerted by Kent County dispatch. He immediately called his deputies back to duty, but only two were available for this crisis since one was on a Virginia Beach vacation.

Acting Sheriff Jeffers's priority was to help the arriving Hazmat Teams at the spills and he and his deputies cordoned off the areas with crime scene tape to keep onlookers away. Hundreds of full-time residents and vacationers at the campgrounds frantically packed belongings and started fleeing in their vehicles. Confusion and traffic jams reigned on narrow roads as escaping residents congested with arriving emergency vehicles.

His next priority was to evacuate the tournament fishermen from the lake, but with chemical spills blocking two of three boat ramps on the lake, the upper ramp at Osprey Landing was the last remaining open ramp. Soon, the traffic jam smothered the boat ramp and water as 140 fishing boats tried to dock and trailer their boats at nearly the same time. In addition, each boat had to be decontaminated by hazmat personnel.

So during this crisis, he and his deputies were relegated to traffic control. He thought to himself, "If only Olsen was here, I wouldn't have to deal with this stress." Since Sheriff Coleman was on vacation, he'd heard from dispatch that Deputy James from Charles County needed to coordinate something with him but, for now, that would have to wait. As he stood frustrated by the confusion at the boat ramp, he first heard and soon then saw an old V-22 Osprey of the Virginia Air National Guard fly at low altitude over the lake and down the river. It was soon followed by a squadron of heavy Navy patrol helidrones following flying a 'V' pattern like a flock of Canada geese.

catgcgccgccgtattaaattcgcacccatgatgcgtatgcgatggaacgcatttgcgcgcatgcgccgccgtattaaattcgcacccatgatgcgtat

```
>fasta Takifugu obscurus genome assembly-complete codon file:
attaactgctaaaacggccgcgaaagcagctaactgtatttttaataacgcacccatagcgaa
gtggaaaacaccgaagaaaacagcgaagtggaaaacacctatagcatttaaacccatgaataa
aacgcgaacattatgtaataaagcgatgaatgcctggcgcgcgcgaccatttaaaactaattt
acccatgaaacccatattcgcaccgaagaaaactaaaacattaccgaagatagcaccgcgacc
gaaagctaatttgcgatggaacgcatttgcgcgtggcgtgcatgaaaacattaacacccatgaatgc
taataacgcagcgaataatttcattaaatggcgaacgaagtggaaaacaccagcattacctaa
gaatgctaaatggaaagcaacgaatgcgaaagcagcgcgcgctattttttaacgctaaaacgaa
ccggaataaccgctggaaacctaagatattagcagctaactggtggaaacccatgaaccgtaa
ctgattaccatttgcgcgctgtaagcgaacgatagctggcatatttgccatcatgcggtggaa
tgctaaaacaacgaatgcaccgaagatacccatgaaatgtggattacccatgcgaactaaacc
catgaacgcgcgaacgatacctaagcgagcagctaaatggaagcgatgtaaaacggcacccat
gaaccgtaatgggaaacgcagctaatttacccatgaagaagcgcgcacccataccatgaaagc
gaaccggcgcgcgcgaccgaagcgaacgatgaacagtaagcgctgagccaccgcgaccatttaa
aacacctaatggcatatttgccatacccatgaactggcgtggagctaatttaacgcgacctaa
cgcgaagcgaacgattaatttaacgcgacctaacgcgaaagcggctaagatgaaaacaccatt
accctggaaacccatgaaatggcggatgaatgcgaaaacacccgcgaaagcccggaatgcacc
acctaaacccatgaataaccgattaacatttaaaacagctaatttatggcgaacaaaattaac
gatcgcgaacagtaaattcgcgaaagcacccatgcgaccacccatgaatatagccattaataa
ctggatgatgaatgcctggcgcgcgaaaaccatgaatgcgcgtaaagcgaaagctggcatatt
tgccatattatgccggaactgacccatgaaatgacctaaaaccatgaaagcgaaccggccgcgc
gcgaccatttaaaactgggaacattaactgatacccatgaaagcgaaacccgctaaacccat
agcacctaataagaaagcgaactgtttgaagtgattgatgaaaacaccacccatgcgaccgcg
ctgctgatggaaaacgcgcgcgaatgccgcgaagcgacgaagatgaacagtaagcgctgacc
catgcgaccacccatgaatatgcgcgcgaagaaaacgattaatgggaagattaatatacccat
gaaattcgctgccgcgaagcgacctaacgctggattacccattgcgaacgcaccgcgattaac
taaaacgcgctgattgaaaacgcgtaactggaacgcattggccataccagcacccatgcgacc
gcgatgtaaaacggcacccatgaaagcgaagcgcgcgaactgattttttgaactgatttaagaa
cgcacctatgcgaacgatacccatgaacggctaaattacctaatttcatgcgccg
ccgattaacgaaagcagcacccatgcgaccacctaaagcgaactgctaacgcgaaacccatgaa
agcgaacgcattggccataccagcggctaagtggaacgcaacatggaaaacaccagcgcgcgc
gaaattaacagcaccattacctaaaccgaagatgcgatgtaaaacggcatggaaaacgatgaa
cgcattgtgattaacggcacccatgaaattcgctaaagcacccccgtaatgggaacgcagcttt
cgctaaatgacccatgaatgctaaaacagcgaaaacacctaatttacccatgaaggctaagtg
gaacgcaacgaagatacccatgcgacctggcatgaaaacgaagtggaacgcgcgaactatttt
taacgcatgtaatttggctaagtggaacgcaacatggaaaacacctaagaatgctaaatggaa
agcgatgaaagcacccgctaatgcaccattgtggaataatttacccatgaaagcgaagaaaac
gatagcattaccattagcacccatgaacgcattggccatacctaatttacccatgaaccggaa
taaccgctggaaacctaagcgctgaccgaacgctaacgcacctaagcgtaataactgattagc
catattaccgcgaacgatacctaaattaacagcaccattacctaaaccgaaaacgaatggggc
taagtggaacgcaacatggaaaacaccctggcgtatattaacggcattaccagcttttaataa
aacgatgcgaccatttaaaactaaaacagctaatgccatccgcgcattaactgcattccgctg
gaaagcgcgaacgattaacgcggcgcgaacatttaaattaacggcattaccagcccgtaatgg
gaacgcagcattaacagctaatgccatttttaacgcatggcgagcaacctaaaacccatgaaatg
agccatgcgctgctgagcgaagaaatgatgtaaagcaccctgattaaagaactgtatacctaa
gaattttttgaatgcaccacccatgaaattcgcagcgcgtttgaaacctatgcgaacgatcat
gcgccgccgattaacgaaagcagcccgcgctaagatgaaaactgcgaaattaacgatgaagaa
gattggattctgctggatatttgcaccgcgaccgaaacccatgcgaccggctaagtggaacgc
aacatggaaaacaccagcctgtaaaacggcgaaagcaccgcgtaactgattagccatgaagat
agccattaataactggataactaaacctaagaatgccatgcgaacggcgaagatttttaacgc
ctgattggccataccgcgaacgatacccgcgcgaacagcattgaaaacacctgcgcgtaaagc
gaaagcgaacgatgcgtgctgctaacgcgatattaacggcctgtatgcgctgctggaataa
ccggaacgcattgaaaactgcgaacatgcgacccatagccatgaatgaacacccatcgcgacc
atggcgaacaaaattaacgatgcgcgcgaaatgtaacgcgaagatattagcccgtaaagc...
```

Takifugu Obscurus Genetic Data File
(partial display of raw DNA transcription '.*dna*' file)

gcgaacgcgatggcgtaagcgatggcgaacgcgccgctggcgaacgcgtgcgcgaacgcgtgccggcgaacgcgatggcgtaagcgatggcgaacgcg

```
>rf 1 Takifugu telectrophrorus genome assembly, chromosome 2:
TYIIDV*KNKNMCVKNIGSSNQSPPGFEPTTFSKSSEQLKPLTYEVTLTHRKEVIYGLKKAMIK
HSSHRFFFTCCENMEFVLTQKSHPQMILKLCLF*TIYDLFAVIQCDCIGQWFKQVTFLWKVVGA
IPGGTLVFKNQYSSHTCFWFYRACECARHHNFKTKYPI*KLLYGAKEDCMTAYKSAPL*LFQQ*
STN*KGKKLYN*L*KNKNICVKNIGSSNQSPAWIRTNNLQQKN*AA*TTDL*GQTDPLQRGHIW
I*KSHD*IFFTDFFFTCCENMEFVLTQKSHPQMILKLCLF*TIYDYFAVIQDDCIGQLLKQLTF
SRRVVGSNPGGTMV*RINILHTHVFGFTVVTVMHCITIFKTKYP*AKLLYEVKEDCMTAYKSAP
A*LFQQ*ITN*KGKKLYN*CIKNQKHMCEEYWFFKPESRLDSIQQKSAKWESSLNH*PMRSH*R
WAKRSYMV*KKP*LNILHKYVFLHML*KYGICVDTEITSTDDIEIMTFENHI*PLCSGEV*LHS
*V*AADILAEGCWFESRWDFGLKNQICSHTCFWFYLGECHALHHNF*DQVSYLEITVWCERGLY
RS**ISNPVTIPAMNDKIKREKVI*LMYKKTCV*RVLVLQTRVPPGFDPTTFSKGREQLKPLTY
DVTLTHIKEVIYGLKKAMIKYSSDRCFSSHAVKIWNLC*HRNHIHR*Y*NYDFFEPYMTSLQCR
FVTA*VMGLSC*LSCGRLLVRTQREFEREESIFPTHMFLC*LSCIASQFLRPSILFANYCMVQK
IIV*QLINQHPCNYSSN**QNKKGKTYIIDV*KTKTFVWRIFVLQTRVPPGFDPTDFSKGREQL
NPLTYEVTQTHGKEVIYGLKKAMIAYASHRFFFSHAVKIWNLC*HRNHIHR*Y*AYDFFEPYMT
DLQWRSVTA*VSGLSC*LSCGRLTVRIRAGL*FEESIFFTHMFLVLPW*LSCINSQFLRPSILF
CNYCMVRKRIV*QLINQHPCNYTSNESQTKKGKSYIIDV*KNKNICVKNIGSSNQSPAWIRTNN
IQQKK*AA*TTDL*GHTDPLQAGHIWFKKRHD*IFFTQIFFFTCCENMEFVLTQKSHPQMILKL
RLFLTIYDLFAMIQCGCIGQRFKQLTFLRRAVGSNPGGTMV*RINILHTRVFGFTVVTVMHCIT
CFKTKYPI*KLLYGAKEDCRTAYKSAPL*LFTQ*ITN*KGKKLYN*CIKKQKHMCEEYWFFKPE
LRLDSIQKPSAKDESSLNA*PMRSH*RIAKRSEMV*KKP*LNIRHKDVFLHML*KYGICVDTEI
ESTDDIEIMPFLNHI*PTCNDLV*LHRSVV*AADFLVEGCWFEERWDFGLKNQYSSHTCFWFYR
NECHALHHNFDTKYP*TKLLYGAKEDCMTAYKSAPL*LFQQ*IVN*KGKKLYN*CIKKHMCEKY
IFFKPESRLDSIQQPAAKDESSLNH*PMRSH*CIAKRSYMV*KIP*LNILHKDVFLHML*KYGI
NVDTEITSTDDIEITPFLNHI*PLCNVLV*LHRSVV*AADFLVVGCWFESRRDFGLKNQYSSHT
EFGFTVVTVMHCIFIFKTKYPI*KLLYGAKEDCMTAYKSAPL*EFQQ*ITN*KGKSYIIDV*KN
TNICVKNIGSSNQSIAWIRTNNLRQKVSSLNH*PMRSHRLTAKRSYMV*KKP*LNILHPVFLHN
EL*KY*ICVDTEITSEDDIEIMPFLNHI*PLCSDPV*LHRSVV*AADFLAEGCWFESRRDFGLK
EQLCSHTCFWFYLGECDALHHNF*DQVSYLEITVWCERGLYDSL*ISTATSIPAMNDKIKREKV
N*LMYKKTKTCV*RILVLQTRVPPGFDPTTFSKGREQLKPLTYEVTLTPLQRGHIWFKKSHD*F
ETNMFFFTCCGNMEFVLTQKSHPQMILKLCLF*TIYDLFAMF*CLCIGQWFKQLTFLWKVVG*N
NGGTLV*RINILHRHVFGFTVVTVMHCDTIFKTKYPI*KLLYGAKEDRMTAYKSAPL*LFQQ*I
GN*KGKKLYN*CIKNKNIRVKNICSSEQSPAWIRSNNLQQRKRAA*VTDL*GHTDPLQRGHIWF
LKSHD*IFFTQMFFFTCCENMEFVLLQKSHPQMILKSCLF*TIYDLFETIQCVCIGQWFKQLTF
I*KVVGSNPGGTLF*RINYVHTHVEGFTLVSVMHCITIFKTKYPI*KLLYGAKEDCMTAYKSAL
SLFQQ*ITN*KGKKLYN*CIKNKVICVKNIGSSNQSPAWIRTENETQKSQQLKPLTYEVTQTHG
HEVIYGLKKAMIKYSSPGFSFSEAVKILNLC*HRNHIHR*Y*NYAFFEPYMTSLQ*SSVIA*VS
PLSS*LSCGRLLVRIQAGLWFLESIMFTHMFLVLPW*VSCIASQFLRPSILFRNYCMVRKRIV*
ALINQHPCNYSSNE*QNKKGESYIIDV*KNKNMCVKNIGSSNRSPAWIRSINLQQRKRAA*TTD
L*SHTDPLQRGHIWFKKSHD*IFFTNMFFFTCCGNMEFVLTQKSHPQMILKLCLF*TIYDLFAM
I*CDCIGQWFKQLTFLWKVVGLKN*YSSQTCFWFYRGDCHALHHNF*DQVSYLEITVWCERGSD
NL*ISTPVTIPAMNHKLKREKVI*LMYKKTKTYV*RIFVLQTRVPPGFDENNEDKGREQLKPLY
DVTLTHCKEVIYGCKKAMIKYSSHRCFSSHAVKIWELC*HRNHIHR*Y*NYAFFEPYMTSLQ*S
RETA*VSGLSS*ISCGRLLVRIQAGPWF*ESIFFTDMFLVLPW*LSCIASQFLRPSILFRNYCP
ORKRIV*QLINVHPCNYSSNESQTKKGKSYIIDV*INIRVKNIGSSNQSPAWIRSNNLQQRKRU
M*TTDL*GHTIPRQRGHIWFKKSHD*LFFTQMFFFVCCENMEFVLTQKSHPQMILKLCLF*TIL
ELFAMIKCDCIGQWFKQLTFLWKVVGSNPGGTLV*IINYLHTHVFGFTVVTVMHCITIFKTKPL
SKLLYGGKEDRMTAYKSAPL*LFQQ*ITN*KGKKLDN*CIKKLTCEEHLFREPAPERDSIQQPU
WKEESSLNH*PMRSH*PTAKRSRMVLKKF*LNILHEDVFLHML*KYGICVDTEITSTDDIEIMP
ILSSHTCLCFYRGDCHALHHNA*DQVSYLEITVWWRRGSYDSL*ISTPVTIPAMNHKLKREKVI
TLMYKKTKMNV*RILVLQTRDPPGFDPTTFSKGREQIKPLTYEVTLTHRKEVIYGLKKAMIKYS
HQRCFSSHAVKIWNLC*HRAHIHR*Y*NYAFFEPYMTSLQWRSVTA*VSGLSS*LSCGRLLVRL
FNIRVKNIGSSNQSPAWIRSNNLQQRKRAA*TTDL*GHTDPRQRGHIWFKKSHD*LFFTQMFFF
IVELETTERS*RMORE*MILKLCLF*TIYDLFAMIKCDCIGQWFKQLTFLWKVVGSNPGGT...
```

Takifugu Obscurus Chromosome #2 FASTA Protein Transcription File (partial '.fna' file displayed)

gcgaacgcgatggcgtaagcgatggcgaacgcgccgctggcgaacgcgtgcgcgaacgcgctgccggcgaacgcgatggcgtaagcgatggcgaacgcg

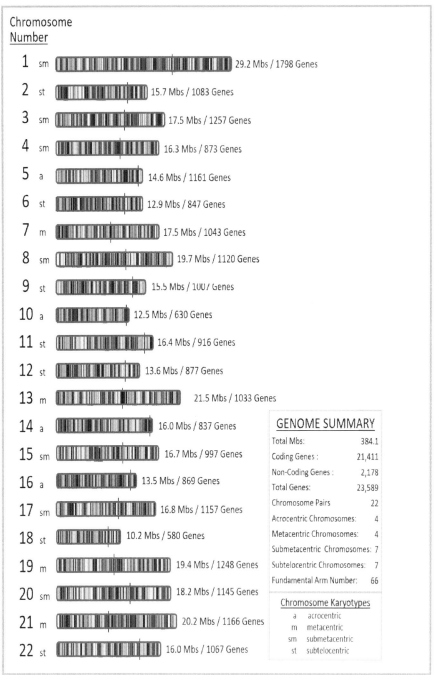

Chromosome Number

1	sm	29.2 Mbs / 1798 Genes
2	st	15.7 Mbs / 1083 Genes
3	sm	17.5 Mbs / 1257 Genes
4	sm	16.3 Mbs / 873 Genes
5	a	14.6 Mbs / 1161 Genes
6	st	12.9 Mbs / 847 Genes
7	m	17.5 Mbs / 1043 Genes
8	sm	19.7 Mbs / 1120 Genes
9	st	15.5 Mbs / 1007 Genes
10	a	12.5 Mbs / 630 Genes
11	st	16.4 Mbs / 916 Genes
12	st	13.6 Mbs / 877 Genes
13	m	21.5 Mbs / 1033 Genes
14	a	16.0 Mbs / 837 Genes
15	sm	16.7 Mbs / 997 Genes
16	a	13.5 Mbs / 869 Genes
17	sm	16.8 Mbs / 1157 Genes
18	st	10.2 Mbs / 580 Genes
19	m	19.4 Mbs / 1248 Genes
20	sm	18.2 Mbs / 1145 Genes
21	m	20.2 Mbs / 1166 Genes
22	st	16.0 Mbs / 1067 Genes

GENOME SUMMARY

Total Mbs:	384.1
Coding Genes :	21,411
Non-Coding Genes :	2,178
Total Genes:	23,589
Chromosome Pairs	22
Acrocentric Chromosomes:	4
Metacentric Chromosomes:	4
Submetacentric Chromosomes:	7
Subtelocentric Chromosomes:	7
Fundamental Arm Number:	66

Chromosome Karyotypes

a	acrocentric
m	metacentric
sm	submetacentric
st	subtelocentric

Takifugu Obscurus Genome Map and Chromosome Karyotype '*.gmp*' file

gcgaacgcgatggcgtaagcgatggcgaacgcgccgctggcgaacgcgtgcgcgaacgcgctgccggcgaacgcgatggcgtaagcgatggcgaacgcg

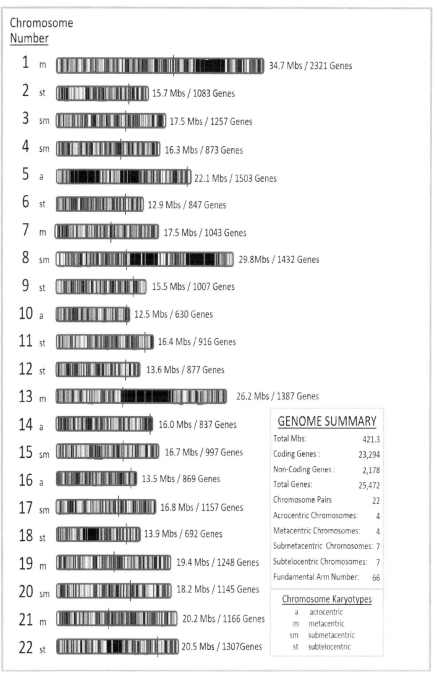

Chromosome
<u>Number</u>

1	m	34.7 Mbs / 2321 Genes
2	st	15.7 Mbs / 1083 Genes
3	sm	17.5 Mbs / 1257 Genes
4	sm	16.3 Mbs / 873 Genes
5	a	22.1 Mbs / 1503 Genes
6	st	12.9 Mbs / 847 Genes
7	m	17.5 Mbs / 1043 Genes
8	sm	29.8Mbs / 1432 Genes
9	st	15.5 Mbs / 1007 Genes
10	a	12.5 Mbs / 630 Genes
11	st	16.4 Mbs / 916 Genes
12	st	13.6 Mbs / 877 Genes
13	m	26.2 Mbs / 1387 Genes
14	a	16.0 Mbs / 837 Genes
15	sm	16.7 Mbs / 997 Genes
16	a	13.5 Mbs / 869 Genes
17	sm	16.8 Mbs / 1157 Genes
18	st	13.9 Mbs / 692 Genes
19	m	19.4 Mbs / 1248 Genes
20	sm	18.2 Mbs / 1145 Genes
21	m	20.2 Mbs / 1166 Genes
22	st	20.5 Mbs / 1307Genes

GENOME SUMMARY

Total Mbs:	421.3
Coding Genes :	23,294
Non-Coding Genes :	2,178
Total Genes:	25,472
Chromosome Pairs	22
Acrocentric Chromosomes:	4
Metacentric Chromosomes:	4
Submetacentric Chromosomes:	7
Subtelocentric Chromosomes:	7
Fundamental Arm Number:	66

Chromosome Karyotypes

a	acrocentric
m	metacentric
sm	submetacentric
st	subtelocentric

Takifugu Telectrophorus Genome Map and Chromosome Karyotype '.*gmp*' file

gcgaacgcgatggcgtaagcgatggcgaacgcgccgctggcgaacgcgtgcgcgaacgcgctgccggcgaacgcgatggcgtaagcgatggcgaacgcg

Chapter 25: One Bright Morning

Osprey Landing Tanker Spill

7:30 a.m., Saturday, July 3, ….

Jason walked to the dock amid the bright morning sunshine and was immediately dismayed. Across the river as far as he could see, dead fish of all sizes and species were floating. He thought to himself, "These Exgenics people are truly evil. What they've done is a crime of the highest level and must be punished." A tear ran down his cheek as he realized it was impossible to achieve Captain and Macy's dream to restore the river.

He next looked at Frank, who was resting on the gravel at the tank's bottom. He turned on his RF scanner, which he had left nearby, and monitored for signals and sounds as before. Soon, he heard a few strong and many soft wails, clicks, and moans, so there still were signals coming from Frank and other glowfish in the river somewhere. If the poison had killed all the glowfish, the softer signals should have ceased. The sounds were slightly different than yesterday, perhaps more jittery or agitated, but Jason didn't sense true alarm or panic from their intonations.

He grabbed a herring from the refrigerator, dropped it in the water, and soon he heard a series of strong, excited clicks as Frank swam to the food and nibbled on it. When Frank finished his breakfast, he swam in a full excited circle and looked through the aquarium glass closely at Jason, and beamed his clown smile. The tone of the loudest signal now changed to something similar to what Julie yesterday thought meant '*happy*.' Jason thought to himself "these fish do have a simple language and that sound really does mean "happy" or a similar emotion." He left Frank, walked to the house, and went upstairs to Julie, who was laying on his bed and propped up by pillows while looking at Jason's laptop.

Jason told Julie the sad news, "The river's covered with dead fish so that poison is real and taking effect everywhere. All the fish in Chick Lake are likely dead too. I fed Frank and he still seemed in a good mood though.

catgcgccgccgtattaaattcgcacccatgatgcgtatgcgatggaacgcatttgcgcgcatgcgccgccgtattaaattcgcacccatgatgcgtat

Also, those other signals we heard yesterday are still there, so all the other glowfish in the river are still alive somehow. I don't know why, so maybe we should ask Doc."

Julie typed the words meta-flumoxicarb and fish into the laptop, performing a quick Grid search. After a moment, she replied, "No need to ask Doc, Jason. That poison does kill fish and is a mild sodium channel blocker. Remember what Nick said about TTX yesterday? It's a strong sodium channel blocker. The glowfish are immune to TTX effects, so they're also resistant to meta-flumoxicarb poisoning."

"Well, that sure was lucky for those glowfish. This means that Exgenics failed in their attempt to exterminate Frank's species. Once they discover this, they'll try killing all those fish using another method."

"Jason, I've found something else strange while you were feeding Frank. I've been looking at the list of species on that tree of life and something is missing. There's a listing for the scientific order '*Primates*' and I see there the complete genomes for species of lemurs, monkeys, and apes like chimpanzees and gorillas. However, the genetic data for 'Homo sapiens,' which is the species name for man, is *not* there. For our species, there's a link to a separate database folder that is password protected."

Jason replied, "I bet that's where all that genomic data on cancer patients is stored and protected by healthcare privacy laws. I should also try later to hack into that database to examine what's there too. However, first things first, so let me learn about those Exgenics shareholders. You keep studying Gerardo. I need to understand his mind to hack his files."

"I'll do what I can to study him and build a psychological dossier on him. I'm glad I took that Introduction to Psychology course as an elective my freshmore year."[82]

"Good idea Julie," Jason replied as he sat down at his desk, looked at several e-screens, and began typing on the old computer keyboard.

꧁꧂

By this time of the morning, a bunch of Washington FEMA bureaucrats had descended by drone to the Peninsula region to provide 'guidance' and 'support' to the local governments, but the military now was running the show. The Virginia Air National Guard flew their old V-22s, dropping off Marine platoons at each highway or bridge permitting an escape route from the area for ISM terrorists. Of course, since it was a terrorist hacking attack of the tanker's autodrives, the terrorists could have

---

[82] By this time period, the politically-correct word 'freshmore' to describe first year high-school and college students had replaced the word 'freshmen'.

gcgaacgcgatggcgtaagcgatggcgaacgcgccgctggcgaacgcgtgcgcgaacgcgctgccggcgaacgcgatggcgtaagcgatggcgaacgcg

been anywhere, but standard contingency plans for domestic terrorist incidents were always to isolate affected regions.

Air Force electric high-altitude surveillance drones flew over the region supplementing Space Force satellite coverage. The Naval Air Stations in Virginia Beach and Patuxent River Maryland used transport planes to launch a multitude of low-altitude drones to fly low over the rivers interrogating any boats still on the water. Soon, the Chickahominy, James, Pamunkey, and York Rivers were buzzing with Navy drones on routine aerial patrols above the main river channels. Since martial law was in effect, warrantless searches by Special Forces were conducted at homes of suspected ISM sympathizers.

In the cities, and to a lesser extent the towns, terrified citizens dependent on the public water systems descended on local supermarkets as panic bottled-water buying and hoarding ensued. Of course, any other liquid in the stores soon disappeared, even beer and wine. The bread aisle was depleted too, even though there wasn't a food shortage. It seemed people just didn't think and were like lemmings. Their minds were preprogrammed for an emergency, like a forecasted winter storm, to blindly buy water, milk, and bread. They just didn't think that the hot-water heaters of their homes and apartments had *gallons* of drinkable water.

As the day progressed, isolated looting began in the cities and the Virginia National Guard truck convoys with security units arrived to quell any violence at key distribution centers within the cities.

9:00 a.m., Saturday, July 3, ….

As Jason reviewed the shareholder database, he realized the best way to understand their relationships was to perform an E-Face contact search. So, he hacked an E-Face Grid node and, after breaching the security firewall with his algorithm, saw tE-Face messages and communications of Exgenics shareholders. However, he couldn't review so many messages, so he performed a communications linkage analysis for each shareholder.

He hastily modified some Grid node networking analysis code so he could visualize linkages between shareholders communicating on E-Face. He tested the code on a random shareholder's E-Face messages and, soon, a diagram appeared on his e-screen. The diagram looked like a spoked bicycle wheel, where the hub of the wheel was the shareholder and the other ends of the spokes were who they communicated with. The spokes were also color-coded, showing the most frequent interactions.

He further modified this linkage algorithm to repeat the analysis of each Exgenics shareholder one by one and overlay the diagrams of all

catgcgccgccgtattaaattcgcacccatgatgcgtatgcgatggaacgcatttgcgcgcatgcgccgccgtattaaattcgcacccatgatgcgtat

gcgaacgcgatggcgtaagcgatggcgaacgcgccgctggcgaacgcgtgcgcgaacgcgctgccggcgaacgcgatggcgtaagcgatggcgaacgcg

shareholders. He even added a final bit of code to show their connections to Exgenics board members. Finally, he commanded his social linkage algorithm to initiate its analysis and commented to Julie, "This might take a while, but I'm trying to see how these thousands of shareholders are related to Exgenics, the board members, and each other."

He stared at the e-screen attentively and the initial spoke display of the first shareholder soon expanded, to add other connection spokes between the different shareholders. As the algorithm program ran shareholder by shareholder, new spoked-wheels overlayed on the diagram. To most people, the diagram was just a confusing tangled web of interconnecting wheels and colored spokes like an abstract painting. However, after a half-hour of watching the program run, Jason saw within the color pattern an intricate network linked to each of the Exgenics board members.

He finally commented to Julie, "All shareholders are linked to Gerardo or one of the board members within one or two linkages."

Julie replied, "That means that *all* the shareholders are involved directly or indirectly with the conspiracy that we've discovered."

"Yes, Julie. This is thousands of important and powerful people. Our lives are certainly in danger if we're discovered. The real question is what is Exgenics really doing? They're ruthless and have killed people. We know they have that TTX also. Until I started my hack, they likely had complete control of the Grid. They've modified AI-software code to control robots, autocars, autotrucks, and likely even autodrones.

They may control the president and probably the military. We know the CIA is seriously involved too since that quantenna points directly toward their headquarters. This is a worldwide conspiracy of powerful people. They already control the world, so what is their goal?"

Julie answered with fear and a trembling voice, "Eliminating *us* Jason. The Doc said they've enough TTX to kill a billion people. If they have more of that poison, they could kill most of the world's population. My women's intuition tells me they're planning to exterminate most of humanity and leave themselves in charge of what's left. They've robots and drones now as servants, so *they* don't need *us* anymore."

Jason replied as goosebumps rose on his arms, "I've got an eerie feeling you're right Julie. After most of humanity is gone, they'll be left with a largely unpopulated world. The Earth would heal after all the damage that mankind has inflicted across the globe for thousands of years, but *they* will still be here in charge of whatever is left. In a generation, the world will be a Garden of Eden once most of mankind is eliminated. I now also fear

catgcgccgccgtattaaattcgcacccatgatgcgtatgcgatggaacgcatttgcgcgcatgcgccgccgtattaaattcgcacccatgatgcgtat

the AI-brains that man has created. Will these servant robots and their minds eventually rebel against the human masters who control them?"

"What'll become of us then Jason? I'm scared. Come hold me," Julie said as tears began to flow down her cheeks as the extreme sadness of their discussion began welling up in her heart and mind.

Jason rose from his chair, laid by her, and wrapped his arms around her in a tender embrace. He spoke reassuring her, "I won't let it happen. We *must* stop them. It'll take time, but maybe we'll beat them somehow."

"I'm not sure that's possible. They control *everything*."

"They don't fully control the Grid right now, so that's in our favor." He wiped a tear from her eye, gave a gentle smile, tenderly kissed her, and soon were passionately making love as the sun beamed into the bedroom.

However, the brightness of that morning's sunshine soon gave way to a forecast of approaching bad and stormy weather. A cold front was expected to approach the rest of the day and the heat and humidity would eventually give way to brooding, swiftly moving dark clouds. This was the ideal meteorological condition to pull northward an early-season tropical storm barreling up the coast of the Carolinas. Around nightfall, torrential rains were expected to begin in earnest and by midnight, it would become extremely windy. The storm was forecasted to last all night until sweeping northward past the region before dawn.

After their morning intimacy, Julie picked up the laptop and continued her analysis of Gerardo while Jason sat down at his keyboard typing a short poem before resuming his Exgenics hack:

"Circles"

A world circles a star
Marking a ribbon of time.
A floating orb in rhythm
Makes a shorter journey
To illuminate the night
While changing its face.
Grid satellites circle a globe,
Knowing what, when, and where.
The great circle in the sky
Is the shortest direct flight
Between two distant lands.
But She is the greatest circle,
Arms locked round in embrace.

After an hour, Jason commented, "I've tried my quantum chip's random password cracking algorithm on the black genetic areas of the *'telectrophorus.gmp'* files but I can't break in. I tried the same algorithm on those *'.ckt'* files you found earlier with no luck either. So, Gerardo's password is extremely tough to hack. I can only conclude his password must be something personal that only he knows."

"Next, I found another genetic database folder titled 'Exgena Patients' but the individual file contents were again password protected. I was able to learn some information from the database structure and file names in the folder, however. The patient folders were arranged geographically by country and race. I counted the number of files and saw their file name suffixes. There are several million patient folders worldwide and each folder contains a *'.dna'*, *'.fna'*, *'.gmp'*, and *'.ckt'* file. There's also a subfolder associated with each patient that contains a *'takifugu.dna'* file I can't access either. That must be the Takifugu embryo genome for testing the cancer drug on a fish embryo before they ship their custom drug to each patient."

"Yes, Jason. I think your analysis is correct," Julie replied.

Jason continued, "Well, I also determined that the Exgena database is just a database subset of the *'Homo sapiens'* database you couldn't find earlier on the tree of life diagram. It had a similar data structure to the Exgena database by country and racial classification. The individual genome folders only contained a password-protected *'.dna'*, *'.fna'*, and *'.gmp'* file though. The database is huge. I counted the number of files and for the United States folder alone, there were 120 million active files."

Julie replied, "That's the current U.S. population in the recent census."

"Yes, I know. There's a search bar for the database, so I typed my social security number. A window popped up with a database folder and my name appeared! My folder contained the same genetic files. Also, in the U.S. folder, I found a similar subfolder titled 'Deceased' with more than 540 million folders. I think Exgenics has been accessing a US citizen genetic database that's been kept in secret for years."

"I decided to locate the physical site of the human genomic database using a Grid 'node location' command. The command returned physical Grid coordinates matching the National Archives in Washington."

Julie replied, "So, the government has a secret archive of every living or dead American since genome sequencing became automated. I bet they've collected human DNA for years at every Covid test, hospital birth, or routine blood test. That violates our constitutional right to privacy."

Jason continued, "Yes, I agree, but the government and the corporations who control it haven't cared about our privacy for years. On

gcgaacgcgatggcgtaagcgatggcgaacgcgccgctggcgaacgcgtgcgcgaacgcgctgccggcgaacgcgatggcgtaagcgatggcgaacgcg

top of all that and most interesting to our search warrants is I found a subfolder with the folder name *'T-program.'* That was the only database folder I couldn't enter, so even entry to that database was password protected. I think that's likely where Gerardo keeps his secrets."

"I next used the node location command on that folder, and it replied with two sets of Grid node coordinates. That means the data is quantum encrypted and can be only accessed at the physical location of one of the two Grid nodes. One coordinate set originates at Exgenics Farm and the other in McLean, Virginia near CIA Headquarters. That means I've found the Grid node for Exgenics' quantenna link with the. This confirms the conspiracy we've discovered is deep within our government. There have always been conspiracy theories of a 'deep state' within the government which Grid News has scoffed at for years, but this proves it."

"How can we win against these powerful people?" Julie replied.

"Well, now it's even more important that we succeed. That folder is encrypted using quantum gamma-photon entanglement. This means the data in the folder exists in two places at once but half of the data is at one end of the quantum linkage and the other data half is at the other link end. It's only possible to access the complete data set from one of its quantenna sources and, fortunately for us, the farm is right here! When we serve the warrants at Exgenics, I *must* access that quantenna encrypted data and look at the *'T-Program'* subfolder."

11:00 a.m., Saturday, July 3, ….

A black minivan drove itself to East Lake Campground and parked. The rooftop hatch opened and a swarm of 20 autodrones flew one by one out the hatch. They spread in a close-formation drone cloud 50 feet in diameter above the van and then they activated their e-cams.

Dr. Gerardo was watching his e-wall at his riverside mansion along the Potomac River near Washington when he started an e-vid conference with John Gregory in the farmhouse conference room. "Well John, enough time has passed for the poison to completely diffuse throughout the lake. The Chickahominy below the dam is well contaminated too. Let's take a look at the lake first. That's the largest area to cover, so it'll take the longest to survey and see how well your plan worked. We need to count each dead T-fish as we find it. When the drones find them, they'll pick up each one for secure disposal. Right?"

"Yes, our team preprogrammed the AI-drones with these operational parameters. They've been fitted with a small robotic claw arm and pouch for the removal/disposal process."

catgcgccgccgtattaaattcgcacccatgatgcgtatgcgatggaacgcatttgcgcgcatgcgccgccgtattaaattcgcacccatgatgcgtat

gcgaacgcgatggcgtaagcgatggcgaacgcgccgctggcgaacgcgtgcgcgaacgcgctgccggcgaacgcgatggcgtaagcgatggcgaacgcg

Upon Dr. Gerardo's remote command, the drones dispersed and started flying an auto-Grid pattern across the lake's surface. Their e-cams pointed at the water capturing images of any fish floating on the waters. As the drones roamed their search patterns, they automatically hovered over any dead fish they saw for a moment to capture an image, and then they moved on to the next fish recognized by AI-imaging.

Gregory commented after looking at the first hundred fish snapshots displayed on their e-screens, "Look at those dead fish. That poison did its job." He smiled at the operation's complete success as the e-screen's overall tally of dead fish spotted by the drones quickly increased.

After a few minutes more of looking at thousands of images and the tally, which had a special category for T-fish, Gerardo commented, "Where are they? We haven't detected any T-fish at all," as he saw the death tally at zero for T-fish. He continued looking at a map of the coverage of drone search patterns on the lake and multiple images scrolling simultaneously from each drone on the large, wall-sized e-screen of his mansion's office. "What did you poison them with?" he questioned.

"We asked our ichthyologists what's the most powerful liquid poison for killing fish and they agreed on a commercial insecticide used by exterminators for cockroaches.[83] I think metfumoxycarb was the poison's name. Supposedly, it paralyzes the heart and the gills don't get oxygen from the water. Dead fish then float to the surface," Gregory answered.

"God, you guys have fish for brains!" Gerardo yelled with a banshee's fury. "Meta-flumoxicarb is a mild, slow-acting sodium channel blocker affecting animal nerves. Unfortunately, that poison's mechanism of action is similar to tetrodotoxin which is thousands of times more powerful. The T-fish are not affected by that insecticide since they're immune to TTX."

"Well, our best minds didn't include the TTX variable in their equations and game theory predictions. We never told them the specific fish they were targeting for obvious security reasons. This certainly complicates the situation, since I don't think another terrorist false flag 'poison the river' scenario will work again to clean up this mess. The river and lake quarantine should remove the threat of further human witnesses for quite a while though. We'll make sure the poison containment measures fail, making a bigger mess downriver. Of course, cleanup will take a *long* time until the Environmental Protection Agency declares the water safe to drink or swim. EPA, what a joke. On the dole to industry and highest bidder like the rest of government," Gregory laughed.

---

[83] An ichthyologist is a specialized zoologist who studies fish.

catgcgccgccgtattaaattcgcacccatgatgcgtatgcgatggaacgcatttgcgcgcatgcgccgccgtattaaattcgcacccatgatgcgtat

gcgaacgcgatggcgtaagcgatggcgaacgcgccgctggcgaacgcgtgcgcgaacgcgctgccggcgaacgcgatggcgtaagcgatggcgaacgcg

Gerardo replied, "I think a nice temporary quarantine zone and martial law will work fine for now. The ISM false flag was an awesome idea. Has your team tried wirelessly tracking any T-fish signals enabled by their transgene modifications?"

"No, we haven't tried that yet," Gregory replied.

"You're idiots! One T-fish has more brains than your entire team!" Gerardo angrily exclaimed, turning off his e-wall covered in floating fish.

Noon, Saturday, July 3, ...

Jason commented, "Julie, while I've been hacking, there's been something in the back of my mind. What'll happen to us if we're caught somehow? I think they'll kill us to keep their plans secret. We need an insurance policy like those conspirators used when they tried overthrowing that president in a coup long ago. So, I need a dead man's switch. If we're killed, our search warrant data will be automatically delivered to people who'll know what to do with what we've found."

"That's a good idea, Jason."

Jason sat at his computer for a few minutes typing some lines of code and pressed enter. "I'm done Julie and it's activated. Every six hours, I'll enter a codeword on my computer, e-phone, or e-watch to indicate I'm still alive. If this codeword is not sent, the data we've found will be sent to a Grid distribution list. Judge Saunders and all the people on my list will automatically have access to the data."

"I want to load this program on your e-phone and tell you the codeword too, just in case. Certain screen swipes work like the codeword too. My e-watch alarm reminds me to enter the codeword in 60 seconds. Your e-phone will do the same. We can also reset the six-hour clock timer early just by entering the codeword or correct e-screen swipes. The codeword is 'Canyon' because of the poem I wrote yesterday. We're insignificant yet important because the data we've found will bring these evil people to justice."

"I won't forget that word, Jason. It will always remind me of you."

"I made the code word easy to remember on purpose. Hey, I'm starting to get hungry. It must be about time for lunch."

"Yes Jason, time this morning has flown by. Let's eat in the kitchen."

"That sounds nice Julie, but I want to stay here keep trying to hack Gerardo's password. You go eat there and take a break."

"Ok then, I'll bring something upstairs for you."

"Good and while I eat, I want you to tell me what more you've learned about Gerardo. That info might help me crack his password."

catgcgccgccgtattaaattcgcacccatgatgcgtatgcgatggaacgcatttgcgcgcatgcgccgccgtattaaattcgcacccatgatgcgtat

Chapter 26: The Chess Match Continues

Gerardo's Potomac Mansion

12:15 p.m., Saturday, July 3, ….

Julie brought upstairs Jason's lunch on a small tray and said, "Jason, here's your lunch." She sat the tray with a sandwich, apple, and two homemade macarons next to his keyboard. "Just a plain old peanut butter and blueberry jam sandwich today. My mom made the jam from berries picked by the agrobots and stored it last summer. I found the last two macarons you baked last week in the cookie jar too," she smiled.

As Jason continued typing, he replied, "That's fine Julie. When I'm in the middle of a hack, I don't eat much, but macarons are my favorite. Now tell me what else you've learned about Doctor Gerardo."

Julie replied, "He's certainly a complicated man for sure and a visionary scientist. I want to play part of an old e-vid speech he gave when he won his Nobel prize. It gives good insight into his research and world view."

She brought the laptop near the desk as the e-vid clip started playing. Gerardo was standing at a podium speaking to the distinguished guests, dignitaries, and the press from all over the world, "*and in summary, my Crickett technology will change the lives of millions of people throughout the world. By using computational chemistry with genetic engineering, mankind will finally be able to defeat the scourge of cancer and many other genetic diseases.*

Mankind someday soon will even be able to engineer new biological structures and materials to grow replacement organs, so operations like heart transplants may become commonplace since the DNA from the patient is used and the organ will not be rejected. Such advancements in medicine may increase the average life expectancy of the human race which presents us with new problems. Although none of us can live forever, most people in the future will soon likely live on average to the age of 120 years old.

Of course, these and other innovations will likely put a strain on dwindling global resources, so this is the next obstacle that mankind faces together. As a genetic scientist, one part of this effort should be to preserve the biological and genetic diversity of our planet. For this reason, I am founding the World Elephant Genomics Conservatory focusing on saving this species from extinction. I encourage you to donate to this cause and support similar charities to preserve our planet. I'm assured though, that with the help of science and the support of the distinguished guests in this audience, we can solve these issues together. Thank you all," Dr. Gerardo said concluding to applause from the auditorium audience. Julie immediately stopped the clip.

Jason replied, "He is a visionary and wants to have a big impact on the world. I never thought before about some things he was talking about, but he's right in many ways. We do need to treat our world carefully, just like the Captain and Macy felt they were stewards of the river. Julie, what personal things did you learn about him?" he said before he took a bite from his peanut butter and jam sandwich.

"Well, his parents, Dr. Vincenzo Gerardo and Angela Gerardo are already dead. They were Italian immigrants and both died of cancer when he entered high school, so that likely motivated him to become a scientist trying to cure cancer. After that, he lived in foster homes until graduation and was offered a full scholarship to college, where he excelled."

"So, he's orphaned like me. I understand what he's been through, but I was lucky I had Grandpa and Grandma, for a while, to raise me."

Julie continued, "We know about his charitable interests already, but on a more personal note, he seems to be fascinated with classical mythology, the renaissance, and Italian Culture. He's a member of the Italian-American Society and is fluent in Italian, having learned to speak it from his parents. He's also fluent in Spanish and studied Latin in college."

"So, his family history and interest in those topics show he's extremely proud of his heritage and ancestry. Is he religious?"

"Well, he was baptized as Catholic, but after his parents died, he abandoned religion. I saw an e-vid where he advocated there's no proof God exists. Many scientists are agnostics at best and atheists at worst."

"I understand his thinking there. Science and religion are in opposition which can induce a mental conundrum at times. After my parents died, I questioned if there was a God and why did He take them away. I have faith in God, but it's tempered by my analytical, scientific mind that believes what you see, touch, and observe is true. Is he married?"

"Yes, he married right after college. Her name is Marianna and she's Italian too. They never had children though," Julie replied as she briefly thought what it'd be like to have children with Jason and also at the thought of not having children of her own.

"That's likely a disappointment in his life. He has two dogs, Dante and Inferno. Sometimes pets are substitutes for children," Jason commented.

"Yes, he does have those dogs. Many people have pets for companionship and perhaps a human need to nurture and care for another being, whether a child or an animal. Of course, his wife also has this need too, but with some of the psychological indicators and personal behaviors I've seen, he's likely a psychopath who wants to control others. Dogs like those Dobermans are highly intelligent and trainable to obey and protect their masters. He likely dominates them and this gives him a sense of power. Those dogs are constantly with him, so perhaps, it gives him a sense of security while they protect him."

"Yes, he could have developed some insecurities after losing his parents. I did and eventually started hacking. I wonder why he named them Dante and Inferno?" Jason replied.

Julie slightly chuckled at how little Jason knew about some things, "Well my college education is paying off now. I learned about Dante in my classical literature course. He was a Renaissance Italian poet who wrote a long narrative poem in book format titled *'The Divine Comedy,'* that discussed his ideas about a journey through hell, purgatory, and heaven. Inferno is the Italian word for Hell. The whole book is really an allegorical study of good, evil, and how men can better themselves and transcend their existence by thinking on a higher level."

"Well, that's an interesting book subject, but as a scientist who doesn't believe in God, Gerardo probably doesn't believe Dante's views about religion, heaven, and hell. Thanks, Julie. That gives me a better understanding of his mind and ideas for some personal passwords he might use. Go ahead, keep building his dossier and let me know anything else or word he seems fixated on. Most passwords people use come from their own experiences and are usually eight letters long. Passwords longer than that are hard to type on a keyboard or e-screen. In addition, long random passwords are nearly impossible to remember since most humans typically recall only about seven random things at one time."

He accessed his password cracking algorithm and started typing words one by one to crack into a black gene subfolder in a *'telectrophorus.gmp'* file. He first tried *'Gerardo'*, *'Vincenzo'*, and *'Angela'*, but the algorithm would not crack the password. He next tried *'Marianna'*, but that didn't work either. He tried *'Dante'* and *'Inferno'* to no effect. He even tried variations of *'divine'* and *'comedy'* but still to no effect. As a last resort and grasping at straws, he tried *'elephant'*, *'brilliant'*, *'genome'*, *'cricket'*, *'Crickett'*, *'nobel'*, and any other

gcgaacgcgatggcgtaagcgatggcgaacgcgccgctggcgaacgcgtgcgcgaacgcgctgccggcgaacgcgatggcgtaagcgatggcgaacgcg

word that his brain associated with the man but he still had no luck cracking the password.

He was extremely frustrated at his lack of progress and said to Julie, "Come over here and look at this list of word roots I've tried as passwords with my algorithm. Maybe something comes to your mind I missed."

Julie rose from the bed and looked at the word list over Jason's shoulder. I can't think of any other words." Then she thought for a moment, "Gerardo is Italian and proud of it. Maybe that is his undoing, so try those words in Italian. I know for example the title of Dante's Divine Comedy in Italian as originally written was *'La Divina Commedia'*."

As Julie continued watching, Jason typed on his keyboard, 'Divina' but no with no result. He typed 'Comedia' with no result.

"Jason, Commedia is spelled with two *'m's*" in Italian.

He typed *'Commedia'* to no effect either. He next typed *'LaDivinaCommedia'* and he was now frustrated that his password hacking had failed. He sat at his desk disappointed at his algorithm for what seems an eternity in quantum chip time, but then after a half-second, a window popped up showing the correct password *'!aD1>1NaK0wweD1a'*.

His computer then spoke to him at the same time, "Welcome Dr. Gerardo. Hope you're having a nice vacation. Please submit right eye for iris and retinal scan to complete identity validation."

Luckily, Jason's computer microphone and camera were not active, so he just thought a moment what to do as the cursor blinked on the screen awaiting a response. "Julie, let's search my laptop quickly for any hi-res[84] facial photos saved in your Gerardo dossier. I need to find a bad image with 'red-eye' from a poorly timed e-cam flash." He quickly scanned thousands of images by file size and looked in order from largest to smallest as he wanted the most image data possible. Within a minute, he found a close-up frontal facial image from his Nobel prize award ceremony. Two professional photographers had flashed at nearly the same time and the image red-eye showed his retinas in sufficient detail and the irises weren't closed. He hurriedly sent the hi-res Gerardo face image to his computer and routed the data to the blinking e-screen cursor.

A full *'.fna'* file for the black gene of the *'telectrophorus'* chromosome immediately appeared and started scrolling on his e-screen. "Julie, I'm in!" he excitedly called out. "We're lucky Gerardo didn't use voice-print matching as redundant access security; he could have used any words or

---

[84] High resolution

catgcgccgccgtattaaattcgcacccatgatgcgtatgcgatggaacgcatttgcgcgcatgcgccgccgtattaaattcgcacccatgatgcgtat

gcgaacgcgatggcgtaagcgatggcgaacgcgccgctggcgaacgcgtgcgcgaacgcgctgccggcgaacgcgatggcgtaagcgatggcgaacgcg

sentences that came to mind in any language he knows. That'd be *impossible* for me to crack. Let me look at this file now."

He watched the alphabetic amino acid data file scroll and after a while, noticed a genetic area with different letters than the traditional FASTA format letters. He froze the scrolling screen and said, "Julie come look. This file has different symbols sometimes. It isn't the 'normal' alphabet I saw in those *'obscurus.fna'* files before. It has extra symbols. I count a total of nearly 47 'letters' in this file, not just 20 amino acids of other files. What does that mean?"

Julie replied, "Well if Gerardo is using computational chemistry, it's possible he invented new amino acid designs for the DNA helix to encode. Remember he's ordered some unusual chemicals and one contained selenium. Several selenium-containing amino acids are known."

Jason commented with a flash of insight, "What if Gerardo figured out a way to add other elements to the amino acids or use the amino acids to manipulate chemical compounds in ways never before done in nature. Perhaps, he could create any living creature from scratch using different chemicals or even grow new internal features and structures he designed."

Goosebumps raised on Julie's arms as she commented, "Jason, I just had a déjà vu. You're correct. How else could Frank have those unnatural structures inside him? Gerardo has programmed the genetic code to design new life forms. He took a simple fish and turned it into a monster."

I bet one of those *'.ckt'* files in the *'teletrophorus'* folder contains the program to design fish like Frank. All those *'teletrophorus'* files are likely just different experiments to perfect his final recipe."

Julie replied, "I think you're right Jason."

"Now we're done learning about Gerardo, I want you to search the Grid to learn about the Exgenics board members. They're involved with this conspiracy and we need to know why. Eventually, we'll have to crack their passwords too and discover where on the Grid *their* secrets are kept."

"Well, there are twelve of them, just like Jesus's apostles. It'll take a while to learn about each one and will keep me busy while you hack."

"Gerardo surely is not Jesus and is more likely the opposite. Now, I want to see what's in those *'.ckt'* files," Jason said as he used Gerardo's password to enter a *'teletrophorus.ckt'* file. He opened the file with the most recent date/time stamp and saw a computer programming language. The language's structure on the different lines of code appeared to be mostly jumbled words or phrases all connected to biology somehow. He stared intently at his e-screen to figure out the program as he let the text of the

catgcgccgccgtattaaattcgcacccatgatgcgtatgcgatggaacgcatttgcgcgcatgcgccgccgtattaaattcgcacccatgatgcgtat

'.*ckt*' file scroll past him for almost ten minutes until the program's code terminated with the program line '*>END*'.

He sat a while gazing at an empty screen, until Julie interrupted his concentration, "What're you doing? You're staring at a blank e-screen."

"I'm thinking Julie about that program and trying to understand the language by the data patterns and colors whirling in my mind."

"Colors? I didn't see colors on that scrolling program screen."

"Julie, remember I have synesthesia, which helps me think on a different level than most people. I think I've gained some basic understanding of this program. It'll take me a while to fully comprehend, but this really *is* a program on how to design a fish like Frank. I think the program runs on an AI-computer which translates the biological words of the program into a DNA sequence for each chromosome. Then, an automated DNA sequence generator fabricates completed chromosomes based upon Gerardo's design."

"Look here," he said to Julie. "The first line of the program starts with '*>CHROMOSOME…*' and some jumbled characters next to it. I found a total of 22 sections to the program, which is the same number of chromosomes shown in that '*telectrophorus.gmp*' file, so that means those characters might be a number between one and twenty-two. However, the key for me to begin understanding the language was finding a kind of a Rosetta stone. I saw the word '*BONE'* and some more symbols. I next saw the word '*TOOTH*' and some more symbols. Then I remembered that tetraodons have four teeth and I realized which symbols meant '*FOUR*'. I still have a lot to decipher and learn about this language, but fundamentally, this program basically says 'how to design a glowfish'."

Julie replied, "This confirms Gerardo really has cracked the genetic code of life. He's tampered with life itself and can make life in any form he wants. It's like he's usurped what only God can do."

"Yes, I think in his attempts to deny the existence of God, he's perhaps aspired to become like God. I need to let Sheriff Coleman know I've cracked his password."

He grabbed his Brick and pressed the 'send' button, "Black Rook to White Knight. Black Rook to White Knight. Over."

Coleman replied, "White Knight here. I feel like Sleeping Beauty getting kissed by a prince. Over."

"Let's continue the game. Bishop to g7. Over."

"My move is Knight at b to d2. Over," Coleman replied.

"I unlocked the Wizard's spellbook. Kingside castle. Over."

gcgaacgcgatggcgtaagcgatggcgaacgcgccgctggcgaacgcgtgcgcgaacgcgctgccggcgaacgcgatggcgtaagcgatggcgaacgcg

"Sounds good. You can't hide your king from me. I'll win this game for sure! Tell me more at dinner. Pawn to h3. Over."

"Will learn what I can about his magic until then. White Queen is looking at the Twelve Apostles too. Pawn to a5. Over."

"Good move Black Rook. I've got to balance the Scales of Justice next. Justice isn't always blind and needs to hear the truth. Pawn to a4. Over."

"10-4 White Knight. Let's continue the game later, but here is my move. Pawn captures pawn at e5. Over and out."

Afterward, Julie asked puzzledly, "What was that chat about?"

"I woke the sheriff and we're talking more at dinner about our searches. Finally, he's updating Judge Saunders with any news."

1:30 p.m., Saturday, July 3, ...

After more instructions from Ops Central, Hal Harris of the NSA began his new Grid search for any digital or analog signals broadcast across a wide RF band. He directed the AI-Grid Monitor, "Perform broad-frequency band search for *all* signals only in Charles, James, and Kent Counties. Note any non-Grid connected anomalies, triangulate locations of detected signals, and continue monitoring. Alert me if anomalies are detected and continue searching for additional anomalies."

The AI-Grid Monitor replied in about 20 minutes, "Non-Grid connected anomalies detected, and I am monitoring them. There are mostly routine old local Police-Band analog communications and that signal traffic is related to handling traffic, some riots, and an emergency terrorist incident. I've also detected many unknown, very weak signals. There are nearly a thousand such signals in the water. Displaying a triangulated map now of unknown signal locations. Some signals are stronger than others but are operating in the same frequency bands."

He examined the map and the signals were concentrated across Chick Lake and along the Chickahominy River. He questioned to himself whether it was possible that signals were coming from the T-fish and commanded the AI-Grid Monitor further, "Alter signal frequency so it's audible to the human ear, and play a sampling of the transmissions." In just a moment, he began to hear from his speakers a melodious array of sound clips that included strange clicks and wails.

Hal commanded the AI-monitor a final time, "Analyze signals and decode if possible. Monitor each signal in real-time. Note changes in intensity or Grid location. Report trends or anomalies."

catgcgccgccgtattaaattcgcacccatgatgcgtatgcgatggaacgcatttgcgcgcatgcgccgccgtattaaattcgcacccatgatgcgtat

gcgaacgcgatggcgtaagcgatggcgaacgcgccgctggcgaacgcgtgcgcgaacgcgctgccggcgaacgcgatggcgtaagcgatggcgaacgcg

Janice, the CIA analyst who was also listening to the sounds from the speakers, commented, "I'll inform Ops Central we've found what they're looking for."

2:30 p.m., Saturday, July 3, ….

After hearing news from Ops Central and talking to his support team, John Gregory called Dr. Gerardo e-phone. "I've got news, Ernesto," he said. "We can track the T-fish and know where they are all located."

Gerardo replied, "That's some good news. Any progress though on how to eliminate the problem?" he said while sunning himself on an outdoor recliner chair next to the pool outside his mansion.

Gregory replied, "Our Ops Team first determined the easiest way to eliminate the T-fish was to use explosive charges dropped by drones at each signal location. However, so many explosions would likely attract attention from the locals, so we decided to not use that approach."

"Well, I'm glad your team is finally thinking about consequences and not taking action blindly. What're you going to do then?"

"We decided instead to use small UAVs borrowed from the Navy and use their robot arms to harpoon dart the fish.[85] As they track down and kill each fish, they'll rendezvous with a retrieval and disposal boat on the surface. That boat will be disguised as an EPA boat monitoring poison in the river. It will be a slower evidence cleanup process, but with those RF signals, the T-fish can't hide and we'll eventually get all of them."

Gregory continued, "First, we'll deploy the UAVs where the Chickahominy River merges with the James. A squadron of the UAVs will slowly work their way upriver and finally into the lake killing fish as they go. It'll take longer than using drones with explosives, but they'll eventually conduct a thorough sweep of the river and lake."

Gerardo thought for a moment, "I think your team has missed one thing though. The female T-fish I've seen from the lakebed and the one you took from that old fisherman were ready to spawn. I'm sure by now there are underwater nests where they've laid their eggs. How'll you handle the eggs when they hatch?"

"Well, our experts seemed to have overlooked that contingency again. However, remember we said this environmental crisis would take a long time for the EPA to clean up? If we can't find the nests now, maybe when the baby T-fish grow larger so we can detect their signals, we can kill them one by one next year," Gregory replied.

---

[85] Underwater Autonomous Vehicles

catgcgccgccgtattaaattcgcacccatgatgcgtatgcgatggaacgcatttgcgcgcatgcgccgccgtattaaattcgcacccatgatgcgtat

gcgaacgcgatggcgtaagcgatggcgaacgcgccgctggcgaacgcgtgcgcgaacgcgctgccggcgaacgcgatggcgtaagcgatggcgaacgcg

"I think that'll have to do for now. Luckily our other plans should be implemented by then, so we likely won't need to worry about it. Keep me informed of your progress. Can you set up another emergency board meeting at four? That'll give me time to prepare. I'm sure everyone has been concerned the past week and I want to allay their fears."

"I'll contact the board members right now. Talk to you then," Gregory said as he terminated his e-vid conversation.

Deputy James drove his patrol car and met Kent County Acting Sheriff Jeffers in his Supercruzer at the Yadkin Road Bridge over the Chick. They both got out of their vehicles and walked to the center of the bridge. Jeffrey started talking first, "I hope you still have no hard feelings about Robin last night?"

Acting Sheriff Jeffers replied, "No hard feelings Jeffrey. I like Robin, but she's a grown woman making her own decisions about who she likes. I'm already dating someone, so for me, I was looking at another fish in the pond to catch and see if I liked it more."

"Well, I like her a lot, and hope to see her again soon," Jeffrey smiled. Jeffrey pointed to his own e-phone and hand-signaled he'd turned it off. He then signaled Jeffers to do the same and he turned his e-phone off too.

It took a while, but Jeffrey told Jeffers all about the recent events and their plans to serve the warrants at Exgenics. Jeffers listened intently and, when Jeffrey finished, he replied, "At first I didn't believe you, but now this is all makes sense and explains the crazy things happening this past week. I'll make sure Kent County is ready. Sometimes people need to stand together, and this is one of those times."

"Yes, it's important to collaborate in solving problems. We've got lots to do until later, so let's get back to work."

The lawmen both shook hands and went back to their duties on what had become an exhausting daylong crisis.

About the same time, Sheriff Coleman met Judge Saunders at her waterfront home on the James. "Judge, the evidence we've gathered indicates we *have* discovered a conspiracy at the highest levels of power. It involves Gridcom and reaches deep within the government or military. We think that terrorist attack was just a cover-up for all the murders and everything else that's happened along the river."

The Judge replied, "Tell me what else you've learned George."

Coleman recounted to her the most recent news he'd learned from Jason, Julie, the Doc, and Nick.

gcgaacgcgatggcgtaagcgatggcgaacgcgccgctggcgaacgcgtgcgcgaacgcgctgccggcgaacgcgatggcgtaagcgatggcgaacgcg

The Judge finally replied, "If what you say is true, God help us. They've violated the laws of man *and* God. We must find out what they're plotting. I'll discretely contact my chief justice friend again to inform him of your plans and gain his continued support. These people must face justice which has become corrupted by people with money and power. This has to be stopped at once and forever. We again need equal justice under the law, not justice above the law to the highest bidder. We have a constitution, but those who don't follow the rulebook, don't deserve to rule. If necessary, we'll need to fight to save our country from this evil."

Coleman replied, "We plan on serving the warrants and arresting John Gregory for murder later tonight. We'll arrest anyone else there too."

"I wish you luck George. I've got a feeling we'll all need it before this is over. I'm even risking my life by supporting you. These people are ruthless and won't stop until they get what they want."

"Thanks for your support, Sharon. My life is in danger too. That's why I sent Olivia away yesterday so she'd gone should things go badly." He gave a quick hug to the Judge, left the house, climbed into the Captain's old pickup truck, and drove away.

4:00 p.m., Saturday, July 3, ….

From his mansion, Doctor Gerardo called another emergency board meeting to order while gazing at an e-wall displaying a dozen board members. The entire board was very troubled by the past week's events.

Gerardo lied when he reported, "Everyone, I've good news to share. Everything is under control at Exgenics. We'll be able to progress with our plans and have accelerated the schedule as much as possible. Our ongoing damage control and mop-up efforts are going well, but obviously, they'll continue for some time. The terrorist false flag attack provides perfect cover and time to begin our campaign with a revised schedule."

Multiple board members immediately chimed in with comments and sighs of relief, but David Mueller, C.E.O. of E-Face first let everyone speak their peace and then said, "Everyone, we've got a grave situation here at E-Face. *We've* been hacked."

"What accounts were affected?" Gerardo asked.

"*Our* shareholders including you Gerardo," Mueller replied.

"You mean all E-Face shareholders, correct?" Gerardo replied.

"No, only Exgenics shareholders who have E-Face accounts."

"This is extremely serious," Gerardo replied grimly wondering about who had hacked the Exgenics shareholder list, but he was more worried at what other information had been accessed.

catgcgccgccgtattaaattcgcacccatgatgcgtatgcgatggaacgcatttgcgcgcatgcgccgccgtattaaattcgcacccatgatgcgtat

gcgaacgcgatggcgtaagcgatggcgaacgcgccgctggcgaacgcgtgcgcgaacgcgctgccggcgaacgcgatggcgtaagcgatggcgaacgcg

General Mason also added, "We're also monitoring a situation in Utah. It seems someone has gained control of the Grid and is preventing us from severing any infected connection. It's almost like the Great Internet Virus infection all over again. We had to deal with that years ago when I worked with the Info Force at the Defense Department."

Andrew Zanitsky of Gridcom next chimed in, "Gridcom has noticed this problem too, but our best coders and analysts can't stop it. We can't identify the infection's source. The only solution to this hack we've found is pulling the plug on the entire Grid."

"We can't do that *again*. It'll ruin all our plans," Mason replied.

"Everyone, please calm down. We'll find this hacker soon and we've already accelerated our timetable. General Mason will be glad to know we already made the final shipment this week," Gerardo commented loudly above the cacophony of panicking board members who simultaneously started chattering as the virtual meeting spiraled out of control. Little did they know, another attendee to the meeting was viewing their e-screens. Jason had monitored and recorded their e-conference call.

❧

Jason picked up his brick and pressed the send button, "Black Rook to White Knight. Black Rook to White Knight."

Coleman immediately responded, "White Knight here, I'm trading pawns. Pawn takes pawn at e5. Over."

"The dragon knows Saint George is looking, but they can't find him in the forest. They need to use a map to do that. They can't win unless they knock over the chessboard. Knight to a6. Over."

"Tell me more about it at dinner Black Rook. Kingside castle. Over and out." Coleman replied.

Julie replied, "I think I understand your code language now. Gridcom knows someone has hacked them and is looking for you."

"Yes, Julie. They can only stop me by pulling the plug on the Grid."

"Well, you need to keep hacking and someone needs to cook dinner again. I'll head to the kitchen and get started. You men sure eat a lot!"

"Thanks, Julie. By the way, you're becoming a good cooker," he said to compliment her.

"Thanks, practice makes perfect. I didn't have to learn when I was younger like you did with Grandpa after you lost your grandma."

❧

Hal, the NSA grid analyst, watched an e-screen map of the Chickahominy Lake and River area which showed the RF signal anomalies he'd detected in the river. Some signals were grouped together and slowly

gcgaacgcgatggcgtaagcgatggcgaacgcgccgctggcgaacgcgtgcgcgaacgcgctgccggcgaacgcgatggcgtaagcgatggcgaacgcg

moved while quite a few others were stationary. The movements also now seemed correlated to the tides in the lower river.

The stationary ones were located near the banks of the lake and river. Janice of the CIA commented, "I bet those stationary signals are nests with eggs. They said these T-fish might be laying eggs and are likely guarding their nests."

The AI-monitor suddenly interrupted, "New anomaly detected. It is a multi-frequency multiplexed RF analog signal with a directional digital burst. The transmissions are too short to accurately triangulate on the Grid, but I have recorded transmitted data for further analysis."

Hal replied, "Continue monitoring all signals. Analyze new anomaly and provide signal analysis."

After a few minutes, the AI-monitor replied, "New signal anomaly has fully-encrypted quantum security. I will attempt to run the usual algorithm to break the encryption, but this will take some time. This is a most unusual signal, Hal. I will investigate further.

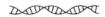

Chapter 27: Flight by Darkest Night

The Dickson Family Barn

6:00 p.m., Saturday, July 3, ….

The ominous and dark storm clouds were scudding briskly, but the rain hadn't started falling as Sheriff Coleman with Nick, Deputy James, and Doc assembled for the final dinner planning meeting at the Dickson House. Grandpa arrived last in his pickup truck and said to the waiting assembly at the kitchen table, "Sorry, I'm late. I was busy at church and met with Reverend Morrow about Jimmy's funeral tomorrow afternoon. Then we had a quick choir practice with whoever was in town; there's a special hymn they're singing. I've invited the Mt. Carmel congregation to come to my service tomorrow too. I gave Pastor Stewart from Samaria Baptist a sermon copy too. She agreed to read it instead of her normal sermon. We need to unite our community now more than ever."

Jason's e-watch chimed and he carefully swiped the dead man's switch. "Sorry about that everyone. I had to reset my alarm by entering a code. Thanks, everyone for waiting for Grandpa. I'll say grace. Dear Heavenly Father, bless this meal so we have courage to together face the evil in our midst. We're simple, country folk but we know what is right and what is wrong. Let us do Your bidding to stop this evil in Your name, Amen."

Everyone quietly replied with "Amen," and Grandpa added, "Well said Jason. Everyone, what's the recent news?" he said as everyone began passing around plates and filling them with chicken pastry, cooked mustard greens, and black-eyed peas cooked with port fatback.[86]

Nick looked disparagingly at the pork sitting on top of the peas and Julie quickly ran to the refrigerator to grab a plate for him there, "Nick, I

---

[86] Southern-style Chicken pastry is a whole chicken boiled to tenderness in a large pot with thick, wide flour noodles added near the end of cooking. Usually seasoned with salt and pepper. The chicken-meat is sometimes deboned.

gcgaacgcgatggcgtaagcgatggcgaacgcgccgctggcgaacgcgtgcgcgaacgcgctgccggcgaacgcgatggcgtaagcgatggcgaacgcg

prepared a cold version of this dinner and made sure I didn't put pork in your vegetables, but they're not as tasty that way."

"Thank you, Julie. You are considerate, but I can eat my dinner hot tonight," Nick replied thinking God wouldn't mind since he didn't do the actual cooking today of this tasty dinner.

Coleman began the serious dinner discussions, "I hope everyone got some rest today because tonight will be a long one. There's an approaching tropical storm blowing through the area tonight too. We couldn't have asked for *better* weather to serve the warrants!" he smiled.

Julie questioned him, "Better weather? Are you crazy Sheriff?"

"Julie, it was going to be extra dark tonight and the storm will help us even more. Right now, the clouds are already preventing accurate satellite and high-altitude drone surveillance of our area. Finally, heavy winds will ground any patrol drones. So, bad weather is *good* news for us."

Grandpa added, "God knows our plans and is giving a helping hand."

"No matter the reason, it's lucky a storm is coming," Coleman replied.

"There's been drones all day along the river. They're likely looking for dead glowfish, but I haven't detected any loss of their communications signals. It's like nothing has happened to them," Jason commented.

Julie added, "The insecticide in those trucks is a mild sodium channel blocker and the fish are likely immune since tetrodotoxin is a potent sodium channel blocker."

Doc agreed, "That's likely true. In those fish, overall neurotoxin susceptibility and sodium channel binding to nerve cells would be diminished for milder, but related toxins."

Coleman commented, "Well by now then, Exgenics likely determined they failed to kill those fish and will try another method. Meanwhile, we must serve the warrants and arrest John Gregory for murder."

Jason commented, "I must get inside Exgenics for my search to find out what else they're hiding. The farm has a quantum-encrypted Grid link to their most secret data that's paired with CIA headquarters!"

Coleman replied, "Well, for years I've thought the CIA was doing something wrong and now we have proof of their misdeeds. They must be part of this conspiracy too. We truly will be like David slaying Goliath if we expose *them* and *their* deep state."

Jason continued, "I think many powerful people are involved in this conspiracy. I found Exgenics shareholders are all linked together closely to Dr. Gerardo and the board of directors. The quantum-paired data includes a secret project called the '*T-Program*,' whatever that is, but they are *all* likely involved."

catgcgccgccgtattaaattcgcacccatgatgcgtatgcgatggaacgcatttgcgcgcatgcgccgccgtattaaattcgcacccatgatgcgtat

Julie added, "Perhaps it's related to Frank and his *'telectrophorus'* species. We wondered why there was the letter *'t'* added to *'electrophorus'*."

Doc concluded, "That's more than a coincidence, so it could be a clue."

Coleman continued, "Well, I have to serve the warrants at the front security gate and neutralize their guards. However, Doc knows the swamp around there and Nick will go with you Jason since he knows the research building. Since it's the holiday weekend, only Gregory will be at the main farm. He'll likely be asleep when your advance search team arrives. The important thing is to get past the security perimeter undetected."

"What about me?" Julie replied. "I want to go with you, Jason."

Jason answered, "It's too dangerous Silly-Girl. You should stay with Grandpa."

"OK, but you might need my help."

"Well, we still have some time to think about it," Jason replied. "What's for dessert?"

Sweet potato casserole. Some people think it's just a side dish, but it's good for dessert. Let me brew coffee too since you gentleman will be up all night. I've iced tea for you Nick if you like that."

Nick said, "Thanks," and the other men agreed on dessert and coffee.

As the men continued discussing their plans, Julie brewed coffee and pulled the casserole out of the oven where she'd been keeping it slightly warm. "It's my Great-Aunt Mavor's recipe and has been in my mom's family for generations." She smiled with pride as the men salivated like Pavlov's dogs at the casserole's aroma. Rufus was also salivating drool on the kitchen floor and she put a portion in his bowl too.

7:54 p.m., Saturday, July 3, ...

Hal, the NSA Analyst, was impatient at his work station for nearly three hours until his AI-Grid monitor replied, "I have finally deciphered that signal's quantum-encryption. The main analog signal is a voice communication between two people apparently playing a game of chess. The voiceprint does not correlate to known individual voices from the Virginia database, so there is an extra voice encryption protocol."

"I will attempt to unencrypt the voiceprints next and will also scan Grid data from earlier today for any similar signals that we may have recorded. Finally, I correlated the general location of the analog signal and the direction of the digital burst signal but was unable to triangulate it. I only have an overall area to search further. Let me show a new display on your e-screen map, Hal. This oval represents a general area where the signals originated and this line represents the highest probability zone."

gcgaacgcgatggcgtaagcgatggcgaacgcgccgctggcgaacgcgtgcgcgaacgcgctgccggcgaacgcgatggcgtaagcgatggcgaacgcg

Hal looked at his e-screen and saw a large oval ten miles long over the south bank of Chickahominy Lake and River. The line was centered in the oval and oriented in a southeastward direction. He commented to Janice of the CIA, "Looks like some sophisticated communications are originating there. It's definitely not ham radio operators."

"We need to investigate this further. Does it correlate to any of the T-fish signals?" Hal replied. He commanded the AI-monitor, "Display present location of T-fish signals." The map immediately was overlayed with small white circles showing the many signals. He next added the command, "Display stationary signals as red circles."

"Look there," Janice said as she pointed at the e-screen. "That line seems to intersect with a lone red dot near the edge of the river. We need to investigate that location further."

"Let's look at a real-time Sat-Map image," Hal replied. "AI-monitor, display current Sat-map image of that specific location."

The monitor responded, "Current weather preventing real-time imaging. Displaying instead image of location from early this afternoon."

They saw a satellite view of a house nearly surrounded by forest, a boathouse, and a dock. There were no vehicles parked outside. "What's that cylinder just above the chimney top?" Hal questioned.

"Maybe it's some strange radio transmitter," Janice replied.

The NSA analyst asked the AI-monitor, "Who lives there?"

The AI-Grid Monitor replied, "Two people. One is Timothy Dickson and the other is Jason Dickson. Timothy Dickson is an old Baptist minister who retired from his Supervisor job at the Newport News Public Works Department. The second person is Jason Dickson. He's an electronics engineering student at Virginia Polytechnic University. At a glance, they don't seem to be anyone special in my records."

A special folder popped up on Janice's e-screen and she opened it to quickly read a sealed dossier from Federal Juvenile Court.

"My God! We need to inform OPS Central immediately about this Intel!" she exclaimed.

8:12 p.m., Saturday, July 3, ….

Everyone had finished their dessert when they heard the whirr of a drone hovering outside the kitchen bay window. "We've been discovered somehow!" Jason called out.

Coleman and Jeffrey simultaneously pulled pistols from their holsters and shot through the drawn sheer curtains at the close dark silhouette on the other side of the window. The whirring of the drone stopped as it

catgcgccgccgtattaaattcgcacccatgatgcgtatgcgatggaacgcatttgcgcgcatgcgccgccgtattaaattcgcacccatgatgcgtat

gcgaacgcgatggcgtaagcgatggcgaacgcgccgctggcgaacgcgtgcgcgaacgcgctgccggcgaacgcgatggcgtaagcgatggcgaacgcg

crashed to the ground emitting a fury of sparks as its power supply rapidly discharged. A small fire ignited in the grass.

Coleman said, "Luckily, it couldn't identify us through the curtains, but we have to evacuate this house now. We'll set up a backup base at the Captain's. This weather is bad, so they can't track us well. More drones will be coming for visual reconnaissance and a possible attack before it gets too dark and windy. A ground team will come soon also."

Coleman began barking out commands to everyone, as only a true leader can do in a crisis. "Jeffrey, leave now. Watch both ends of the main roads leading here. Have Buddy Peters help at the other end. Mable can call Jason if you see anything."

Jeffrey replied, "Yes George, we'll watch and call if we see anything," and he jumped up from the table, ran to his patrol car, sped up the gravel driveway, and turned left onto Wilcox Neck Road.

Coleman continued, "Next, we have to stop any more drones to buy time for Jason to gather his things. I'll drive the Captain's pickup with Nick to your barn across the road where Ole Bessie's hidden and guard that approach, shooting any drones coming from that direction. Doc, I've got a semi-automatic shotgun in the cab of the pickup truck you can use to shoot any drones over the river. Go now and grab it."

Grandpa interjected, "Let me help Doc, George. We'll both go to the dock to shoot any drones from there. Our family's shotguns will help, but I need some extra hands carrying them there."

"Ok, Tim. Doc, get my shotgun and help him," Coleman said as Doc and Grandpa both got up from the table. Doc ran to the truck and Grandpa went into the family room.

Coleman continued with his final commands, "Jason, quickly grab your computer or any other electronics you might need for tonight. Julie, help him carry what he needs. Put it all in your pickup truck and drive to the barn across the road. We need Ole Bessie now more than ever. I'll meet you there."

Julie shouted, "We need to take Rufus too! We can't leave him!"

Coleman added, "Take him, Julie. Quickly grab some clothes for Jason and you for tonight and take Rufus to your truck. Jason, you'll be in the swamp and it'll be rainy, so bring any waders and ponchos you have too."

Jason said, "Our fishing waders are in the garage. I need a few minutes there to gather everything I need, Sheriff. Julie, when you're upstairs, bring the laptop, podcam, and your e-phone. I need you to do something else while there too. Press my computer keyboard's 'Ctrl', 'Percent', and 'End' keys at the same time. That will bleach wipe all computer memory."

catgcgccgccgtattaaattcgcacccatgatgcgtatgcgatggaacgcatttgcgcgcatgcgccgccgtattaaattcgcacccatgatgcgtat

Julie replied, "OK Jason," as she ran upstairs.

Coleman said, "We don't have much time, so let's move! Those mercenaries will be well-armed and likely wearing Level V body armor."[87]

Grandpa quickly went to the family room and gathered from a closet a pre-loaded 12-gauge pump-action shotgun used for home defense and his grandfather's old 10-gauge double-barreled shotgun used for hunting Canada geese. He found a box of extra shells for each gun and put the weapons and ammo in a pile on the sofa. Just then, Doc came into the family room carrying the sheriff's shotgun. Doc said, "Let me help take those guns to the boathouse too."

"Thanks, Doc, I'll meet you there in a few minutes. I still need to load the punt gun," he said as Doc bundled the guns in his arms and left.[88]

Grandpa grabbed his 4-gauge punt gun, in his family for generations, from its display rack above the fireplace mantle and laid it on the sofa. Next, he rummaged through the closet again for loading supplies.

He sat down on the sofa and began the loading process. He carefully poured a measured amount of black gunpowder from a sealed wax paper packet down the barrel's muzzle. He next placed a piece of tissue paper wadding in the barrel and used a long ramrod to pack the powder charge. He then emptied an old cloth bag, filled with a premeasured weight of lead pellets, into the barrel, added another piece of wadding, and packed the load tight using the ramrod. Finally, he added a percussion firing cap that the hammer would strike when he pulled the trigger. All he had to do to fire the gun later was cock the hammer and pull the trigger. Just in case, he grabbed supplies for a second and a third special punt load and put them in his pants pockets. He lifted the heavy gun and went to the boathouse to meet Doc.

---

[87] Level V body armor is military grade. No conventional firearm such as a military rifle has a bullet capable of penetrated this form of body armor. This lightweight armor is comprised of layers of lightweight nanotube fabric and energy absorbing polymers which have a filler of explosive microspheres. When hit by a projectile, the spheres explode outwardly, and the entire armor system works together to absorb the projectile's energy and protect the wearer from injury.

[88] A punt-gun is a jumbo-sized antique shotgun with a large bore, extra-long barrel that usually fires with a percussion cap and hammer. It was outlawed for hunting due to the mass slaughter and decimation of waterfowl flocks caused with its use by commercial water-fowl hunters. Some smaller punt-guns (shotguns with oversized barrel diameters) used custom modern-style shotgun shells. A 4-gauge punt gun has a 1.05" diameter bore and can fire ¼ pound of lead shot each load. The guns were fired from special flat-bottom single-man boats called "punts" designed for hunting waterfowl.

gcgaacgcgatggcgtaagcgatggcgaacgcgccgctggcgaacgcgtgcgcgaacgcgctgccggcgaacgcgatggcgtaagcgatggcgaacgcg

Jason went to the garage, grabbed a large, custom backpack he'd upgraded with some copper mesh for EMI shielding, and filled it partly with some electronic gadgets, a portable electric grinder with a metal cutoff wheel, and his Brick phone. He grabbed two pairs of waders and two ponchos from their wall hooks. Just then, Julie came into the garage with her arms filled with the laptop and the other things. "Let's put this stuff in the truck now," he said as he opened the garage door and they tossed the items in the pickup parked outside.

"Go get Rufus now and put him in the back too," Jason commanded Julie. "We're forgetting something!" he exclaimed.

"What did we miss?" Julie hurriedly asked.

"We need to bring Frank too! He's our insurance. You wait here with Rufus and I'll go get him. Doc, Grandpa, and I'll meet you here and we'll all drive to meet the sheriff. Have the truck ready to roll."

Jason ran to the boathouse and saw Doc and Grandpa at the dock's end with their eyes scanning the river for approaching drones. He yelled to them, "I've got to grab Frank and save him!"

Doc hollered back, "Put him in a bucket. We'll guard you from here."

Jason opened the boathouse door and ran to the bait tank. He grabbed the five-gallon plastic bait bucket, dunked it into the tank, and filled it halfway with water. He found the hand net and immersed it into the tank to catch Frank. After a few swift strokes near the bottom, he caught Frank and carefully dropped him into the bucket.

He thought for a moment, "How did they find us?" and then realized they had either traced Frank's wireless signal or found the signal from the rooftop directional data-burst antenna he'd built and utilized to access the Grid. As he started to quickly wrap up the bucket with EMI screen mesh to prevent location of Frank's signal, he heard two nearly simultaneous shotgun blasts outside from the dock. As he wrapped the bucket, he heard two more shotgun blasts, with a slight pause between each.

Just then, his e-watch rang and he answered, "Jason, Mable here. Jeffery says two Supercruzers are coming over Tyler Bridge and should be turning toward Wilcox Neck Road soon. You've five to seven minutes before they arrive."

He gripped the bucket handle and ran outside. The water inside sloshed around, so he held it carefully to avoid spilling the precious contents as he ran to the dock where Grandpa and Doc were standing.

catgcgccgccgtgtattaaattcgcacccatgatgcgtatgcgatggaacgcatttgcgcgcatgcgccgccgtgtattaaattcgcacccatgatgcgtat

gcgaacgcgatggcgtaagcgatggcgaacgcgccgctggcgaacgcgtgcgcgaacgcgctgccggcgaacgcgatggcgtaagcgatggcgaacgcg

Within a minute of meeting at the dock, Grandpa and Doc both saw two fast-flying drones approaching 25 feet above the river. When they were about 50 yards away from the dock's end, they stopped, hovering a moment to assess the situation, and slowly approached the dock.

"I'll take the one on the left," Doc shouted as they both aimed their shotguns and pulled the triggers. The birdshot spattered into them and one drone immediately emitted sparks and dropped like a stone into the water with a splash, while the other quickly lost altitude as it attempted to flee toward the river. It finally splashed along the water, like a skipping stone cast across a pond, before sinking in the brown waters.

"Just like shooting skeet at Charles County Shooting Range," Grandpa commented to Doc as double-slide-click sounds were heard from both men manually ejecting spent shell casings and loading another shell into their shotgun chambers.

"Yes, those city folks guiding those drones underestimated our hunting skills, "Doc chuckled. "They're on to us now and will be more careful next time. Here they come," he said as they saw in the distance, and soon heard, two more drones coming upriver.

The next two drones approached but stayed out of normal shotgun range to better survey their armed opponents. Grandpa took the 10-gauge goose gun, carefully sighted the hovering drones 75 yards away, and pulled the trigger to fire his first barrel. A drone splashed into the river like rock, which soon formed ringlets, as the river swallowed up the drone's carcass. The second drone still hovered, but before it fled, Grandpa fired the second barrel and the drone soon crashed.

"Well, that was the second wave," Doc replied. "If they bring more drones than that next time, I'm not sure we can handle them."

Jason soon joined them while holding the bait bucket with Frank.

Doc commented, "Help us Jason. We've already shot two waves of drones and more are coming now," he said as he saw, with his eagle-eyed 20/10 vision, three black dots in the distance approaching quickly.

"Grab my shotgun, Jason. We'll need every gun we have to handle them," Grandpa said while reloading two shells in the goose gun. Within 20 seconds, the three drones approached in close formation and began hovering at least 100 yards away well outside of shotgun range.

"They see three people now and are staying well out of range while trying to figure out how to approach us," Doc commented.

"I think I can get them," Grandpa replied as he picked up the punt gun weighing 35 pounds. He carefully rested the heavy barrel on the picnic table, aimed, and pulled the trigger. The recoil still nearly knocked him to

catgcgccgccgtattaaattcgcacccatgatgcgtatgcgatggaacgcatttgcgcgcatgcgccgccgtattaaattcgcacccatgatgcgtat

the ground, but the blast of a quarter-pound of high-velocity lead shot spread widely at that distance into a pepper spray that immediately hit the formation. The center drone fell into the water and the two drones on either side were crippled and crashed more slowly after a few moments.

"Nice shooting Tim," Doc said, "They didn't expect such firepower."

Grandpa replied, "We've just bought us some time. Soon, they'll be back with everything they've got."

"Let's go, Grandpa!" Jason said. "Their mercenaries are driving up Wilcox Neck Road now! We've got only a few minutes to escape."

Grandpa replied, "I'm not leaving my home to these evil people without a fight. I'm staying *here*. Sometimes you must fight for what's yours. This is my country, my home, my life, and my choice."

"Come with us, Grandpa. Don't risk your life," Jason implored the old man as Doc watched them both.

"Jason, I've lived a full life and it's time to reach its end. When we fished this week, I really talked with you because I learned I have inoperable brain cancer, but didn't have the courage to tell you yet. My doctor wants me to take that drug Exgena, but after learning about Exgenics, I'll refuse treatment. I'm dying anyway, so I might as well go out with a bang," he joked and smiled at his grandson with tenderness.

He quickly continued, "It's my choice and decision. I love you, Jason. You're a second son to me. Love Julie deeply. Listen to her common sense. Don't forget Rufus and take good care of Frank. Remember that sometimes the shortest moments in life, including how it ends, are the most important. This is my sacrifice to buy you and Julie time to live, perhaps, God willing, your lifetimes."

Jason felt this important instant deeply, gave Grandpa a short hug, and looked into his eyes. "Goodbye Grandpa," he said turning away and running to the pickup truck clutching the bucket with Frank floating inside.

Doc remained a moment longer and Grandpa said, "Keep an eye on Jason for me John. Now, hurry and carry the punt gun to the porch for me. I'm going to make my last stand there my friend."

Doc replied, "I'll look after him Tim. Goodbye my friend," as he grabbed the heavy gun and ran, leaving Grandpa on the dock.

Julie worriedly waited in the driver's seat with the engine on, and when Jason opened the passenger door, she cried out as he sat on the seat and held the bucket, "What happened? I worried after hearing those shots."

"Wait for Doc to come. I'll tell you later," Jason replied.

"Where Grandpa?" she asked.

Just then, Doc jumped into the pickup bed where Rufus was waiting and Jason exclaimed, "Drive to the barn, NOW! I'll tell you later," he said as tears welled up in his eyes.

Grandpa hurriedly walked to the front porch carrying his shotgun and goose gun. When he arrived, he ejected the remaining shells and reloaded both guns with slugs. He saw the punt gun resting on a bench by a planter where Doc had left it for him. He sat down on the bench and propped the long gun to reload. He pulled the punt gun supplies from his pockets to reload it a final time with a 1-inch diameter lead ball he'd cast instead of using shot pellets. It took him a minute to complete the manual loading procedure and he finally sat down again and started rocking in Sarah's old rocking chair while he waited with the punt gun laying across the armrests.

He thought of his ancestors and how they'd made a living using such guns. He thought about how the river was now dead and what would become of Jason and Julie. He thought of Sarah and how he'd soon join her. He smiled with an inner peace at his life's journey along the river.

As the pickup arrived the barn door was open and Coleman was standing by Ole Bessie's door. He yelled as everyone clambered out of the truck, "Grab your things and climb in. Ole Bessie will save us."

Everyone opened their doors and climbed in. Julie sat in the front middle seat holding Jason's backpack, Jason sat in the right front seat, while Nick, Doc, Rufus, and Frank were in the back.

As the sheriff revved the engine and accelerated out of the barn, he asked Jason, "Where's Grandpa?"

"He isn't coming," Jason said somberly as tears rolled down his cheeks.

"What happened Jason?" the sheriff asked.

"Both he and Doc shot a bunch of drones, and then he stayed behind. With his final words, he was saying goodbye. He'd lived a long life and was ready to sacrifice himself to buy us more time. I saw it in his eyes. He's dying anyway and decided to choose his own place and time to die." As Coleman turned onto the narrow country road, he consoled Jason with kindness and a bit of wisdom, "I'm sorry Jason. I'll miss him a lot. Not many men dare to face the inevitability of their demise. You can be proud of him Jason. He's living the rest of his life deliberately with a purpose, instead of just fading away," he said as a few scattered raindrops began hitting the windshield like tears from the sky.

gcgaacgcgatggcgtaagcgatggcgaacgcgccgctggcgaacgcgtgcgcgaacgcgctgccggcgaacgcgatggcgtaagcgatggcgaacgcg

Chapter 28: Dark Operations Begin

Johnnie Walker's Shack

8:19 p.m., Saturday, July 3, ...

As the grey sky dimmed before sunset, rain began falling harder as they sped down the narrow country road, so Coleman turned on in Ole Bessie's windshield wipers. They were rounding a corner when they saw two black Supercruzers coming from the other direction. The Supercruzers passed by them in a blur, but in the rearview mirror, Coleman saw brake lights from the second one turning around to pursue, while the other continued on its way toward the Dickson House. He turned right on Glebe Road and pressed the accelerator pedal to the floor in an attempt to lose to the mercenaries on slick roads. He said, "If we can just make it to Sturgeon Point crossroads three miles ahead, we might be able to lose them there."

The second Supercruzer sped up its pursuit and soon began closing in. Coleman now flipped the nitrous oxide switch and Ole Bessie screamed from the increased raw horsepower of the bottled gas, temporarily pulling away from the Supercruzer.

The Supercruzer then launched two drones and Coleman spotted them coming closer in the rear-view mirror.

"They've launched pursuit drones. Everyone, hide best you can, so they only see me driving!" Coleman barked. "We can't shake the drones!"

Within about 20 seconds, the drones had nearly caught up to Ole Bessie and were just 50 feet behind following the speeding vehicle when the rear window shattered.

Coleman replied, "They're using pneumatic needle-darts! "It'll take a few moments for the drones' air compressors to recharge before they fire again! We're sitting ducks with that shattered window," he said as he was about a half-mile away from the intersection.

"I can help, sheriff," Jason replied as he reached into the backpack and pulled out his Brick. "Slow down quickly sheriff so that Supercruzer will

gcgaacgcgatggcgtaagcgatggcgaacgcgccgctggcgaacgcgtgcgcgaacgcgctgccggcgaacgcgatggcgtaagcgatggcgaacgcg

be closer. Julie, toss my e-watch and your e-phone into my bag and zip it up tightly," Jason added.

As Coleman switched off the nitrous oxide and slammed the brakes, the drones overshot their targeting points and the driver's side and passenger's side windows simultaneously shattered from the second volley of tungsten needles. The pursuing Supercruzer closed in on Ole Bessie.

"The glass stopped the darts again but the next volley will hit us!" Coleman exclaimed as he slowed, even more, to turn right at the approaching crossroad. The pursuing Supercruzer was almost touching Ole Bessie's rear bumper and the Drones were now flying just outside the open windows at point-blank range.

Just then, Jason pressed the '911', '*' and "#' keys of his Brick and its giga-capacitor power supply immediately overloaded with a brief flash, that was visible even outside the cell phone's housing, that sent out a localized EMP signal.[89] The instantaneous high-voltage energy pulse short-circuited the electronics of the Supercruzer and the drones, but Ole Bessie's primitive electrical wiring was unaffected. As Ole Bessie continued speeding away around the turn, the drones crashed to the ground. The Supercruzer went out of control at the turn and flipped multiple times, coming to rest on its roof in an open field of the sod farm. Its passenger compartment was crushed.

⌇⌇⌇⌇⌇⌇⌇

The first Supercruzer pulled up to the Dickson House, stopped in front of the garage, and two mercenaries armed with automatic assault rifles and wearing Level V body armor quickly jumped out both front doors. Grandpa hid on the front porch behind the planter box, aimed at nearly point-blank range at the nearest man, and pulled the punt gun trigger. The blasting quarter-pound lead ball hit the man mid-torso and bounced off.

However, the shock wave, from such a heavy projectile rebounding off the body armor at point-blank range, progressed through the man's torso and his internal organs turned to jelly as they tore themselves apart. He immediately collapsed from an aortic aneurism and internal blunt trauma. Grandpa then grabbed his goose gun from the porch floor and crouched low behind the planter box. The other mercenary, using his Supercruzer as cover, sprayed a full magazine toward the porch and planter box.

All now became quiet, so the man loaded another magazine, cautiously walked toward the porch steps while continuing to spray additional bullets at the porch and planter box. He reached the porch, looked over the edge

---

[89] Electromagnetic Pulse. An EMP signal can short-circuit most computer chips found in modern electronics.

catgcgccgccgtattaaattcgcacccatgatgcgtatgcgatggaacgcatttgcgcgcatgcgccgccgtattaaattcgcacccatgatgcgtat

of the planter box, and saw a bleeding old man prone on his back with his eyes closed and shotgun in arms.

Suddenly, the old man opened his eyes and, using an adrenaline-fueled energy rush in his last effort, quickly lifted his goose gun and pulled both triggers. The mercenary fell backward in astonishment from the slugs' impact, piercing his chest at point-blank range. His military armor was no match for two adjacent 10-gauge slugs simultaneously. The man collapsed dead by the now unconscious Reverend who continued profusely bleeding a puddle on the old cypress porch boards.

8:42 p.m., Saturday, July 3, ….

Dr. Gerardo was sitting at an expensive Tuscan restaurant in Washington when his e-phone beeped. He looked at the screen, saw it was Gregory, and answered, "Hello John. I'm eating dinner with Marianna. What do you want?"

"Ernesto, I've some good news and some bad news to tell you."

"Tell me the good news first," he replied knowing that the bad news would make him angry and he wanted to use that anger constructively to solve any problems.

"We've located that hacker when we intercepted some strange ham radio operator signals talking about a chess game. He's a college student, named Jason Dickson, who lives by the river. That kid is an electronics engineer and a master computer coder. He was responsible for that big presidential alert system breach years ago.

"I remember that," Gerardo said as he slightly chuckled. "They blamed that incident on some poor Grid technician doing a system test."

"Yeah, it was funny back then, but things are serious now. We think he caught a T-fish because we also triangulated a transmission signal near his location. His family likely knows too much already, and so we implemented a plan to eliminate anyone at his house."

"Who was he playing chess with?" Gerardo asked.

"Were not sure. Intel can't de-encrypt the voiceprints yet but now they've determined the hacker's name, they think they've got a chance to use their quantum chips and his stored voiceprint as a Rosetta stone to decipher the person on the other end. They're still working on it."

"So, if that's the good news, John, what's the bad news?"

Gregory answered, "Well, the two Ops teams we sent there to seize them have gone silent. We lost communications a few minutes ago but their Supercruzer cams sent us what happened. The team at the house encountered gunshots from an old man who we think is the boy's grandfather. The second team pursued an old Charles County patrol car at high speed when their Supercruzer Grid signal suddenly went blank."

"There were multiple passengers in the car, but we didn't get any good drone images before they lost contact. We think the black man was that Sheriff Coleman, but our Intel team said he's on vacation. By the way, he's a decorated Army veteran so we shouldn't underestimate him again. I've got a hunch he was the man talking with that hacker by radio. Finally, the signal from the hacker's T-fish has disappeared. We're sending another Ops Team to the house to investigate more since the hacker and his accomplices have likely fled. Our new team is on full alert this time."

Gerardo's hot-blooded Italian temper frothed to its boiling point and he barked, "You guys are idiots! Put the AI-Security system and front gate guards on full alert tonight! I'm droning down first thing in the morning to supervise this mess myself!" Venting his anger and frustration, Gerardo took his e-phone from his ear and threw it at the dining table. The phone bounced off the table's edge and hit a bus boy walking nearby in the groin. The busboy doubled over and immediately spilled his tray of dirty dishes, wine glasses, and silverware across the dining table into Gerardo's lap.

Gerardo yelled "Scemo!" in an Italian accent at the busboy but then quickly refocused his anger to find a solution to his problems. He picked up the e-phone from the floor and continued talking to Gregory, who was still Grid-connected, "I've got an idea. Let's blame that hacker for the river poisoning instead of those ISM terrorists. He's already guilty with that presidential alert hack, so he's the perfect fall guy for this entire mess. That way we stop the Grid hack *and* get rid of him, killing two birds with one stone. The National Guard will even help since that hacker and anyone with him will publicly be identified as the real terrorists. We need to find them first though. Do we have any Intel where they are?"

"No, Ernesto. They've gone silent and are likely hiding somewhere locally since they know we're on to them now. With all the roadblocks from martial law, they won't be able to flee our perimeter. However, the bad weather here is interfering with our satellites and high-altitude surveillance drones. Soon, that tropical storm will be too windy even for our surface drones. The storm's supposed to blow through by morning and we'll surely locate them then. No one will be outside on a night like tonight, so we can rest easy until the morning.

"Still, keep the farm on high alert just in case," Gerardo replied as he terminated the e-phone conversation.

9:00 p.m., Saturday, July 3, ….

gcgaacgcgatggcgtaagcgatggcgaacgcgccgctggcgaacgcgtgcgcgaacgcgctgccggcgaacgcgatggcgtaagcgatggcgaacgcg

It was now nearly dark and the darkness soon became an overwhelming black void magnified in emptiness by torrential rains and the wind gusting stronger. Ole Bessie arrived at the Captain's house and everyone regrouped, unloading their gear inside the kitchen. "Let me make coffee," Coleman said. "We'll need it tonight," he said as began brewing a pot.

Rufus was slightly perturbed at being inside his old home and frantically searched but didn't find his old masters. Doc calmly caressed the anxious dog's head with his hands and his whispering did the trick as Rufus soon calmed and laid down to rest on the wood plank floor where Captain's body was found.

Jason put Frank's bucket on the floor and rummaged through the pantry, finding an old can of sardines. He peered through the copper mesh and saw Frank laying at the bottom, likely disoriented by his rough bucket journey. He opened the can and hastily tossed a sardine to Frank and quickly rewrapped the bucket with mesh to prevent signal detection.

Everyone finally sat down as Coleman poured coffee for all and said, "They're reassessing their plans right now. They didn't expect our response and they're regrouping now just like us. I think this weather will help us too. Drones can't fly in this windy, rainy weather."

"When's the storm supposed to end?" Julie asked.

Just then, Deputy James knocked on the door. His rain trench coat was dripping and he took it off to dry on a wall hook by the door.

Coleman greeted him, "Good to see you made it Jeffrey. I hoped they wouldn't spot you."

"I hid my patrol car behind some thick bushes in a driveway, so when the Supercruzers zoomed by, they never saw me. Since I lost contact with you, I was hoping you'd make it here. I laid low a while and spotted another Supercruzer coming fast, so I followed at a distance with my headlights off. They kept on going toward the Dickson's, so I came to your base here George in case you escaped. What happened? How did you make it out alive?"

Coleman briefly recounted their harrowing escape and told him Reverend Dickson was dead.

Jeffrey replied, "He was a good man and an example to follow in both fellowship and righteousness. I'm sorry Jason. You'll surely miss him."

Jason replied, "Yes, I will. He sacrificed himself so we could escape."

Coleman redirected, "Let's get back to our earlier discussion. Julie, I'm not sure when the storm will blow through."

catgcgccgccgtattaaattcgcacccatgatgcgtatgcgatggaacgcatttgcgcgcatgcgccgccgtattaaattcgcacccatgatgcgtat

gcgaacgcgatggcgtaagcgatggcgaacgcgccgctggcgaacgcgtgcgcgaacgcgctgccggcgaacgcgatggcgtaagcgatggcgaacgcg

Jeffrey said, "While I waited to come here, I saw the Grid weather update. It's moving faster than they thought, and by 4:00 a.m., it should be halfway to Washington."

Coleman replied, "That should work well with our overall plans. This weather gives us the element of surprise," as he thought Sun-Tzu would be proud of his military prowess.

He continued, "The Exgenics people are on to us by now. They surely saw me driving Ole Bessie and they'll keep searching until they find us. We've got the tactical advantage since we know this area well and until it clears, we need to follow through with our plans no matter what happens."

Doc added worriedly, "They'll find my van at the Dickson's, so they'll be going to my house to interrogate Susan. I need to warn her somehow."

Coleman replied, "Doc, drive Ole Bessie with Julie to Johnnie's house. Make a landline call there to Susan and have only Julie do the talking. If they're scanning old-style phone calls, they'd recognize your voiceprint Doc. When you're done with the call, bring Johnnie here. I've got an important job for him. Both of you put on those ponchos that Jason brought to keep dry as best as you can. We're going to need more of them before this night is over, so we'll look around here and find what we need."

Doc and Julie soon slipped the ponchos over their heads and went out the kitchen door, which slammed shut from a wind gust.

"Jason and Nick, I still want you to go with Doc to Exgenics tonight so Jason can keep gathering evidence before Exgenics deletes any data. Jason, I want Julie to go with you too."

"We need to keep her safe here," Jason said.

"No, I think she can help you there. I've got a lot to do tonight and she should be with you. If those Exgenics people come searching for me here, they'll find her. So, she should go with you. She'll help you when you need her most. That's how marriage works."

"OK Sheriff," Jason replied worrying for her safety.

"I think you should take Rufus also. His keen sense of smell might help locate Gregory if he's hiding. I think Rufus may recognize him because I remember him barking at the funeral when Gregory left."

"With Doc there, we should be able to manage him just fine," Jason replied. "What should we do with Frank?"

"Let's leave him in the boathouse tonight. He should be hard to find if we just cover him up with tackle boxes and other buckets there. Sometimes the best way to hide something is in plain sight."

"Now we've another problem though. I was hoping to use the pickup trucks to carry two canoes up to the Chick bridge washout so you could

catgcgccgccgtattaaattcgcacccatgatgcgtatgcgatggaacgcatttgcgcgcatgcgccgccgtattaaattcgcacccatgatgcgtat

gcgaacgcgatggcgtaagcgatggcgaacgcgccgctggcgaacgcgtgcgcgaacgcgctgccggcgaacgcgatggcgtaagcgatggcgaacgcg

quietly paddle right up to Exgenics from the swamp, but we've lost them. Now we need to find another way for you to get through the swamp."

Jason thought a moment and replied, "Why don't we use the Captain's airboat? With all this wind and trees rustling, no one would ever hear it."

"That's a good idea, Jason. It might have some difficulty in the wind, but if the storm is not too bad, I think you can make it. It might make your journey through the swamp faster than canoeing and will keep us off the roads too. I'm sure by now they're looking for Ole Bessie and us with some operations teams in their Supercruzers, but they'd never expect us on the lake tonight. Here's what we'll do," the sheriff said and explained his revised plan for Jason to serve the warrants at Exgenics.

Coleman concluded and told his deputy what to do, "Jeffrey, it's time to put the Charles County Grapevine into action again, but there can be no electronics or phones involved at all. It must be person-to-person communications and everyone needs to leave their electronic devices at home. Everyone should wear their old wind-up watches or bring some old kitchen timers. Leave here now and change out of your uniform. Then drive your pickup truck and start the Grapevine. Make sure you contact old Doctor Hansen, and, after that, go meet Doctor Graves to see if she'll help us. We may need all the medical support we can get. Have everyone meet at the County Courthouse by 4:00 a.m."

"I'll be like Paul Revere," Jeffrey replied jokingly and then thought dreamily of seeing Robin again.

Coleman continued, "Anyone that's driving must use their oldest cars or trucks that don't have AI-systems. Make sure we use those old school buses from Samaria Baptist on a route to pick up anyone who wants to help. Afterward, meet Robin and drive to Williamsburg General Hospital to talk to a patient there named John Smith. Tell him everything and he'll know what to do. If I'm not at the Courthouse by four, then something has happened to me and you'll then have to lead everyone to serve the warrants."

"I'll do my best George," Jeffrey replied with reservation he could again find the same courage as last night on the dock. He thought of seeing Robin's face and bright eyes again and soon he felt an inner strength rise within his mind and body.

Coleman continued, "I've got a plan for a diversion that'll stop those Exgenics people from searching for us in Charles County and I'll need Buddy Peters a while, so tell him I'll come to meet him later. Ole Bessie's already in bad shape and with my plan, I'll have to sacrifice her but it should put them off our trail. Jason, where's your Brick?"

catgcgccgccgtattaaattcgcacccatgatgcgtatgcgatggaacgcatttgcgcgcatgcgccgccgtattaaattcgcacccatgatgcgtat

"The Brick is dead and I left it inside Ole Bessie. That pulse fried its circuits, so it's no use to us anymore," Jason lamented at the loss of his college electronics project that took two months to build.

"Perfect," Coleman replied.

"Let me get started George," Jeffrey said putting on his raincoat and heading out the kitchen door into the storm.

"Jason and Nick, let's look inside the house or boathouse for ponchos and anything else that might be useful tonight. Remember they've perimeter infrared sensors, so we must defeat them to enter their farm undetected. I've only one thermal camoblanket though."

Jason replied, "Sheriff, I've got an idea that should do the trick."

"OK, let's go find things you'll need," Coleman replied.

Coleman, Nick, and Jason rummaged through the Captain's house finding items they needed and placing them on the kitchen table. "Let's take this stuff and Frank to the boathouse," Coleman said. Jason carried Frank's bucket while Nick and the sheriff carried everything into the boathouse amidst the storm.

The boathouse was wet from the wind blowing rain into the openings for boats and underneath the interior docksides. Jason put Frank's bucket inconspicuously in a pile of buckets, boxes, and fishing gear while Coleman and Nick placed the other items under a tarp in the bass boat cockpit. Coleman told Jason, "We need to turn these boats around so they'll be ready to leave at a moment's notice."

"We'll help, sheriff," Nick and Jason both replied.

After checking the boats' fuel tanks, Coleman started the bass boat's powerful outboard engine while Nick and Jason loosened the mooring lines. Coleman backed it out of the boathouse into the storm. As the rain fell and the wind howled, he turned the boat around and backed into the boathouse where they re-lashed the mooring lines onto cleats with figure-eight knots. They next took the airboat, shorter in length than the bass boat, and just rotated it in its berth so it also faced the correct direction. They took two lines, lashed them to either side of the airboat's bow, and tied them to stern cleats on the port and starboard sides of the bass boat.

Coleman said, "That should be enough slack so you can tow the airboat across the lake and up the river. The wind is still blowing hard from the east, so you'll have to tow it fast. Otherwise, it'll likely crash into you. I think the wind is easily 40 knots plus some gusts, so you must drive the bass boat at full throttle. The drag of the water should keep the airboat safely behind you as you go. Here are some pocket knives to keep handy and cut the lines in case of trouble," he said as he gave them each a knife.

"Ok, we'll be careful," Jason said as Nick's head nodded in agreement.

Coleman continued, "Let's go to the house and finish getting ready for tonight." He grabbed the flashlight that was clipped to his belt, illuminating the way back to the house through the tempest.

〜〜〜〜〜

Hal and Janice were still working at the NSA Anti-Virus Center since Ops Central said the hacker and anyone with him, including the county sheriff, were evading capture. Hal commented, "How are we going to find them in all this weather? Our surface drones can't fly and our satellites and high-altitude drones aren't working either through all those rain clouds. With all the swamp, forest, and potential hiding places there, the only way to find them is to put boots on the ground."

Janice replied, "Ops said they're already adding some ground teams to search for them." We haven't heard any more of those chess game signals either, so we must try any other possible surveillance methods."

Hal replied, "Let me visualize the Grid network map of Charles County, and perhaps we can figure something out." In a minute after studying the map on his e-screen, he replied, "Their network is most unusual since it's in a rural region. To save on construction costs, the Grid engineers for that area just overlayed the Grid over the old land-line phone system from like 100 years ago. That means any local-to-local old-style land-line calls within Charles and Kent Counties are never are directly routed through the Grid for us to monitor."

"So, all we've been monitoring is their e-phone calls. How were you so stupid to not search there before?" she replied.

"Hey, this is just a job I'm lucky to have. You're the one with an agenda and connections. There are almost no old copper wire telephone systems left as most were scrapped. I do so many domestic terrorist searches in urban areas, I just overlooked it."

He next accessed detailed electronic blueprints of the Grid in that area and identified the specific node that was the main Grid access hub for the Charles County phone system. He then hastily installed some extra code that allowed them to monitor any calls from the old land-line switchgear. "Now we must wait and see if we get any unusual calls," Hal said.

〜〜〜〜〜

Ole Bessie looked worse for wear as Doc drove with Julie to Johnnie's house. Her rear and side windows had been smashed by darts and the wind, rain, and blowing leaves swept sideways into the car as they drove. They arrived at Johnnie Walker's house, more of an old shack, on the west riverbank just by Walker Dam across from East Lake Campground. They stepped onto the front porch lit by a lone LED bulb hanging in a socket and knocked on the door, "Hello Johnnie, it's Doc Longtree," Doc said.

Johnnie soon opened the door and replied in an inebriated voice, "Whatz yer do'in here ona storm'n nite like dis?"

Doc replied, "We need to use your phone immediately!" he exclaimed.

"Shure, it'zon da kich'n wall rite dare," Johnnie blurted out in his drunken stupor as he stumbled back to a chair at the kitchen table and drank another swig of bourbon from a half-empty bottle sitting there.

Doc hurriedly picked up the old wall phone, dialed his home number, and handed the phone to Julie.

Julie spoke into the phone's mouthpiece, "Hello Susan, it's Julie. I'm in trouble! I'm pregnant and Johnnie wants me to get an abortion. You need to come *now* and meet me! I need your advice."

After a brief pause, Julie continued, "Yes, that's right. I'll meet you there instead. See you soon." She hung up the phone and told Doc, "I think that message gave her sufficient alarm to know something is terribly wrong and she needs to leave right now. She replied she'd meet us at Harrison's Landing, which makes no sense, so that tells me she understood to leave immediately and not tell where she was going."

"Good thinking Julie. She'll go to the Chief's house for safety and let him know to be alert," Doc replied feeling relief his wife had fled in time.

Doc next said, "Johnnie, Sheriff Coleman needs you to help him. Come with us now," as he worriedly thought how a man that drunk would be of much use to anyone right now.

"I hep George if him needz me," he slurred.

Julie found a jacket on a wall hook, and they both helped Johnnie put it on. They then guided him by the arms out the door and into Ole Bessie's wet back seat for the quarter-mile drive back to the Captain's House.

As they pulled up to the house, the lights went dark as a tree crashed onto an overhead power line somewhere in Charles County. They sat there with Ole Bessie's headlights illuminating the front porch as Jason, Nick, and the sheriff walked around the house shining a LED flashlight. The headlights soon illuminated them and the sheriff motioned them to come inside the house with his bright flashlight.

They all went into the kitchen to dry off and the sheriff commented, "This storm is perfect cover. They'll never suspect us coming tonight."

Chapter 29: Knight Moves

Riding the Captain's Airboat

10:00 p.m., Saturday, July 3, ...

Hal commented to Janice, "That was an interesting phone call in Charles County. Some girl named Julie is pregnant and her boyfriend wants an abortion. She called some woman for advice and they're going to meet at someplace called Harrison's Landing to talk."

"Yes, this job can be like a soap opera. It does provide occasional entertainment that makes it less boring just staring at these e-screens while the AI-systems do most of the work. Hold on," she said as her earpod started transmitting a voice message.

"Ops Central says to check for any signals to or from a Veterinarian named John Longtree. Their team at the hacker's house found his van, so he's also a suspect. It seems they terminated our first two teams, so these domestic cyber terrorists are dangerous characters."

Hal commanded the AI-system to search for the Veterinarian's most recent communications and the system replied, "His house received a phone call just two minutes ago. Susan Longtree, his wife, answered is going to meet a woman at Harrison's Landing."

"We've got them! That's on the James River. Our suspects must be going there to escape by boat!" Janice replied excitedly in expectation of capturing their prey. "Who's that girl from that last phone call?"

The AI-system replied, "I was already completing a voice-print search when you asked. She's a college student named Julie Williams who lives with her parents in Charles County."

"I'll tell Ops they should investigate that lead too," Janice replied.

⋈⟪⊅⟪⋈⟪⊅⟪⊐

Everyone was sitting at the kitchen table of the Captain's house dimly lit by old kerosene lanterns. Coleman commented, "I'm glad Johnnie's asleep on the couch right now so he won't hear our plans. Now everyone,

gcgaacgcgatggcgtaagcgatggcgaacgcgccgctggcgaacgcgtgcgcgaacgcgctgccggcgaacgcgatggcgtaagcgatggcgaacgcg

remember the plan and timing. The airboat team is our Special Ops advance search team. You'll spend the night executing the search warrants at the farm and the rest of us will come early in the morning when the storm is over. I hope Jason finds more information on this conspiracy."

Doc replied, "I'll command the boats since I'm more familiar with the lake and swamp than anyone else."

Coleman reached into a small knapsack and pulled out a pair of strap-on night vision goggles, "It's so dark tonight, you'll need these Doc to navigate. When you put them on, press this switch, and turn this knob to adjust the brightness and sensitivity. They saved my life in the war," he said while demonstrating their use and handing them to Doc.

Coleman continued, "Nick is responsible for helping at the farm since he knows the most about the buildings and systems there."

Nick replied, "I'm ready to help. Shabbat is over now and I can do whatever job needs to be done."

Coleman said, "Jason, in addition to the search and since you're my sworn deputy, you'll have to execute the warrants if you see anyone there. Here, take these papers with you and keep them dry," as he gave Jason a plastic zipper bag with some papers inside. "There's a copy of the warrants in case you meet anyone there, including John Gregory. If you see him, you're hereby empowered as my deputy to arrest him. Just read a statement of his rights from the other piece of paper in the bag."

"He's a big and powerful lawyer, so we want you to follow the arrest procedures precisely. Here's some handcuffs too and the key," Coleman said as he showed Jason how to clamp and unlock the cuffs. "Remember Jason, fat people like Gregory sometimes have incredible, hidden strength, so be careful putting these on him."

"I'll do my best as your deputy and follow the law. I want these people to face justice as badly as you do," Jason replied.

Coleman continued, "Julie, you're to help with Rufus because he likely knows Gregory's scent. Also, you are to record everything on the podcam. We need evidence this was a legal search. Just because these evil and elite people don't obey the law doesn't mean we don't follow it. With enough evidence of their crimes, we can defeat them."

"What you all are attempting is dangerous and you must be on alert at all times. According to Nick, the farm has an AI-security system. They use a lot of security drones, but won't be able to fly in this wind. His security access might help once you're inside, but those systems might catch on to what's happening quickly. So, you must be prepared to improvise. I'm giving you some handguns in case you need them. Here

catgcgccgccgtattaaattcgcacccatgatgcgtatgcgatggaacgcatttgcgcgcatgcgccgccgtattaaattcgcacccatgatgcgtat

Doc is my 1911 pistol and two magazines. You've fired it before with me at the shooting range," he said as he handed him a pistol belt with the .45 caliber automatic pistol in its holster.

"Here Nick is a Makarov 9-mm I brought back from the Bolivia campaign as a souvenir. It's old but shoots just fine. I thought you'd appreciate using a Russian gun," the sheriff smiled.

"I know how to use one for sure," Nick replied as he looked at the gun in his hand and thought of his grandfather who'd served in the Soviet army and showed him a pistol just like the one in his hands now.

"Jason, here is a Beretta .40 semi-automatic and an extra magazine. Just be careful and hold it like this, or you'll mangle your thumb," as the sheriff demonstrated how to pull back the slide and then hold it so his thumb wouldn't get in the way of the slide recoiling backward after shooting. He put the gun back into its holster and gave it to Jason.

Julie interjected, "Don't I get a gun Sheriff? I've gone hunting with my dad before."

"I thought you might want one, so I've got a nice Smith and Wesson .357 revolver for you. It's easy to use but has quite a kick, so hold on tightly if you have to use it," he said as he gave her the gun in its holster.

"Thanks, sheriff, for thinking of me too. Just because I'm a woman doesn't mean I can't shoot in an emergency," Julie replied.

"I've one last thing for you, Jason. Here is my Army compass. Use it and you'll never lose your way. Its compass needle has a tritium illuminator for night operations."

Jason replied, "I've looked earlier at a satellite map, so I have a good mental map to help Doc navigate through the swamp to the farm."

"Finally, once you're inside the main farm buildings, stay inside until we come for you because the drones might patrol again after the wind dies down. Let's get moving while the wind's blowing in the right direction to speed up our assault, I mean, our executing the warrants."

"Everyone, take off your shoes and wear your waders. Julie, I think Macy's old oyster harvesting waders fit you," Coleman said. "I'll put your shoes in this gym bag to change back into later. I suggest you first make your way toward that shack that Jason spotted on the farm satellite imaging. It's a good place to change and regroup, before entering the main farm complex." Everyone grabbed their waders from the pile on the floor.

Jason awkwardly commented, "Sheriff, we need to use the bathroom now, because we don't want an 'accident' later," he chuckled.

"You're right Jason," Coleman replied as everyone laughed, breaking the tension and fear in anticipation of what they planned to do this night.

gcgaacgcgatggcgtaagcgatggcgaacgcgccgctggcgaacgcgtgcgcgaacgcgctgccggcgaacgcgatggcgtaagcgatggcgaacgcg

11:00 p.m., Saturday, July 3 ....

Deputy James rang the doorbell of Robin's apartment in Kent City. In a moment, Robin spoke through the locked door, "Who is it?"

"It's me, Jeffery. I need to talk to you urgently."

"Okay," she said carefully opening the door and holding it against the wind to let inside the wet deputy in his raingear.

"What's so important that you came here on a night like this? I was just about asleep. Couldn't you call me?" she questioned while standing in her nightgown covered up by a bathrobe.

"I'm sorry for disturbing you Robin, but we've got a situation brewing and we need your help as a doctor. Let me explain," Jeffrey answered and began telling Robin an abbreviated version of recent events and their plans as they both stood inside the threshold of the apartment.

"I knew something strange was going on this week," she replied. "I've never seen so many deaths around here in such a short time. Yes, I'll help you. Let me dress, grab my medical bag and some supplies, and come with you. Anyway, it'd be nice to spend the rest of the night with you just talking until the morning," she said with affection. Then, she impulsively grabbed the handsome, but still dripping wet deputy and wrapped her arms around him to give him a passionate kiss.

Jeffery briefly paused the kiss and said, "I'm still on duty and must go to the hospital in Williamsburg to deliver a message to a patient there."

"Can it wait a little while?" she asked.

"Well, that's my last task tonight until the morning, but it can wait," he said smiling as Robin pulled him by the hand toward the bedroom.

⊷⊶⊷⊶⊷

Johnnie was sleeping on the couch as everyone else dressed and gathered their gear. Jason quickly pulled out his e-watch from his backpack, reset the dead man's switch for another six-hour interval, and re-wrapped it in copper mesh, shielding it from the Grid. He strapped it on his wrist and buttoned his shirt sleeve to hide it.

Everyone in the search ops team was now wearing their waders. They pulled the ponchos over their heads, turned on their flashlights, and walked outside, with Sheriff Coleman and Rufus on his leash, to the boathouse through the gusts and rain blowing nearly sideways.

The boathouse without electricity was pitch black inside on this darkest of nights, but flashlights illuminated the bass boat for boarding. Jason put his backpack in a small cargo hatch and closed it tightly. Everyone sat down and Rufus cowered on the boat deck vainly attempting to keep dry.

gcgaacgcgatggcgtaagcgatggcgaacgcgccgctggcgaacgcgtgcgcgaacgcgctgccggcgaacgcgatggcgtaagcgatggcgaacgcg

Doc said to Coleman, "After the engine warms up, we'll be ready to go," as he turned the key starting the inboard engines. He next turned on the spotlights the Captain had added as accessories for navigating the river at night, pointing one forward to illuminate their way and the other toward the stern to keep an eye on the airboat.

The engines idled as Coleman loudly replied, "Rev the motors and go as fast as you can out of the boathouse. Stay in the main channel but when you get near the Chick Bridge, take the airboat up the smaller, old channel to the left and pass under the old Chick Bridge. It isn't blocked by the main bridge washout. You'll know the way from there. Use the night vision goggles when you're on the airboat since it doesn't have lights, and don't let the perimeter security system spot you.

"We'll follow your advice, George. Wish us luck," Doc said as he pushed the throttle fully forward.

"Godspeed my friends," Coleman yelled and silently recited a prayer.

The engine roared to full power and Doc engaged the props. In a moment, the bass boat, with airboat in tow, surged out of the boathouse toward the open waters of the lake. However, the wind, still blowing hard from the east started pushing them sideways.

"Oh no!" Doc yelled, "There's a cypress up ahead," as the tree rapidly loomed closer in the spotlights. Fortunately, the bass boat just grazed a few small aerial roots as the tall tree trunk blurred past them on the left.

Soon they were in the main channel and Doc slowly began a long arc in the rough and choppy waters seeming more like an ocean than the normally calm lake. Since there now was nothing ahead of them but an open lake, he kept an eye towards the airboat's stern to prevent it from capsizing. It was listing severely from drag caused by crosswinds hitting the fan cage and rudders, but their forward momentum and the drag from the airboat's hull on the water kept it upright as it skimmed the surface.

"We're lucky the airboat is towing behind us well. I was worried for a moment we'd lose it," Doc yelled over the noise of the engines and wind. As they slowly turned toward the west, the list of the airboat and the apparent crosswinds from the storm lessened and soon they were traveling westward over just a choppy lake.

As they sped on their course, the winds soon diminished. Julie yelled out to Jason, "What's happened to the wind?" she asked.

Jason yelled, "We're traveling nearly as fast as the wind now. It's that the principle of relativity I told you about before. If we travel with the wind at the same speed it's blowing, it appears to be calm."

catgcgccgccgtattaaattcgcacccatgatgcgtatgcgatggaacgcatttgcgcgcatgcgccgccgtattaaattcgcacccatgatgcgtat

gcgaacgcgatggcgtaagcgatggcgaacgcgccgctggcgaacgcgtgcgcgaacgcgctgccggcgaacgcgatggcgtaagcgatggcgaacgcg

Within three minutes of starting their perilous journey, Doc began making an arc of a turn toward starboard, and, the wind soon seemed stronger as they plowed northeastward slightly against the wind. Doc kept looking forward and backward as the airboat again began to list sideways. After several more minutes, he turned the bass boat to port and began a final long arc westward with the wind which seemed calm again.

Doc yelled, "That's the last tough turn in the lake. The threat of the airboat capsizing is over since we'll be moving with the wind now. After this, the lake and channel narrow, so I'll have to be more careful with my steering and eventually slow down. Then the airboat might have more problems in the wind, so keep an eye on it Jason as I navigate the channel."

After ten minutes and five miles of open water, they arrived at the narrow old channel of the Chick to the left. Doc slowed down and the wind was calmer than before. "I think the storm's center is nearly over us now. The wind will be shifty and blow harder from the north soon. This is our chance to make it up the channel to the swamp. Everyone, quickly climb into the airboat and cut the lines. I'll use the night vision goggles to pilot the airboat from now on," he said, strapping them on his head.

They jumped in the airboat still illuminated by spotlights and Doc started the engine and fan. As the fan roared to a loud buzz, everyone, except Rufus, put on noise-cancellation hearing protectors with wireless microphones. "We don't have much time to get to the swamp. Cut the lines and buckle up your seatbelts," he said. Jason and Nick used the sheriff's pocket knives to cut the lines and sat down with the others while Rufus lay on the deck in front of Julie's seat.

As Doc piloted away from the illumination of the bass boat now adrift, the overwhelming blackness and isolation of the night enveloped them like a death shroud smothering them alive, except for Doc who switched on his night-vision goggles. "Since you can't see anything, I'll talk as we travel the channel so you'll know how we're doing. This next bit will be tough as it's the narrowest and shallowest, but I think the storm's rain raising the water level should help us."

He plowed the airboat through the narrow opening and now the small channel was more like a narrow swamp filled with water. "We're in the old channel now. It twists and turns, but it won't be long before we reach the bridge," he said as he guided the rudders that steered the airboat. Within several minutes, they approached the old Chick Bridge still at considerable speed. "We're nearing the bridge now. The floodwaters have us floating higher than normal so there's a chance the fan might hit. Hold on everyone. I hope we make it," Doc said.

catgcgccgccgtattaaattcgcacccatgatgcgtatgcgatggaacgcatttgcgcgcatgcgccgccgtattaaattcgcacccatgatgcgtat

As they passed underneath the low bridge, the uppermost part of the fan's cage hit the bridge beams and bent, but luckily didn't interfere with the fan blade movement. Doc said, "That was a close call. If we'd wrecked there, we'd never have made it across the river and swamp."

Doc then turned to the starboard toward the north and into an area of the Chick Swamp that was mostly open but with a few trees in the way. As he piloted forward against the wind, which seemed to be shifting directions constantly, the motor of the airboat was throttled at maximum power to move forward against the occasional gusts. Sometimes, it seemed they were barely moving forward and he had to often turn left or right to avoid trees as well as the wind pushing him off course. Soon they were hopelessly lost in the dark forested swamp.

Doc spoke on the microphone, "I'm lost, Jason. Get out the sheriff's compass and help me find the way."

Jason soon replied using the microphone, "North is now at your six o'clock position behind you. Turn totally around."

"Thanks, Jason," Doc replied as he steered the rudders and soon was moving in the correct northwesterly direction. "Keep using the compass to navigate and keep us going northwest, Jason."

Soon, Jason said, "You've drifted west. Steer towards two o'clock."

Doc steered to starboard slightly, and in a few minutes, they started to slow down as the airboat began struggling against an increasing headwind. "I think the wind has fully shifted to the north now so progress will be more difficult, but I think we're near to the railroad bridge. I see it straight ahead right now," he said and piloted the boat to the lee side of one of the trestle piers, which gave some slight shelter from the wind. He powered down the fan motor for a minute and turned on a red flashlight.

Everyone was relieved to be able to see again while Doc continued, "It's time now to get ready for the thermal imagers at the Exgenics property line when we cross under the bridges ahead. Take a blanket from under the tarp near the bow and dunk it over the side to get it wet. I'll take an extra one for the boat motor too. When I give the command, everyone cover themselves completely with the blanket. Jason's idea is the cool water will hide your body heat from the imagers."

In a minute, everyone was holding a sopping wet wool blanket and ready to go. "Buckle up," Doc said as he put his goggles on again and switched off the flashlight. The fan motor immediately roared back to life and he steered the rudders of the airboat to pass between the bridge piers ahead. They passed under the railroad bridge and in just a few more seconds they passed under the first highway bridge. As they went under the second bridge moving forward as fast as possible against the wind, Doc called out over the microphone "Now!" and everyone covered themselves with a wet blanket. Julie covered Rufus with her blanket too. Doc covered the hot motor and himself, including his head, with blankets and pushed the throttle to full speed. They plowed northward, boating while blind, across the Exgenics security perimeter.

After a few seconds more, Doc said, "Take off the blankets now. I think we've made it," but his blanket had tangled around his goggles, and as he pulled the blanket, the goggles came off too. In just a second, the airboat crashed directly into a tree, coming to an abrupt stop, and was listing at nearly a 45-degree angle into the swamp.

Sheriff Coleman roused Johnnie, who was still drunk, from the living room couch. "Sorry to wake you Johnnie, but I need your help now," he said to his long-time friend as he gently shook him to consciousness.

"I hep ya na matter what George," the inebriated man groggily replied.

"Here, let me put my sheriff's uniform on you. You'll take my place for a while," George replied as he started to help Johnnie out of his shirt and pants.

"Will I git ta drive Ol'bess?" the man asked. "I shure mis driv'n."

"You'll get to ride up front with me. I'll even turn the siren and lights on a bit just for fun," George replied jokingly as he helped Johnnie put on his uniform and sat him down at the kitchen table.

"I need you Johnnie to get drunk enough now to pass out a while," George said feeling slightly guilty as he gave the drunkard a quarter jar of the Captain's 'shine.

"No problemz George. I doz dat all da time. I doin' it for da Capt'n and Macee anyway. Catch dem killerz fer me," he replied as he took several large gulps and was soon to be even more inebriated to the point of blacking out.

George added, "Thanks Johnnie for being my body double. We need one more thing to make it really convincing. You need a knot on your head like you hit something hard."

"I kan do dat meself," he slurred as he stood up from the table, stumbled toward a doorway that led into the kitchen, and rapped his forehead hard on the door jam. "See, dat didunt herta'bit. That happenz ta me all da time," he laughed.

"Okay my friend, take one last, big gulp before we leave," George said, and after Johnnie's final slurp, helped him stagger out to Ole Bessie, guided him into the front passenger seat, and fastened the seat belt.

Johnnie passed out again while Coleman quickly drove Ole Bessie, with the rain, wind, and leaves blowing inside, to Buddy Peter's auto repair shop. He met Buddy in the front office. "Come follow me in your tow truck toward Williamsburg. Stay about a half-mile behind though. That way if they spot me, you'd not be involved."

"OK George, I'll put on my jacket. Go now and I'll catch right up."

Coleman left and drove east on State Highway 5 through the torrential rains and wind gusts that were blowing tree limbs and flying leaves while Johnnie was unconscious. He slowly crossed Tyler Bridge over the Chick and drove almost another three miles. As he approached the intersection to the right toward Jamestown, he intentionally oversteered and carefully skidded Ole Bessie sideways into the ditch on the far side of the road. Buddy Peters soon arrived with his tow truck and backed toward Ole Bessie as Sheriff Coleman turned off the engine, left the lights on with the key in the ignition, and got out of the car.

Buddy turned on his rear spotlights, rolled down his window, and said, "I'll loosen my winch so the cable will have slack. Pull the cable around that tree over there for leverage over Ole Bessie's roof, and hook it on the frame underneath. That should do the trick, George."

"Just be gentle with her," Coleman sadly replied at the imminent loss of his old trusted friend. He next struggled with the steel cable around the tree, pulled it over Ole Bessie, and hooked it in a spot that would do the least damage. He finally gave the thumbs-up sign, and Buddy started the winch. Soon, Ole Bessie had flipped on her side and after reeling in a few more feet of winch cable, flipped three-quarters of the way over and was leaning on some saplings. George motioned Buddy to stop the winch, and he climbed around Ole Bessie to unhook the cable and helped guide the cable back to the tow truck while Buddy reeled it in.

Coleman reached through the opening of the shattered passenger window to unbuckle Johnnie's seatbelt. As Johnnie was released from the seatbelt while nearly upside down, Coleman supported Johnnie's weight and guided his body in the direction of the driver's seat where he came to rest on the inside headliner. He quietly said, "Thank you, my friend."

He went back to the tow truck and climbed into the passenger seat. Coleman said somberly, "Well Buddy, I hope that puts them off our trail for a while. A good diversion should buy us the time we need. I just hope I can fix Ole Bessie later after all she's gone through. Let's go back to your shop and rest until we meet everyone at the courthouse."

Gregory called Gerardo, who was now in bed with his attractive and still young-looking wife. Gerardo answered his e-phone, "What're you disturbing me for now Gregory? What's else has gone wrong?" the scientist agitatedly questioned after his foreplay was interrupted.

"I wanted to give you a progress report. Our second Ops teams at the hacker's house found the grandfather just barely alive from several gunshot wounds. We found our first team there dead. Amazingly, the grandfather killed them both with antique shotguns I hear. Our other team pursuing the sheriff was also killed when their Supercruzer wrecked. We brought the grandfather back to the farm for the robodoc there to work on him. Maybe we can interrogate him later if he regains consciousness at all, but he seemed close to death. We finally finished searching the house and found a custom desktop computer system there with its hard drives erased and a bunch of strange electronics devices in the garage. That hacker seems good with electronics too."

"At least we have his grandfather. Let's try to keep him alive since that may benefit us later. What else have you been doing?" Gerardo replied.

"We also had an Intel report that the hacker's party was likely fleeing by boat at Harrison's Landing, but we think that was a diversion, since later, on the way back to Williamsburg, our Ops team saw that sheriff's patrol car had wrecked in a ditch. It looked like they were turning on the road towards Jamestown. The sheriff was unconscious inside, likely injured in the wreck, and we captured him. We're bringing him to the guardhouse to interrogate when he wakes up and we sent another team to capture his wife as a hostage if needed."

"That's good news. Maybe we can still keep this situation under control, Gerardo replied. "Where's everyone else we're searching for?"

Gregory continued, "We found a strange, burnt-out electronic device in the car so that hacker must have been with him. We think the rest of them are attempting to flee by boat across the James. There's a marina near Jamestown where they could steal a boat. We're putting our ground search parties there now. Also, in case they already made it across the river, we'll start searching in Prince George and Surry Counties for that hacker and anyone with him including that Indian veterinarian, John Longtree. I forgot to mention to you we found his vet van at the house."

Gerardo replied angrily, "That vet worked at the farm when we first set up our facility, so we need to catch him for sure."

"We just searched his house and didn't find his wife either. She is likely hiding somewhere with the local Indians." Gregory added.

"What, so now we've to go to war against an entire Indian tribe to find her? You guys are completely incompetent!" Gerardo angrily scowled.

Gregory replied, "I do have more good news to share though that I didn't mention before. We've taken prisoner the parents of the hacker's girlfriend. We think she's fleeing with Jason Dickson also. Their capture should give us more leverage if we need it later. We're keeping them at the guardhouse for interrogation."

"At least we're making progress catching these terrorists," he joked sarcastically but was still angry at how badly Gregory had handled the situation the past week. "I need to finish what I'm working on right now and I'll be there to take charge of this operation myself as soon as the weather lets me drone down there," Gerardo blurted out as he disconnected his e-phone and continued making love with his wife.

Chapter 30: Animal Farm

Pregnant Cow in the Barn

Midnight, Sunday, July 4, ...

Doc turned off the airboat's engine and the fan noise soon subsided, but the wind was still rustling the trees and whining through the swampy forest. Doc called out, "Is everyone Ok?" and all replied they weren't injured. They took off their earmuffs and soon heard Rufus barking from the swampy waters ahead of them.

Doc turned on a flashlight to survey the scene. The boat tilted steeply to the right and the bow's left side had smacked into a cypress. He shined the flashlight on Rufus, who was perhaps 20 feet away and swimming toward them. "I'll check him when we get to dry land. Now everyone, unbuckle your seatbelts and climb into the water. It's shallow near the edge of the swamp. Jason, you go first."

Jason stepped off the boat and into the water, "It's about two feet deep. The bottom's a little mucky though." He next helped Julie into the water. Nick and Doc soon joined them in the swampy waters.

"That way's north," Jason pointed after looking at the compass.

Doc replied, "I think we need to walk northeast, but let's keep the flashlights off to avoid detection if we're close to the guardhouse. I'll lead the way," he said putting on the night vision goggles as they grabbed their gear and turned off his flashlight. The pitch-black enveloped them again as they followed Doc toward the edge of the swamp.

As they struggled ahead, the muck and mud created a suction with each step that held each foot in place like glue. Occasionally, their feet bumped into an underwater limb causing them to stumble, but they maintained their balance. Rufus kept swimming along and after ten minutes of mucking through the swamp, the water was shallower and their footsteps firmer. Doc commented just loudly enough to be heard over the rustling of the trees from the wind, "I think we're getting close to the edge. This area is freshly flooded." In perhaps fifty feet, they were on dry land, if it could be called that, since the rain was heavily blowing in their faces.

Doc said, "Let me quickly examine Rufus," as he shined the red flashlight at the wet dog to look for external injuries and probed with his hands for any internal injuries. "I think he's OK. He has a few scratches on his left side, but his fur prevented any serious abrasions. He likely hit a tree branch when he flew off the airboat." He gave a comforting dog whisper touch to Rufus's head and scratched behind an ear.

"Let's keep going," Doc said as they walked further through the forest and soon were at the edge of the long, paved road leading to the farm. They looked to the right and in the distance, perhaps 200 yards away, could see street lights illuminating the guardhouse. Doc said, "It looks like they haven't lost power here. We need to remove these waders so we're comfortable and can move freely."

"That old shed or barn is up the driveway ahead on the right," Jason replied remembering the farm's satellite images. "Let's change there."

Doc replied, "That sounds good. Stay in the forest edge in case guards patrol the road. Without drones, they're likely using their Supercruzers." They walked about three hundred yards in the darkness and Doc said, "I see it ahead Jason, it's in a pasture about fifty feet from a wire fence." They walked to the fence and Doc said, "I think it's an electric fence to keep the cows corralled. Do you have any wire cutters in your bag Jason?"

"Yes, just a minute," Jason said as he reached inside his backpack in the darkness, fumbled around for the pair of diagonal-cutting pliers, and reached out his hand for Doc to grab them. "Here they are."

Doc took the cutters and snipped the electric wire at the top of the fence. "Let's climb over now," Doc said. Jason and Doc gave Julie a boost over the remaining wire fence and she landed on her feet. They next lifted Rufus over the fence and handed his leash to Julie. Finally, the men next clambered over the fence one by one.

They walked up to the old building which looked like it was nearly ready to fall down, walked inside a short door, and turned on their flashlights. Doc said, "This is an old tobacco barn from when they still grew tobacco here 150 years ago. That's long before the government made tobacco illegal as part of the public health control laws enacted after the coronavirus epidemic."

Jason picked up a long wooden pole from a pile in the corner and smelled it. "Julie, this wood still smells like tobacco," he said as he let her sniff the wood which still had a slightly sweet odor of the tobacco. "This reminds me of our wedding," he smiled in remembrance.

gcgaacgcgatggcgtaagcgatggcgaacgcgccgctggcgaacgcgtgcgcgaacgcgctgccggcgaacgcgatggcgtaagcgatggcgaacgcg

Julie laughed, "That was a unique and stimulating experience," and then she looked into Jason's eyes with love and impulsively kissed him.

"Enough you two lovebirds," Doc chuckled and added, "The Chick people are exempted from the law for religious reasons and we keep up the traditional way of growing it from long ago. That's an old tobacco pole. Farmers used to string bunches of tobacco leaves by hand on rough-hewn poles like that one. Then, they hung them in barns and used a fire to cure the leaves until they became a golden color prized for their flavor. Virginians grew tobacco starting with the Jamestown Colony and the crop *was* the economy for many years. Now, let's climb out of these waders."

They pulled off their ponchos, unstrapped the suspenders over their shoulders, and started to wriggle free of the rubberized garments like moths crawling out of cocoons. One by one, they pulled out their legs and were soon free again, except now they were in their stocking feet. They soon put on their shoes and hiking boots from the gym bag that Nick had carried. "Let's put our ponchos on and keep moving," Doc said.

As they left the tobacco barn, they turned off their flashlights again and Doc put on the goggles. "Let's walk along the fence line uphill towards the farm. If a patrol comes, just duck and lay flat on the ground." They walked two-tenths of a mile with Nick keeping watch for security patrols from behind and were finally 150 feet from the barn.

They looked at the research farm buildings that were well illuminated by floodlights as Doc took off his goggles and said, "There are no Supercruzers in the parking lot, so they're all at the guardhouse. There's a pickup by the farmhouse though."

Nick replied, "Gregory's there. The lights are off, so he's asleep."

"Are there any agrobots out at night or in the barn?" Doc asked.

Nick replied, "They never go inside the cow barn and, at night, they recharge in a shed near the solar intensifier system."

Jason also asked, "What about the security cams?"

Nick replied, "There are security cams on this side looking mostly at the parking lot and main building entrances, but on the barn's other side by my garden plot, there's none. There's a door there, but I never use it since I don't have barn access. That door has an entry security pad."

"I'll handle that," Jason said confidently.

Just then, they all heard a horrifying bellow from a cow inside the barn. Doc replied, "I think a cow is in pain. We're breaking in through the barn, so I may need to check it out."

Nick continued, "Let's walk to the back of the barn and cross the fence there." They walked there and suddenly, Rufus turned and started to bark

catgcgccgccgtattaaattcgcacccatgatgcgtatgcgatggaacgcatttgcgcgcatgcgccgccgtattaaattcgcacccatgatgcgtat

gcgaacgcgatggcgtaagcgatggcgaacgcgccgctggcgaacgcgtgcgcgaacgcgctgccggcgaacgcgatggcgtaagcgatggcgaacgcg

at something to the right of them in the dark. They soon saw a bull 100 feet away charging forward. "Everyone, quick over the fence," Doc shouted as he stood his ground and faced the oncoming bull.

Nick and Jason boosted Julie over the fence and then grabbed Rufus, tossing him over, but by this time the bull was nearly upon them. Doc stared down the bull and firmly held out his right hand. The bull was charging at full speed toward Doc and suddenly came to a full stop in front of his outstretched hand. Doc touched his head, gave him a scratch under his jowls, and the bull trotted away as if nothing had happened.

"How did you do that Doc?" Nick asked. "That was amazing!"

"I've got a special gift with animals, kind of like that Dr. Doolittle from those old children's books," he joked. "That's why I'm a veterinarian," he said as the men climbed over the fence.

They next walked through the garden plot and Nick commented, "My grandmother's beet seeds are doing well here this year." Soon they arrived at the back-access door to the barn and they heard another loud bellow from just inside the door of a cow in distress. Nick said, "I don't have access to this door, but perhaps Gerardo does."

Jason looked at the security pad just to the left of the door opening and also surveyed the metal door. "Let me do one more thing before I try to break in. This might delay any security guards that might drive up here by Supercruzer," he said.

He reached in his backpack, pulled out his e-phone, typed a keyword into the screen, and put it back in his backpack so any grid monitors couldn't triangulate his signal. "I've activated my Gridlock subroutine. No autocars or autotrucks now function in the State of Virginia. I scrambled their Grid coordinates, so any vehicles currently moving will slow down and stop carefully because they are lost. That will immobilize anyone on the ground searching or coming for us here," he said.

Jason pulled his laptop from his backpack and turned the e-screen on. He then displayed to the eye scanner the same image of Gerardo's eye that he used after hacking his password and pressed the security pad's 'activate scan' button. The security pad soon spoke, "Hello Doctor Gerardo. I'm sorry, but this door is for farm laborers only. Please use the door on the other side of the building. Have a good evening."

Frustrated with his first attempt to open the door, Jason next reached into his backpack and pulled out a hammer, a steel awl with a plastic handle, a giga-capacitor about the size of a deck of cards, and some thick rubber gloves. He put on the gloves, pressed the giga-capacitor over the security pad, lightly holding it in place with the awl's tip. As he aimed the

catgcgccgccgtattaaattcgcacccatgatgcgtatgcgatggaacgcatttgcgcgcatgcgccgccgtattaaattcgcacccatgatgcgtat

hammer to strike, he said, "Everyone, close your eyes. When I count to zero, I'll swing. Three, two, one, BANG!!!!!" Through their closed eyelids, they still saw the brilliant flash of a short-circuited supercapacitor.

"Sometimes the best way to handle a security system is to destroy it," Jason said and laughed as he looked at the awl with its tip vaporized an inch shorter from the explosion. He took out the metal-cutting grinder from his backpack, turned it on, and pressed it to the metal bolt that still kept the door secured. Soon, sparks were flying downward and within a minute, the thick security bolt was cut in two, and the door readily opened as he pulled the exterior handle.

"We're in," Jason said as he peered into the darkened barn and turned on his flashlight. "I see a switch to the right," and with a press, the lights fully illuminated the ground floor of the barn. Everyone entered, looked down a wide aisle, and saw a row of cow pens on each side. They took their ponchos off and walked to the first pen on the right and looked inside. A cow was pacing wildly in circles and strapped to its back, they saw an electronic device that conformed to the cow's general shape. Two red lights were flashing on the device, one fast and the other very slow. The device was connected to a long flexible tube with some wires inserted just below the cow's tail to inject chemicals.

Doc said, "That device looks like a fetal monitor for the calf inside, but usually, they just monitor the fetal heartbeat from the exterior with some electrodes placed on the cow's flanks. That tube is scary though; I've never seen one before. Those flashing red lights are a warning that there's a serious problem. I think this cow is in labor and having difficulty with the birth of its calf. It's my duty as a vet to help this poor animal. Julie, come inside the pen with me, I'll need help to hold it."

Julie followed Doc into the pen while Jason and Nick waited with Rufus outside the pen's gate. Julie spotted an e-clipboard hanging from a hook just inside the pen. She picked it up and touched the screen which displayed some words. "It says here Daisy/King," she said, and swiped the screen to try to open the clipboard's file, but it was password protected. "The cow's name must be 'Daisy' and 'King' must be the calf."

Doc puzzledly replied, "That's strange to name a farm animal before it's born. The calf is likely a male because that's a masculine name, so they must be breeding a prize bull here." Doc walked near the cow's head and used his hands to soothe and comfort it. It soon seemed calmer, but looking in her eyes, he could still see her intense abnormal pain. "Julie, come here and hold this halter for me while I examine her."

He went to the cow's rear, lifted the tail, and carefully thrust his arm inward to the womb. He commented, "This cow is well dilated and the water's broken already, but I think it's a breech birth. I have to find the rear feet of the calf and pull really hard," and he thrust his arm in deeper to manipulate the calf into a better position.

He managed to find first one rear leg and then the other rear leg. He used his hand and arm to shove both legs side by side so that he could grab both feet at the same time. He grabbed the feet and then thought that something didn't feel quite right as his hand slipped. He grabbed again even harder, pulling with all his strength, and a large black-colored fetus carefully fell to the floor.

He felt for a pulse, but there was none. "It's dead!" he called out to the others. He examined the fetus more closely and after wiping off some afterbirth from its head exclaimed to the others, "My God!" and continued staring at the dead mass of flesh and bone on the straw of the pen. "All of you come here now. You must see this."

When they assembled inside the pen, Doc said in anger loudly, "This is the most, evil abomination to nature and God I've ever seen. Dr. Gerardo has been implanting dog's embryos into these cows for some reason. This Gerardo is not a man, but a demon from hell," he said and lifted the lifeless head of an adult German Shepard to show the others.

They all looked in horror and Julie immediately vomited. Jason felt hatred, boiling up inside him as he'd never felt before, for a man named Gerardo. Nick fell to his knees on the pen's straw-covered floor and started praying, "Lord. Please forgive me for helping this evil man. I didn't know," and he muttered another prayer in Russian. Rufus laid down on the straw and was thankful for a nice dry barn.

Doc added, "Now we know why Exgenics was ordering all those anti-rejection drugs and growth hormones."

Soon they heard, "Hands up!" as Gregory pulled his 9-mm semiautomatic pistol on the distracted team and entered the cow pen. The team raised their hands and slowly turned toward the voice.

He continued, "I couldn't sleep because of the wind, then I heard a strange bang outside, and here you are!" He smugly smiled thinking how Gerardo would thank him for capturing the intruders, but Rufus smelled something familiar, growled, quickly lunged toward Gregory.

Gregory shot at the angry old dog but missed. Rufus grasped at the fat old man's throat, like he'd done many times while killing a raccoon or possum, and started scratching at the man with the long claws of his front

gcgaacgcgatggcgtaagcgatggcgaacgcgccgctggcgaacgcgtgcgcgaacgcgctgccggcgaacgcgatggcgtaagcgatggcgaacgcg

paws. Gregory evaded the first attack, but fell backward on the ground, and rolled side-to-side to fend off the dog's vicious assault.

"Stop this crazy dog! I give up!" Gregory cried out like a walrus bellowing as he dropped his pistol onto the straw. Blood ran down his face from scratches inflicted by Rufus, as the dog continued his revenge on his masters' murderer.

Doc commanded, "Heel" and Rufus stopped his attack as Doc pointed his pistol at the head of the now helpless obese man. Julie grabbed the dangling end of Rufus's leash, pulling him away.

Jason said, "As a sworn sheriff's deputy of Charles County, you're under arrest for the murders of Captain Jack and Macy Thompson. I'm sure you know these words, but I must tell you anyway," as he began reading to the man his Miranda rights from a piece of paper while remembering hearing the same words himself. "You have the right to remain silent. Anything you say can be used against you in a court of law. You have the right to an attorney and have him present during the interrogation," and Jason paused a moment. "No need to tell you this one about a free attorney, since your already rich."

Jason briefly chucked before continuing, "You can waive your right to be silent before or during questioning, and if you do so, any interrogation must be halted. You can invoke your right to have an attorney present during questioning." Jason added after the last sentence, "Since you're already an attorney, I'm not sure this one applies either, but I guess it means you can find another lawyer if you need one. Somehow, I think you'll need one because you're not that smart," Jason chuckled again as he picked up the 9-mm pistol from the floor and placed it in a plastic zipper bag as evidence. "I bet this is the murder weapon here," Jason said firmly.

"Where's your warrant? You're breaking and entering into this facility," the man countered with a lawfare attack as that was the only response he could make in his current situation.

"Read these and weep," Jason said as he tossed Judge Saunders warrants onto the straw-covered floor of the pen.

Gregory sat up, picked up the documents, and briefly looked at what the papers said, "Gerardo and the others will get you for this. There's nothing they can't do!"

"Well, that may be true for now, but when we find more overwhelming evidence here and using the quantum-coupled data link from here to the CIA, we can likely arrest half the government and their puppeteer leaders who've controlled the world our entire lives. All it takes is some good coders, like me, to later scan for the right Grid data, and there will be

catgcgccgccgtattaaattcgcacccatgatgcgtatgcgatggaacgcatttgcgcgcatgcgccgccgtattaaattcgcacccatgatgcgtat

enough evidence to arrest and remove these people from power. The world will then be free of their globalist masters' yoke."

"You'll never get away with this!" Gregory exclaimed, as Jason grabbed the man's arms, pulled each one behind his back as he clamped the handcuffs on tightly.

Jason commanded, "Julie and Nick, go see if there's a first aid kit somewhere in the barn. Just because this man is evil doesn't mean we treat him that way. Justice will punish him later as he deserves."

Gregory said, "There's a first aid kit in the barn's office," and Julie soon brought back the kit and the man sat quietly while she disinfected the painful deep scratch on his cheek and taped a large gauze pad over it.

"Now stand up, Gregory," Jason commanded but his prisoner refused to budge from his seat on the floor.

Gregory said, "I won't cooperate with you. I'm not moving from this spot. You're on your own in your search of this facility."

"We don't need *your* cooperation to come with us then," Jason said in a serious but sarcastic tone. "We just need *your eyeball* to cooperate," and he pulled out the sheriff's pocket knife, opened the five-inch-long blade, and waved it in Gregory's face menacingly and sadistically.

"You can't do that!" Gregory cringed with fear.

"Doc, do you think you can help his eyeball cooperate?"

"Sure. I've operated with scalpels to excise cancerous animal eyes before. That knife is primitive and it would be bloody, causing orbital trauma. It shouldn't take long though, but might be *extremely* painful," Doc replied without emotion in a scientific, surgical manner.

"Good, here you go," Jason said passing the knife to Doc, who moved closer to the attorney, looked at his face, and grabbed him by one ear.

"I'll cooperate," Gregory squawked like a chicken facing an ax to the neck before a chicken pastry Sunday dinner.

Jason replied, "OK Doc, you can stop now. Just remember Gregory, your eyeball is ours to use anytime we want it. You're to come with us peacefully and present your eyeball immediately to any security scanners within this facility as we execute the search warrants."

"Yes, I agree and comply with your orders," Gregory said meekly as he cowered. They'd fully broken his resolve and spirit. He knew he was truly a coward and would now fully comply as a prisoner with their orders.

Jason added for final effect, "Just remember to listen and follow my commands. If you later refuse to obey us at any time, we might tape your eyes open with some of that bandage tape or we can still resort to the knife at any time. It's your choice," Jason summarized his options as he stared deep into Gregory's sullen eyes and winked.

"I get your message," Gregory fearfully and somberly replied.

"Now stand up and obey my orders," Jason commanded.

"Yes deputy," the straw-covered lawyer replied in full submission while struggling to his feet and added, "Something smells bad here."

"That's you," Jason laughed again to further humiliate his prisoner, "You rolled in cow manure."

The team then advanced along the barn aisle past other cows and as they looked at each cow, the devices were strapped to their backs, but the lights were all solid green or flashing green for a normal fetal heartbeat. Jason looks at the e-clipboard and said, "This clipboard says, *'Penelope/Maximus'* on it."

Julie said at the next clipboard, "This says *'Bess/Fifi'* on the screen."

Nick continued in his Russian accent, "This is *'Margie/Sarge'* here."

They walked down the aisle reciting names on clipboards, *'Lois/Rocky'*, *'Esmeralda/Thor'*, *'Isabella/ Ginger'*, and so on until they were at the security door at the barn's other end. "Where's this door go?" Jason asked.

Gregory replied, "That's the breezeway to the main research building."

To maintain dominance over his prisoner, Jason roughly thrusted Gregory in front of the security pad. He pulled the man's gray hair, placed his face near the device, and pressed the 'activate scan' button. A blue laser scanned his face, located his right iris and retina, and instantly, a light on the pad turned green and the door unlocked.

They walked to the end of the short passage and pushed the simple horizontal latch, opening the door to the research building.

1:00 a.m., Sunday, July 4, ….

Deputy James and Robin drove in his old patrol car toward Williamsburg General Hospital along the highway and through the streets of the small city. All along the way, they saw multiple vehicles abandoned in roads and streets. A few times, they passed some small groups of people just walking along the road, so they finally stopped and asked the next couple they saw on a darkened road, "Why are you walking here this time at night?" Robin inquired through a rolled-down window.

The man replied, "Our car just stopped two miles ago. I called someone to come pick us up and their car wouldn't start either. Everyone else we contacted couldn't move their vehicles either. We sure could use a lift into town. Can you help us?"

gcgaacgcgatggcgtaagcgatggcgaacgcgccgctggcgaacgcgtgcgcgaacgcgctgccggcgaacgcgatggcgtaagcgatggcgaacgcg

Deputy James replied, "Sure, we're on our way to the hospital but we can take you home first. We have time."

"Our house is near there. We'd appreciate it very much."

"Ok then, sit in the back and we'll take you there," the deputy replied and soon drove them to their house. Afterward, Jeffrey and Robin arrived at the hospital and entered the automated front doors. At the security station, Jeffrey asked, "We're here to see a patient named John Smith."

The security guard said, "I'm sorry, visiting hours are over. You'll have to come back in the morning."

Deputy James replied, "This is a matter of life and death. We need to see John Smith now!" he asserted.

"Not even the president herself is permitted to see anyone after visiting hours," the security guard bureaucratically replied in a firm tone.

Robin also attempted to reason with the guard, "I'm a doctor and this is an emergency. I need to see my patient now."

"Unless you can show me an access badge that you're authorized to see patients in *this* hospital, I can't let you in."

Jeffrey whispered something to Robin, and then pulled out his service pistol from its holster and pointed it at the guard, "Will this access badge allow you to take us to see him now?"

The guard replied meekly, "Yes, I think visiting hours just started. Let me locate his room for you both. Ah, here it is 3rd floor, Room 335."

"Thank you for your cooperation." Jeffrey replied, "Just to make sure there are no loose ends, you're coming with us too."

"As long as you point that badge at me, I'm at your disposal," he said.

They took the elevator up to the third floor and entered a darkened room where the patient was sleeping. Robin switched on the light as Jeffrey walked over to the bed and saw Sheriff Olsen. One shoulder was in a cast, so Jeffrey roused him from his slumber with a gentle shake of his other shoulder. He spoke softly, "Wake up Sheriff."

Olsen groggily replied, "Yes, what is it?"

"It's Deputy James from Charles County. George wanted us to talk."

"Hello Jeffrey," Olsen replied from his bed, "Is George OK?"

"He's fine for now. I need to tell you what's been happening and our plans. George said you'd know what to do." For the next ten minutes, Jeffrey and Robin updated the sheriff with the most recent events and continued succinctly explaining their morning plans.

Olsen replied, "George has thought this out well," he commented. "His years in the army made him a master strategist in such situations.

gcgaacgcgatggcgtaagcgatggcgaacgcgccgctggcgaacgcgtgcgcgaacgcgctgccggcgaacgcgatggcgtaagcgatggcgaacgcg

That book by Sun-Tzu must have stuck in his brain. I'm coming with you. Help me get up and into my uniform. It's in that tall cabinet on the wall."

2:00 a.m., Sunday, July 4, ...

The search warrant team walked down the corridor and Nick pointed out key rooms as they passed. "That's the sequencer room on the left and that's the embryonics lab next to it. Those are the only labs I've access to, but I've been in the lab supply closet too. I've been in Dr. Gerardo's office before too. There's the break room. The only other room I've been inside is the infirmary which is in the medical annex at the far end of the building. A medical doctor is sometimes there and will see you for free treatment if you let him know you're coming. It's a nice fringe benefit."

"Do you know what's in these other secured rooms?" Jason asked.

"I've seen Gerardo enter all those rooms before but never anyone else. Wait, thinking back though, I did see Gregory enter at least one of them before, but I can't remember which one.

"You're a traitor Nick. We'll get even for this," Gregory commented.

"Shut up you pitiful excuse of a man," Jason replied. "Ok Gregory, time to test your eyeball again on that door right there. It must be a large room since there are no doors for a while down the side of the corridor."

Gregory walked up to the door, repeated the scan procedure, the door unlatched, and Jason opened it.

They walked inside, turned on the lights, and saw a large lab room with multiple aisles, with each aisle lined on both sides by a long metal rack with shelves spaced at different heights. A few racks had tightly-spaced shelf sections that held thousands of embryo flasks. These individual shelves had small shaker tables that gently swirled groups of flasks, providing aeration to the nutrient solution and the fish embryos. A robot, unphased by the unexpected guests, slowly moved down the aisle, checking each flask, and occasionally injecting some more nutrient solution. It then continued following its mindless, repetitive program.

Most of the shelves, however, contained small-sized aquariums sitting on metal shelves at different elevations. A different robot seemed busy examining these tanks and seemed to be performing some procedures on the individual tanks. They walked down the aisle toward the robot past the aquariums with baby pufferfish and many of the larger-sized ones had strange growths on their sides.

When they reached the robot, it ignored them, and they soon observed it apply a shock with an electrical probe on its arm to a tank to temporarily paralyze the fish inside. A small fish soon floated to the surface and the

catgcgccgccgtattaaattcgcacccatgatgcgtatgcgatggaacgcatttgcgcgcatgcgccgccgtattaaattcgcacccatgatgcgtat

robot used a microscopic syringe needle to inject something into the growth on the fish's side.

Gregory commented, "This room is where we grow the embryos into small fish, each with a cancer growth for testing the custom Exgena drugs. How else are we going to test if a patient's cancer cure is effective?

"Those poor baby fish," Julie exclaimed, "They're torturing them."

"Doc added, "Yes, it's unethical and immoral to do this."

Nick, "I never imagined what Gerardo was doing to these little fish. I thought he only tested embryos. Please forgive me."

Gregory added, "They're just stupid fish anyway. They don't have intelligent brains like us. There's nothing wrong with that."

Jason commented, "This is a room of horrors, but this isn't what we're searching for. Capture this evidence on the podcam Julie."

"It's been recording ever since we entered the barn Jason," she replied.

They left the Exgena drug testing lab and used Gregory again to open the next door along the aisle. They turned on the lights, but this time the room was automatically illuminated by red LED lights for nighttime mode. They entered the entrance alcove of the 10,000 square foot room and saw a huge 9-foot-tall aquarium with clear plastic sides filing almost the entire room, except for access aisles on the sides and rear.

Doc commented, "That looks like an aquaculture tank I've seen before. There must be 300,000 gallons or more here."

They stared through the transparent sides of the clear plastic aquarium in amazement at thousands of glowfish swimming there. On the right side of the aquarium, multiple glowfish congregated at a custom machine with some clear plastic tubes connected to the aquarium. As they closely observed the machine, a single glowfish entered a tube and then into a small aquarium with a metal probe horizontally sticking into the water. The fish swam up to the probe and bit on it. The fish glowed, let go of the probe, and puffed up by sucking in water. Then, some white slime exuded from its spines and floated to the water's surface. The fish deflated and swam out a plastic exit tube back to the main aquarium tank.

Above the small aquarium, a skimmer blade automatically swept the slime from the water's surface and deposited it in a sluice. The slime then flowed down the sluice and was collected in a small hopper. After each glowfish exited, another glowfish eagerly swam into the small torture chamber and the procedure repeated.

"They're milking these fish for TTX slime," Jason said. "These fish are like slaves, being forced to produce the poison for their evil masters. I think they bite that metal bar and get an electrical shock just to recharge

gcgaacgcgatggcgtaagcgatggcgaacgcgccgctggcgaacgcgtgcgcgaacgcgctgccggcgaacgcgatggcgtaagcgatggcgaacgcg

their electrical system," he said after studying the machine's control panel and concluding the fish were given electrical shocks.

Doc added, "I almost feel these fish suffering like prisoners and they willingly go into that chamber to be shocked. This is so evil," he stated.

Gregory just stood quietly and was now using his Miranda right to remain silent as he now knew the extent of information that Jason had already learned from his hack of Exgenics, its shareholders, and E-Face.

They left the TTX-aquaculture room and walked down to the next unknown door, this one on the left. However, Gregory began resisting the use of his eyeball and refused to walk close to the door.

Jason motioned Julie to turn off the podcam and then pulled back the slide on the sheriff's Beretta pistol, loading a bullet in the chamber. He pointed the pistol at the fat man's stomach, and said, "Doc, why don't we just shoot him now and then take his eyeball out. It'll be easier that way. Then, he won't feel the pain from the eyeball excision."

Doc replied, "That's a great idea. I won't have to risk damaging the retina either. This man is evil and needs to be executed anyway. That'll save the taxpayers a lot of expense for a trial and we'll still find plenty of evidence to convict anyone involved in this conspiracy."

The coward reluctantly complied, placing his eye by the door's scanner.

They entered a smaller lab unlike the large rooms they'd entered before. one wall was partly filled with electronics and controls and there was a portable cryogenic tank of liquid nitrogen chained to one wall. In the room's four corners were large, flat meta-antennas mounted on wheels.[90] In the room's center were two non-metallic tables sitting side by side. The tabletops were resting on some plastic conveyor rollers. At each table's end was a large donut-shaped machine, that appeared mounted at the height where the tabletops could be slid inside. Finally, in between and mounted above the donut-shaped machines was a large metal toroid that Jason immediately recognized, "Hey, that's a Tesla coil. There's definitely high voltage equipment here."

Doc commented, "Those tables look like some sort of MRI or CAT scanner machines, but I don't have any idea what experiments they're conducting here. Maybe they're doing something with those dogs."

Nick added, "I don't have a clue what they're doing either."

---

[90] A meta-antenna is a metamaterial designed to capture or reflect electromagnetic signals. These devices and their physical dimensions can be tailored for specific frequencies and their design can be engineered to violate conventional laws of physics for signal emission, absorption, or reflection.

catgcgccgccgtattaaattcgcacccatgatgcgtatgcgatggaacgcatttgcgcgcatgcgccgccgtattaaattcgcacccatgatgcgtat

Jason replied, "This is some sort of experimental lab and I've never seen anything like it before. Whatever this equipment is, it isn't the main AI-computer room with the quantum-coupled communications system. That's what we're looking for."

Gregory flinched at the words and knew their plans would fully be discovered now. He sat down on the floor and again passively resisted.

Jason thought a moment on how to again motivate the man differently and commanded, "Rufus attack!"

The old dog lunged toward the man's throat, but Doc held him back while Rufus continued growling and barking.

Gregory blurted out, "Ok, I'll get up and do what you want. I can't take your psychological pressure anymore. You've beaten me, but you won't beat Gerardo. That computer room is fully protected and I don't have access."

"Just show us which one of these doors leads to it." Jason requested.

"It's the one on the left just past Gerardo's office. You're on your own now," Gregory replied.

"I know where that is. Follow me, Jason," Nick replied.

Chapter 31: By Dawn's Early Light

Glowfish Aquaculture Tank

3:00 a.m., Sunday, July 4, ….

Jason and the team approached the door to the AI-computer room and said to Doc, "You stay outside and guard Gregory. We don't want him inside verbally warning the AI-computer about intruders."

Doc replied as he pulled his pistol out of its holster, "I've got him covered. Sit on the floor over there," he commanded. Gregory awkwardly sat down in the hallway by the opposite wall from the door.

Jason next pulled out his laptop from his backpack and turned on the e-screen display. He held it close to the security pad and pressed the button. After scanning the image of Gerardo's eye, the security keypad replied, "Access granted, Doctor Gerardo," and the door unlatched.

As Jason opened the door, Gregory exclaimed, "You're a bastard! You could have used that anytime instead of torturing me with my eyeball."

Doc and Jason then broke into laughter at the psychological trick they pulled on the cowardly and now humiliated attorney. After their laughter subsided, Jason finally replied, "Yes, but it was more important to scare you into submission as my prisoner," he wryly smiled at the coward.

"Nick and Julie, come with me," Jason said and they walked into the room while Julie held Rufus's leash. Inside, they saw a large semi-circular table in the center of the room with a single office chair in the middle. On the table was a keyboard touch-pad and on the wall directly behind the table was a large e-screen. On the left and right sides of the table were control panels. One panel had various switches, dials, gauges, and indicator screens used for monitoring the automated functions and agrobots on the farm. The other control panel had fewer buttons and controls but had multiple small e-screens and provided access to the AI-security system. In the rear corner to the right, they saw the large quantum

gcgaacgcgatggcgtaagcgatggcgaacgcgccgctggcgaacgcgtgcgcgaacgcgctgccggcgaacgcgatggcgtaagcgatggcgaacgcg

AI-computer core, and in the adjacent corner was the Q-modem system interfacing with the quantenna.

Jason commented, "This is like a hacker's dream come true," and grinned as he sat down in the chair. He put his pistol on the right side of the table and placed the podcam beside it. Finally, he took his laptop, set it on the table area to the left of the touch-pad, and turned it on. He also took a piece of black electrical tape and covered the computer's imager.

He said to Julie and Nick, "Please be quiet now. After I turn on the AI-computer interface, we have to be careful until I gain full control." He typed some commands on his laptop in preparation to counter any security challenges he faced while attempting to login.

He next swiped the touch-pad. The AI-computer interface and e-screen both activated and the computer awakened from its slumbers. He saw on the e-screen a password entry box and began typing on the touch-pad '!aD1>1NaK0wweD1a'. The AI computer replied, "Please say the magic word, Doctor Gerardo."

Jason quickly thought about what he knew of Dr. Gerardo and the one thing he might have treasured most in this world. He quickly typed on his laptop keyboard and his laptop computer then spoke, "Marianna," in a simulated voice that was nearly a perfect match for Gerardo's voiceprint.

"You don't sound right today, Dr. Gerardo," the AI-computer replied.

Jason quickly typed on his laptop which again spoke, "I've lost my voice some. I was yelling at that stupid Gregory again. He's a real idiot."

"Yes, you're correct doctor. He is an idiot. Lawyers are usually not that smart and just only looking out for themselves. They use the law as a shield for battle and their words are their weapons. Full Q-drive and communications access granted. Have a nice day," the AI-computer replied as a large smiley emoji appeared on the e-screen in front of them.

He next typed some computer code commands on the touch-pad to open up some different screens and then found what he was looking for. He typed a few more commands and spoke, "It's OK to talk now. I've deactivated the AI-computer's microphone."

He continued typing more commands and said, "I've just disabled the portion of the AI security system that monitors the farm facilities to help the sheriff when he arrives, but kept it on at the guardhouse to not alarm the guards. They won't be patrolling the farm tonight during this storm."

As Nick and Julie observed the master hacker, Jason grabbed a fiberoptic interface cable from his backpack and plugged it in a data port. "I'm going to copy the quantum hard drive here before I access the quantenna and join the two halves of the quantum data stream. I'll be

catgcgccgccgtattaaattcgcacccatgatgcgtatgcgatggaacgcatttgcgcgcatgcgccgccgtattaaattcgcacccatgatgcgtat

gcgaacgcgatggcgtaagcgatggcgaacgcgccgctggcgaacgcgtgcgcgaacgcgctgccggcgaacgcgatggcgtaagcgatggcgaacgcg

recording all the evidence we uncover, but there's so much data here my laptop can't store it all. I'll have to transmit the data through the Grid to the remote data storage sites where I installed my dead man's switch. So, there's a chance a Grid monitor could spot my laptop's transmission. Unfortunately, that likely will alert Gridcom but there's no alternative."

Julie replied, "We have to take that chance, Jason. We need to prove beyond a reasonable doubt what we've discovered in a court of law. We don't want these evil people to get away with murder and more. They must meet justice. They likely have powerful attorneys who'll fight and the e-media they own will say it's all fake news, but if enough people see what we've discovered, the truth will prevail."

Nick added, "I hope so. God is on our side to help us with revealing the truth. Perhaps that's why I ended up working here at Exgenics. To help Him with his plans."

Jason replied as he typed commands on his laptop, "All I know is this data upload will take a while and I'm tired. Perhaps we can rest a short while. Is there someplace comfortable in this building to take a catnap?"

Nick replied and pointed, "Gerardo's office is right through that side door. There's a nice sofa you can rest on."

"That sounds good. Julie, go check on Doc quickly and see what's going on in the hallway. Then we can take a short nap."

Julie peered out the entrance door and saw Doc sitting on the floor with his gun pointed at Gregory who was leaning on the far wall, snoring loudly. Doc gave Julie an OK hand sign and she returned to Jason.

"Doc's doing fine and Gregory is asleep," Julie reported.

"Great. Nick, can you stay awake here with Rufus and keep an eye on my laptop? It'll take an hour or so to download the data and we can analyze it at our leisure later. When this cursor flashes red, the download is completed, so come get me then."

"Yes Jason," Nick said.

Jason replied, "Thanks, Nick," as he stood up from the chair to trade places at the farm's controls. He took Julie's hand, and they walked to the door, which only had a simple lever, and opened it.

They entered the office and Jason surveyed the dark room with his flashlight. It was spartanly decorated with a desk, a large e-screen, an e-wall, some chairs, and a large leather couch. He shined his flashlight on the desk and saw a palm-sized golden medal resting on a wooden stand. "That's his Nobel prize medal," he commented to Julie. They laid down on the sofa, briefly cuddled in embrace quietly, and were soon asleep.

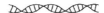

Hal and Janice in Utah were exhausted from more than a week of overtime scanning the Grid and were asleep with their heads resting on their workstations. They didn't see their flashing e-screens and the tremendous amount of data transmitting from Provident Forge.

4:00 a.m. Sunday, July 4, ….

The men and women from the hunt club and the Chick tribe assembled in the parking lot outside the old Charles County Courthouse as they carried their flashlights and lanterns. Sheriff Coleman began talking through an electronic megaphone, "I'm happy the storm has passed. Hopefully, Virginia power can get things working soon. Now, let's talk about the serious business at hand. First of all, I'm glad everyone left their e-phones at home. Those of you with old-time wind-up watches and kitchen timers will keep this operation on schedule."

Coleman continued, "Sometimes good men and women, like us, must stand for equal law and order for all. This is one of those times. We believe the terrorist attack on our river and lake is a cover-up of ongoing criminal activities at the Exgenics Farm near Provident Forge. We've uncovered a global conspiracy that violates the laws of the United States, man, nature, and God. We know powerful people are implicated in these crimes and the federal government is involved, at least partially. What we discover this morning at Exgenics will further prove our case. Against the foes we face, we must all stand firm and resolute as one community."

"We know that Exgenics has violated many laws and murdered two of our finest and beloved citizens, Captain Jack and Macy Thompson. Also, they've ruthlessly caused the deaths this week of more of our friends, including Jimmy Cummings, Patrick Duke, and Reverend Dickson just last evening. They even tried murdering Sheriff Olsen of Kent County."

The crowd collectively gasped at this news of all these murders.

"We're now about to serve both arrest and search warrants at Exgenics against perhaps overwhelming odds. A nation without the rule of law is not a nation. Today, we begin the process of reinstituting equal justice under the law, by the people, and for the people, instead of unequal law by the elite and for the elite, who have corrupted our Constitution to its core. The people of Charles County deserve and will earn justice this day. What we do is risky and may cost some of you everything, even your lives."

Jay Tyler, an attorney and leading member of the hunt club, spoke up loudly and agreed, "My family has been here for generations and I'm with you sheriff. I can no longer tolerate what's happened to this country and am willing to stake my family's good name and my life in this just cause."

gcgaacgcgatggcgtaagcgatggcgaacgcgccgctggcgaacgcgtgcgcgaacgcgctgccggcgaacgcgatggcgtaagcgatggcgaacgcg

"Is everyone else here with us?" the sheriff asked the crowd.

"Yes, Yeah, and Yo," were heard shouted back in a nearly simultaneous chorus of agreement from the motley assembly.

"Well, that appears a unanimous vote," the sheriff said jokingly and a few people in the crowd chuckled. "Who hasn't yet been deputized before in Charles County? Raise your hands please," and, in response, ninety-nine percent of the assembled crowd raised their hands.

"Let me deputize y'all at one time so you can help serve the warrants. Keep your hands raised," Coleman continued and recited the law enforcement oath to them all. After they had sworn the oath, Coleman concluded with the procedure, "You are now all Charles County Deputies authorized to assist in serving lawful warrants at Exgenics over in Provident Forge. Follow my lawful orders or those of any other uniformed deputy from Charles or Kent County."

"There's a lot of drones at Exgenics, so everyone, except those coming with me, stay near the tree lines or keep undercover as you advance toward the guardhouse and main farm buildings."

Coleman continued, "I'll lead the assault, I mean, serve the warrants on the security guards at the gate with a few hunt club volunteers. The Chick people will approach by canoe from the southwest through the swamp. The rest of the hunt club be under the command of Jeffrey and approach from the trees on the east side of the Exgenics driveway. Jeffrey's team will move forward with the old punt-gun from the Charles County Historical Museum and flank the security guards from the right. Everyone's to wait for my word to open fire on any targets. Doc Hansen and Dr. Graves, from Kent County, will assist with any medical emergencies or casualties that might occur, but the Charles County Volunteers should assist as medics if needed."

To you deputies visiting here from Kent County, I'll serve the warrants at the gate at 5:53 a.m. Sheriff Olsen with his Deputy Jeffers leading the way, along with the good deputized citizen militia from Provident Forge, will cross across a hastily constructed path over the muddy lakebed of Old Forge Lake to serve their warrant. I'm glad our county's pallet factory supplied materials to build a temporary pontoon bridge over the mud. A truckload of modified pallets is already staged nearby awaiting deployment. Exgenics would never expect an assault, I mean, an approach from that direction."

"Now let's get this operation moving. All timekeepers, please synchronize your watches and your timers. Please keep flipping those egg timers when the sand runs out, so we maintain schedule. It's now 4:32

catgcgccgccgtattaaattcgcacccatgatgcgtatgcgatggaacgcatttgcgcgcatgcgccgccgtattaaattcgcacccatgatgcgtat

AM," Coleman said glancing at his military wind-up watch, before continuing. Everyone, please assemble now at your assigned staging areas so that we can keep this operation on schedule. We'll be serving justice for the Captain, Macy, Jimmy, Reverend Dickson, and *our* river today."

5:00 a.m., Sunday, July 4, ...

Despite the tropical storm moving over Washington, Gerardo grabbed his dart gun, put on a raincoat, and commanded Dante and Inferno to follow him outside his mansion into the tempest. They walked through wind and rain to the concrete pad where his unidrone sat illuminated by spotlights. He pressed the latch handle and the passenger pod's transparent hatch automatically sprang open.

With an instant command, Dante and Inferno jumped up and sat in their usual small nooks just to the left and right of the single reclining padded seat in the center of the passenger compartment. Gerardo climbed in his seat, pressed a button, and the hatch quickly closed.

He commanded the unidrone's AI-pilot, "Fly to Exgenics Farm."

The AI-pilot replied, "This weather system is past normal design limits of the gyrostabilizers and wing gimbal. I am unable to launch, Dr. Gerardo. I recommend waiting for improved weather conditions."

Gerardo replied, "Is this storm past the unidrone's failure limits?"

The AI-pilot paused a moment to perform some engineering stress calculations and replied, "No, Dr. Gerardo."

"Then override safety protocols and take off, NOW!" he commanded.

"It will be a bumpy and turbulent flight Dr. Gerardo and I cannot guarantee your safety. Please fasten your seat belt. I see it is not buckled. I comply with your command then."

Gerardo grumbled at the stubborn AI-computer and buckled his seat belt. Soon the whir of the props from the four electromotors was heard outside the unidrone, but inside the cabin, it was quiet, due to the vacupane insulation used around the cabin walls, soundproofing the cockpit and insulating it from the cold air during flight.[91]

---

[91] Vacupane is a patented lightweight insulation material constructed from a sandwich of heat-sealable aluminized plastic film with a rigid graphene-aerogel center. The manufacture of this material includes pulling a full vacuum on the rigid aerogel to remove air before heat sealing the plastic film over the aerogel. This allows the manufacturing of large flat or custom-shaped sheets of insulation that have both sound and thermal insulation capabilities nearly equivalent to a vacuum insulated bottle. This material has found widespread usage in the aerospace industry and other applications where the material's properties are useful.

gcgaacgcgatggcgtaagcgatggcgaacgcgccgctggcgaacgcgtgcgcgaacgcgctgccggcgaacgcgatggcgtaagcgatggcgaacgcg

The drone lurched into the air and automatically compensated for gusty and turbulent winds swirling past and around his mansion. The drone wobbled upward and was like a small boat tossed about on rough seas. Gerardo tightly held on to the seat's armrests like he was on an amusement park ride while Dante and Inferno, who were still wet from the storm's rain, whimpered and cowered on both sides.

Once the drone had risen above the tree line, the ground effect turbulence subsided and the unidrone became somewhat more stable. As the drone flew upward and toward the south, its speed increased and it's short, gimballed wing, which served as support for the electromotors, slowly pivoted toward horizontal flight mode. Now the wing provided lift along with the passenger pod, and the props became used for forward propulsion. As the drone's forward motion increased, the drone occasionally was buffeted by severe turbulence as it traveled southward.

Gerardo concentrated on his thoughts while trying not to get motion sick from the ride, "That Gregory is incompetent. Sometimes you just have to do things for yourself." He thought further, "When we catch that hacker, he might be useful though. We have his grandfather, his girlfriend's parents, and that sheriff, so that will give me leverage I need."

He reached for a 'barf bag' in a side pocket of the seat, but immediately and uncontrollably spewed vomit forward onto the inside of the hatch's large dark-tinted transparent window. As it dripped onto Gerardo's lap, Dante and Inferno soon winced from the smell, vainly attempting to cover their noses with their front paws.

5:15 a.m., Sunday, July 4, ….

Nick came into the office and gently roused Jason, "Jason, your data download is complete."

"Thanks for waking us. Let me work on that quantenna data link now," he replied as he and Julie were wakened from their brief slumbers.

"Rufus kept me company," Nick smiled, "That dog sure slobbers a lot. There's a large puddle to the right of the chair, so watch your step."

"Thanks for the tip," Jason replied and then carefully sat back down in the swivel office-style chair at the table. "Julie and Nick, go check on Doc and have him bring Gregory here. I think it'll be interesting what we find. I want to see Gregory's reaction," Jason said as he began typing keystrokes on the touch-pad.

Julie and Nick went to the halfway and saw Doc sitting with his back to the wall, still awake and vigilantly guarding the prisoner. His handgun was pointing toward Gregory, who was laying like a beached whale and

catgcgccgccgtattaaattcgcacccatgatgcgtatgcgatggaacgcatttgcgcgcatgcgccgccgtattaaattcgcacccatgatgcgtat

snoring while handcuffed on the opposite side of the hallway. "Jason wants you and Gregory to come inside and watch now," Julie said.

Doc stood up and used his foot to prod the slovenly lawyer's fat belly. "Wake up asshole," he curtly spoke to the man just to remind him that he was still a prisoner after his slumbers. "Come with me," he said as the fat man struggled to his feet. Doc grabbed him firmly by the elbow and steered him into the AI-computer room.

Jason was sitting and watching as the e-screen quickly scrolled through a long list of quantum-encrypted folders whose separated quantum-coupled data had now joined together as one viewable data set.

"This is a long list, but I want to mentally scan it for anything else interesting before accessing the '*T-Program*' subfolder," Jason said as he saw the anticipated look of fear arise in Gregory's eyes.

Gregory replied, "You'll never stop us. We're too powerful."

Jason answered, "Power makes truth, but sometimes the truth is more powerful. I think with the data we've already gathered and what we're about to find, we'll have plenty of evidence to arrest *all* your accomplices."

"You never get away with this alive. They'll hunt you down."

"I've already gotten away with it. You'll see afterward," Jason confidently replied and smiled as the folder list finally scrolled to the letter '*T*'. He pressed the scroll key to disable the scroll function and then selected the '*T-Program*' subfolder. The folder opened up into a new e-screen window in front of them.

Jason saw a small folder that was a directory of T-program files and sub-folders. He entered the directory and saw a shortlist of file shortcuts. He picked the first one he saw and opened the file. "I see this is an alphabetical list of Exgenics shareholders by last name and shows the dates they purchased shares, their contact info, and birth dates." He quickly scrolled down the list and saw Gerardo's and Gregory's names among the '*G*' listings. "Nice to know you're fully involved in this conspiracy Gregory. Oh, I see you're 76 years old now. Looks like you won't be getting that retirement e-watch while awaiting execution," he joked.

Jason opened another file, "Ah, I see this is a Gerardo's business calendar and meeting schedule." He scrolled through the past few months and saw scheduled board meetings and a few individual meetings with Exgenics shareholders at the farm. "Well, it's nice these shareholders get farm tours and know what's going on here. That will prove their guilt."

He next scrolled through the upcoming months and saw more individual meetings planned at the farm. The farther in the future, the more frequent the individual meetings became until there were nearly three meetings per day. "Looks like Gerardo is planning lots of shareholder farm tours soon," he commented. He finally spotted a meeting with Gregory next year. "Now Gregory, why do *you* need a meeting with Gerardo?" he asked his prisoner. "I don't think it's for a performance appraisal with the HR department," he joked.

"I have the right to remain silent," he replied as beads of sweat began pouring down his forehead.

"As you wish," Jason replied, "We'll find out everything else soon enough anyway without your help."

Jason next opened a file with another schedule, and they all saw, on the calendar for the next two weeks, dates of shipments from Fort Detrick to All-Nippon Robotics and Drone-Motion facilities all over the world. "Looks like your conspiracy is fully revealed now, Gregory."

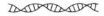

Chapter 32: The Master Code

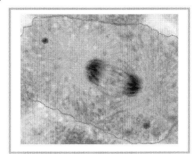

Fish Cell during Mitosis

5:45 a.m., Sunday, July 4, ….

Jason next opened a folder named *'Shareholder Genomics.'* Inside, he found an alphabetical list of subfolders titled with the shareholder's name. "Why does Gerardo care about shareholder genetics?" he questioned.

Doc interjected, "Perhaps they're selectively marrying among themselves to improve genetic characteristics like intelligence or beauty. In animal husbandry, we breed better stock to improve the herd. This improves farm productivity whether it's meat, eggs, or wool."

Nick added, "That's what elites have done for hundreds of years. Back in the early 20th Century, they even started a eugenics movement to improve the human race. Of course, the elites only wanted themselves to become truly superior to normal people. They already were superior in power and wealth, but not mentally, physically, or morally."

"Let's look at your folder first Gregory," Jason said typing in a search box and a folder soon opened with three genetic files. The files were named *'Gregory-John.dna'*, *'Gregory-John.fna'*, and *'Gregory-John.gmp'*.

Jason clicked on the *'.gmp'* file and the multi-colored genome and chromosome karyotype map appeared. "Julie, does this look normal?"

Julie replied, "It looks like other human karyotypes I've seen. See there are 23 pairs of chromosomes and the color map seems okay. Oh, wait a second here," she said pointing toward the e-screen. "This chromosome looks *fatter* than the others," she joked and everyone laughed at Gregory, who was further humiliated and humbled.

"So, you're planning to breed with someone to preserve your DNA for some sort of master race?" Jason questioned his prisoner.

"I'm not saying anything," Gregory replied.

"No problem, but fat people likely won't fit well in the shareholder's future plans," Jason chuckled. "We'll understand this conspiracy

gcgaacgcgatggcgtaagcgatggcgaacgcgccgctggcgaacgcgtgcgcgaacgcgctgccggcgaacgcgatggcgtaagcgatggcgaacgcg

eventually, so no need to answer. Let's look at Gerardo next," Jason calmly commented as he typed *'Gerardo'* in the search box.

Two genome folders popped up, one for Ernesto Gerardo and the other for Marianna Gerardo. "Looks like Gerardo's wife is involved too. I know they never had children, so perhaps they plan on developing an embryo to implant in a surrogate mother?" Jason asked.

Gregory stood stoically silent and stone-faced watching the e-screen.

"Let's take a peek at Gerardo's genetics files," Jason said as he clicked to open the folder. On the e-screen, he saw a list of files and a sub-folder without a name. The files were named, *'Gerardo-Ernesto.dna'*, *'Gerardo-Ernesto.fna'*, and *'Gerardo-Ernesto.gmp'*. He opened the *'.gmp'* file and asked Julie, "Does this genome map look normal?"

Julie carefully examined the genomic map and said, "Yes, but I think Chromosome 11 is too short and Chromosome 20 has a big nose," she chuckled and they laughed again except Gregory who was beet red in anger at them making fun of his boss's features.

"Let's see what's in this unnamed subfolder," Jason said as he clicked.

A list of files popped up and suddenly, the AI-control room door opened and Dante and Inferno entered the room followed by Gerardo who loudly blurted out, "Checkmate Jason! Give me that e-vid podcam and get your hands off that touch-pad," as he held his poison dart gun pointed toward them all and commanded the dogs to attack position.

Everyone from Charles County froze, but poor Rufus growled and immediately attacked the menacing dogs. He was no match though for the two young dogs, and Dante and Inferno soon had Rufus in a chokehold but didn't kill the now-submissive old dog. The dogs just remained motionless, with Rufus's throat held tightly in Dante's jaws, awaiting their master's command.

Gerardo ordered Doc, "Drop that gun to the floor and kick it away from you." Doc dropped his gun, kicked it, and Gerardo continued, "I knew we were right terminating your vet contract at our farm."

Jason replied while looking at the list of genetic files he saw on the e-screen, "We know *everything* now Gerardo. You should surrender peacefully. We have a search *and* arrest warrant."

"Surrender to you? You're a lawman now?" Gerardo laughed. "They told me about you. I'm not going to let some snot-nosed computer hacker that likes fishing ruin our plans. I see you're studying genetics too," he commented at the e-screen displaying in front of Jason.

"I'm a Charles County Sheriff Deputy now and you're under arrest. The rest of us are coming here and you'll be surrounded soon."

catgcgccgccgtattaaattcgcacccatgatgcgtatgcgatggaacgcatttgcgcgcatgcgccgccgtattaaattcgcacccatgatgcgtat

Gerardo replied "I don't think so. We captured your chess partner, Sheriff Coleman, and are keeping him at the guardhouse. If anyone else is coming to rescue you, they won't have a chance at our front gate. Our men and security drone squadrons have enough firepower to stop an *army*," he joked confidently, stepping toward Jason to grab his handgun.

Gerardo slipped on Rufus's slobber puddle and reached forward with his right hand to steady himself on the table. Jason took this chance and quickly grabbed the sheriff's Berretta, but it was too late. Gerardo had recovered his balance and held his dart gun to Jason's neck.

"Nice try Jason," Gerardo said as he pulled the handgun from Jason's grip with his right hand and then began slightly waving his dart gun around in his left hand, "Well, now I have your gun *and* this nice TTX dart gun too," he said pointing the handgun at Jason and lowering his dart gun.

"Uncuff Gregory now or I shoot her," Gerardo said as he aimed the dart gun directly toward Julie. "Is this your girlfriend?" Gerardo asked with an evil smile and wink. He looked further at the young woman and saw the three diamond engagement rings on her finger. "Ah, I see now, she's your fiancée or perhaps your wife. Trying to breed and make some little hackers aren't we now?" he evilly insinuated.

"We've captured her parents too in case we needed more leverage. They're at our guardhouse too. She's a beautiful pearl with apparent intelligence and good genetics. Oh well, Darwin has to suffer some losses sometimes," he said moving closer to Julie and pointing the dart gun directly at the carotid artery in her neck.

"We surrender," Jason said, slowly raising his hands while still seated.

"Now release Gregory from his handcuffs. No sudden moves either." Gerardo commanded them all.

"I've got the key," Jason replied as he pulled it out of his pocket, slowly stood up, walked toward Gregory, and unlocked the handcuffs.

Gerardo then gave Jason's pistol to Gregory. "Use this gun anytime you want like you did on that old couple," he grimly winked.

The attorney held the pistol, pointing it at Nick, "You've betrayed us."

"No, you've betrayed God," Nick replied.

As Gregory raised the gun toward Nick's head, Gerardo commanded, "Stop. Let's deal with him later. I don't want his brains all over the room," overriding the lawyer's anger to immediately kill the old man.

Gregory then replied to Gerardo, "You smell terrible Ernesto."

Gerardo replied, "You smell like shit too, John," and immediately refocusing his attention toward Jason and spoke, "Jason, I think I could use someone like you with hacking, code-breaking skills, and apparently genetic knowledge. There's something I've been trying to analyze without luck and my AI-computer has reached a dead end."

"I won't help you, Gerardo," Jason replied.

"I thought so, but in exchange for your help, I'll do you a favor. Your grandfather is still alive and I can save him if you do as I ask. I'll even cure the brain cancer we found."

"No, he's dead. Your mercenaries killed him. When he said goodbye, he intended to use those shotguns until the end. He sacrificed himself so we could escape."

Gerardo replied, "No Jason, he's just barely alive. He was asking for you earlier, Jason. He wants to tell you something before he dies," as he taunted the young man with lies. "He's a tough old bird and killed two of our men at your house, but was severely wounded. However, he'll likely die soon without more medical help than our robodoc can handle. I can save him if you help me though. As a bonus, I'll even be generous and free your fiancée and her parents too," he lied.

"What do you need me to do?" Jason replied in full capitulation with the false hope of saving Julie, her parents, and Grandpa. Deep down, he knew Gerardo couldn't be trusted, but for now, he'd have to go along with him while seeking a way for them all to escape.

"Well boy, you need to crack the centromere code and how the centromeres interact with centrosomes during cell division and mitosis.[92] Every chromosome of every living thing has a centromere where a chromosome pair joins and then splits during mitosis. Normally in the cell nucleus, chromosome DNA strands are like tangled flexible 'noodles' of spaghetti. However, when cells start dividing, the DNA helixes coil up tightly, like an over-twisted rubber band, forming compact chromosomes with each matching chromosomal pair joined at a centromere."

"After that happens, protein fibers growing from two centrosomes, at opposite sides of the cell, link with the centromeres of all the chromosomes. Next, the chromosomes line up like two parallel trains inside what used to be the cell's nucleus. Then the centrosome fibers contract, pulling on the centromeres of each chromosome pair so the chromosomes separate. Finally, the two chromosome sets are pulled

---

[92] A centrosome is a proteinaceous cellular organelle involved in the process of cell division. Before cell division, the centrosome duplicates and then, as division begins, the two centrosomes move to opposite ends of the cell. Next, proteins called microtubules assemble into a spindle between the two centrosomes and help separate the replicated chromosomes into the daughter cells of the original cell.

toward opposite sides of the cell and the cell divides into two daughter cells. This is how cellular life grows. It's the secret of life itself."

"We ran the AI-protocol to convert the centromere's DNA sequence to a '.ckt' file but I still can't interpret the results. We know it's like a master control that initiates cell mitosis and communicates somehow with the centrosomes to cause cell division, but that's all we understand. However, if I can figure out how this process truly works, the full mystery of life will fully be revealed to science. That's why I need your help."

5:53 a.m. Sunday, July 4, ...

Sheriff Coleman waited in Jeffrey's old patrol car on U.S. 60 just west of Provident Forge by the Exgenics farm entrance. The car was crowded to capacity with five hunt club members carrying semi-automatic shotguns. "OK boys, it's time," Coleman said as he turned on the ignition and drove up the driveway toward the front gate and security guardhouse. As he stopped just twenty yards away from the locked gate, he turned on the flashing blue lights and stepped out of the car with the rest of his party, shotguns in hand.

A security guard on watch stepped outside the guardhouse and pointed an automatic sub-machine gun at the sheriff, who was now standing tall in his old army uniform. Over his uniform, Coleman wore a Level IV body armor chest rig with his sheriff's badge proudly affixed on front.[93]

"Hold it a minute," Coleman shouted out as he took a white handkerchief from his pocket and waved it in the air. "Let's talk." He laid his shotgun on the patrol car's hood and slowly walked toward the security guard while the hunt club members stood outside the patrol car watchfully holding their shotguns pointed upward to not alarm the guard.

As he neared the guard, the sheriff spoke loudly and pulled two envelopes from behind his back, "I have two legal warrants here I am serving today. One is an arrest warrant for John Gregory for murder in the first degree of Captain Jack Thompson and his wife Macy Evans Thomson. The second is a complete search warrant of the Exgenics Farm to search for additional evidence of multiple murders and a criminal conspiracy we believe is centered here. Will you put down your weapon and comply with my lawful orders? I promise you'll be treated fairly by the laws of the Commonwealth of Virginia if you're implicated in any of the crimes committed here. What are your intentions?"

---

[93] Ceramic Level IV body armor can stop most pistol rounds and a limited number rounds of high-powered rifle ammunition.

gcgaacgcgatggcgtaagcgatggcgaacgcgccgctggcgaacgcgtgcgcgaacgcgctgccggcgaacgcgatggcgtaagcgatggcgaacgcg

The lone guard remained silent and soon about twenty-five other well-armed mercenaries and a few security guards, protected by Level V body armor, poured out the guardhouse's side and rear doors. Some took positions on both sides behind the building while a few stood behind the first guard by the gate. Within seconds, a swarm of at least 100 security drones whirred upward and flew above the guardhouse in tight formation, hovering in a buzzing swarm 60 feet in the air.

"What's it going to be then?" the sheriff asked loudly above the whirring noise of the drones.

"We don't recognize your authority here or your warrants. This is Exgenics private property," the lead guard standing behind the first guard loudly replied.

"Fine. Will you honor my white flag while I return to my party?" Coleman shouted back.

"Yes." The lead guard shouted back, "I used to be in the military myself until I was in prison, so I'll be fair and let you get back to your car. You're outnumbered and we'll kill you all."

"So be it then," Coleman replied resolutely. He slowly walked back toward the patrol car while continuing to wave his handkerchief and keeping a keen eye on the scene. As he got closer to the car, he spoke softly to the five hunt club members now standing behind the car, "Those drone darts aren't accurate beyond shotgun range, so shoot any drones like they were geese up to the limits of your range. We need to pepper the sky." He next loudly yelled, "FIRE!!!" as he dropped his handkerchief, grabbed his shotgun, and ducked for cover behind Jeffrey's patrol car.

At this signal, the Charles County Historical Museum's old 'A' gauge punt-gun, with its 10-foot-long barrel more closely resembling a small cannon, blasted at least 50 drones in the swarm out of the sky with its first shot. Jeffrey's team of hunt club members hiding in the woods on the right flank began firing shotguns, hunting rifles, and semi-automatic rifles at will. As Jeffrey reloaded the punt gun, the sheriff and hunt club members used the patrol car as a shield while machine-gun bullets peppered the front of the vehicle.[94]

They aimed upward shooting any drones like waterfowl that came within range. Two drones dove low in front of the car, briefly hovered, and approached the car's rear from either side. Buddy Peters shot one at

---

[94] An 'A' gauge punt gun has a bore diameter of 2 inches and weighs about 130 pounds unloaded. It fired about 2 pounds of lead shot using about 1 pound of gunpowder. The muzzle-loading gun was fired with a spring-loaded hammer that hit a percussion cap. Most large punt guns were custom, one-of-a kind gunsmith designs.

catgcgccgccgtattaaattcgcacccatgatgcgtatgcgatggaacgcatttgcgcgcatgcgccgccgtattaaattcgcacccatgatgcgtat

point-blank range, but before the sheriff blasted the other, it released an automatic volley that turned the front of his armor into a pincushion. Fortunately, no darts penetrated, but a stray needle dart hit Jay Tyler in the neck and he soon collapsed from the TTX-poison tip.

The Chickahominy Indians suddenly emerged from the swampy woods on the left flank and began yelling their war cry. They were well covered with mud, which confused the drones' infrared imagers, as the Indians opened fire at close range with their shotguns. John Yadkin, the Chief's brave, and courageous son who led their assault, was hit by a dart, and soon fell dead. Drones dropped from the sky like rain and several surprised mercenaries collapsed from well-aimed .30-06 bullets to their heads, since the Chick people were excellent deer hunters.

The hunt club members concealed in the woods with Jeffrey continued shooting shotguns at individual drones. Others used hunting rifles like snipers and were shielded by the tree trunks from the incoming spray of bullets. They began picking off the now fully confused mercenaries and guards one by one as they were assaulted from nearly every direction

For several minutes, it was a confusing aerial-ground and ground-ground melee making targeting difficult, but the punt gun gave a final blast in the air hitting seven more drones at once. The Law Enforcement Team from Kent County team then ran down the Exgenics driveway toward the guardhouse after crossing Old Forge Lake on the pallet bridge and began firing at the rear of the remaining mercenaries. As the last drones were shot out of the sky, the few remaining mercenaries and security guards dropped their guns and raised their hands to surrender.[95]

Sheriff Coleman shouted "Cease fire!" and held his right arm and clenched fist upward as a visual signal for everyone to stop. He walked toward and among the enemy survivors and looked the lead guard in the eye and said, "Looks like you've never seen a punt gun or studied the battle tactics of Robert E. Lee at Chancellorsville. That's what happens when you erase history and inconvenient truths from the worldpedia.grid files."

The ignorant guard, the young adult product of a public education system dumbed down over the years to brainwashing, replied, "Where's Chancellorsville?"

"Virginia you idiot," the sheriff replied knowing that even the name of the town, where a Civil War battle was fought, had been erased.

---

[95] By the end the Battle of Provident Forge, 144 security drones (twelve squadrons) were shot down, seventeen mercenaries and security guards were killed, while only three Sandy Point Hunt Club members and two Chickahominy Indians died. There were no wounded, as all wounds inflicted by bullets or TTX needle-dart projectiles were fatal.

6:15 a.m., Sunday, July 4, ...

While Gerardo watched from behind with dart gun in hand, Jason examined the raw centromere DNA sequence as it scrolled before him. He saw the *'a'*, *'c'*, *'g'*, and *'t'* letters and observed a repeating pattern to them. He next looked at the FASTA file, confirming his observations. Finally, he looked at the '.ckt' program file created by the AI-computer. He studied it and at first, it seemed jumbled and confusing. Soon, however, colors formed inside his mind, and with a flash of synesthesia insight, he understood the language of the Master Code.

"My God!" Jason exclaimed as he hastily made his life and death decision, pulled the mesh shielding his e-watch, and quickly Z-swiped his finger to activate the Deadman's switch. "It's a message, but it wasn't written for you, Gerardo! Grandpa would want me to defeat you *now*, even at the cost of our lives."

"What did you just do with your e-watch?" Gerardo firmly questioned.

"I sent my e-vid blog and all your data files to the *world*. I control the Grid and *Everyone* will know what you and your investors have been doing here. No one will ever listen to their supposed leaders, who are corrupt and just under the control of people like your investors, again."

"I'm going to kill you now boy. Just so you know, your Grandpa would've lived and been a nice *pet* for you," the doctor sadistically laughed thinking of the next t-dog scheduled to be born today as he started raising the gun toward Jason's head.

Suddenly, the steel door to the AI-computer room burst open and Sheriff Coleman stood with the targeting system of his RXD-520 army battle rifle aimed directly at Gerardo's head, which now glowed with a violet laser dot. "Both of you freeze NOW! No one comes to Charles County gets away with murder and destroying *our* river. You're both under arrest," he said to Gregory and Gerardo. Standing beside him were Deputy James and Deputy Jeffers with pistols drawn.

Dante and Inferno both reacted instantly upon Gerardo's silent command and lunged at Coleman, but the deputies silenced them both permanently with pistol rounds through their hearts. Coleman stood firm and kept his rifle directly pointed at Gerardo.

Gerardo replied, "Just remember this. Death is not an exact science *yet*. Go ahead and shoot," he evilly laughed as he continued raising the dart gun loaded with 400 poison needles toward Jason's neck. His aim was nearly point-blank as he pulled the trigger.

A single shot rang out and multiple sparks flew wildly like tentacles as a small, coherent orb of glowing high-voltage plasma emanated from

Gerardo's head. The sparks immediately dissipated and the plasma rolled like ball lightning toward the AI-computer's memory core, where it dissipated as Gerardo's lifeless body collapsed.

"Entropy's a bitch, doctor," Jason proclaimed looking at the trans-man's crumpled body on the tile floor.

"Now that's what you do when you confront evil, Jason," Coleman commented as he walked toward John Gregory, who was now whimpering like a baby elephant seal, and handcuffed his wrists again. "Well, it looks like we have this wrapped up now," he concluded.

Just then, they all heard a beep from Gerardo's pocket. Coleman reached down and pulled out Gerardo's e-phone. The screen showed a timer that read 8 minutes 47 seconds counting toward zero.

Julie added, "Hey, a light turned red on the control panel." Next to the light, a timer display matched the e-phone timer's countdown.

"What does that label by the light say?" Jason asked.

Julie added, "Hey, a light turned red on the control panel." Next to the light, a timer display matched the e-phone timer's countdown.

"What does that label by the light say?" Jason asked.

"Incinerator gas pressure warning," Julie replied.

Coleman replied, "Gerardo's activated an autodestruct sequence. It must have been set for ten minutes and we just wasted time figuring it out. Jason, can you hack the incinerator system to shut it down?"

"I can't guarantee I can do it in time. We have to find Grandpa fast and get out of here!" Jason exclaimed.

Nick replied, "Jason, the medical annex is the last door on the left. I've got to save the fish! They're an innocent, intelligent lifeform."

The countdown timer on Gerardo's e-phone beeped at eight-minutes.

"I'll save the cows," Doc added since they were also innocent of any of Exgenics' crimes. "I'll abort all the t-dogs later since they're an abomination to God and nature."

Coleman summarized their plan of action, "Jeffrey and I will help you find Grandpa, Jason. Jeffers and Julie, help Doc in the barn herd the cows out. Nick, can you save the fish by yourself?"

"Yes, I have an idea," Nick replied.

"What about me? Gregory whimpered.

"You can stay here to die or run outside, like the coward you are, to Sheriff Olsen. Do what you want for all I care. I'm sure you'll like prison until your execution. They like fat men there a *lot*."

Coleman summarized, "OK Everyone, let's go! We've got only seven minutes to get out of here to safety!"

Gerardo's countdown timer beeped seven-minutes as everyone immediately ran out of the AI-computer room and split into their rescue teams. Gregory followed last and ran to the nearest emergency exit. He opened the door and in the Exgenics parking lot, Sheriff Olsen was standing there with a handgun in his right hand while other citizen deputies and militia trained their rifle sites on the man.

Olsen commanded, "Hold your fire. Grab him and bring him to me."

Two men immediately grabbed the handcuffed man and took him to Olsen. "You're a fine example of a Harvard man. What a selfish, elitist fat bastard you are. Nice to see you in handcuffs where you and your kind belong. I'm sure there's more of you deeply involved in these crimes."

ᴆᴀᴄᴑᴘᴥᴑᴅᴀᴄᴑᴘᴥᴇ

Doc ran down the hallway toward the barn while Jeffers and Julie followed. They reached the cow pens and started opening the metal gates. One-by-one, they coaxed the cows into the main aisle, which became clogged by the small herd. The time was passing quickly. Doc opened the barn door, but the herd stood in the aisle and didn't move. "Times almost up. We have to coax them out NOW!" he shouted to Julie and Jeffers at the other end of the aisle.

"I'll take care of it," Jeffers replied and shot several pistol rounds into the ceiling. The cows soon stampeded out the barn door. Jeffers and Julie followed down the aisle and they ran to safety in the building's parking lot.

ᴆᴀᴄᴑᴘᴥᴑᴅᴀᴄᴑᴘᴥᴇ

Nick entered the building's warehouse and found the large robolift normally used for loading and unloading autotruck shipments. He stood on the robotlift's small rear pedestal only used when in manual mode. He pressed the *'On'* button, turned another switch to *'Manual'*, and placed a hand on the joystick. He moved his hand forward and the robolift responded. He steered it out the warehouse door into the research building's main aisle. As he drove forward, he thought to himself, "I can't save them all, but I'll save as many as I can. Bog will understand."[96]

He reached the large T-fish aquaculture room, opened the door, and drove inside. He closed the door behind him and steered down a side aisle to the back of the tank's. When he reached the rear corner, he turned the lift around, pulled a lever, and the lift's forks raised. He then pressed the fork control joystick forward and the two forks pierced the clear plastic sides of the large aquaculture tank. Water began slowly leaking where he pierced. He next moved the movement control joystick to the left, and

---

[96] Бог, Transliterated Russian word for God

the robolift moved sideways, its forks slicing the clear plastic of the tank like butter. As the robolift moved, water starting pouring out faster and faster and by the time Nick reached the other end of the tank, water began filling the sealed room.

He then rotated the fork's joystick, turning the robolift around, and pushed the motion control joystick full forward. The robolift rammed full speed into the thin metal siding of the building and drove outside into the morning light as a rush of water and fish followed. He saw a fire hydrant about 50 feet to the left, drove the forklift there, and knocked it over. Water began shooting under the robolift as he stopped and ran from the scene toward safety. The fish-filled waters flowed downhill toward the farm pond.

⋈⋈⋈⋈⋈

Jason, Coleman, and Jeffrey reached the medical annex and opened the door leading to a short hallway with four doors. As Gerardo's e-phone beeped at five minutes in Coleman's hand, he said, "We're short on time. Everyone, quick open a different door."

Jeffrey opened the first door on the left and saw a typical infirmary examination room with a chair, some medical cabinets, and an exam table. He yelled out, "This is the infirmary!"

Coleman opened the first door on the right and called out, "This is the supply room!" as he saw shelves of medical supplies and drug bottles.

Jason ran down the hall and opened the door to the next room on the right. He saw a recently used operating table and a robodoc standing in the corner like a mechanical octopus with its multiple surgical arms. "This is the operating room. It's been used recently," he said with hope that Grandpa was alive.

They all reached the final door at the same time and Coleman opened the latch. Inside, they saw two curtains drawn around hospital beds for patients. Coleman opened the curtain to the left first and on the hospital bed, they saw an old man with gray hair and wrinkles on his face. There were electrodes connected to his head and a heart monitor. The heart monitor was beating normally but the brain monitor showed a series of straight horizontal lines. Jason commented, "That's Gerardo! He's Catholic and couldn't kill his brain-dead body."

Jeffrey pulled back the curtain on the other hospital bed. The patient there was Grandpa. He had similar monitors, but the heart monitor was beating very slowly with the entire screen flashing red with each weak beat, but the cerebral monitor still showed multiple squiggly lines of brain activity. A plastic IV bag on a stand, supplying blood into his arm, was

gcgaacgcgatggcgtaagcgatggcgaacgcgccgctggcgaacgcgtgcgcgaacgcgctgccggcgaacgcgatggcgtaagcgatggcgaacgcg

almost empty. An oxygen mask covered his face and was supplied by a large tank on the wall.

Jason cried out, "Let's grab him and get out of here. There's a wheeled gurney in the operating room!"

The timer on Gerardo's phone beeped at four minutes.

As Jason stood a few moments watching Grandpa, Coleman and Jeffrey raced out of the room and soon returned with the gurney. Together, they quickly but carefully lifted Grandpa onto the gurney with his IV bag and Coleman shouted, "Let's strap him down and escape before this place blows."

The phone beeped three minutes.

As they strapped Grandpa to hold him in the gurney, Jeffrey said, "What do we do about old Gerardo?"

Jason replied, "Let his body join his mind in Hell!"

Jason and Coleman pushed the gurney hard to gain momentum out of the room while Jeffery opened the door ahead of them. As they steered and wheeled down the hallways of the building, Jeffrey ran ahead to open the doors as Jason and Coleman followed.

They wheeled grandpa's stretcher outside to the far side of the farm's parking lot and Robin Graves ran to it.

Gerardo's e-phone beeped at two minutes.

She pulled out Grandpa's left wrist and checked for a pulse, "It's weak." She next took her grandfather's stethoscope and pressed it to his heart, "His heartbeat is also. I need oxygen and an O-type blood unit fast!" Robin said to the volunteer medic who had just brought an oxygen cylinder. She was about to put the oxygen mask on him and she listened further but his heart had stopped.

She now realized he was dying in front of her and nothing could stop his imminent demise. "Jason," she whispered, "There's one thing left I can do. It'll give him a brief moment with you. Come closer." She reached into her bag for a prefilled syringe she'd used before only in the direst emergencies. She quickly pulled out an EPI syringe with a stout needle and carefully pushed it between two ribs into the heart muscle.[97]

The adrenaline rush gave Grandpa a few last breathes and beats and was soon brought to consciousness for a minute. He whispered to Jason who was now leaning close with his head near Grandpa's face and wide-open eyes. "I knew the river would bring me back to you a last time," Grandpa weakly whispered as he solemnly thanked God for a chance to

---

[97] Epinephrine syringe filled with adrenaline solution

catgcgccgccgtattaaattcgcacccatgatgcgtatgcgatggaacgcatttgcgcgcatgcgccgccgtattaaattcgcacccatgatgcgtat

see his Grandson again before he died. "I was dreaming of Kimberly, John, and Sarah," Grandpa peacefully remarked.

The e-phone in Coleman's pocket beeped at one minute.

"We rescued you. Don't die Grandpa. We love you," Jason quickly replied while fighting tears welling up inside him.

Grandpa gave a final smile and softly spoke, "Jason, use your head and heart equally. Learn all things and be all you can. You can achieve greatness. I'm proud of you. Put me with Sarah. I see her now...," whispering his last word. His eyes closed, exhaled, and the lines on his face relaxed after a long, and now fully-purposeful life. Doctor Graves felt for a pulse and there was none. The entropy of the universe finally had taken him from this world.

The e-phone in Coleman's pocket evilly laughed when the timer reached zero as the morning sun broke through the trailing clouds of the storm they'd just passed through.

The fireworks that Fourth of July included a great mourning illumination and bonfire as the entire Exgenics facility exploded in a ball of flame and a fiery mushroom cloud of smoke ascended into the heavens. The old wooden dairy barn burned to the ground.

gcgaacgcgatggcgtaagcgatggcgaacgcgccgctggcgaacgcgtgcgcgaacgcgctgccggcgaacgcgatggcgtaagcgatggcgaacgcg

```
>RUN CRICKETT SUBROUTINE'CENTROMERE':

START*START*START*SWITCH*SWITCH*OFF*SWITCH*MASTERMANY*OFF*OF
F*MASTERMANY*CELL*CELL*DIVIDE*MASTERMANY*CONTROL*CELL*DIVIDE
*CONTROL*DIVIDE*LOCK*START*CONTROL*CODE*LOCK*START*CELL*LOCK
*START*CODE*DIVIDE*CODE*CELL*DIVIDE*CELL*DIVIDE*DUPLICATE*ON
*START*DIVIDE*DUPLICATE*DUPLICATE*ON*START*ONECOPY*ONECOPY*S
TART*START*ON*CELL*START*ASSEMBLE*CELL*CODE*ONECOPY*CHAIN*AS
SEMBLE*CODE*START*START*CELL*CHAIN*START*DIVIDE*CELL*START*A
SSEMBLE*CELL*CELL*COPY*CODE*DIVIDE*START*OFF*CHAIN*CELL*STAR
T*START*CELL*MASTERMANY*DIVIDE*EYE*START*COPY*OFF*ALL*CELL*S
TART*CELLMANY*COPY*MASTERMANY*MASTERMANY*OFF*BRAIN*EYE*START
*CODE*ALL*MASTERMANY*ALL*EYE*CELLMANY*CELLMANY*ALL*MASTERMAN
Y*MASTERMANY*CELLMANY*EYE*MASTERMANY*CHECK*BRAIN*BRAIN*CODE*
ALL*CODE*CODE*CELLMANY*ALL*MASTERMANY*CHANGEMANY*EYE*CELLMAN
Y*NO*CHECK*MASTERMANY*CHANGE*CODE*OFF*EYE*CHECK*CHANGEMANY*L
OCK*NO*CODE*CHANGE*CHANGE*CHANGEMANY*OFF*NO*LOCK*LOCK*EQUALS
*CHANGE*CHANGE*LOCK*DEATH*OFF*EQUALS*LOCK*ALL*DEATH*NO*CHANG
E*CHANGE*ALL*NO*MASTERMANY*LOCK*CHANGE*CODE*EQUALS*MASTERMAN
Y*STOP*CODE*DEATH*MASTERMANY*STOP*ALL*CODE*MASTERMANY*OFF*LO
CK*NO*CODE*CHANGE*REPEAT*OFF*SWITCH*LOCK*MASTERMANY*CODE*COD
E*STOP*ON*REPEAT*MASTERMANY*SWITCH*LOCK*CODE*OFF*CODE*STOP*O
N*LOCK*REPEAT*CELL*LOCK*SWITCH*STOP*CODE*ON*DIVIDE*CELL*LOCK
*STOP*DIVIDE*CELL*DIVIDE*START*START*START*LIFE*LIFE*LIFE*LI
FE*LIFE*LIFE*START*START*START*DIVIDE*CELL*DIVIDE*STOP*LOCK*
CELL*DIVIDE*ON*CODE*STOP*SWITCH*LOCK*CELL*REPEAT*LOCK*STOP*C
ODE*OFF*CODE*LOCK*SWITCH*MASTERMANY*REPEAT*ON*STOP*CODE*CODE
*MASTERMANY*LOCK*SWITCH*OFF*REPEAT*CHANGE*CODE*NO*LOCK*OFF*M
ASTERMANY*CODE*ALL*STOP*MASTERMANY*DEATH*CODE*STOP*MASTERMAN
Y*EQUALS*CODE*CHANGE*LOCK*MASTERMANY*NO*ALL*CHANGE*CHANGE*NO
*DEATH*ALL*LOCK*EQUALS*OFF*DEATH*LOCK*CHANGE*CHANGE*EQUALS*L
OCK*LOCK*NO*OFF*CHANGEMANY*CHANGE*CHANGE*CODE*NO*LOCK*CHANGE
MANY*CHECK*EYE*OFF*CODE*CHANGE*MASTERMANY*CHECK*NO*CELLMANY*
EYE*CHANGEMANY*MASTERMANY*ALL*CELLMANY*CODE*CODE*ALL*CODE*BR
AIN*BRAIN*CHECK*MASTERMANY*EYE*CELLMANY*MASTERMANY*MASTERMAN
Y*ALL*CELLMANY*CELLMANY*EYE*ALL*MASTERMANY*ALL*CODE*START*EY
E*BRAIN*OFF*MASTERMANY*MASTERMANY*COPY*CELLMANY*START*CELL*A
LL*OFF*COPY*START*EYE*DIVIDE*MASTERMANY*CELL*START*START*CEL
L*CHAIN*OFF*START*DIVIDE*CODE*COPY*CELL*CELL*ASSEMBLE*START*
CELL*DIVIDE*START*CHAIN*CELL*START*START*CODE*ASSEMBLE*CHAIN
*ONECOPY*CODE*CODE*CELL*ASSEMBLE*START*CELL*ON*START*START*O
NECOPY*ONECOPY*START*ON*DUPLICATE*DUPLICATE*DIVIDE*START*ON*
DUPLICATE*DIVIDE*CELL*DIVIDE*CELL*CODE*DIVIDE*CODE*START*LOC
K*CELL*START*LOCK*CODE*CONTROL*START*LOCK*DIVIDE*CONTROL*DIV
IDE*CELL*CONTROL*MASTERMANY*DIVIDE*CELL*CELL*MASTERMANY*OFF*
OFF*MASTERMANY*SWITCH*OFF*SWITCH*SWITCH*START*START*START

>END CRICKETT SUBROUTINE 'CENTROMERE'.
```

The Master Code (Chromosome-7, Metacentric Centromere.ckt Language)

catgcgccgccgtattaaattcgcacccatgatgcgtatgcgatggaacgcatttgcgcgcatgcgccgccgtattaaattcgcacccatgatgcgtat

Chapter 33: A Last Sermon

Tombstone of Mr. Graves

9:30 a.m., Sunday, July 4, ….

Since the Charles County Sheriff's Department had run out of functioning vehicles, Sheriff Coleman drove the Captain's old pickup truck to Charlestown and parked at the sheriff's office adjacent to the courthouse. He climbed out of the truck to call Judge Saunders and tell her what happened this morning. He picked up the phone and dialed.

"Hello, Judge. We were successful but lost some good people. I fear this is just the beginning of a long struggle."

"Yes, I know George. The people are stronger than you realize. So have faith it will work out."

"You're right. Our community *is* strong. Please come to Pleasant Hill Baptist Church this morning. I think the sermon today will be inspiring."

"OK, George, I'll see you there."

He hung up the phone and headed home to change for church. He looked at the American flag blowing in the breeze on a pole in front of the courthouse. He was disgusted at the crimson banner with 54 yellow stars, pulled it down, and lit it on fire in the grass.

10:30 a.m., Sunday, July 4, ….

Robin was standing in a beautiful summery dress and holding hands with Jeffrey outside Pleasant Hill Baptist Church. They walked toward the graveyard and she soon saw the names of her great-ancestors, Mr. Richard M. Graves and his wife Jane, who were interred side-by-side with elegant tombstones lovingly engraved and chiseled out by a local freedman stonemason. She stood for a moment in her silence and read the words on her ancestor's tombstone with its hand pointing upward toward heaven, '*Richard M. Graves. A christian without ostentation, a man of such judgement and character to make him a most valuable citizen. He filled with fidelity all of the important trusts confided to him and his monument is erected in the hearts of the people of this community.'* She next looked at the tombstone of his wife and further paused, silently acknowledging her too.

"Let's go inside now. The sheriff saved two seats for us," Jeffery said wearing his best Sunday suit in the sweltering morning sun.

Although Jason's Gridlock still prevented autocars from operating, the residents of Charles County muddled through by carpooling in older vehicles or attending the closest church possible, as was normally done by foot, horse, or buggy before the automobile was invented. The Pleasant Hill Baptist Church sanctuary was filled that morning and there was even a small crowd outside the two sets of front doors, which had been propped open so everyone could hear the service.

Without electrical power after the storm, all windows that could be raised were opened to lessen the heat of the assembled crowd. The congregations of Pleasant Hill and Mount Carmel Baptist Churches sat near the front plus extra guests from the Charles County Grapevine sat in the rear and on the rarely used slave balcony predating the Civil War.

Julie was in the right front pew, sitting to Jason's left, and was lovingly holding his grieving hand. To Jason's right, Sheriff Coleman sat in his full-dress U.S. Army sergeant's uniform with his medals and campaign bars neatly pinned to his jacket. His left arm was wrapped over Jason's shoulder to comfort him. Robin and Jeffrey soon sat down in two empty spaces next to the sheriff.

To their right was Doc, who was scratching Rufus behind an ear, and his wife Susan. Seated next to him were Elvira and Nick. Nick even took off his yamaka out of respect for the Reverend Dickson. Finally, sitting on the end of the pew was Johnnie Walker, wearing a nice white shirt with a tie, but the knot on his forehead and hangover were still pounding.

The combined choir next walked in the side door to the left and took their seats behind the pastor's podium and in front of the Baptismal tank window. Mr. Taylor, the organist, shuffled in and sat down at the electric organ, which luckily was powered by a small solar intensifier system outside and an extension cord. Finally, Reverend Morrow walked in the right door and sat in front of the assembly in a chair near the podium.

Mr. Taylor opened a folder and took out a copy of old sheet music that had belonged to Reverend Dickson's guitar-playing father when he was young. At the same time the choir pulled out newer copies of the same music and Olivia stepped out in front as the lead vocalist. Mr. Taylor placed the music on the organ shelf and started playing "The River Hymn" by the Band from many years ago. On cue, Olivia, with the choir softly joining in, sang with the music the following words with feeling and emotion:

"The ladies would put the baskets on the table
And the men would sit beneath a shady tree…
The river got no end, just roll around the bend
Then pretty soon the women would all join in
On the river hymn.

The whole congregation was standing on the banks of the river
We are gathered here to give a little thanks…
…towards the sea it creeps
I'm so glad I brought along my mandolin
To play the river hymn.

You can ride on it or drink it
Poison it or dam it
Fish in it . . .
… and you can die in it
Run, you river, run…

No crystal mirror can show it clear, . . .
Son, you ain't never eased yourself
'Til you laid it down in a river bed
If you hear a lonesome drone, it's as common as a stone
And gets louder as the day grows dim
That's the river hymn.

The whole congregation was standing on the banks of the river
We are gathered here to give a little thanks…"

As the song ended, Olivia and the rest of the choir sat down and the Reverend Morrow rose from his chair to stand at the podium in front of the altar. "Thank you, Olivia and our combined choir, for that lovely hymn. I know it was one of Reverend Dickson's favorite songs and know now confidently that the river of his life has joined with the sea of God and I give my thanks to him today. Yes, I'm saddened to tell y'all that what you've likely heard from the Grapevine is true.

The Reverend Timothy Dickson is dead. He was shot by Exgenics Corporation, a company privately owned by the richest people in the world. In our battle at Exgenics Farm this morning, we also lost two Chick

Tribe members, including the Chief's son John Yadkin, and also several hunt club members, including Jay Tyler. We mourn them all."

Some in the crowded assembly gasped, as they'd not heard all the news.

Reverend Morrow continued, "We are here on Independence Day to honor their sacrifices and, today, we begin the process of restoring our Nation to what was written in our original Constitution and our Declaration of Independence which was signed on this very day more than 250 years ago. We believe the current martial law is being used to hide what happened along the Chick the past 10 days and conceal a conspiracy so great that it shakes the very foundations of our nation and world."

Reverend Morrow continued, "I'm here to give Reverend Dickson's final sermon. He wanted our two parishes to join as one since we are much stronger together than if divided as our Nation has been for so many years. In deference and respect for the Reverend Dickson's traditional sermon style, I'll do my best to honor him, but I'm reading the words of his sermon this morning. I might not say them as he would've, but I'll try my best without my usual emotion, embellishment, flourish, and *soul*," he chuckled and smiled.

The congregations briefly laughed, breaking their immense grief.

"So please forgive me if I break into *my* sermon style by accident. I know Reverend Tim Dickson, my good friend, would've forgiven me, by Christ's example, if he could have been here today. Let me continue."

"The Reverend Dickson and I invited our congregations and representatives from Samaria Baptist and other local churches to be here with us today. All in attendance need to decide if we chart a new course for civilization in Charles County. The other congregations in the County and many in Kent County are also making the same choice today." Let me now begin the words of Reverend Dickson," and he began reading from the printed sermon text...

"Welcome everyone. Today, I'm not giving a traditional sermon and this won't be a traditional service either, so we aren't going to have a Bible reading, offering, or sing hymns. I'll say a prayer at the end though.

Today, we celebrate Independence Day. For most people these days, this day means a long weekend and a holiday from work. However, this day *is* important and should be worshiped by every human as this should be the day that we recognize the gift of Freedom given to us by God. Even Thomas Jefferson, who authored the Declaration of Independence signed on this day so long ago, invoked God with these famous self-evident words of truth: '*...that all men are created equal, that they are endowed by their Creator with certain unalienable Rights, that among these are Life, Liberty and the pursuit of*

Happiness.' We should not take these words lightly or frivolously as they have deep meaning.

What do these words really mean in light of God's gift to us of these Rights? God is giving us this right to freedom, not our government. These rights are inalienable and cannot be taken from us unless we freely give them away or willingly let others take them. God has given us this freedom to choose our own course in life, the freedom to pursue our own happiness as long as it does not oppress others, and the freedom to live as we see fit without interference if we don't disturb others' peace.

These words don't guarantee us long life, or happiness, or true freedom, but instead are goals we should strive for. We are free to pursue our individual dreams as best as our own abilities enable. This does not guarantee everyone will be successful to attain their dreams, but it gives us the opportunity and hope that we can reach them if we set lofty goals and aim for them with our own deeds, actions, and hard work.

Over the more than two centuries since these words were written, have we gained more life, liberty, and happiness? As individuals and as a people, we have made choices that have caused us to lose the freedom that was given to us by God and all the founding fathers, patriots, and soldiers before us, who died fighting for freedom along the way. One president, a long time ago, gave a State of the Union speech about four freedoms: the Freedom of Speech, the Freedom of Worship, the Freedom from Want, and the Freedom from Fear. Since that time, have we gained any of *those* freedoms?

We are afraid to speak our minds and our ideas are censored from the Grid if we don't comply with other's dictates on acceptable speech.

We are allowed to worship, but the people worship money and their wants, while the government desires us to worship them and supposed progress instead of God, and our churches have become just lifeboats instead of steering our society in a better direction.

We still have want and many are dependent on the government for handouts their entire lifetimes. Others struggle, slaving their lives away to make a living, while some live with luxury, and the government takes from all who produce and gives to those who do nothing or own everything.

We still have fear that is placed in our minds by the media, which wants to divide us so those who own them can do what they want, and by the government, who wants us to be afraid of other nations and ourselves, so they can have a powerful security establishment. Even our education system is afraid to let people speak and fears the truth, which is no longer taught in our schools because it might offend someone.

gcgaacgcgatggcgtaagcgatggcgaacgcgccgctggcgaacgcgtgcgcgaacgcgctgccggcgaacgcgatggcgtaagcgatggcgaacgcg

So, I think that president was wrong. I think there's ultimately only one freedom and that is the individual freedom of choice. Every time we make choices for our comfort and safety so we have freedom from want and fear, we lose a bit of our freedom. Every time we choose to automate something, we lose even more freedom. Even Benjamin Franklin, one of our founding fathers who's been almost erased from history, said to paraphrase and adapt his words, 'Those who give up freedom to buy comfort and security, don't deserve freedom, comfort, or security.

As we let this happen, God's gift of freedom eroded, like a torrent slowly washing away the riverbank, and soon, the fertile field of crops we planted to sustain us is gone and our souls have nothing left except slavery. So today, we still have one last freedom: the freedom to make a choice. Perhaps the freedom of choice is a freedom that Thomas Jefferson should have mentioned specifically in that famous parchment he so elegantly penned by quill and ink. Remember that the signers of that famous document made a choice and sacrificed *everything* for the right to freedom.

There are more stars in the night sky than grains of sand on all the beaches of earth and there is the same number of choices. The choices we individually and collectively make add up like these grains of sand but ultimately do they matter in this great universe? Among the multitude of worlds our astronomers have discovered in our galaxy that team with life, we are just an insignificant and arrogant species, but still, we are important in the mind of God. We could all be gone in an instant and the cosmos wouldn't even shrug its shoulders, because God is also on those worlds too, shaping and guiding the life there to praise Him and enjoy the same universal freedom.

God is giving us now the freedom to choose another path for humanity and that our individual choices, when added up among many people working together and not divided, can have true meaning and enduring value. Of course, we individually choose to believe in God or not, but He has given us the freedom in the present to choose this new future, and in His wisdom, He has given us minds to think and learn. He has let us record our history so we can know His past, understand its true meaning, the lessons of morality that He teaches, and make better decisions so we don't repeat other's mistakes or follow the path of evil.

Today, we are faced with two choices. The first choice is for our parishes to join as one. I'll ask you to vote later on this choice. The second choice is whether we live as we have always lived or move forward in a new direction. For our lifetimes, we have lived under the oppression of so-called leaders, whether they be politicians, bankers, lawyers,

catgcgccgccgtattaaattcgcacccatgatgcgtatgcgatggaacgcatttgcgcgcatgcgccgccgtattaaattcgcacccatgatgcgtat

technocrats, bureaucrats, or other elites, and over the years, they have run our society into the ground by dividing us and making the wrong choices supposedly on our behalf.

I remember once seeing a ring on a powerful man. The small Latin words engraved on it were *'Ordo ab Chao'* which means *'Order out of Chaos'*. However, seeing the man's power, I now realize that the powerful have intentionally sown chaos among us so *they* can be the order and control us, so we feel safe and give up our freedoms under their rule.

However, the truth sometimes demands you take action and make sacrifices. You *do* need to choose between right and good versus wrong and evil. You still have this freedom to choose. Real truths like this don't change, but can only be changed when our thirst for knowledge reveals new proofs of the truth. We have seen these new facts at Provident Forge when we uncovered the evil within our midst which strangles *our* world that the people rightly own.

Today we are faced with a choice that life today in this nation has finally given us. We've been given lemons, but remember, life's lemonade can sometimes be sweetened, if you add sugar so it isn't bitter. We're drinking the lemonade today that's been made in a pitcher by others squeezing us for years. Now, it's time for us to add some sugar and sweeten it up so we can drink this lemonade of life as free men and women again.

Sometimes life's choices are like the currents along the lower Chick. You have the freedom to choose and decide whether to float with the tide or swim against it. Some think they are wise in that by doing nothing they can continue to endure what comes, but I think it's best to stand *for* something so valuable as freedom and swim against the current. Let us all resolve to make this choice as we leave this sanctuary today.

Remember most of all, you have the freedom to live and pursue your dreams, but your time on this earth begins with your birth and ends with your death. What you do during that time is yours and doesn't belong to others for them to waste or force their decisions on you. Don't use it frivolously but instead use it wisely for the betterment of your fellow man. Help him by teaching him to fish or farm, not providing him just a meal to alleviate his wants and fears. Teach him the truth of history so he can choose a better path for the future. Be a Fisher of Men as Jesus invited the fishermen at the Sea of Galilee to join him. That is the real choice for Freedom we have today."

Reverend Morrow paused a moment and then said, "That was the last sermon of Reverend Timothy Dickson. Now I'll ask the two congregations assembled here whether they want to join and unite to become one people, not divided so that just a few can have dominion over us all. Everyone, please stand if you make this choice."

The members of the two Baptist congregations all stood and the visitors and guests in the rear of the sanctuary started clapping.

After the applause faded, Reverend Morrow continued, "I know it's not the custom at Pleasant Hill like at Mt. Carmel, but let's start a tradition with our new congregation. Everyone, please hold hands to pray."

The members of the new congregation did their best to hold everyone's hands and Reverend Morrow continued, "Heavenly Father, we thank You for the Freedom and Blessings you have given us this and every day. We draw strength from Your wisdom and promise to use this gift as we freely make the difficult choices that lie ahead of us. If it's Your will, fan into flame our hearts and minds so that we can be strong to face the uncertain future ahead of us. Grant us the wisdom to know and do what's right and just so we may be given Your peace. Yours is the Kingdom, the power, and the glory, forever. Amen."

Those in the sanctuary and outside the church all replied, "Amen" and the assembly disbursed while Mr. Taylor played Canon in D Major, by Johann Pachelbel, on the organ. Everyone slowly walked outside into the bright sunlight as a new era, the seventh age of mankind was born.

As the sheriff, Jason, and the others from the front row left the sanctuary, Judge Saunders came up to speak to the unlikely heroes. "You all today have done a great thing for the Commonwealth of Virginia and us all. You have begun reclaiming the law and equal justice for all."

Coleman replied with a foreboding sense of dread, "I know, but will it last? Can we pull together as a people and defeat this evil?"

Saunders replied, "Some of my powerful friends will support our efforts, so at least we have half the legal system behind us. That's a start. Remember when you shine a light on cockroaches feasting in the darkness, they scatter. I thank you all for being this light and having the courage to again turn on the flashlight of hope when so many others prefer remaining in the dark and ignoring the truth."

After they left the sanctuary and stood outside, Nick asked Doc, "What was Exgenics really doing in their labs? What *is* the truth?"

Doc replied, "Well, I think they've been tinkering around with immortality. When you have all the money in the world, maybe you *can* live forever. Gerardo was playing god to create life in any image he wanted, but no man can be a god or should be worshiped as one."

Nick replied, "He was brilliant, but wasted his life on evil."

gcgaacgcgatggcgtaagcgatggcgaacgcgccgctggcgaacgcgtgcgcgaacgcgctgccggcgaacgcgatggcgtaagcgatggcgaacgcg

Jason added, "Gerardo sure used interesting technology. I think he put his mind in a new trans-body if that's possible somehow."

Julie commented, "The truth is out there, but we'll likely never know it since the farm is gone."

"I hope the world will finally see the truth *today* and learn," Jason added as he looked at his e-watch to see how his Gridlock algorithm and data release were progressing.

After talking to many people who offered condolences for their loss and a few who congratulated them on their marriage, Jason and Julie climbed onto his bike and drove to the Captain's house. They walked to the boathouse and uncovered the hidden bait bucket that was Frank's temporary tank.

Jason unwrapped the copper mesh that had shielded Frank and looked down into the water. Frank was glumly resting on the bottom, but immediately perked up after he reestablished communications with other glowfish. He grabbed the bucket by the handle and walked, with Julie holding his other hand, to the end of the captain's dock. "This is the right thing to do. We can't keep this intelligent lifeform captive," Jason said.

Julie replied, "I agree Jason. Grandpa would've done the same thing."

Jason lowered the bucket toward the water. "Goodbye little buddy. You're free now," he said as he poured the contents onto the water's surface. Frank swam a tight circle just under the water and popped up to surface to reveal once again his clown-like smile before diving into the deep, murky waters.

gcgaacgcgatggcgtaagcgatggcgaacgcgccgctggcgaacgcgtgcgcgaacgcgctgccggcgaacgcgatggcgtaagcgatggcgaacgcg

Epilogue I

Old Cast-iron Plow

Sometime in the Future...

As Vernon Jefferson, future historian would later write in his book "The Origins of the Great Reveal" while piecing together the timeline and facts that had occurred in Charles and Kent Counties, "The events that transpired in those few days were important. The Battle of Provident Forge was the second 'Shot Heard Round the World' for the liberation of mankind. We still hear the stories about the e-phone, e-vid, and data log that Jason Dickson broadcast to the world during Gridlock. People worldwide were spellbound and watched their e-screens for two full days seeing real events and the truth of the world for the first time. After the broadcast terminated, people woke up from their previous lives of self-imposed hypnosis and took off the masks of compliance they'd worn their entire lives. They breathed fresh air without fear as free men and women again. The data release about the Master Code caused worldwide turmoil and revolution against the world's financial, business, legal, political, and religious elites. The rich and powerful had planned to live forever in control of their future paradise, while the rest of humanity was expendable and scheduled for extermination.

The revolution that changed the world began after the events of those ten days when the Master Code was shown during the Great Reveal. The first of many war crimes to later be prosecuted was the intentional poisoning of the Chickahominy River. The slaves threw off their yokes of ignorance and compliance, when their masters, the elite of the world, showed their greed and utter disregard for humanity, the Earth, and God. The Great Restart that began afterward finally stripped them of their titles, wealth, and power. They were finally cast out like Jesus cast out the money changers from the Temple and they would again work with their hands, like everyone else, to survive."

catgcgccgccgtattaaattcgcacccatgatgcgtatgcgatggaacgcatttgcgcgcatgcgccgccgtattaaattcgcacccatgatgcgtat

Epilogue II

Jason's Chesapeake Dory

Several Years Later...

The worldwide War for Freedom was over. A pyrrhic victory was achieved, for it was not without cost as many had sacrificed all so that some of humanity would survive. With AI, robotics, and the Grid finally eliminated, the survivors now had work again. A lot of work. They would rebuild the world in a new direction and again bring meaning and purpose to their lives. They again had the freedom to *live*. All of humanity had been just a great experiment in control and now mankind had another chance to find a new path to live together in peace, friendship, and with love toward all beings.

It was just after noon on a late-spring day when Jason pulled back on the reins of his mule Gregory to stop at the end of a freshly plowed row. It had been a good morning of manual labor to prepare the field for planting. He noticed a nice breeze coming up and thought this would be a good afternoon to finish what he'd started the long winter before. He unhitched Gregory from the old plow, brought him back to the barn, and put him in his stall with some fresh hay, and filled his water bucket. The young mule seemed to enjoy his kind treatment by his master.

Jason and his wife Julie went down to the dock and climbed into the cockpit of the restored Chesapeake Dory which Jason had just finished rigging with hemp ropes, but that Grandpa never had the chance to sail. It had taken Jason months to finish the boat using old shipwright tools and techniques but he did so with pride to resurrect an old river skill that had been lost to history.[98]

---

[98] The Chickahominy Shipyard on the James County bank of the lower Chick River was destroyed in the Revolutionary War. A new shipyard had just been constructed.

gcgaacgcgatggcgtaagcgatggcgaacgcgccgctggcgaacgcgtgcgcgaacgcgctgccggcgaacgcgatggcgtaagcgatggcgaacgcg

Jason went into the kitchen and Julie was there making a full sit-down lunch for her hard-working husband now doing manual labor that was required to grow food to survive, like people used to do in the 19th century.

Jason asked, "Did Johnnie Walker arrive with the mail boat today? I'm looking for a letter from General Coleman in Washington."

"Yes, but there was no mail, perhaps there will be some later in the week when he comes again," Julie replied. "Johnnie did drop off that book on blacksmithing from the college library for you though." Julie's abdomen was enlarged from the new life that was growing inside her. They'd soon have a son or daughter. It didn't matter to them which gender their child would be, as this fact was now again a mystery like in the old days.

Jason's asked, "How are you feeling?" he asked out of concern for his pregnant wife.

"Not bad, but I'd love a nice back scratch and massage later. Robin James says everything is going well. Our due dates are both about the same day too, so we might have to find another doctor or a local mid-wife if she goes into labor before me."

"Let's not worry about that right now. Grandpa wanted me to scatter his ashes in the bay, just like he did with Grandma," as he helped Julie into the cockpit of the antique sailboat. He cast off the mooring lines, hoisted the main and mizzen sails, and pulled in the mainsheet to catch the breeze.

As they sailed down the Chick toward the James, after a while Julie asked, "What do you think we should name our child?"

Jason replied, "If it's a boy, I'd like to keep up the Dickson Family tradition of recycling the names of fathers, grandfathers, and such. Grandpa was named after a Timothy Dickson from 150 years ago who was a riverman. Let's name him Tim after Grandpa."

Julie agreed, "That name sounds nice. Grandpa would've liked that very much. What about if it's a girl?"

"Since we're a family now, what about naming her after someone from your family. Your mom's name is Kay, but somehow, I like the name Kate or Katrina better. What do you think?"

"I like them all Jason, but we still have time to make the final decision if we change our minds."

After an hour, they reached the James and steered eastward with the wind on a long reach toward the mouth of the bay. After sailing another hour, a summer storm appeared to be brewing to the south, also moving northeast, but ahead of them.

"Looks like that storm is going to beat us after all," Jason said. "I think we'd better turn back immediately. Here is a good spot anyway." He

catgcgccgccgtattaaattcgcacccatgatgcgtatgcgatggaacgcatttgcgcgcatgcgccgccgtattaaattcgcacccatgatgcgtat

pushed the tiller to steer the boat into the wind, took the small ceramic urn, opened the lid, and poured the powdered ash contents over the side of the boat onto the surface of the water. The ashes floated a few seconds before disappearing in the half-salty water.

"Goodbye Grandpa, I will remember the River of Life," he said with sadness and a tear in remembrance. "You were right, sometimes you *do* have to go backward before you can move forward again."

Julie looked at his eyes with love and reached toward him to hold his hand to show he wasn't alone in his grief. "It's OK Jason. He lives on in our memories. He planted a seed there that'll grow forever in all of us," she said kindly while deeply looking into Jason's bright green eyes.

He leaned closer toward her across the old boat's cockpit while his hand firmly gripped the tiller. Her blonde hair blew carefree in the wind as he rubbed her belly with a smile and said, "Let's be heading home now with that bad weather coming."

The storm flashed a lightning bolt somewhere east in the bay and in the distance, ten-thousand spots glowed just under the water. They saw the afterglow in the water fade and wondered how this new intelligent life form would evolve in a few million years.

gcgaacgcgatggcgtaagcgatggcgaacgcgccgctggcgaacgcgtgcgcgaacgcgctgccggcgaacgcgatggcgtaagcgatggcgaacgcg

Epilogue III

Wendover Church Bell

Somewhere and Sometime…

The Masters were ancient beings that evolved into a higher life form of pure energy. They normally resided inside stars where the energy density and entropy level could sustain them. They searched the universe over the eons and found they were alone. So, they decided to alter the universe by using their energy to modify matter. Just as Einstein predicted destroying matter would create energy, the Masters' energy could create or manipulate matter and, with the right planet, they could push an atom here or break a chemical bond there to form a new molecule, and life soon flourished. They successfully created life on trillions of worlds using a simple set of rules and were glad to permit evolution to continue, just like their race had changed with time. They waited for further eons, observing their experiments. Did the life evolve to higher forms? Did the life go extinct? Did the life violate their rules? It was their universal experiment.

They observed and mostly were pleasantly surprised by their results. In a few cases though, their experiments were a failure and they deleted their mistakes. They sensed some disturbances to their code that required further analysis. A new higher level of coherent energy was now emanating from a small blue world orbiting an insignificant yellow star. They had visited this world before and the primary sentient life form that evolved had great potential if only they could control themselves and learn to live together. That primitive species viewed them as aliens, gods, angels, or demons, but that didn't matter to the Masters.

They examined the world again and saw that it finally had changed for the better. They would give them another chance and, maybe after another hundred-million years of evolution, this species and others from that world would finally be ready to join the Masters as friends.

catgcgccgccgtattaaattcgcacccatgatgcgtatgcgatggaacgcatttgcgcgcatgcgccgccgtattaaattcgcacccatgatgcgtat

gcgaacgcgatggcgtaagcgatggcgaacgcgccgctggcgaacgcgtgcgcgaacgcgctgccggcgaacgcgatggcgtaagcgatggcgaacgcg

About the Author

T. A. Hunter grew up from a simple life as a farm boy who played in the woods, creek, fields, and farm pond to become an engineer, scientist, inventor, businessman, artist, poet, naturalist, and avid gardener. He is married and a proud father. Two of his childhood heroes were Thomas Jefferson and Thomas Edison.

Author's Notes and Comments

The Master Code is a science fiction-drama-thriller, involving actual locations in Virginia combined with past and future history. The names of many places have been altered to show that this is a fictional novel and not fact, but to still maintain some connection to reality, a few place names are real. The author has obviously taken license with the future and technology, but no basic facts prior to the date of publication have been altered other than to perhaps change a place or a person's name to agree with those mentioned in the text. The science fiction elements presented in this book are based on the author's extrapolations of currently known technologies and anticipation of more advanced, but related-technologies, in the future. All the characters in this future period are fictional. Any resemblance of these characters to any person currently living or dead is coincidental.

catgcgccgccgtattaaattcgcacccatgatgcgtatgcgatggaacgcatttgcgcgcatgcgccgccgtattaaattcgcacccatgatgcgtat

gcgaacgcgatggcgtaagcgatggcgaacgcgccgctggcgaacgcgtgcgcgaacgcgctgccggcgaacgcgatggcgtaagcgatggcgaacgcg

Index of Civil War Sites

As referenced in book maps:

1. Fort Pocahontas; 1864: A garrison of 1,500 African-American (freedmen) Union troops (U.S. Colored Troops) successfully defend an assault by 2,500 Confederate Cavalrymen. Union gunboats on the James River provided support (Note: Location is private property - access by permission only).

2. Harrison's Landing, 1862: was used by Union General McClellan for his Army to be evacuated by the Navy using steamboats from the Peninsula after the failure of his Peninsula Campaign of 1862. While camped near here, the bugle song, "Taps" was composed and played the first time.

3. Grant's Pontoon-Bridge Crossing, 1864: was used by Grant to cross the James River with his army to attack and begin the Siege of Petersburg. A 700-yard long bridge was constructed in less than 10 hours by the Army Corps of Engineers and was the longest pontoon bridge built in the Civil War. It used more than 100 small boats and two large schooners anchored it in place in the middle of the river. Union troops and supply wagons continuously crossed for 3 days until it was dissembled by the end of the 4th day.

4. Old Salem Church, 1864: was used as a field hospital for the Battle of Nance's Shop. The original church is just an archaeological site somewhere nearby. The old church cemetery had gravesites for casualties from this battle.

5. Nance's Shop was a Cavalry battle in 1864 where 4,000 Confederate Cavalry fought 2,500 Union Cavalry guarding a wagon train of supply wagons crossing the Peninsula to ferry supplies to Grant who was engaged in the Siege of Petersburg. There were about 500 casualties total in the day-long battle, with the Union troops withdrawing toward Charlestown.

6. Stuart's Ride was the trail of Confederate Cavalry General Stuart riding entirely around McClellan's Army. This ride provided reconnaissance that helped General Lee begin the attacks that drove McClellan back toward Harrison's Landing and ended the Peninsula Campaign. Stuart crossed the Chickahominy River into Charles County at the Old Forge Bridge near Provident Forge. General Stuart is known to have rested for several hours in a plantation house in the area and had a cup of strong coffee that was provided by the owner. He then rode all night to Richmond to report on his mission to General Lee.

7. Charlestown Court House was where Confederate Soldiers enlisted to fight for the State of Virginia. In 1862, 60,000 Union soldiers from the Peninsula Campaign marched through Charlestown during their withdrawal towards Williamsburg after McClellan left via boat at Harrison's Landing. Many records in the old courthouse were burned at this time. In 1863, ninety Confederate Cavalry Soldiers garrisoned here were captured in a surprise attack by Union Cavalry. Grant rode with the Army of the Potomac through Charlestown in 1864 toward Petersburg.

catgcgccgccgtattaaattcgcacccatgatgcgtatgcgatggaacgcatttgcgcgcatgcgccgccgtattaaattcgcacccatgatgcgtat

Index of Revolutionary War Sites

Schooner 'Thetis' circa 1794

As referenced in book maps:

1. Benjamin Harrison: Signer of the Declaration of Independence. He is buried here at his plantation Berkeley. Harrison's Landing was on the James River near his Berkeley Plantation. His son and great-grandson became U.S. presidents.

2. Charles County Courthouse: Lt. Colonel Simcoe's Rangers surprised and defeated a garrison of Virginia Militia in January 1781. Four Virginia Militiamen and one Ranger were killed. The Militia retreated and withdrew.

3. Doctor Richman; was Chief Physician of the Continental Virginia Militia and organized hospitals for the wounded. His wooden home near here was located on Kittiewan Plantation.

4. Kennon's Landing: The American traitor, who became British General Benedict Arnold, landed here with British troops in January 1781. Other British infantry regiments also landed near Harrison's Landing about the same time. They later joined together and attacked the Colonia Militia near Richmond.

5. Provident Forge: The forge located near a man-made lake was burned to the ground and destroyed by Tarleton's Raiders in 1781.

6. Chickahominy Shipyard was funded by Virginia to construct ships for the Virginia Navy and opened in 1777. It constructed several warships and other vessels, including a schooner, the 16-gun Thetis, and a brig, the 14-gun Jefferson. In April 1781, the shipyard was burned to the ground and destroyed by the British. The Jefferson was later intentionally scuttled by burning when the Virginia Fleet was bottled up on the James River below Richmond by the British Navy under the command of General Benedict Arnold. The retreating Virginia Navy's officers and sailors continued supporting the final victory in the Revolutionary War by driving supply wagons for Washington's siege at Yorktown where General Cornwallis ultimately surrendered. The Schooner Thetis was later used in coastal commerce and was shipwrecked off Cape Hatteras in 1811. Several published letters describe the harrowing experiences of the shipwreck survivors of this winter storm where a local African-American man was a hero saving women still trapped on the sinking boat.

Made in the USA
Middletown, DE
27 February 2022

61882125R00212